Relentless

www.booksattransworld.co.uk

Also by Simon Kernick

The Business of Dying
The Murder Exchange
The Crime Trade
A Good Day to Die

For more information on Simon Kernick and his books,
see his website at www.simonkernick.com

Relentless

SIMON KERNICK

BANTAM PRESS

LONDON · TORONTO · SYDNEY · AUCKLAND · JOHANNESBURG

TRANSWORLD PUBLISHERS
61–63 Uxbridge Road, London W5 5SA
a division of The Random House Group Ltd

RANDOM HOUSE AUSTRALIA (PTY) LTD
20 Alfred Street, Milsons Point, Sydney,
New South Wales 2061, Australia

RANDOM HOUSE NEW ZEALAND LTD
18 Poland Road, Glenfield, Auckland 10, New Zealand

RANDOM HOUSE SOUTH AFRICA (PTY) LTD
Isle of Houghton, Corner of Boundary Road & Carse O'Gowrie,
Houghton 2198, South Africa

Published 2006 by Bantam Press
a division of Transworld Publishers

A catalogue record for this book is available from the British Library.
ISBN 9780593054710 (cased) (from Jan 07)
ISBN 0593054717 (cased)
ISBN 9780593054703 (tpb) (from Jan 07)
ISBN 0593054709 (tpb)

Typeset in 11/16pt Times by
Kestrel Data, Exeter, Devon

Printed in Great Britain by
Mackays of Chatham plc, Chatham, Kent

1 3 5 7 9 10 8 6 4 2

Papers used by Transworld Publishers are natural, recyclable products made from
wood grown in sustainable forests. The manufacturing processes conform to the
environmental regulations of the country of origin.

For my daughters, Amy and Rachel

Part One

SATURDAY

1

I only heard the phone because the back door was open. I was outside breaking up a fight between my two kids over which one of them should have the bubble-blowing machine, and it was threatening to turn ugly. To my dying day, I will always wonder what would have happened if the door had been shut, or the noise of the kids had been so loud that I hadn't heard it.

It had just turned three o'clock on a cloudy Saturday afternoon in late May, and my whole world was about to collapse.

I ran back inside the house, into the living room, where the football was just kicking off on the TV, and picked up on about the fourth ring, wondering whether it was that perma-tanned bastard of a boss of mine, Wesley 'Call me Wes' O'Shea, phoning to discuss a minor detail on a client proposal. He liked to do that at weekends, usually when there was a football match on. It gave him a perverse sense of power.

I looked at my watch. One minute past three.

'Hello?'

'Tom, it's me, Jack.' The voice was breathless.

I was momentarily confused. 'Jack who?'

'Jack . . . Jack Calley.'

This was a voice from the past. My best friend when we were at school. The best man at my wedding nine years earlier. But also someone I hadn't spoken to in close to four years. There was something wrong, too. He sounded in pain, struggling to get the words out.

'Long time no speak, Jack. How are you?'

'You've got to help me.'

It sounded like he was running, or walking very quickly. There was background noise, but I couldn't tell what it was. He was definitely outside.

'What do you mean?'

'Help me. You've got to . . .' He gasped suddenly. 'Oh Jesus, no. They're coming.'

'Who's coming?'

'Oh Christ!'

He shouted these last words, and I had to hold the phone away from my ear momentarily. On the TV, the crowd roared as one of the players bore down on goal.

'Jack. What the hell's happening? Where are you?'

He was panting rapidly now, his breaths coming in tortured, wailing gasps. I could hear the sound of him running.

'What's going on? Tell me!'

Jack cried out in abject terror, and I thought I heard the sound of some sort of scuffle. 'Please! No!' he yelled, his voice cracking. The scuffle continued for several seconds, and seemed to move away from the phone. Then he was speaking again, but no longer to me. To someone else. His voice was faint but I could make it out easily enough.

He said six words. Six simple words that made my heart lurch and my whole world totter.

They were the first two lines of my address.

Then Jack let out a short, desperate scream, and it sounded like he was being pulled away from the phone. There followed a succession of gasping coughs, and instinctively even I, who'd lived my life a long way from the indignities of death, could tell that my old friend was dying.

And then everything fell eerily silent.

The silence might have lasted ten seconds, but was probably nearer two, and as I stood frozen to the spot in my front room, mouth open, too shocked to know what to say or do, I heard the line suddenly go dead at the other end.

The first two lines of my address. The place where I lived an ordinary suburban life with my two kids and my wife of nine years. The place where I felt safe.

For a moment, just one moment, I thought it must have been some sort of practical joke, a cruel ruse to get a reaction. But the thing was, I hadn't spoken to Jack Calley in four long years, and the last time had been a chance meeting in the street, a snatched five-minute conversation while the kids – much younger then, Max just a baby – shouted and fidgeted in their twin pushchair. I hadn't had a proper chat with him – you know, the kind friends have – in, what, five, six, maybe even seven years. We'd gone our separate ways a long time ago.

No, this was serious. You don't put fear like that into your voice deliberately. It's a natural thing, something that's got to come from within. And this most definitely had. Jack had been terrified, and with good reason. If I wasn't mistaken, and I would swear to God that I wasn't, I'd just heard him breathe his dying breaths. And his last words were the first two lines of my address.

Who wanted to know where I lived? And why?

Let me tell you this: I am an ordinary man with an ordinary desk job in a big open-plan office, leading a team of four IT software salesmen. It's not a huge amount of fun and, as I've already suggested, my boss, Wesley, is something of an arsehole, but it pays the bills and allows me to own a half-reasonable detached four-bed house in the suburbs, and at thirty-five I've never once been in trouble with the boys in blue. My wife and I have had our ups and downs, and the kids can play up now and again, but in general, we're happy. Kathy works as a lecturer in environmental politics over at the university, a job she's held for close to ten years. She's well liked, good at what she does and, although she probably wouldn't like me saying so, very pretty. We're the same age, we've been together eleven years, and we have no secrets. We've done nothing wrong; we pay our taxes and we keep out of trouble. In short, we're just like everyone else.

Just like you.

So why did some stranger want to know our address? Some stranger who wanted it so badly he was prepared to kill for it?

Fear kicked in, that intense terror that starts somewhere in the groin and tears through you like an express train until it's infected every part and is ready to develop into outright panic. The instinctive flight mechanism. The sick feeling you get when you're walking empty streets alone at night and you hear foot-steps coming from behind. Or when a man smashes a beer glass on the corner of a bar and demands to know what the fuck you think you're looking at. Real fear. I had it then.

I replaced the phone in its cradle and stood where I was for a long moment, trying to think of a rational explanation for what I'd just heard. Nothing presented itself, and yet at the same time even the most paranoid explanation didn't make sense either. If someone wanted to speak to me, then they presumably knew who I was. In which case they could easily have found out where I lived without asking a man who barely knew me any more. They could have looked in the phonebook for a start. But they hadn't.

'Daddy, Max just hit me for no reason.' It was Chloe coming back into the house, grass stains on the knees of her jeans, her dark-blonde hair a tousled mess. At five, she was little more than a year older than her brother Max, yet vastly more sensible. The problem was, he'd already overtaken her in bulk, and in the anarchic world of young kids bulk tends to win through in arguments. 'Can you go and tell him off?' she added, looking put out, as innocent of danger as all children are.

Someone was coming here. Someone who'd just killed my oldest friend.

The last I remembered, Jack Calley had been living five or six miles away, just outside Ruislip, where London finally gives way to the Green Belt. If he'd called me from near his home then the person he'd given my address to would be about a fifteen-minute drive away at this time of day. Maybe less if the traffic was quiet and they were in a hurry.

'Daddy, what are you doing?'

'Hold on a sec, darling,' I said with a smile so false it would have embarrassed a politician. 'I'm just thinking.'

It was two minutes since I'd put down the phone and I could hear my heart beating a rapid tattoo in my chest. Bang bang, bang bang, bang bang. If I stayed here, I was putting my family at risk. If I left, then how was I ever going to find out who was after me, and why?

'Hey, sweetie,' I said, keenly aware of the strain in my voice, 'we've got to go out now, round to Grandma's.'

13

'Why?'

I squatted down and picked her up. 'Because she wants to see you.'

'Why?'

Sometimes it's best not to get into a dialogue with a five-year-old. 'Come on, darling, we've got to go,' I said, and strode outside, carrying her in my arms.

I saw that Max had abandoned the bubble-making machine in the middle of the lawn and was now at the bottom of the garden, his head poking out of a makeshift, canvas-sided camp at the top of the climbing frame. I shouted at him to come out because we had to go. His head immediately retreated into the camp. Like a lot of four-year-old boys, he didn't like to do what he was told. Usually this wasn't much of a problem. I tended to ignore it and let him do his own thing. Today it was a disaster.

Jack's words played over and over in my mind. 'Oh Jesus, no. They're coming.' The urgency in them. The fear. They're coming.

They're coming here.

I looked at my watch. 3.05. Four minutes since I'd picked up the phone. Time seemed to be moving faster than it usually does.

'Come on, Max, we've got to get moving. Now.'

I ran over to the climbing frame, still holding onto Chloe, ignoring her complaints. She tried to struggle out of my arms, but I didn't let go.

'But I'm playing,' he called out from within the camp.

'I don't care. We've got to go now.'

I heard a car pulling into the road out front. This was unusual. The housing estate we live on leads nowhere and is simply a horseshoe-shaped road with culs-de-sac sprouting off it. Drive

14

along it and eventually you end up right back close to where you started. Our house was on the corner of one of the culs-de-sac, and a car came down it once every twenty minutes at most.

The car slowed down. Stopped.

I heard a car door shut, further down in the cul-de-sac. I was being unduly paranoid. But my heart continued to thud.

'Come on, Max. I'm serious.'

He giggled, blissfully unaware of my fear. 'Come and get me.'

I put Chloe down and reached inside the camp. Max retreated as far as he could go, still giggling, but his expression changed when he saw the look on my face.

'What is it, Dad? What's wrong?'

'It's all right, nothing's wrong, but we've got to go round to Grandma's quickly.'

He nodded, looking worried, and scrambled out.

I took them both by the hand and, trying to stay as calm as possible, led them through the house and out to the car. They were both asking questions, but I wasn't really listening. I was willing them to go faster. In the distance, I could hear the cars out on the main road. Above me came the steady roar of a passenger plane circling beyond the unbroken ceiling of white cloud. The neighbour's new dog was barking and someone was mowing their lawn. The comforting sounds of normality, but today they weren't comforting at all. It was as if I was in some sort of terrifying parallel universe where danger loomed on all sides, yet no-one else could see or understand it.

I strapped the kids into their car seats, then realized, as I was about to get into the driver's seat, that I'd better take some overnight gear for them, just in case they were out of the house for any length of time. I tried to think what I was going to say when I turned up at my mother-in-law's with them. The best

15

man at my wedding just phoned me for the first time in years; then, as we were speaking, he got murdered, and now his killer's after me. It sounded so outlandish that even I would have questioned my own sanity, if I hadn't been so damn sure of its authenticity. And Irene had never liked me much either. Had always thought her daughter, with her strong academic background and her Cambridge degree, was too damn good for a glorified computer salesman.

3.08. Seven minutes since I'd picked up the phone.

I was going to have to tell Irene that something had come up at work. That maybe it was best if the kids spent the night with her. And then what? What happened tomorrow?

I told myself to stop trying to analyse everything and to just get moving.

'Stay in the car, OK? I'm just going to get some overnight stuff.'

They both started to protest, but I shut the door and ran inside and up to each of their bedrooms, hastily chucking together pyjamas, toys, toothbrushes, everything else they were going to need, and shoving them in a holdall, knowing with every step that I was racing against time.

3.11. As I came running out of the house, I recalled the gurgling, coughing noise Jack had made as he was being attacked. The sound of death – it had to be. But who wanted to kill a middle-of-the-road solicitor like Jack Calley, a man who was doing well but hardly setting the world on fire? And, more importantly – far more importantly – who wanted to find out from him where I, lowly salesman Tom Meron, and my family lived?

As I reached the car, I cursed. Both kids had unclipped their seatbelts and were fooling around. Chloe had clambered through the gap in the front seats and was now playing with the steering wheel, while all I could see of Max were his legs sticking up in the air as he hunted for something in the back. They were both laughing, as if there was nothing whatsoever wrong with their world – which there wasn't. It was just mine that was going mad.

I opened the door and flung the overnight bag past Chloe onto the passenger seat. 'Come on, kids, we've got to go,' I said, picking her up and pushing her back through the gap in the seats. 'It's very important.'

'Ow! That hurt.'

'Get back in your seat, Chloe. Now.'

I was sweating as I ran round to the back passenger door, pulled it open, yanked Max up and shoved him bodily into his seat. With shaking hands, I strapped him back in, then reached over and did the same to his sister.

'What's happening, Daddy?' asked Chloe. She looked frightened, not used to seeing her father acting so strangely.

I'm not a panicker by nature. There's not much in my life that would instigate panic, if I'm honest, which was why I was now finding it hard to stay calm. This all felt like a bad dream, something that should have been happening to someone else. An elaborate hoax that would end in laughter all round.

But it wasn't. I knew it wasn't.

I scrabbled around in my jeans pocket for the car keys, found them and started the ignition. The dashboard clock read 3.16, but I remembered that it was four minutes fast. Eleven minutes since the call. Christ, was it that long? I reversed the car out of the drive and drove up to the junction, indicating left in the direction of the main road. The relief I experienced as I pulled away and accelerated was tangible. I felt like I'd escaped from something terrible.

I was being stupid. There had to be some sort of rational explanation for what I'd just heard. There just had to be. 'Calm down,' I muttered to myself. 'Calm down.'

I took a deep breath, feeling better already. I'd take the kids to Irene's, drop them off, phone Kathy, then just drive back home. And there'd be no-one there. I'd look up Jack Calley's number, call and see if everything was all right. From the safe cocoon of my moving car, I began to convince myself that Jack hadn't actually been hurt. That the ghastly choking hadn't been him dying a lonely death. That everything was fine.

A one-hundred-yard-long, relatively straight stretch of road led from the entrance of our cul-de-sac to the T-junction that met up with the main road into London. As we reached it, I slowed up and indicated right. A black Toyota Land Cruiser built like a tank was moving towards us down the main road at some speed. I could see two figures in caps and sunglasses in the front seats. When it was ten yards away, the driver slowed dramatically and swung the car into the estate, without indicating. I was about to curse him for his lack of courtesy, when I noticed that the side windows of the vehicle were tinted, and I felt a sense of dread. An unfamiliar car driving onto the estate only eleven minutes after Jack had called me. At a push, Jack lived eleven minutes away. The timing was too coincidental.

I watched its progress in the rearview mirror, a dry, sour taste in my mouth, fear causing my heart to rise in my chest. Our cul-de-sac was the third one down on the right, just before the road bent round sharply. The Land Cruiser passed the first cul-de-sac, then the second.

Fifteen yards short of ours, the brake lights came on.

Oh no, no. Please, no.

'Daddy, why aren't we moving?'

'Come on, Daddy. Come on, Daddy.'

The Land Cruiser turned into our cul-de-sac, then disappeared from view. I knew then as much as I knew anything that its occupants were coming for me.

I pulled onto the main road and accelerated away, the voices of my two children and Jack Calley – desperate, dying Jack Calley – reverberating around my head like distant, blurred echoes.

2

'You know, I'd prefer it if you called in advance, Tom,' admonished Irene Tyler, my formidable mother-in-law.

It was 3.35 p.m. and I was seven miles away from home and the occupants of the black Land Cruiser, and hopefully safe. At least for now.

'I'm sorry, Irene. Something's come up. An emergency.'

I led the kids into the hallway of her grand Victorian semi-detached home that sat on a quiet, tree-lined street of equally grand homes, all of which boasted intricately painted, Swiss-style façades. It was the house where Kathy had grown up, and the type of place to which she'd always aspired to return.

'What kind of emergency?' she demanded, raising a sceptical eyebrow.

Irene Tyler was an unnerving woman. A former secondary school headmistress, she had a dominating presence that was assisted by her powerful build and broad shoulders. I always felt that she would have made an excellent prison warder, or a trainer of gladiators had she been around in Ancient Rome. She wasn't unattractive to look at for a woman of seventy, but you get the picture. She wasn't someone you'd last long against toe to toe.

But the kids liked her, and they ran up and hugged her now, chuckling delightedly as they clutched her ample form while I tried to think of a suitable excuse for being there. As a salesman of some twelve years' standing, I was quite a proficient bullshitter, but a combination of my mother-in-law's brooding presence and the fear that was coursing through me in waves made thinking up a plausible story next to impossible.

'It's just something with work,' I said. 'I've got to go in. One of our major clients is playing up. You know how it goes.'

Although, of course, she didn't, being a retired civil servant. However, this wasn't an entirely unusual scenario for me. In the past few months Wesley O'Shea had experienced several entirely imagined client emergencies which had resulted in him calling his team leaders into work on a Saturday to help 'brain-storm' the problem. I was sure he only did it to make himself feel important.

Irene didn't look convinced. But then she'd never really trusted me. Like a lot of people, she thought there was some-thing a bit dodgy about anyone who sold things for a living. Plus, the concept of people outside the retail trade and the emergency services working on a Saturday didn't sit too easily with her. This time, however, she let it go, and asked where her daughter was.

'She's at work as well,' I explained, putting down the over-night bag next to the ornate grandfather clock that dominated the entrance to the Tyler household. 'Down at the university. She's researching for a paper she's writing.'

I had to phone Kathy. Make sure she didn't go home. I couldn't remember what time she said she'd be finished, but thought it probably wouldn't be yet.

'So, when are you going to pick the children up?'

'Can we stay for tea, Grandma?' asked Chloe, pulling at her grandmother's dress.

'Course you can, darling,' she said, smiling at last as she stroked Chloe's long hair.

'I don't know what time either of us is going to get back. I've packed some things for them.'

'So, you want them to stay the night?'

'Yes. Please. I'll pick them up first thing tomorrow.'

'Why are you going to work on a Saturday afternoon, Daddy?' asked Max.

'I think you ought to tell your boss that you have commitments outside work too,' said Irene in a tone that brooked no dissent.

'It's a one-off,' I answered quickly, experiencing a sudden, unstoppable urge to get away from this interrogation and find out what the hell was going on with my life. I made a play of looking at my watch. 'Listen, Irene, I've really got to make a move.' There's a Land Cruiser with blacked-out windows at my house. It contains men who want something from me, something they're prepared to kill for, even though I have no idea what it is. 'I've got a long night ahead, and I don't want to be late.'

She nodded, the glint of suspicion flickering in her dark eyes, then leaned down so she was level with Chloe and Max. 'So, what shall we do, children? Do you want to go down to the river and feed the ducks before tea?'

'Yes, yes, yes!' they both cried.

I could feel sweat running down my brow and I knew that Irene would have spotted it and drawn her own conclusions as to why it was there. I kissed the kids goodbye but they were already thinking about going to the river to feed the ducks and their reciprocation was perfunctory. I nodded to Irene and thanked her, conscious that I was avoiding her eye. Then I was out of her front door and down the pathway to the car.

I jumped inside, drove to the end of Irene's road so that I was out of sight, and speed-dialled Kathy's number. The phone rang five times before going to message. I wasn't entirely surprised she wasn't answering. If she was working in the library she'd have the phone off, and I knew she didn't like to be disturbed unless it was urgent. I didn't leave a message but instead tried her office extension. I listened as it rang and rang before finally the voicemail came on.

For a few seconds I wasn't sure what to do. Then I put the car into gear and drove back in the direction of my house. I was sure now I wasn't being paranoid, but I still wanted to check which house the Land Cruiser was parked outside, and whether it was, as I expected, my own.

As I drove, I thought of Jack Calley. We'd known each other since almost the very beginning. He'd moved into our road in the late seventies when we were both eight years old, and had made his presence felt immediately. He was big for his age with a thick, ridiculously long mop of naturally blond curly hair that made him look a bit like Robert Plant in his Led Zeppelin days. His dad had died a few months earlier and they were moving down from East Anglia so that his mum could be nearer her own parents. My mum and dad took an instant dislike to him – I think it was probably the hair. And because they didn't want me spending time with him, I inevitably did.

We hit it off immediately. For a kid who'd just lost his father, he was remarkably full of life, maybe because he felt he always had something to prove. Jack was an adventurer, the kind who always wants to climb the highest tree, to perform the greatest dare. He was the first boy in the school to ride his bike down Sketty's Gorge, a near vertical slope in our local woods at the bottom of which was a thick wall of stinging nettles. I only tried it once and got stung to pieces, but it remained Jack's party piece; he was always doing it. It demonstrated his devil-may-care attitude. It made him exciting company. And never once did he fall off.

We spent our whole childhood as friends and, although we drifted apart when he went off to university to study law and I got my first full-time job as a photocopier salesman, we renewed the friendship in our twenties, which was a good time to be hanging round with a man like Jack. He'd turned into a tall, handsome guy with plenty of charm, and a fair bit of money too. He tended to draw women to him, and because we were out together so much in the bars and clubs of central London and the City, they got drawn in my direction too. Sometimes, occasionally, I felt I was getting his cast-offs, but, like most men, I never let my dignity get in the way of sex. In those days I was in awe of Jack Calley a little, and appreciated the fact that I was his friend.

Marriage, specifically mine to Kathy, had been the catalyst for our friendship to become more distant. Gradually, we saw less and less of each other. Jack found himself in a relationship with a high-flying female lawyer, and Kathy fell pregnant with Chloe. It was a time of upheaval, and our meetings were reduced to once or twice a year, until eventually they fizzled out altogether. I always felt that this was more Jack's doing than mine. I'd left a couple of phone messages for him that hadn't been returned, and emails I'd sent, although answered enthusiastically with talk of getting together some time soon, never seemed to come to anything. As far as I could recall, we hadn't even sent each other Christmas cards for the last couple of years.

Half a mile short of home, I decided to break the law by calling Kathy's mobile while driving. Again, there was no answer, something that was now beginning to worry me. I wanted desperately to talk to someone about what was going on, and she was the one person I could rely on to come up with either a rational explanation or at least a viable plan as to what to do next. Because if someone was after me, they were still going to be after me tomorrow, and the next day. And the day after that. Which meant I had to find out what the hell it was they wanted.

It was just short of five to four when I turned into the estate. Usually when I make this turning it fills me with a deep sense of satisfaction because it means I'm almost home, at the end of a hard working day. The pleasant, well-kept 1960s houses with their neatly trimmed front lawns always seem so welcoming, an oasis of quiet amid the noise and traffic of suburban London. Today, though, I felt nothing but deep trepidation over what I might find here.

But when I drove past my cul-de-sac without slowing and glanced across at it, I saw that the Land Cruiser with the blacked-out windows was no longer there. I continued round the bend at the bottom of the hill and went another couple of hundred yards before turning round. As I came back the other way, I looked over again. The Land Cruiser was definitely nowhere to be seen. Perhaps they'd found out I wasn't there and had simply left. The Henderson boys opposite, two raucous tykes of seven and nine, were out on their driveway washing their father's car. Martin Henderson once told me that he got them to do it by making the whole thing a game. One cleaned one side, one cleaned the other; whoever did the best job won the game. The beauty of it was that there was no prize for winning, so Martin got a spotlessly clean car for free. The normality of the scene was painful.

I slowed down and stopped a few yards past the cul-de-sac entrance, parallel to the wall that ran alongside my back garden. I got out of the car, leaving its engine running, and walked over to a spot where I could see through the ivy-covered trellising at the top of the wall. From this position I had a view across my back garden and into the dining room at the back of the house. The dining-room door was open, and I could see the hallway and the front door beyond it.

I stared for about thirty seconds. There was no movement. My house looked empty. I thought about going back inside and trying to find Jack's number, but there didn't seem much point. I knew he wouldn't be answering his phone.

A man in a cap and glasses crossed the hallway, moving purposefully, and disappeared into my study. He was dressed in black, and I thought he was wearing gloves too. He was only in my field of vision for a couple of seconds. I could almost have imagined it, but I knew I hadn't.

There was a man in black in my house.

I waited, watching. Nothing moved. In the background I could hear my car's engine ticking over. I felt like some sort of peeping tom, even though I was looking into my own house. I also felt the first flash of anger. Some bastard had broken into my home and was strolling about as if he owned the place.

As I silently cursed him he appeared again, stopping in the hallway. I pushed the ivy out of my field of vision but still couldn't get a good look at him. He was medium height and medium build, and was holding some of my files that he must have pulled out of the filing cabinet. There was nothing exciting in there, just bills and old tax returns, stuff like that. What the hell was this guy looking for?

As I watched, he opened up one of the files, leafed through the contents and, apparently satisfied that there was nothing in there of any use, casually dropped it to the floor, spilling papers across the carpet, before starting on another one.

'You bastard,' I hissed, then made a decision.

Jumping back in the car, I dialled 141 on the mobile so my number couldn't be traced, then 999. When the operator came on I told him I wanted the police, and was put through to the police control room.

'I'd like to report a burglary in progress,' I told the woman at the other end, giving her the address. 'The suspect's armed with a knife and I think he may have attacked the occupant.' I was trying to sound as alarmed as possible, something that was no great feat in the circumstances. 'A woman lives there alone with young kids. I think they might be in there with him.'

She seemed suitably concerned, which was the idea. I wanted the police there in five minutes, not two hours after the guy had left, which would probably have been the case if I hadn't been bullshitting. When the woman asked for my name, I told her to hurry as I'd just heard a scream. Then I hung up and put the car into gear.

It was time to find Kathy.

3

It was usually a twenty-five-minute drive to the university campus where my wife delivered her lectures on environmental politics (a subject in which I have to admit I have no interest whatsoever), but today I managed it in twenty. Traffic was quieter on the roads than normal, and I was hurrying. Half-way through the journey, I tried Kathy's mobile for a third time. Still no answer. The same with the office extension. She'd now been non-contactable for forty minutes. Not unusual, but worrying given everything else that was happening. This time I left messages on both phones, telling her to call me as soon as possible. I made no attempt to tone down the urgency in my voice. I wanted to make sure she didn't go home. I didn't like to think what might happen if she ran into our uninvited guest, but I had a strong feeling he wouldn't be very welcoming.

The university campus was a set of bland 1960s redbrick buildings with oversized black roofs that looked like they didn't fit properly, and which were dotted to one side of a much larger building that stretched from one end of the site to the other. On the other side of this main building was a large car parking area

27

which, because today was Saturday, was only about a quarter full. I parked as close to the main entrance as I could and hurried inside.

There was one woman manning the main reception desk but she was busy dealing with an enquiry by two Chinese students, and she completely ignored me. A bored-looking security guard of pensionable age sat on a chair beside the desk on duty in the reception foyer, supposedly to vet people who came into the building – a post created after the rape of one of the female students several years earlier. His vetting skills must have been on the blink, though, because he barely gave me a second look as I turned right and made my way along the corridor, past the lecture halls on my left and a café and Internet area on my right. It was in this building that most of the university's lectures and tutorials took place, but it was relatively quiet today, with only a few students dotted about.

I looked out of place, being at least a dozen years older than everyone else, but no-one challenged me as I made my way in the direction of the library and the politics department. I was just another irrelevant old guy. And yet I could have been anyone. I could have been the rapist from a couple of years ago, but no-one seemed to care. There's a degree of truth in the maxim that people only notice what they want to notice; a lot of the time they simply ignore what's going on around them, so absorbed are they in their own lives. I was beginning to wonder if I'd been like that too recently, and had therefore missed something important. Something that could have told me what was going on.

As I cleared the café and Internet area, the number of people dwindled, and when I turned left and mounted a staircase to the first floor I found that I was on my own, my steady footfalls echoing on the linoleum. The corridor was completely silent, and it struck me that it would have been easy for a rapist to strike in a place like this, somewhere that initially felt safe because it was often alive with people, but which could just as easily turn into a place of darkened hallways with lines of doors beyond which anyone could lurk.

I felt nervous. Not for myself – no-one knew I was here – but for Kathy, having to come and work here alone. She'd told me they'd installed CCTV cameras throughout the building and that they were constantly monitored by a security company, so there was no need to worry. But I knew that not even cameras stop the more foolish criminals, or the ones who can't control their urges. If this were the case, Britain, which has more CCTV cameras than any other country in the world, would be a relatively safe and peaceful society. And it isn't.

At the end of the corridor was a set of double glass doors which marked the entrance to the university's Department of Political Studies. They were shut, and beyond them I could neither see nor hear any signs of activity. The silence here was complete.

I stopped and looked at my watch. It was 4.25 p.m. Beyond the glass was another corridor that led down to an arch-shaped external window at the back of the building. There were four doors on the left side of the corridor, only one on the right. Kathy's was the second on the left, and I noticed it was closed, as were all but one of the other doors.

I pushed the double doors and they opened. As I stepped through, they closed behind me with a loud bang that cracked across the silence like a gunshot. I flinched, resisting the urge to shout hello, and went over and tried Kathy's door.

It was locked, which was strange. I knew I hadn't made a

mistake. Her name was engraved across it on an expensive-looking stainless-steel nameplate: DR KATHERINE C. MERON PH.D. The C stood for Cynthia, a name she hated. It made me wonder why she'd had it included. I tried the door again, just to make sure. It remained locked.

My mouth felt dry. Something wasn't right. The silence felt heavy and unnatural. I couldn't even hear the sound of traffic outside. Then I remembered. The walls here were very well insulated so that the academics could get on with their work in peace, unsullied by the constant racket of urban life the rest of us have to put up with.

Turning round, I went over to the door that led into the department's library. The lights were off and it looked empty. I turned the handle and stepped inside, shutting the door quietly behind me.

It was a big room, probably fifty feet square, with a walkway running down the middle from the door to a bank of windows at the far end. About a third of the space was taken up by large rectangular worktables, some with PCs on them, all of them empty. There were no bags or coats to suggest that anyone was around, no books out and opened, and the screens on the computers were all blank. The tables gave way to lines of floor-to-ceiling shelves full of books that ran left to right and were bisected by the walkway, and which blocked out much of the natural light, giving the room that gloomy feel you often get in libraries. There was a line of further tables at the very end of the room by the windows. They too were empty.

This time I did call out. 'Hello, is anyone here?'

No answer.

I pulled the phone from my pocket and speed-dialled Kathy's mobile yet again. At the same time I walked over towards the lines of bookshelves filled with political tomes that took up much of the space ahead of me. I was unsurprised but increasingly unnerved when it went to message again. If she wasn't here, where on earth was she?

I had to keep calm, I knew that. Maybe she'd left for the day and forgotten to switch the phone on. But of course that meant she might already have got home and run into whoever it was who was rifling through our belongings. Whichever way I viewed it, things were not looking good.

As I pocketed the mobile, something on the floor caught my eye. Just in front of one of the shelves. Difficult to see against the deep green of the carpet.

A stain, no more than a couple of inches across.

I swallowed hard, bent down, dipped a finger in it and flinched at its wetness. I inspected the upturned fingertip. There was no doubt about it. No doubt at all.

Blood.

And it was fresh.

Slowly my gaze moved along the carpet. There was a second stain, smaller than the first, then another. Thick droplets of blood. A trail.

My body stiffened. Please no. Please not Kathy. Not my wife, a woman who's never hurt anyone. Anything but that. 'Keep calm,' I said, aloud this time. 'Don't panic.'

I looked up and saw a door facing me at the end of the bookshelf, fifteen feet away. It was about a foot or so ajar, and all I could see beyond it was darkness. I looked again at the carpet. The blood trail ran right along it towards the door. I stared at it, trying to detect movement.

My mobile started ringing. No, it wasn't mine. It was someone else's. A different ringtone. Mine was pretty normal; this was

31

more jaunty. Annoyingly so. And it was coming from beyond the door.

Then it stopped.

The silence was so heavy that I could almost feel it weighing down on me. My instincts told me to run, to get the hell out of there. But what if it was Kathy who was bleeding in there? It wasn't her mobile, I knew that. But that didn't mean it wasn't her behind the door.

I took a step forward. Halted. I was unarmed. What on earth was I going to do if I was confronted by someone? I needed to get help. Now.

The door flew open and a tall figure dressed in a sky-blue, paint-flecked boiler suit, black balaclava and gloves stood in front of me. He held a knife in front of him. It had a yellow handle and a long curved blade, similar to that of a filleting knife. The end of it was stained dark with blood.

For a split second neither of us moved, each studying the other. Only five yards apart. I didn't have time for fear. Instead, I experienced a single, nightmarish jolt of shock that froze me to the spot. And then suddenly he exploded out of the door, coming at me with huge purposeful strides, the knife raised high in a killing arc.

Instinctively I grabbed a book from the nearest shelf and flung it at him, then turned and ran, but in my panic I went the wrong way and found myself facing the windows at the far end of the room rather than the door. There was no time to double back, he was right behind me, so I took off up the walkway in the direction of the windows, the sound of his breathing and the rhythmic patter of his boots clattering on the laminated plastic of the walkway spurring me on.

There was a wooden trolley full of books next to one of the

shelves and I grabbed the end of it as I passed and yanked it out into the walkway behind me. I heard him clatter into it, and the sound of books falling to the floor, then him knocking it to one side, the delay to his progress giving me perhaps an extra second and a half. I didn't dare look round; I was too busy concentrating on getting to the windows. I could see that they had handles and guessed – prayed – that they opened outwards. The library was high up, twenty feet above the ground at least, maybe more. It didn't matter. I had to get out.

I ran between two round reading tables in front of the windows and pulled desperately at the first latch I came to. It didn't move. The damn thing was locked. I could hear my pursuer's footfalls gaining. I swung round and he was there, right in front of me, five feet away and still running, the bloodied knife thrusting forward at waist height. Ready to fillet me.

I heard myself cry out in fear, but at the same time I had enough instinct for survival to grab the nearest chair and charge into him, forcing its legs into his face and upper body as I tried to get him off balance. He stumbled backwards, lifting his arms defensively, and this gave me time to move into a more open space. Out of the corner of my eye I saw an open door marked TOILETS. A potential escape route, but there was no time to give it much thought as I pressed my advantage, advancing fast and thrusting the chair at him once again. But this time he was ready. He jumped nimbly to one side and grabbed one of the legs, twisting it away from me.

We wrestled with the chair for several more seconds, but I was now more exposed and he suddenly lashed out with the knife, just catching the exposed flesh of my arm below the elbow. I felt a sharp burning sensation but no pain. My adrenalin was pump-ing too hard for that. I gritted my teeth, saw the thin gash he'd made through the material of my shirt bubble up with blood, and then I was having to dodge him as the knife skimmed through the air again. It caught me in the middle of my cheek as I twisted my face away. Another burning sensation, and I could feel a drop of blood running down onto my neck.

The reality of what was happening now hit me. I was fighting for my life. This man was trying to kill me, and all the time the room was deathly silent.

He tried to get his leg round the back of mine so he could trip me up, then yanked at the chair again and drove the knife at my midriff. This time as I twisted away, banging hard against the nearest bookshelf, I let the chair go, giving it as much of a shove as I could manage under the circumstances. I don't think he was expecting that because he stumbled backwards and almost lost his footing.

That was my chance. I turned and ran like I've never run before, aiming straight at the door marked TOILETS, knowing that if I fucked this up, I was dead. I have a morbid fear of being stabbed to death. Of being opened up by a hot blade and watching my blood and my life ebb away, unable to do anything about it. It's been with me ever since a guy we went to school with was fatally knifed in a local nightclub a decade ago. Two thrusts, both straight to the heart. The doormen threw him out, not realizing what had happened, and he died on the pavement outside. This was the fate that awaited me. A lonely, terrifying, messy death.

As I moved through the open door, I slammed it shut behind me. My mind registered two more doors: one to the left, one opposite. I took the one opposite. The men's. Behind me, the main door flew open again. He was still on my tail.

I charged into the men's, saw a row of stalls directly in front of me, swung right, slipping on the tiled floor but somehow keeping my balance, and kept going round the corner where there were a number of individual urinals arranged against the wall in a rough semicircle. Directly above one was a narrow window, maybe eighteen inches high and three feet across. There was an ancient latch at the bottom of it, the paint almost entirely peeled off. I ran forward and jumped up onto the urinal, flicking the latch off its guard in one movement, and using both palms to knock open the window. Then I was scrambling through, head-first, my legs flailing. As my upper body lurched out into the open air, I could see a flat roof six or seven feet below me where the building had been given a single-storey extension. Safety. I was halfway out, arms outstretched, already prepared for impact, when I heard the scuff of his boots from inside and felt him grab my leg and pull up the material of my jeans in an effort to expose my calf. As the blade touched my flesh but before he could make an incision, I lashed out with the other leg and could tell by the impact that I'd caught him in the face. For the first time I heard him cry out, and I kicked again, like a donkey, then put the flats of both hands against the outside wall and launched myself forward into thin air, as if making a championship dive.

The roof shot up to meet me and I hit it in an unsteady handstand, pain shooting up my wrists. My legs hovered precariously in the air then made a rapid descent, and I ended up somersaulting over, the roof's material digging into my scalp. It didn't even strike me to look back, to check whether my assailant was coming or not. I half-crawled, half-ran, over to the edge of the building and, using my hands as a pivot, swung myself over and slid down the wall, jumping the last couple of feet to the ground.

I was in a small paved area enclosed by a brick wall some ten feet high. In front of the wall were two lines of car-sized green wheelie bins, the majority of them overflowing with rubbish. There was a strong smell of refuse. Beyond the wall, I could hear the sound of a car coming past. Freedom.

I stood where I was for several seconds, panting heavily, then heard movement on the roof above me. It was like being trapped in a nightmare. The bastard was still coming.

Summoning up my remaining strength, I ran between the lines of wheelie bins and tried to haul myself up on one that had been positioned adjacent to the wall. I failed with my first attempt. I'm no longer as fit as I used to be. My gym membership lapsed three years ago, and now the occasional game of tennis in the summer is my only real exercise. Bizarrely, as I went to try it a second time, I made a vow to renew the gym membership if ever my life returned to normal.

This time, with a grunt of exertion, I managed it, flopping onto the bin's plastic top on my belly before struggling to my feet, pulling myself up the last couple of feet to the top of the wall and scrambling over, unable to see my pursuer in the half-second timeframe I had before the view behind me disappeared.

I hit the pavement feet-first and saw that I was in an unfamiliar residential street of terraced housing. A car came past but the driver didn't seem to notice me. I'd lost my bearings, having never exited the university this way before. All I knew was that I was a long way from my car.

Panting loudly, I ran across the road and headed back in the direction of where I thought the car park was situated. I must have looked a sight. I could feel the blood from the wound on my face now running down onto the collar of my shirt, staining it. The arm wound, meanwhile, was bleeding even more heavily.

It burned, as if someone was inserting white hot needles into the skin, and I looked at it for a moment as I half-staggered, half-ran down the street, my mouth open, sucking in air. For the first time, I felt sick. What was happening to me? What had I done to deserve this?

An attractive woman of about thirty in a long gypsy skirt and halter top stepped out of her house, took one look at me and immediately rushed back in again, shutting the door behind her. This was London. The place where it's always best to mind your own business and step away from trouble. A friend of Kathy's had been mugged once, about five years ago, outside Oval tube station at four o'clock in the afternoon. She'd tried to hold onto her handbag and her two attackers had kicked her to the ground and spent several long minutes wrestling it from her while raining down resistance-sapping blows. During that time she estimated that some fifty people walked past. Most had hurried away. A couple slowed down to get a better look. No-one had intervened. Kathy had sworn that had she been one of those passing she would have done something. 'I wouldn't have been able to live with myself if I hadn't,' she'd told me. 'If you turn your back, it's the same as admitting that you've been defeated, and I could never do that.' This was typical of Kathy. She was a woman with principles, a woman who cared. But where was she now? And, more importantly, had it been her blood on the carpet back in the library with that madman?

I had to locate her. Get to her soon.

Still running, I rummaged in my pocket for the phone. Please answer this time. Please.

Another car came past. This time the driver slowed, and as our eyes met, his widened dramatically. I kept going, ignoring the pain in my lungs. Behind me I heard the car stopping, and him getting out.

'Mate!' he shouted. 'Mate! Are you all right?'

I didn't want to speak to him. I didn't want to speak to anyone other than my wife. I had to get to her. I tugged out the phone, but heard the man's footsteps coming behind me.

No, not again. Was he one of them? The bastards seemed to be everywhere. In my home – my fucking home. At my wife's work.

I accelerated, and as I came to a crossroads I stumbled into the road, the phone in my hand, ignoring the shouts of the man behind me. I heard the roar of a car to my right. A blast of a horn, and then an angry screech of tyres. Out of the corner of my eye I saw a huge white shape bearing down on me and I knew I was going to get run over. I could just make out the blue lights on its roof and then it hit me with a bang that was all but drowned out by the sound of the skid. I tumbled over the bonnet, bounced off it once, then seemed to slide off the other side, falling onto the road in a fetal roll a few feet from the front passenger door.

The door opened and I came face to face with a pair of well-polished black police-issue boots. 'Hello hello hello,' I said, and then, for some wholly inexplicable reason, I started laughing, the movement making my body sear with a dozen different pains.

For the moment, I could stop running, and I felt a surge of relief that lasted as long as it took for the police officer to bend down, pull my arms painfully round behind my back, and tell me I was under arrest on suspicion of murder.

4

DI Mike Bolt's team of National Crime Squad detectives operated out of the middle third of a nondescript 1970s two-storey greybrick building with a corrugated-iron roof that made a terrible racket whenever it rained heavily. It was situated on a bland, sprawling industrial estate just off the A4 in Hayes, and a couple of miles east of Heathrow airport. The sign in the window said WHITEHOUSE DESIGN CONSULTANCY, and neither of the companies on either side of them – a printer's and a recruitment agency – had any idea that the men and women coming out of the front door were plainclothes police officers. They kept themselves to themselves and retained a low profile, which was the way to operate when you were involved in the murky world of organized crime.

Today, however, the only occupant of Whitehouse Design Consultancy was Bolt himself, and the crime he was working on had nothing to do with the organized variety, at least on the surface of it. It also might not have been an actual crime. At that moment in time, it was difficult to tell.

The case was the apparent suicide of a senior member of the

judiciary. Because of the victim's high profile, and the fact that his suicide note had been typed and unsigned, a decision had been taken at the highest level to launch a thorough investigation into the circumstances surrounding his death. And because Bolt's team had just come off a very successful case in which they'd broken up a major money-laundering ring, they'd been chosen to carry it out.

So, rather than enjoying the fishing trip with a couple of old Flying Squad buddies that had been planned for months, Bolt was instead spending his Saturday afternoon sitting in his drab open-plan office, with a view that took in a power tool wholesaler's and a vegetable oil importer's warehouse, poring over the initial autopsy report which had been faxed through an hour earlier. There was a lot of crap about body temperatures, chemicals and stomach contents, but the gist of the report was that the victim had died between 8 p.m. and 4 a.m. two nights earlier, the cause of death an overdose of dilantin, a type of sleeping pill. Further tests were needed to confirm how the drug had been administered, but mild bruising on the underside of the victim's left arm suggested that he had probably injected it.

Bolt sighed and sat back in his chair. None of this told him much. His first instinct when the team had been assigned the case the previous morning, after the victim's maid had discovered the body, was that it had indeed been a suicide. The reasons for this were as follows. One, there were no signs of forced entry into the Mayfair townhouse where the body had been found, and it was a secure building, with strong locks on the front door, no rear access unless you traipsed through someone else's house first, and a sophisticated alarm system with panic buttons in every room. Two, there were no signs of a struggle. The victim was lying on his side in bed with the covers off, clad in fashionable silk pyjamas and a towelling robe, his features peaceful. It was a perfectly natural position to die in. As well as this, everything in the room looked untouched. There were no overturned lamps or drawers pulled out, nothing that would invite suspicion.

What was bugging the people on high, though, was the suicide note. The fact that it was typed rather than handwritten was one bone of contention. Apparently, the victim was particularly proud of what one fellow judge had described as, quote, 'the curved, flourishing style of his handwriting'. Another of the victim's former colleagues had suggested that the letter, at only two lines long, was too short. The dead man was a methodical thinker, which probably had something to do with his legal background. He liked to seek out and provide explanations for events, and would, they argued, have wanted to give the public something a bit more substantial than the fact that he couldn't take the pain of living. Finally, the letter was unsigned, which had led to some questioning its veracity.

None of this swayed Mike Bolt. A lot of suicide notes were short. Some were only one line long. Sometimes they weren't signed either. The thing was, people didn't tend to be thinking straight when they chose to put an end to their own lives.

But a job was a job, and to this end Bolt had set the team to work interviewing friends, family and colleagues of the victim, to build up a picture of his private life. The victim had been divorced for more than twenty years, was childless, and his wife now lived in the Cayman Islands. At some point someone would have to talk to her. Not surprisingly, there was no shortage of volunteers among the nine people he had working under him to take on that particular job, but, should it be needed, he'd be the one jetting off over there for a couple of days. He might even try to fit in some game fishing; he'd heard the marlin were good round that neck of the woods. There was no point being the boss unless you got some perks.

At the moment, though, they were concentrating on the many people who knew him in south-east England. Bolt had already interviewed a judge and a senior politician today, one in central London, the other at his family seat in Hampshire. Now he was waiting for his colleague, DS Mo Khan, to pick him up for their 5.30 interview. When that was done, he was finished for the day. He'd already planned the night ahead. Back to his apartment in Clerkenwell, a good hot shower and a takeaway sea bass in tamarind sauce from the Thai place round the corner, followed by the latest of the *Miss Marple* remakes on ITV. Tonight it was 'The Body in the Library' and, thankfully, he couldn't remember whodunnit even though he'd read the book twice. People laughed at him for watching *Miss Marple*, and *Poirot*, and even bloody *Wycliffe*. But what they didn't understand was that he liked to escape from the bleak, cold world of violent crime he inhabited every working day, where murders were cruel events, often committed for the most mundane of reasons. And where escapism was concerned, nothing beat the sofa, a couple of drinks and the late, great Agatha Christie.

He checked his watch. Five to five. Mo should be here soon. He was currently doing a second interview with the victim's maid, who lived in Feltham. She'd been in a bit of a state the previous day, so there were a few things they had to go over in more detail, particularly relating to the company the victim kept in his own time. Mo had a theory that he was gay, but Bolt had told him to go easy on this line of questioning with the maid. She was Filipina and a devout Catholic, so might take offence at any aspersions being cast on the honour of her employer.

He pushed the autopsy report to one side and sat back in his chair, drinking from the mug of coffee he'd made earlier and looking out of the window at the aircraft-hangar-sized warehouse opposite, which was used to store nothing but tens of thousands of gallons of vegetable oil. Bolt often wondered what would happen if that place caught fire. Occasionally, he fantasized about it: this whole bleak estate disappearing in a great ball of foul-smelling flame. It would mean his team being freed to look for some decent premises, preferably closer to the centre of town.

The open-plan office where Bolt was sitting now was ugly, and cluttered, with too many desks for the available floorspace, and very drably decorated. However, it did have one thing going for it: a frankly magnificent thirty-six-inch plasma TV mounted on one of the faded chipboard walls that had the sharpest picture Bolt had ever seen. At that moment it was being graced by the England football team who were playing an excruciatingly dull friendly on very low volume against a country Bolt hadn't even heard of. They were halfway through the second half and the score remained anchored at 0–0.

There was an interesting story about that TV, far more interesting than the one currently being played out on it. It had once belonged to a charming old gentleman by the name of Henry Pugh who'd chopped up his wife, Rita, into six manageable pieces one winter's night several years earlier before depositing her arms and legs in Highgate cemetery near the spot where Karl Marx resides, her torso in the Regent's Canal near the junctions of Upper Street and City Road, and, with what you might call a measure of thoughtlessness, her head in a children's playground in Stoke Newington. When Pugh was arrested, he immediately pleaded guilty and left instructions with his solicitor

43

for all his worldly possessions to be passed to his sister. She then held a macabre bring-and-buy sale that included a set of Japanese kitchen knives with one missing (the murder weapon) and Pugh's state-of-the-art plasma screen, which he'd bought shortly before the murder and whose purchase had, allegedly, led to the argument that ended in his wife's death. One of the team, DC Matt Turner, who always had an eye for a bargain, had snapped it up for £200, a snip when you think the knives went for over five hundred, after a bidding war between rival collectors of gruesome memorabilia.

Bolt's mobile rang, the first time for almost an hour. He picked up. It was Mo.

'Where are you?' Bolt asked.

'About ten minutes away.'

'Have you seen the time? Our meeting's at five-thirty, and I don't want to give him a chance not to be there. It's been hard enough getting him pinned down in the first place.' The victim's lawyer had been a pain from the start, twice moving interviews due to work commitments, and only fitting them in today when Bolt had threatened to arrest him for obstruction.

'Well, to be honest, boss, there's not quite the level of urgency there was,' said Mo.

'What do you mean?'

'I mean, Jack Calley won't be going anywhere. He's dead. And whoever's got him that way tried to make it look like suicide.'

Bolt cursed. This really changed things. So much for his theories.

'Look at it like this, boss,' said Mo. 'At least he'll be there when we turn up.'

5

I was taken in the back of the police car to Colindale hospital. The two arresting officers, a young white man and an even younger black man, gave me no further details about who I was meant to have murdered. Nor would they remove the handcuffs, even though I was bleeding, or let me use the mobile to call Kathy. They emptied out my pockets and put the contents in a clear plastic evidence bag that was deposited in the glove compartment.

'I'm trying to find my wife,' I told them desperately, amazed by their indifference. 'Her name's Kathy, Katherine, Meron. That's why I was at the university. Can you just confirm that she's all right? Please?'

'We can't confirm anything at the moment, sir,' said the white man, who was driving.

'Except that you're under arrest,' added his colleague helpfully.

I tried to reason with them but they told me, politely, to leave it until the interview. The black officer then radioed the station and told the operator he had a suspect in custody for the university killing. He described me as an IC1 male identified by the documents I was carrying as Thomas David Meron, age thirty-five, brown hair, blue eyes, five ten.

'But I haven't killed anyone,' I told the driver as his colleague kept talking. 'I was attacked by a man with a knife in the university library. That's where these cuts are from. I think he may have attacked my wife. Can you at least tell me if the victim's a woman or not?'

'We can't say anything at the moment,' answered the driver.

'The killer's still loose,' I pleaded. 'You should be looking for him.'

'We'll be checking every avenue, sir, don't worry.'

I replied that of course I was worried. My wife was missing, and I wanted to make sure she wasn't the victim.

This time he ignored me.

I was in the hospital for about twenty minutes. Unlike everyone else in the casualty department, I was whisked straight through to a small, windowless room that smelled of antiseptic where a doctor who was even younger than the two coppers stitched me up. By now, the wounds were really hurting. The one on my jawline throbbed hotly, and I was afraid to see what my face looked like. Like a lot of men, I'm pretty vain. I don't think I'm God's gift to women exactly, but I've been told I'm pretty good-looking, and I've not done badly with the opposite sex over the years. The idea of being scarred for life scared me – one of quite a few scaring me at that moment.

The doctor put dressings on the wounds and gave me some painkillers. When he looked at me it was with a mixture of distaste and trepidation. He saw a patient in need, but also a suspected murderer.

'I didn't do anything wrong,' I told him. 'I'm innocent.'

It was hardly an original line, and I guess, like the cops with me, he'd heard it plenty of times before. He didn't reply. Instead he turned to the white police officer and told him that I was now fit to be questioned.

The black police officer reattached the handcuffs, then took me by the arm, his hand scraping against the wound on my forearm. I flinched, and he gave a perfunctory apology. I could tell he didn't mean it.

'Have you got a mirror?' I asked the doctor. 'I need to see what my face looks like.'

As soon as I said it, I regretted doing so. It looked like I was more interested in my own injuries than what had happened to Kathy, which wasn't true. I just needed to know. The doctor nodded curtly and found a small round mirror on his desk which he held up in front of my face.

I flinched again, more noticeably this time. It was bad, very bad. My hair looked like it had been styled by Edward Scissorhands, my face like it had been used to clean a slaughterhouse floor. Smudged and uneven flecks of blood, sweat and dirt covered it. Further dark rivulets of blood, resembling thick spiders' legs, had solidified on my neck where they'd run down from beneath the gleaming white dressing that covered my jawline. My eyes had become grey and haunted, the pupils little more than retreating pinpricks. I looked exactly like I felt.

As I was led away, I saw from the clock on the whitewashed wall that it was five o'clock in the afternoon. In the space of two hours, my life – so ordinary, so mundane, so desperately missed – had been torn irreparably apart. Two hours earlier, I'd been a normal working man living a pleasant, easy life. Now, my wife was missing, and very possibly dead; there were people after me

47

for a reason I had no knowledge of; and I was about to be charged with murder.

What I didn't know was that this was only the beginning. Things, if you can believe it, were about to get one hell of a lot worse.

6

'Do we know what happened to Calley?' Bolt asked Mo as they drove up the M25 in traffic that was surprisingly light for the time of day.

Mo shook his head. 'There are very few details at the moment. I called his house just to make sure that he was going to be there when we turned up, and another cop answered it. That was just before five, and then I called you. I explained who I was and why I was phoning, and he told me they'd found Calley's body in some woods a couple of hundred yards behind his house, hanging from a tree by his belt and looking like he'd had some help getting up there. When I asked what made them think that, he said there were definite signs of a struggle.'

'Less than forty-eight hours after his biggest client dies in mysterious circumstances. Do you think it's a coincidence?' Bolt was interested in Mo's opinion. They'd worked together two years now, and after Bolt himself, Mo was the most experienced officer in his young team.

'There's no doubt it looks suspicious,' he answered. 'Have you found out what work Calley did for our victim yet?'

'That's one of the things I was hoping to find out today,' said Bolt. 'When I asked him on the phone yesterday, he gave me the usual client confidentiality bullshit, but Calley specialized in investments, stuff like that. He was a financial lawyer, so I'm guessing he helped our man hide his money from the Inland Revenue.'

Mo chuckled. 'A financial lawyer. Now there's a job that sounds lucrative.'

'Too right. But it sounds like one that could make you some enemies as well. We're going to have to dig a little deeper into his business dealings.' Bolt sighed. 'You know, I had plans for tonight.'

'It's *Miss Marple*, isn't it?'

'That's right. "Body in the Library".'

'It's a wild life you lead, boss.'

'You only live once. How about you? Anything happening that's now going to have to wait?'

'The usual. Breaking-up arguments, nappy changing, midnight feeds.'

'Shit, I bet you're glad Calley's dead, aren't you? Gives you an excuse to stay out.'

Mo chuckled again. 'I wouldn't go that far, boss, but let's say it's a very dark cloud with a small silver lining.'

They came off the M25 at junction 17, Maple Cross, and proceeded through a maze of back roads in the general direction of Ruislip before turning off onto a narrow, tree-lined lane that wound its way through a mixture of woodland and fields dotted with the odd detached cottage and executive home, until finally a loose group of four houses, spaced well apart, appeared on the right-hand side as the road straightened and widened. The houses backed on to a wooded hill and faced a wide, green, undulating field in which a herd of sheep grazed peacefully. It was a lovely rustic English scene, rare this close to London, and one that was only spoiled by the row of police cars and vans parked outside the third house along, and the line of yellow scene-of-crime tape running across the road. An older couple, presumably the neighbours, were standing outside the second house, talking to two note-taking detectives, while several white-overalled scene-of-crime officers milled about beside one of the vans.

Mo drove past the neighbours and parked up behind one of the police cars. 'Nice house,' he said admiringly, looking up at the two-storey whitewashed cottage with the thatched roof and latticed windows that had belonged to Jack Calley. A very swish-looking black BMW 7-Series was parked in a spacious gravel driveway that would have amply accommodated another three of them.

'That's what you get from being a financial lawyer,' said Bolt, getting out of the car.

A uniformed officer who looked about twelve approached them, cap under his arm. Bolt noticed he was already going bald on top, and felt sorry for the poor sod.

'We're here to talk to the SIO,' he explained as he and Mo produced their warrant cards and introduced themselves.

'National Crime Squad, eh? Do you reckon it's gangland?'

The young officer looked excited and Bolt didn't have the heart to put a pin in his balloon, so he said that it could be.

'Where's the body?' he asked.

The young uniform pointed behind him, up into the woods. 'Follow the path and you'll get to him. The SIO's up there too.'

They went to the back of one of the vans, where a SOCO officer gave them the kit of overalls, hoods, gloves and booties, and once they'd put everything on they headed up the path that ran round the side of Calley's house and into the shadows of the beech trees.

The two of them made an odd pair. Bolt was a tall, rangy man in his late thirties with the broad shoulders of a rower, closely cropped ash-blond hair that was just beginning to fleck with grey, and a face you wouldn't choose to argue with. It was long and lean in shape, the features hard and naturally well defined, and clearly belonged to someone who knew how to handle himself. There was a vivid S-shaped scar running almost the length of his chin, and two more scars, like shapeless runes, on his left cheek – relics of a life-changing night three years earlier. Yet the overall result remained somewhere close to handsome. His eyes were his chief selling point. His former wife had called them the most striking she'd ever seen, and although she could probably have been accused of bias, they did draw people, being perfectly oval and a lively cerulean blue, and when he smiled, which was often enough these days, they became surrounded by deep laughter lines.

Mo, by contrast, was a small, stocky guy with a head that sometimes appeared too big for his body. It was topped by a frizzy mop of curly hair that couldn't seem to decide whether it was black or silver, and had ended up being an unkempt combination of the two. He was a couple of years younger than Bolt, but could probably have passed for forty. His face was round and jolly and he had big bloodhound eyes under which sat heavy bags, that had become more pronounced in recent years due to the trials and tribulations of his young family. He had three sons under the age of five and a daughter of ten who thought she was a teenager, and it showed in the air of permanent exhaustion that surrounded him. Without cigarettes and copious quantities of coffee, it was doubtful he'd be able to function, and people often asked him why he'd punished himself by waiting so long after his first child before suddenly producing three more. His reply was that he hadn't planned any of them; they'd just come when they were ready, and rather than being a punishment, to him they were a blessing. Mo loved his kids deeply, and part of the reason he made such a good cop was because, underneath the somewhat cynical exterior, he believed in what he was doing and wanted to create a better society for them to grow up in. Of everyone in the team, he was probably the hardest working, and had never once shied away from over-time, paid for or not, which was the reason Bolt enjoyed working with him.

The path, which was little more than a dirt track, led up a moderate, fairly straight incline and was muddy in patches from the recent rain, revealing a number of partial and com-plete footprints, several of which had already been enclosed by phosphorescent-scene-of-crime tape. A line of it stretched up the edge of the path, and they had to keep to its right to avoid contaminating any possible evidence. As they made their way along it, they could see that the prints belonged to at least three sets of shoes. Occasionally, they were scuffed where someone had obviously slipped. It didn't take much to figure out that Calley had been chased by two people, probably men by the size and style of their shoe markings.

They rounded a corner and the path became a wider, flatter gully, and it was here that they came face to face with the body of the man himself. He was hanging from one of the lower branches of a gnarled beech tree on the left side of the path about ten yards away, his feet dangling a few inches from the ground, a leather belt around his neck. He was dressed in jeans, trainers and a white England rugby shirt, the front of which was flecked with spots of blood. It looked as if he'd received a facial injury but it was difficult to tell from the position of his head, which was leaning forward so that he was facing the ground. A thick fringe of dark blond hair hung forlornly down over it like a curtain.

Five or six men and women, all in identical white suits, milled around the body, taking photographs and samples in the undignified, if necessary, manner that characterizes all major crime scenes. As Bolt and Mo approached, one of the men standing on the edge of the scene turned and came down towards them, an inquisitive expression on his face. He was a tall man in his fifties, with a well-kept moustache, a seriously receding hairline and a vaguely regal manner that suggested the possibility he was ex-military.

'Can I help you?' he asked, stopping in front of them. The question wasn't delivered in an unfriendly manner, but he wasn't smiling either.

'I'm DI Mike Bolt, NCS. This is my colleague, DS Mo Khan.' Mo nodded. 'We were coming here to interview Jack Calley.' Bolt looked over at the body. 'I'm guessing we're a little too late.'

'You are. I'm DCI Keith Lambden, Ruislip CID, the SIO on this case.' He put out a hand and they shook. 'Can I ask exactly what you were going to speak to Mr Calley about?'

Bolt gave him a brief rundown of their own case and Calley's relationship with their supposed suicide victim. Lambden's eyebrows rose when they mentioned the Lord Chief Justice's name, but he didn't speak.

'Is there anything you've found so far that could link the two cases, Keith?' asked Bolt, looking over again at the body.

'Far too early to say,' replied Lambden. 'He was only discovered an hour ago by a woman walking her dog, which was lucky as this isn't really a well-used path. We got here at half past four, and we've only just finished sealing everything off. The doctor's given a preliminary time of death of between two thirty and three thirty, so he's not been this way long.'

'It looks from the prints like two people were chasing him,' said Mo. 'Those trainers slipped twice in the mud on the way up here.'

'Three times actually, and you're right, it does seem like it was two people. We've checked out the downstairs of Mr Calley's house and the side door was wide open. There's also a fresh partial footprint at the end of his garden by a gate that leads directly on to this path. The gate was also open. It looks like the suspects confronted him in his house and he managed to escape out of the side door through the conservatory, which goes out into the back garden. They chased him up this path and caught him here. There was some sort of struggle. He ended up with a bleeding nose and facial bruising, and you can see where his shirt's been ripped.' He pointed over at the body and they both saw that there was a large tear running underneath the arm of the rugby shirt where he'd obviously been grabbed. 'My guess is that one of them held him while the other put the belt round his neck and either strangled him then and there and hung him up afterwards, or put him up there while he was still alive and let him die like that.'

They all fell silent. Whichever way any of them cared to look at it, it was a particularly nasty way to go.

'They were certainly determined to make sure they killed him,' said Bolt. 'But no-one saw anything?'

'We'll be making the usual appeals for witnesses but no-one called us until the dogwalker who found him.'

'Poor bastard,' said Mo, getting back to his feet. 'I guess we can rule out robbery. They wouldn't have bothered chasing him up this path if they just wanted to burgle his house.'

'And nothing appears to be missing from it either,' said Lambden. 'My guess is that he knew his killers. There's no sign of forced entry at the front of the house.'

'A professional hit, then, boss?' suggested Mo.

'Well, it doesn't appear as though there was anything random about it. What do you think, Keith?'

'Again, too early,' answered Lambden, with a hint of reproach as if they were enthusiastic young rookies running ahead of themselves. 'All we can be certain of is that the people who did this were physically strong, and very nasty indeed. Not the sort you'd want to meet on a dark night.'

Bolt moved closer to the body. He waited while the police photographer took some close-up photos of Calley's corpse, then inspected it from a couple of feet away, ignoring the pungent odour that clung to it.

Calley looked young, maybe early thirties. He was good-looking too, with clean-cut, middle-class features and a big build. A man who should have been, and probably had been, a success story. Not the sort you'd associate with being a victim of crime. The dead man's features were slack, the mouth turned down a little at each corner in a mildly doleful expression, the eyes gazing blankly in Bolt's general direction.

Death, like the onset of age, terrified Bolt. He wasn't a Christian, having become convinced that the world's secrets could be better explained by science than spiritualism while still in his pre-teenage years. He believed then, as he did now, that when a person died, that was it for them. The end of their journey, the big sleep. It was this lack of faith in something beyond which made him fear it so much. Sometimes he truly wished he could embrace religion, as many do when age takes them closer to the end, but he knew that it wouldn't work. His own beliefs were too deeply ingrained. Standing here, viewing sudden, unexpected death at first hand, brought the fear right back to the forefront of his mind. A few hours ago, Jack Calley had been a wealthy young man with everything to live for. Now he was simply a sack of deteriorating meat without soul or function.

Something caught Bolt's eye, and he leaned down, squinting.

'What is it?' asked Mo from a few feet away.

'Do you mind if I move the body, Keith?' he asked DCI Lambden.

Lambden asked the photographer if he was finished, and the other man replied that he was. 'OK,' he said, 'but be careful. I don't want anything contaminated.'

Bolt ignored Lambden's irritable manner. He was used to the territorial instinct of provincial detectives whenever they dealt with him and his colleagues, as if they thought the arrival of the National Crime Squad at a crime scene was some sort of official slight on their reputation. Slowly, he used both gloved hands to prise apart the upper portion of Calley's thighs. The other two men had come closer, and they noticed it immediately.

'What on earth's that?' exclaimed Lambden in a voice that was an octave higher than it needed to be. Mo just exhaled. He'd worked organized crime for several years now and was well used to seeing signs of torture on both the living and the dead.

The crotch of Calley's jeans was badly blackened and charred where a number of separate burns, each approximately the size

56

of a two-pence piece, had been made. Someone, it seemed, had slowly and deliberately held a naked flame to his groin, and not just once either. Four, possibly five times, the marks merging together.

For a while no-one said anything. The other SOCO officers and the photographer came over and looked at this discovery, and the photographer took a couple of pictures. Bolt picked up one of Calley's arms and inspected the wrist. There was a faint but noticeable line of reddish skin about half an inch thick running round the wrist like a bracelet. He checked the other wrist. There was the same colouring. Ligature marks.

'He must have had some real enemies,' said one of the SOCOs.

'Either that,' said Bolt with a sigh, 'or he had something someone wanted very badly.'

7

When I was seventeen, Jack 'n' me and two other friends got arrested on suspicion of stealing a car. We hadn't stolen it. It was a crappy old white Ford Escort van and it belonged to Jack. Having been the first to pass his driving test, he'd bought it fourth or fifth hand for about a hundred quid, and on most of the summer nights of that year he'd come and pick up the rest of us in it. Whoever he picked up first – almost always me, even though he'd moved more than a mile away by that point – got the front seat, while the other two had to make do with sitting on a mangy old rug in the back among the rusty tools, bits of car and all the other crap that had accumulated there over the months. We called ourselves 'The Van Gang', and our nights consisted of driving round looking for something to do, which could involve a visit to one of the few country pubs that would serve us, or a girl's house, or just a detour off somewhere isolated so we could do our bit for teenage rebellion by puffing away on a couple of joints and while away the time giggling inanely. They were good days, all in all, more innocent than they sounded, and though my involvement with drugs was pretty brief, I don't recall it ever giving me any ill effects.

Anyway, the indicators on Jack's van didn't work, and one night near the end of summer when we were driving around aimlessly, he made a right turn, naturally without signalling, in front of a police car parked in a layby. The cops came after us and pulled Jack over. They were an officious-looking pair and the lead guy looked more like an accountant than a defender of law and order. But I remember being scared, even though I had no dope or anything else illicit on me. It was just the thought of being on the receiving end of the attention of the police, as if they could somehow find out about all my other youthful indiscretions and bring me to account for them.

The first question the accountant copper asked was whether the vehicle belonged to Jack.

'Yes,' he'd replied.

'Can you give me the keys, please?'

'Well, the thing is, officer, I lost them a while back and I've been using this.' He removed a pocket-sized screwdriver from the ignition and showed it to the officer.

Incredibly, this version of events was absolutely true (Jack's van really was a heap of shit), but no police officer in his right mind was going to let us go having seen that, and because the police computers were a lot slower in those days and it took a lot longer to access the registration database, we were promptly arrested, even though Jack made a manful and genuine attempt to explain his innocence. I could tell at the time that the police were quite pleased with their collar. Four arrests in one go would look good on their record, and the paperwork meant that they could go back to the station for a while. I could also tell that they were inclined to believe Jack's story, mainly because of his pleas and the fact that, when it came down to it, we looked and sounded like students rather than car thieves.

We were held for a total of four hours, which was the time it took to process the paperwork, followed by a forty-five-minute wait while the necessary checks were made. During that time, as it became obvious that they were only really interested in us as a statistic rather than for any crime we'd committed, I found myself relaxing. They didn't bother putting us in the cells but let us sit together in one of the interview rooms, where we passed the time playing a cramped game of charades until it was time to go. With the vehicle impounded, however, for being un-roadworthy, there was no way home, and after drawing lots we were forced to call my dad for a lift at 4.30 that morning. He collected us but he was none too pleased about it, and he hadn't spoken to Jack for months after that.

I thought back to that time now as I sat in the interview room of a different police station, alone this time, and with the charge of murder hanging over my head. It was, as you can imagine, a very lonely place to be. The police officers who'd brought me here were most definitely not inclined to believe my story, and nor was the custody sergeant who'd booked me in.

They'd done everything professionally, but with the cool, distant air of men who were never going to be convinced by the pained, unimaginative pleas of their suspects. I'd demanded my one phone call and had been taken to a phone in one of the corridors, where the black officer waited while once again I tried Kathy's mobile, and once again it went to message. I'd left another, explaining my predicament and begging her to get in touch as soon as possible.

I'd also demanded a lawyer. Politely but firmly. I was beginning to get angry now. I was still scared, of course, both for myself and Kathy. But I was also extremely pissed off that I was being held against my will for something I hadn't done, and with no-one showing the slightest sign of listening to my story, or of letting me know anything concerning the fate of my wife.

'Do you have one, or would you like us to call someone?' the custody sergeant had asked wearily.

Had he asked me that question at any time in the last twelve years up to three hours earlier, I would have said Jack Calley, and I would have been sure that he'd sort things out for me. Jack was like that. He inspired confidence. For the first time in a long time I needed him, and I was too late.

'I haven't got anyone. I need you to call a lawyer.'

The custody sergeant had nodded and said he'd make the necessary arrangements.

In the meantime I was taken by my two arresting officers down to one of the interview rooms, and here I was now – half an hour, an hour later, it was impossible to tell for sure – waiting and wondering whether my wife, the mother of my children, was still alive, or whether I was to be accused of her murder. Wondering too why Jack Calley had phoned me, and why he'd been attacked and probably murdered before the call was completed. And why a man in a balaclava had attacked me with a bloodstained knife in the politics department of the university where my wife worked.

The door to the interview room opened and a pleasant-looking fat man of about fifty with shoulder-length grey hair that was so thick it could have contained buried treasure came into the room. He was wearing horn-rimmed glasses, a navy-blue pinstripe suit, complete with a waistcoat that stretched and strained over his ample belly, and a smile that was the first I'd seen in a while. His features were soft, his face curiously owl-like, and in one dainty hand that had clearly never been sullied by manual work, he carried a battered leather briefcase which looked as if a pack of dogs had been at it. He banged it down on the table and thrust out a hand.

'Mr Meron,' he said in a lilting Scottish baritone that could have used a bigger audience, peering at me over his glasses. 'I'm Douglas McFee, the duty solicitor. I understand you requested my help.'

I stood up and took the proffered hand, surprised that the palm was lined with sweat. 'Thank you for coming. I think I'm going to need it.'

Douglas McFee smiled again and sat down opposite me. He put the briefcase on the floor and placed his elbows on the table and his hands together, as if in prayer, the tips of his fingers stroking his bottom lip. His expression was surprisingly intense, yet at the same time it remained amiable.

'Now,' he continued, 'why don't you tell me how you came to be arrested running down the street very close to a murder scene, distressed and bleeding from several cuts?'

'Before I tell you anything, can you tell me if my wife's OK? If she's the person I'm meant to have murdered . . .' I trailed off, not sure what else to say.

He gave me a sympathetic smile. The sight of it made me want to weep. Did someone at last believe me? 'I think I can put your mind at rest there,' he said.

I felt a rush of relief. 'Really? It's not her?'

He shook his head. 'No, the woman the police suspect you murdered is not your wife. Her name is, or more accurately was, Vanessa Blake.'

Relief was now mixed with shock. 'Vanessa?'

'You know her?'

'Yes, I do. She's a politics lecturer at the university. Like Kathy, my wife. She's been there for years.'

I'd never liked Vanessa. She was a couple of years younger than Kathy, attractive in a very severe way, and unequivocally gay. She didn't like men and made no secret of the fact, and I'd often thought she'd tried to turn my wife against me. In fact, I think she'd had a thing for Kathy. And now she was dead. But I didn't really have time to think about her passing. I was too relieved for that.

McFee inclined his head solemnly as he delivered the bad news, recounting it like a particularly enjoyable ghost story. 'Her body was discovered by a student in an adjoining room to the library where you encountered the masked man who attacked you with the knife. She'd been stabbed repeatedly. The student was naturally very shocked, but she was able to call the police. This must have been only minutes after you left the building because it was officers responding to that initial emergency call who arrested you.'

I put my head in my hands and took several deep breaths before re-emerging. The wound on my jawline suddenly started throbbing. 'Thank God Kathy's all right. It's terrible about Vanessa, she was a good person, but I'm glad it was her and not Kathy. I know that sounds terrible, but you know what I mean? Are you married, Mr McFee?'

'I have a long-term partner so, yes, I understand what you're saying.'

'Jesus, I've been so scared.'

'That's the good news,' said McFee, who had a habit of speaking very slowly, 'if good news it can be called.'

I stiffened. 'There's bad news?'

'Unfortunately, there is. The murder weapon, a filleting knife with a six-inch blade, was recovered at the scene.'

I was finding it difficult to breathe. 'And?'

'And I've just been informed that your wife's fingerprints were recovered from the handle.'

8

Bolt knew that neither he nor Mo was welcome at the Jack Calley crime scene. DCI Lambden made an effort to be polite – after all, there were some tenuous links between the NCS case and his own, so he had to at least accept the presence of two men from that investigation – but it was obvious to all concerned that it was, indeed, an effort. Lambden didn't see where the torture angle fitted in either and was initially dismissive of it as a factor in the murder of Jack Calley. 'We don't know that it's got anything to do with anything,' he said carefully. 'It might be that he burned himself by mistake. It's too early to jump to any conclusions.'

In Bolt's mind, there were two reasons for Lambden's reticence. One, the DCI was a bit of a plodder and had been caught out by the violence of this case. The second was professional rivalry. Bolt, this NCS big boy, had waltzed in, been on the scene for five minutes, and had made a potentially major discovery. And like most people, Lambden didn't like it.

Fair enough. Bolt could see his point. He wouldn't have much liked it either.

'My guess,' he told Lambden and the other assembled officers, 'is that we'll find evidence in the house that he was tortured. The marks on his wrists suggest he was tied up recently. The suspects overpowered him inside the house and then subjected him to some sort of torture, presumably to get information. He escaped, they chased him up here, and, because they were unable to continue the interrogation out in the open, they finished him off.'

'And if he was tortured, what do you think it has to do with your case?'

This was a good question, and one that Bolt had been thinking about ever since he'd got up here. 'Maybe nothing, but we have to remember he was the solicitor of the Lord Chief Justice, who committed suicide in unusual circumstances less than forty-eight hours ago. Now, suddenly, he's been killed by at least two men and it looks like a professional job. This wasn't a robbery, we can be sure of that, and it's very unlikely to be a case of mistaken identity. The killers spent time with this man; they knew who he was. Which means he was targeted specifically. It may well be he's got lots of enemies, I don't know. Like you, I know nothing about him, but I don't like the timing, coming so close after our man's topped himself.'

Lambden didn't say anything for a moment, then nodded slowly. 'We're going to be checking Calley's background and movements very thoroughly, and obviously we'll let you know our findings if there's any relevance to your own investigation.' He turned to one of the other overalled officers. 'Do you want to empty his pockets, Bill? Put everything in an evidence bag.' Bill, an older detective with a bushy moustache, did as instructed while Lambden turned back to Bolt. 'Is there anything else you need to see?' he asked.

'We'd like to take a look in the house if we can.'

The DCI didn't look too pleased at this, but knew better than to make a fuss. 'Of course, but please don't get in the way of my men down there.'

Bolt didn't rise to the bait. 'We'll be on our best behaviour,' he said.

As he turned to head back to the house, he saw Mo watching Bill intently as he emptied the front pockets of Jack Calley's jeans. Bill removed a credit card wallet, a set of keys, a crumpled ten-pound note and some loose change.

'Did you find a mobile near the body, sir?' Mo asked Lambden.

The DCI shook his head. 'There wasn't one here. If it's not in his pockets, I'm sure it'll be back at the house.'

'It'll be very useful to find out who he's been calling these past few days,' said Mo, with as much as diplomacy as he could muster, 'and who's been calling him.'

'We'll be dealing with that in due course.'

Once the two NCS men were on the way back to the house, Mo gave a concise description of DCI Keith Lambden. 'The guy has no vision,' he said. And then, as an afterthought, 'He's also a stuck-up arsehole.'

Bolt sighed in agreement. 'There's never any shortage of them. I reckon we need to take matters into our hands and get on to Jean.'

DC Jean Riley was the youngest of Bolt's team at only twenty-four, and his most recent recruit. She had excellent contacts with the liaison people at the UK's various phone companies and network providers, and was therefore always given the task of chasing up the phone records of suspects. She'd been supplied with the dead judge's landline and mobile numbers earlier that morning and told to get details of the calls logged to and from them. However, because their team was small, she'd also had to travel to Suffolk to interview the politician's sister, so it wasn't a surprise that she hadn't come back to him yet. The events here, however, meant that she was now going to have to redouble her efforts. Phone records can be difficult to get hold of. They take time and, thanks to Britain's Data Protection Act, they usually involve paperwork and high-level authorization. But in reality, if you're willing to push hard enough, you can usually get results.

Bolt pulled out his mobile and called Jean's number.

She answered on the second ring. 'How's everything going, sir?'

'We've had a few developments,' he said, telling her what had happened to Calley. 'Where are you now?'

'Back at HQ. I didn't get much out of our victim's sister in Lowestoft. She was quite a friendly old girl, married with four grown-up kids, but she only saw him once a year at Christmas, and it doesn't sound like she was very close to him. She said he was a bit pompous.'

'That doesn't surprise me. He always seemed it on the telly. Any joy on the phone records?'

'I've got them here in front of me,' she said. 'Landline and mobile. He seemed to mainly use the landline. I've been going through them for the last twenty minutes and there doesn't seem to be anything untoward.'

'How about calls to or from Jack Calley?'

'Hold on a minute, let me have a look.' Bolt waited a few moments while she checked. She hummed a tune – it sounded vaguely like 'Diamonds are Forever' – while she worked. 'There are three calls to the Renfrew, Calley and Partners office number made from the landline in the last six weeks. Two were about ten minutes long, the last one four minutes nine seconds. Made on Monday afternoon.'

'Nothing untoward there. What about the mobile?'

'I'm checking again, but . . .' She paused. 'No, nothing.'

So, there was no hurried series of calls between the Lord Chief Justice and his solicitor, no lengthy conversations. Bolt should have been pleased as it supported his theory that the politician had committed suicide. If this was so, he could go home, get his takeaway, crack open a nice bottle of Shiraz and settle down to watch the great Miss Marple at work. See how it was really done. Yet he was oddly disappointed. Two killers had brutally murdered a young man in the prime of his life. The young man in question might have been a lawyer (a profession for the most part made up of conmen and charlatans, in Bolt's opinion), but that wasn't the point. The type of person who can torture a man and then string him up to die deserves to be put away for life, and Bolt wasn't entirely sure that DCI Keith Lambden was the best person to make this state of affairs come about.

'Can you do me a favour, Jean?' he asked.

'Of course, sir. What is it?'

'Can you get the records for Calley's office and home numbers, and his mobile?'

'Have you got his mobile number?'

'Not yet, but you can get hold of it, can't you?'

'If it's registered in his name, yes, but it'll take a while.'

For the first time, he thought he detected disappointment in her voice. He knew she had a boyfriend, a guy her own age in the civil service, and wondered if they had plans tonight. Probably, and he doubted if they involved watching *Miss Marple*. He thought about letting it go. Jean was a good, enthusiastic worker and he didn't want to take advantage, but he also wanted answers and it was still only twenty to six. If she worked fast, she could still get a good night out.

'If you can see what you can do, that'd be great.'

'Do you think there's a link between our case and this, then?'

'If there is, I want to make sure we find it,' he said, and hung up.

By now, they were back at the front of the house. More police vehicles had arrived, including a dog unit which would be used to ascertain what route the killers had used in making their escape – something Bolt hadn't asked about. The tracks on the path had all been going up so it seemed likely that they'd fled into the woodland after finishing off Calley. The front door of the dead lawyer's house was guarded by a uniformed copper, and SOCO officers moved in and out of it, carrying their paraphernalia.

They showed their warrant cards to the uniform and stepped inside.

The interior of Jack Calley's place was less spacious than

it looked from the outside but still impressively done in a minimalist style that was all the rage these days but made it appear virtually unlived in. The floors were varnished wood; the walls cream; the occasional rugs alternated between black and white; the hall and dining-room furniture expensive combinations of mahogany and cast iron. The whole thing seemed to Bolt to belong to a man with a phobia about dirt. A plasma TV that was bigger and flashier than the one in the team's HQ hung on the living-room wall like a futuristic ornament, facing a pair of linen sofas that had been symmetrically positioned in a perfect yet rather pointless V-shape.

Bolt and Mo spent the next half an hour inspecting the house while trying not to get in the way of the dozen or so SOCO officers who swarmed over it looking for tiny clues – traces of DNA, strands of clothing, anything, in fact, that would help to identify the two killers. A search of a house like this would take anything up to three days, and if there were leads here, they would be found. The technology available to the police was getting more advanced every year and it was getting to the point where only the most intelligent of criminals could operate successfully. This was, of course, a good thing. It was nice to see the bad guys getting caught, and with such incriminating evidence implicating them that any denial was rendered pointless, but something of the job of detective had been lost too. The crime was no longer such a puzzle, the detective no longer such an important part of the process. Often, their job was done for them, by the CCTV operators and the guys from SOCO. Sometimes, Bolt had to admit, it wasn't so much fun as it used to be.

In the master bedroom, where Calley's kingsize futon took up much of the floorspace, they found what they were looking for.

A pair of neckties had been knotted through the wooden frame on each side of the bed's head. These had obviously been used to restrain him, and the several small black marks on the brilliant white sheets in the middle of the bed confirmed their suspicions that it was here that a naked flame had been applied to Jack Calley's groin. Two SOCO guys were on their hands and knees examining the floor around the bed, and it was clear there wasn't much else the NCS men could do.

'So, what do you think happened, boss?' asked Mo as they stood well back looking down at the futon, the SOCO guys studiously ignoring their presence.

'My guess is that when Calley let his killers in, they dragged him up here. Used his own ties to secure him and then went to work with the lighter, or whatever they were using to extract their information.'

'But somehow he manages to escape, get down the stairs and out the back door, even though there are two of them and they've tied him to the bed?' Mo sounded sceptical.

'You think he had some help?'

He shrugged. 'They were torturing him here and he ended up dying two hundred yards away. So something's not right.'

Bolt looked down at the futon again. He imagined Jack Calley helpless and screaming on it while his killers went to work, and was inclined to agree.

9

As they moved out of Calley's front door back into the open air, Bolt's mobile rang again. It was Jean, and she wasn't hanging about.

'I've got hold of the liaison officer at O_2, dragged him away from a corporate do at the football,' she said. 'O_2 are Calley's network provider, and he was making calls on his phone today. Nine in all, to seven different numbers. The last one was recorded only three hours ago, at one minute past three. It lasted thirty-three seconds.'

'What about incoming?'

'The last incoming call was a lot earlier. One sixteen, and it was from a Michael Calley, so I'm assuming a family member.'

'OK, that's fair enough. Can you tell me who the recipient of Calley's last call was?'

'Yes, it was to a residential landline in the name of a Tom and Katherine Meron.'

Bolt pulled a notebook from his pocket and wrote this information down, taking Meron's number and address from Jean. He told her she'd done a good job, and rang off.

Mo lit a cigarette while Bolt filled him in on what Jean had told him.

'Do we know anything about this guy Meron?' he asked when Bolt had finished.

'Nothing at the moment.'

'Do you think we should see what we can find out?'

Bolt looked at his watch. It was quarter past six, and there was a chill in the air. The sky was overcast with dark clouds on the horizon, and it looked like rain. At that moment, his apartment in the heart of the city seemed like a very inviting place to be.

'Sure,' he said, letting curiosity get the better of him. 'Why not?'

10

The door to the interview room opened and two men in dark suits stepped inside, moving slowly like they were actors trying to maximize the effect of their entrance. The older one, who was mid-forties or thereabouts, with hair that was a mixture of red and grey and a moustache that was just red, introduced himself as DCI Rory Caplin. His colleague, DC Ben Sullivan, was a taller, well-built man of about thirty with a neat head of short black hair and a deliberately imposing manner. He looked at me with barely concealed contempt, an expression that seemed to come naturally to the cold, tight features of his meticulously barbered face. There was, of course, no shaking of hands.

By now, my lawyer, Douglas McFee, was sitting next to me, and he gave the detectives the sort of friendly, paternal smile that he'd been using on me all evening. I didn't feel this was a very good sign. Whenever I see defence lawyers in interviews on the TV they're invariably ruthlessly confrontational in their dealings with the forces of law and order, not grinning at them. Given my luck so far today, I suppose I should have been thankful they didn't all jump up and high-five each other. DCI Caplin gave McFee little more than a curt nod before pointing a remote control at a tape machine built into the wall. A red light came on and it immediately clicked into life.

'Interview of Thomas David Meron on suspicion of murder of Vanessa Charlotte Blake,' said DCI Caplin in a surprisingly soft Northern Irish accent, 'commencing six twenty-one p.m. on Saturday May twenty-first.' He mentioned the names of the other people present, then fixed me with a gaze that was in equal parts sympathetic and untrusting. It was an impressive combination. 'What were you doing at the university today?' he asked me.

I didn't answer for a moment. I was still thinking about what McFee had told me only a matter of minutes ago: that my wife's fingerprints had been found on a knife used to murder one of her colleagues. I didn't even know she'd ever been fingerprinted. It was one more worrying thing to take in on a day that had been full of them.

McFee nodded, to let me know I could answer the question, and I told the truth: I'd been looking for my wife.

'Do you often go and see your wife at work?' It was DC Sullivan speaking now. He leaned forward as he spoke, his expression now mixing puzzlement with the contempt.

'No,' I answered.

'When was the last time you visited her there?'

I looked at McFee, and he nodded again, allowing me to answer. 'I can't remember,' I said. 'Months ago.'

'This year?'

'I don't know. Probably not.' I was conscious that I sounded nervous, which was because I was. And I wasn't stupid. I could tell where they were going with these questions. 'There's a good reason why I went today.'

'Is there a good reason why you sustained two knife cuts to your face and body, Tom?' asked DCI Caplin.

'Yes,' I said, willing myself to remain calm. 'There is.' And I told them how I came to be attacked, noting the sceptical look on Caplin's ruddy face and the frankly incredulous one on Sullivan's, as if I was telling them that I'd been attacked by a marauding band of goblins led by Harry Potter. Mind you, the more times I told it, the stranger a story it became, even to my ears, and I remembered that McFee hadn't looked entirely convinced either when I'd told him earlier.

Caplin nodded slowly. 'So, this masked man who assaulted you, he was the only person you saw. You didn't see the victim, Miss Blake, or your wife when you were at the university?'

I shook my head. 'No.'

'Where do you think your wife'll be now?'

The $64,000 question. 'I really don't know. I've tried to call her on her mobile phone but she's not answering.' I knew that this didn't sound good for Kathy, but it wouldn't take long for the police to find out about my attempts to contact her. 'But one thing I do know is that she's innocent. I was attacked by a man with a filleting knife with a yellow handle, and he must have been the person who killed Vanessa.'

They didn't argue with this version of events. Instead, they started questioning me about Vanessa. My relationship with her. My wife's relationship with her. I was vague. I said I didn't really know her that well, which was true. I said my wife got on fine with her as far as I knew. Their technique followed a pattern. Caplin would try to draw information out of me slowly and with comparative gentleness, while now and again Sullivan would chip in with a series of aggressive questions. It was the classic good cop/bad cop technique, and it surprised me because, unlike the ruthless lawyer business, I only thought they did that sort of thing in the movies and on TV shows. It wasn't very effective either, mainly because I was telling the truth.

Occasionally they tried to trip me up by asking the same question twice but in different ways. However, because I wasn't attempting any bullshit, I parried them without too much trouble, and with only limited help from McFee, whose enthusiasm for my case seemed to be plummeting faster than frozen airplane turd.

'You ought to be out there trying to find the man who attacked me and killed Vanessa,' I said when there was a pause in proceedings. 'And helping me find my wife.'

'We are trying to find your wife,' said Sullivan accusingly.

'She didn't do anything. I promise you.'

'Why are her prints on the murder weapon, then?'

They had me there. Whichever way I looked at it, and I was looking at it in every way possible, I couldn't explain that cold fact away. 'I don't know,' I said eventually, trying too hard to keep the defeat out of my voice. As I spoke, I looked at McFee, but he seemed to be inspecting something on the ceiling with rapt interest. For a long moment I felt completely and utterly alone in the world.

'Why don't you tell us the truth?' demanded Sullivan, leaning forward again, his narrow eyes boring into mine.

I met his gaze. I had no choice. 'I am. I promise you. I am telling the truth.'

'You've got to see things from our point of view, Tom,' said Caplin quietly, folding his arms and rocking back in the chair in a way that was peculiarly avuncular. 'No-one else saw this man you're talking about, yet we have several witnesses at the university today who saw a man fitting your description running away from the scene.'

'My client's not denying he was there, or that he ran away, DCI Caplin,' put in McFee.

'No, I'm not. I was there.'

Caplin casually lifted an arm to halt any dissent. 'The point is, we *know* you were there, and we know the victim was there. We also know, because you've told us, that the injuries you received are from the murder weapon, but the only witness to the alleged masked man you talk about is you.'

'We're putting it to you, Mr Meron,' said Sullivan, 'that the masked man didn't exist.'

'Well, I'm putting it to you that he did. How the hell do you think I got these injuries?'

Sullivan allowed himself a little smirk. 'As far as we can see, there's only one way you could have got them, Mr Meron. They were inflicted by your wife during a violent struggle. Either because you interrupted her attacking Vanessa Blake, or because, more likely, she interrupted you.'

'This is ludicrous, gentlemen,' put in McFee, going to town on the word 'ludicrous' with his lilting Scottish burr. 'My client's already told you what happened.'

'But the problem is, Dougie,' said Caplin, pronouncing the name 'Doogie', 'we don't believe him. It's an extremely far-fetched story.'

'No more far-fetched than the one you're peddling,' I said. 'I hardly knew Vanessa Blake. I've met her maybe five times in the past five years, and that's probably an exaggeration. And if I was disturbed by my wife and attacked her, then why didn't you find her?'

I was pleased with the incisiveness of this latter question. It made a mockery of their theory, but to my dismay, neither man made any attempt to accept this. Instead, they simply ignored it.

'But this masked man business,' continued Caplin, making a dismissive gesture with the hand he'd lifted a few moments earlier. 'You're going to have to come up with something better than that. It makes us think you're hiding something. It'd be best for everyone concerned if you just told us what really happened.'

Sullivan turned his beady eyes on McFee. 'You'll be doing your client a favour if you get him to talk, Doogie.'

'My client's already told you what happened, Mr Sullivan,' McFee repeated, though his enthusiasm seemed to have finally hit the depths and I got the feeling that he'd be happy just to get home to his long-term partner.

It was clear that none of the men in the room believed my story, and not for the first time that day I began to get really angry. When Sullivan asked me for the second or third time in that accusing tone of his where I thought my wife was, adding that I'd be helping both of us if I told them, I finally snapped. 'Fuck this,' I said decisively. 'I've had enough. I've told you everything I know, and it's blindingly obvious that you haven't got any real, tangible evidence linking me to this crime. Also, my wife didn't kill anyone. Full stop. I've known her more than ten years, and I've never seen her violent once. She's a good-hearted person from a good family who can't stand the sight of blood, had absolutely nothing against Vanessa Blake, and has never been in trouble with the police. Now, you're holding me on suspicion of Vanessa's murder, right?'

It was Caplin who answered. 'We're questioning you in relation to that, yes.'

'Well, on what evidence are you holding me? If I killed Vanessa Blake, then why aren't my fingerprints on that knife?'

'Because you wore gloves,' answered Sullivan in a way that suggested this was an entirely stupid question.

'I'm assuming you've got CCTV footage of me from the university. Am I wearing gloves in it?'

'They could have been in your pocket. You could have put them on when you reached the scene.'

'But I didn't. I wasn't wearing gloves at all today. I haven't worn a pair for months.' I was on a roll now, no longer intimidated by the questions being flung at me, the anger at the injustice of my situation still seething inside. 'So, if I wasn't wearing gloves, and my fingerprints aren't on the murder weapon, can you tell me on what evidence you're holding me?' I turned towards McFee. 'Tell these men that I'm not saying anything else until I know exactly why I'm being held. If the reasons aren't good enough, I want to be released now.'

When I turned back in the direction of the two detectives, I saw that Caplin was holding up a small resealable plastic bag. 'Do you recognize these?' he asked me. 'They were found near the scene.'

I could see through the clear material that it was a pair of black leather gloves. I looked more closely, but I didn't really need to. I might not have worn them for the last couple of years but I recognized the diagonal stitching on the fingers immediately, and as I did so my heart jumped high in my chest.

The bloody things were mine.

11

Bolt and Mo were just coming off the M4 near Heathrow, heading back to HQ, when Bolt got another call on his mobile. He pulled the phone from his pocket and checked the number on the screen. He didn't recognize it, and said a curt hello, not wishing to give out his name over the airwaves to someone he didn't know.

'Is that Mike Bolt?' asked an unfamiliar female voice.

'Who's speaking, please?'

'My name's Tina Boyd. I'm a former police officer.'

Bolt knew the name straight away. Tina Boyd had been relatively famous in the small, incestuous world of the Metropolitan Police. She'd even made the cover of *Police Review* in happier times, being just the kind of young, attractive, go-getting female cop the Brass love. Before it had all gone wrong. Now people called her 'The Black Widow'.

'I'm guessing that you're *the* Tina Boyd,' Bolt said, exchanging glances with Mo. 'From the cover of the *Police Review*.'

'That's me, yes.'

'I was sorry to hear about what happened.' Bolt knew he was going to have to bring up her past at some point, and decided he might as well get it out of the way now. 'My understanding was that you were a very good copper.'

'I did my best,' she said, clearly not interested in exchanging pleasantries. 'I'm calling because I understand you're dealing with the suicide of the Lord Chief Justice.'

'That's right,' answered Bolt carefully, surprised that she'd found out about his involvement. It wasn't that it was a top-secret investigation, but there was no publicity surrounding it either.

'I have some information.'

Bolt felt his copper's antennae perk up. 'What kind of information?'

'Not the sort I want to talk about on the phone, but it's something you're definitely going to want to hear about. I would have called you earlier but it took some string-pulling to get hold of your number, and I also wanted to check you out to see if you were trustworthy enough to be given this information.'

'I'm assuming I passed that test.'

'You did,' she said, without a trace of humour. 'And that's why I'm on the phone.'

'And I'm very keen to hear what you have to say. Forgive me for asking, but how did you come by this information?'

'I'll tell you everything when I see you, but I promise I'm not wasting your time.'

'I'm intrigued. When can we meet up?'

'Are you in London tonight?'

'I can be easily enough.'

As he said this, Mo pulled the car up outside their building. There were no cars in the spaces and it looked empty inside. Jean had obviously gone home.

'I live in Highgate,' she told him. 'There's a pub called the

80

Griffin, just off the high street. How about meeting me there? Can you make eight?'

Bolt looked at his watch. It was just short of seven o'clock, and already his mind was whirring. 'Let's make it nine. I've got a few things to do first.'

'OK, nine it is. And something else. I don't want what I tell you to be on the record. This is just a lead for you. No mentioning my name or anything like that, at least not for the moment. And I need your word on that. Otherwise everything's off and you can forget I called.'

Bolt was surprised. This didn't sound much like a police officer talking, even a former one, as she now was. 'All right, it's a deal,' he said, knowing that if it came to it, he might have to reconsider the terms of his agreement. 'But I may bring one of my officers with me, a man who's also completely trust-worthy.' He winked at Mo when he said this, and Mo smiled a little and pulled a face that was full of mock flattery. 'Is that all right?'

There was a pause while she thought this through. 'OK,' she said reluctantly. 'I'll see you at nine, then.'

'One question,' he said, before she hung up. 'We've just come from the scene of a very violent murder, which happened only hours ago. Off the record – and this is one hundred per cent off the record – the victim was the Lord Chief Justice's personal lawyer. Could this possibly have something to do with the in-formation you have for us?'

There was an audible intake of breath at the other end of the phone, and then another silence. Finally she spoke. 'Possibly,' was all she said before hanging up.

'Well?' said Mo as Bolt pocketed the phone. 'What did *the* Tina Boyd want?'

'She wants to meet up. She has a lead. It sounds like it might be a big one.'

'All happening today, eh? Now even the Black Widow wants to get in on the act.'

'You don't have to come with me if you don't want to. You've put in enough hours on this case already today.'

'What? And let you get all the glory? No, boss, I won't let you slave away on your own, and if it's a decent lead, I want a part of it. Are we meeting Boyd in a pub?'

'We are.'

'And it's an unofficial chat, right? So I can have a drink?'

'I guess so.'

'Then I'm in. Let me check in with the other boss. Let her know what's happening.'

Bolt watched as Mo climbed out of the driver's seat and phoned home. He had only met Mo's wife once, when he'd gone round there to pick him up for a job. He remembered her as a short, well-built girl with a very attractive moon-shaped face which lit up when she smiled, and who seemed to be permanently surrounded by young kids. She was very friendly, with a calm, easy-going manner, and Bolt had thought at the time that she seemed to be perfect for the trials and tribulations of motherhood. Mo clearly adored her, kissing her on the head and ruffling her hair in a surprisingly affectionate manner as he'd said goodbye, before kissing and making a fuss of each of his kids in turn. Bolt had seen in the look she'd given him that she felt the same way.

And now he was keeping them apart. Bolt knew that one of the reasons Mo had agreed to work with him tonight was because he felt sorry for him. Everyone who knew about the life-changing event that had happened three years ago, and which had left Bolt with physical and mental scars that would probably never heal, felt sorry for him, and it inevitably made them treat him differently. Of all the people he worked with, only Mo Khan was able to seem perfectly natural in his presence, and this was one of the reasons he liked him so much. But even Mo couldn't help letting the knowledge affect his behaviour on some occasions, such as this one. The irony was, Bolt would have been happy to carry on alone tonight. He enjoyed his own company, always had. It was why he was coping now, and why he'd continue to do so.

He got out of the car and unlocked the office door. He wanted to check whether the police national computer system, the PNC, held anything on either Tom or Kathy Meron. At the same time Mo, who'd been pacing up and down in front of the building, came off the phone.

'Is Saira all right?' Bolt asked him.

Mo nodded. 'She's fine. Happy not to have me getting in her way. I told her not to wait up.'

Bolt could tell he didn't mean it. There was a look of disappointment on his face that he was trying hard to hide, but he couldn't quite manage it. It was obvious that Saira had given him a bit of a hard time, and he couldn't blame her.

As he moved through the office doorway, he only hoped their lead was worth it.

12

Fifteen minutes later they were driving through the back streets of west London, heading north in the direction of the Meron residence, which was about fifteen minutes east by car from where Jack Calley had been murdered. The PNC had given Bolt the information that Thomas David Meron had never been in trouble with the police, but his wife, Katherine Cynthia, did possess an ancient conviction for obstruction, earned at the age of eighteen during a student demonstration in Cambridge city centre. A whopping £25 fine had been the result. Hardly the work of a major criminal.

But the timing of the call from Calley was bothering him. The police surgeon at the scene had stated that he'd died no later than 3.30 p.m. that afternoon. Calley had therefore been confronted by the men who'd killed him at some time before 3.30. They'd come into his house, forced him up the stairs, tied him to the bed and tortured him. The whole process must have taken at least ten minutes, probably longer, because somehow Calley had managed to get free, which presumably meant he'd been left on his own for a time. There'd then been a chase that must have lasted a further five minutes before he was finally butchered on the forest path. The absolute latest they could have come for their victim was, by Bolt's reckoning, 3.10, nine minutes after he'd made that last call. But that was if he'd died at exactly 3.30, which seemed very unlikely, given that the surgeon's time range spanned an hour. So it was possible the call had been made after he'd been confronted. If so, the Merons had to be involved somehow.

It was ten to eight when they pulled up outside Tom and Katherine Meron's house. A high conifer hedge bordered the front of the property, obscuring the view of the house. Next to the hedge was an empty two-car driveway in need of re-tarmacking that led up to a double garage. It wasn't immediately obvious where the entrance was.

The sounds of lawnmowers and kids playing in unseen back gardens drifted across the cool breeze as the two detectives stepped out of Mo's car. The earlier wall of cloud had thinned and broken in places, revealing slithers of pinkish blue sky that glimmered in the last of the setting sun's rays.

They found a wooden security gate with intercom system in the top corner of the drive that had been hidden by the angle of the hedge. It wasn't usual to see a gate like this on a suburban estate property. Usually only the rich and paranoid bothered with them. Bolt wondered if it might signify something. He pressed on the buzzer. There was no answer. He pressed a second time.

'Do you think it's worth vaulting over and having a look, boss?' asked Mo.

But Bolt never got a chance to answer him. There was a sound of footsteps behind them and a confident female voice asked, 'Can I help you, gentlemen?'

The two men turned round and were immediately confronted by a pretty uniformed policewoman in her mid-twenties. She was about five feet three and of commensurate build, and looked as if she'd have had some difficulty handling things if they'd been a pair of villains who'd decided to turn nasty. Then a second uniformed officer, a male, slightly older, approached from a house across the road from where they'd obviously been watching the Merons' address.

Bolt gave her his best smile and produced his warrant card. Mo did the same. They introduced themselves and Bolt asked her name.

'I'm PC Nicki Leverett,' she said, inspecting the cards carefully, and making doubly sure that the photos that appeared on them corresponded to the faces in front of her. Bolt thought that the country's crime rate would probably be slashed by 20 per cent if everyone was as careful as she was. 'And this,' she added as the other uniform approached, 'is my colleague, PC Phil Coombs. Phil, these guys are from the National Crime Squad. They're looking for the Merons.'

Coombs nodded curtly, and grunted a greeting. He looked like a man with an inferiority complex, as well as a bit of an unrequited crush on his colleague.

'We need to speak to them in connection with a murder inquiry,' explained Bolt.

PC Leverett nodded. 'You're talking about the girl at the university. I didn't know the NCS were involved in that.'

Bolt shook his head, caught out by this sudden revelation. 'No,' he said, 'I don't know anything about that.'

'A woman was murdered over at the university today,' Leverett explained. 'Mr Meron was arrested in connection with it, and they're looking for his wife. Apparently, she worked

86

with the dead woman. We were told to come over and keep an eye on the place, in case she returned.'

'Have you got the university victim's name?'

She told him, but he didn't recognize it.

'How long have you been here, Nicki?' asked Mo.

'Since five thirty, but you're the first people to show up.'

'This is actually our second time here,' said PC Coombs. 'We got called out to a burglary here earlier on this afternoon. It was an anonymous tip-off on a nine-nine-nine. The caller said the burglar was still inside. When we got here, we clambered over that gate and took a look, but it was a false alarm. We were here within fifteen minutes and there were no signs of forced entry, and all the doors and windows were shut and locked.'

'And no witnesses saw anything suspicious?'

He shook his head. 'We did a door-to-door on the neighbouring properties and no-one saw anything.'

Bolt and Mo exchanged glances. What all these events meant, and what they had to do with the suicide of the Lord Chief Justice, was anyone's guess. But there was a single, loose link connecting them, and that link was the Merons. The wife might be missing, but the husband was in custody. They needed to speak to him.

Nicki Leverett gave them the number of the station where he was being held and Mo stepped away to call the CID there to make sure they held on to him.

Less than a minute later, as Coombs was telling Bolt about his desire to join Special Branch and hunt down terrorists, Mo came striding back, his phone still glued to his ear. The expression on his face was grim.

'Bad news, boss,' he said. 'They've only gone and released him.'

13

When it was obvious I wasn't going to tell my interrogators any more, they reluctantly brought the interview to a halt. They gave me ten minutes alone with Douglas McFee, who said he'd do his utmost to get me released because of the obvious lack of evidence linking me to Vanessa's murder. He looked like he actually meant it too – not least, I was sure, because then he could go home. After that, the two detectives came back and led me down to the cellblock, where I was given an empty cell at the end.

'You're going to have a bit of time to think now,' said Caplin, holding open the metal door. His expression remained wearily sympathetic. 'I want you to use it to decide whether there's anything more you want to tell us about this case, because if you're holding anything back, it'll be a lot better for you if we hear it from your lips rather than having to find it out for ourselves. Do you know what I'm saying?'

'I've told you everything I know,' I said, and turned away as the cell door was shut behind me and the key turned in the lock.

It was a small room, ten by ten feet, with a single barred

window high up on the dull grey wall, and a strip light overhead. A cast-iron cot screwed into the floor was the only furniture. A yellow plastic sheet covered the mattress, and it made an unpleasant crinkling sound when I went over and lay on it. I stared up at the ceiling and tried to make sense of what was happening to me. I knew that Kathy couldn't have had anything to do with the murder, not least because I'd run into the man who must have been the killer, and he was a lot bigger and stronger than my wife. Not that I would have thought her capable of it anyway. She was too good a person for that. I mean, she gave money every month to Great Ormond Street Children's hospital; she bought the *Big Issue* from homeless people; she wept when she saw footage of famine victims on television; and, being a political person, she railed against the government corruption and Western double standards that brought such situations about. She was, I would swear on my own life, not a killer. But that still didn't explain what her fingerprints were doing on the murder weapon. Nor did it explain where she was now and why she hadn't been answering her mobile for the last four hours.

It struck me then that I could easily find out whether Jack was dead. It would only take a quick word with Caplin and Sullivan; they'd be able to make the necessary enquiries. But if he was dead and the call he'd made to me came to light, then I might find myself in more trouble. It seemed a lot better simply to keep my mouth shut and my head down, and hope they let me go. Then I might be able to find out what the hell was happening out there, and also how a pair of my gloves that I hadn't worn for at least two winters had ended up at the scene, which was something else I couldn't for the life of me explain.

I'd lied about the gloves, telling the police I'd never seen them before, and as I lay on that bed I wondered how on earth they'd got there. I also wondered whether I really knew Kathy. I'd always thought so, but now, after the events of this afternoon, I was feeling a lot less sure. Maybe she had some sort of secret life. Maybe Vanessa had actually converted her to lesbianism, and the two of them had been having a relationship. Kathy certainly worked long hours and was away from the house almost as much as I was, so there would have been an opportunity. But once again, that didn't explain what a man in a balaclava had been doing waiting for me at the library, and it didn't throw any light on why Jack had called me for the first time in years, and why somebody had murdered him as we spoke.

When I thought of it like that, it all seemed so bizarre as to be almost laughable, but the throbbing of the cuts to my face and arm brought back to me the seriousness of what was happening. A man had tried to kill me today. On top of this, two people I knew had died violent deaths in separate incidents, and it looked like me, Kathy, or both of us were being set up for at least one of them.

I realized that up until now I'd never really appreciated life because it had always been nicely set out for me. I had two beautiful, healthy children, a pretty, good-hearted wife, a nice house and a well-paid job that wasn't exactly back-breaking. Yet I couldn't remember the last time I'd woken up in the morning and thought of myself as truly happy. Life could always be better – that had been my underlying feeling. I could earn more money; I could have more free time; I could be thinner, better looking, more desirable to women. Never once had it crossed my mind that, as well as being better, life could also be a lot worse. And now, lying here with my wife missing, my house burgled and a murder charge for a crime I didn't commit hanging over my head, I'd learned to appreciate it all only after it was too late.

The key turned in the lock and I sat up on the bed in a sudden movement that made my vision turn fuzzy. It cleared as the door opened and Douglas McFee came into the room, battered brief-case in hand, a big smile on his round face.

'I've good news, Tom,' he announced chirpily, the word 'news' seeming to last for ever.

'You've located Kathy?' I'd asked McFee to try her mobile for me again and, although reluctant, he'd promised to do so.

The smile disappeared as he approached the bed, stopping a few feet away. 'I'm afraid not. But it's something you'll be pleased with anyway. The police have decided to see sense and release you on bail. They may want to question you again so have asked you to remain at your current address for the time being. And you're to tell them if your wife makes contact. I know that sounds hard, but it'll be for the best. If she is innocent of any crime – and, of course, I'm sure she is – then it's best that she comes forward to clear her name.'

'What's the time?' I asked him, not bothering to reiterate Kathy's innocence. I could tell he hadn't bothered to phone her either, the cheap bastard.

He looked at his watch. 'Five to eight.'

So, where did I go now? Kathy was nowhere to be found, my children were with my mother-in-law, and my house felt pretty much out of bounds. It didn't leave a lot of places. I felt like I needed a drink. Maybe a couple. There are few things that beat the consumption of alcohol in a crisis.

I got to my feet and followed McFee out of the cell and through the corridors into the station's main reception area. It was a small, drab space dotted with posters warning potential criminals of the supposedly dire consequences of their wrong-doing. Along the length of one wall were bulletproof Perspex screens behind which the police dealt with their customers. The latest, two rat-faced teenagers in the delinquent's uniform of big trainers, baggy jeans and hoodies, were being booked in by the same custody sergeant who'd dealt with me nearly three hours earlier. Their expressions were boredly defiant. Unlike me when I'd been brought in, there was no fear on their faces either.

A younger copper appeared on the other side of the screen and took me to one of the other windows, where I was booked out. In the background, the phone was ringing. No-one made any move to answer it.

'Thanks for your co-operation, sir,' said the young copper as he got me to sign for the bag containing my possessions. He sounded so chirpy I thought he was going to add a 'Don't go being a stranger now', but somehow he managed to resist it.

I grunted something in reply, and asked if there was any chance of a lift over to the university to pick up my car.

'I'm afraid we're rather short-staffed tonight, sir. We can call you a taxi if you like.'

The old saying that there was never a copper around when you needed one rang truer than ever. 'Forget it,' I said. 'I could probably do with the walk.'

I gathered my stuff together, turned on my mobile and walked out of the double doors with Douglas McFee in tow. When we were on the steps, he handed me one of his business cards and told me to call him if the police needed to question me again. 'I'd offer you a lift, but . . .' he added.

'But what?'

'Unfortunately, I'm expected home. Graham's cooked a special meal. Sea bream baked in rock salt, which won't keep, and the university's in the wrong direction. Take care, Mr Meron.' With that, he gave me a comradely pat on the arm and hurried off down the steps, making me feel more like a leper than ever.

I followed him down, and walked through the car park to the gate, imagining him and Graham munching away on a huge wet fish in their cosy parlour. For some reason I couldn't quite fathom, I pictured McFee wearing a pair of clogs and a well-worn smoking jacket.

I was also thinking that as well as a drink I was going to buy a pack of cigarettes and have my first smoke in almost ten years. My mood was beginning to change from terrified and confused to why-the-hell-not mode. But as I reached the gate, I heard someone shouting my name. I turned round and saw McFee standing by his car with his keys in his hand, waving over in my direction. It was him doing the shouting. Then I saw why. He wanted me to stop. Not, I suspect, because he'd had a change of heart and wanted to give me a lift, or offer me a fish supper. More likely it was because two uniformed officers were hurrying down the steps in my direction, looking very much like they wanted to speak to me.

My first thought was that they'd finally located Kathy, and I was already preparing to walk back to them, when a second thought crossed my mind. What if whoever was trying to set me, or her, up had planted further evidence, giving them a fresh opportunity to do what they'd wanted to do these last three hours, and charge me with a killing I'd had nothing to do with?

I had twenty yards on them, and I made a snap decision.

Run.

I turned and charged through the open gates and out onto the high street, where evening revellers were just beginning to gather. Dusk was turning to darkness, and I welcomed it. I didn't look round, but I knew they were coming after me. One group of blokes in their twenties clustered outside a pub gave a cheer as I came hurtling past, and people stepped out of my path. Without warning, I did a jackknife turn and sprinted across the road, causing at least one car to brake suddenly. This time it didn't hit me, thank God, and I kept going, darting up a side street, then up another, now finding myself in a plush-looking residential area of whitewashed Georgian townhouses. My lungs hurt; my cuts hurt; pretty much every part of me hurt. This really was turning into a bad day.

I must have run two or three hundred yards when finally I slowed, and looked back. The street behind me was empty. Panting with exhaustion, I stopped and leaned against a low garden wall. Inside the house beyond I could see two middle-aged couples in the front room eating dinner. One of the men was filling glasses with a bottle of red wine. He was laughing at something, and I saw that the others were laughing too. Without a care in the world. I was only five yards from them yet they didn't even look my way.

And because I was taking the time to feel sorry for myself, I only vaguely heard the car as it came down the street and pulled up beside me. I thought about taking off again, but knew that there was no way I was going to outrun them, even if I had any strength left. I'd done too much running for one day, and it was clear that they were suddenly very keen to re-interview me.

So I turned round, ready to tell them that I wasn't going to say a word until they provided a better lawyer than Douglas McFee. But, of course, I never got the chance. A blurred figure in a cap was coming straight at me, taking up my whole field of vision, and before I could react or even get a glimpse of his face, he punched me once, very hard, in the stomach. As I doubled over, he grabbed the back of my shirt and shoved me onto the back seat of a car, squeezing in behind and slamming the door shut behind him. There was a second man in the driver's seat. He was also wearing a cap, and without a word he pulled away from the kerb.

I tried to look at the man next to me, but now I could see that he had a black pistol with a short barrel in one gloved hand. He pushed it against my temple, forcing my head against the window, and for an awful, bowel-loosening second I thought he was going to pull the trigger. Then he spoke.

'When I pull the gun away, you're going to lean over and put your head between your legs and keep it there,' he said evenly. 'If you try to look at either me or my colleague, then before the end of the night you're going to die. Do you understand?'

I told him I did.

'Good.' He removed the gun and I did exactly as I was told, instinctively closing my eyes. A second later, I felt a blanket being flung over my head and upper body. 'As long as you tell us everything we want to hear, you'll be free in a couple of hours.'

His words were meant to be encouraging, but since I still didn't have a clue what it was they wanted, they weren't.

14

Bolt cursed when he heard they'd released Meron. 'I thought he was being held on a murder charge.'

Mo shrugged. 'They said there wasn't enough evidence to hold him.'

'How long ago did they let him go? Do you know?'

Mo asked the question into the phone. 'Literally just now,' he told Bolt. 'A couple of minutes, that's all.'

'Tell them to see if they can see him anywhere. And if they can, get them to arrest him again. It's essential we talk to this guy.'

Calmly, Mo relayed the information into the phone, and waited while the officer he was speaking to reacted to it. A few seconds passed, then it was Mo's turn to curse. 'Are you sure? In that case, can you get some people out there looking for him? Sure, I know you've got resource problems. We've all got them.' He pulled a face at Bolt and made the universal hand gesture to illustrate his opinion of the person at the other end of the line. 'Well, if you can do something . . . Sure, sure . . . Thanks.' He flicked the end call button on the phone and put it back in his jeans pocket.

'He's gone?'

Mo sighed. 'Yeah, he's gone. They went out after him but he ran, and now they're saying they haven't got enough people on duty to try to locate him.'

They were still standing on the Merons' driveway with PCs Coombs and Leverett, and Bolt turned to them now. 'If Mr Meron turns up here, can you call us on this number?' He handed out business cards with his mobile number on them to the two officers. 'Have you got a photo of him anywhere?'

'The people over the road have,' said PC Leverett.

'Well, maybe they can let us have one.'

The people over the road were a vaguely harassed couple called the Hendersons whose two young boys were charging about like wild animals, refusing to go to bed. Both Martin and Suzette Henderson described the Merons as a perfectly ordinary, friendly couple who they couldn't imagine getting involved in crime of any sort. Martin managed to find them a photo of the two of them taken at a barbecue the previous summer held in honour of their youngest son's birthday.

The photo seemed to reflect the Hendersons' description. The Merons were indeed an ordinary-looking, if quite photogenic, pair in their mid-thirties, both smiling at the camera in front of a bright yellow and orange bouncy castle. He had his arm round her, and was holding a can of Fosters in his spare hand, while she had hold of a glass of red wine. They didn't look like the sort of people who got mixed up with murder, but that didn't mean that they hadn't. As a young PC, Bolt remembered arresting a sweet-looking white-haired old lady of seventy-two who attended church every Sunday without fail, and was known as Nan by the neighbourhood children, to whom she would often distribute sweets. She'd even offered him a cup of tea after he and his colleagues had turned up to take her away for burying a meat cleaver in the back of her husband's head, almost killing him. It turned out that she had an unusually high sex drive, and the husband had been refusing to service her needs. Things had got out of hand, and she'd lost her rag, something which under questioning she'd put down to a build-up of nervous tension caused by a lack of orgasms. It takes all sorts, Bolt reflected.

As the two NCS men were leaving, Martin Henderson came out after them.

'I don't want to make a big issue of this,' he said quietly, as they stopped to hear what he had to say, 'because it may not mean anything, and I don't want to get anyone in trouble.'

'Go on,' said Bolt.

Henderson sighed. 'It's just that things have been a bit strange with Tom and Kathy lately. I've seen him driving out late at night, then coming back in the early hours, and she's been around a lot less than usual.' He paused. 'There's also been fights. Big screaming matches, and they've never had them before. One time, Tom was even walking round with a black eye.'

'How long's this been going on?'

'A while. A few months now.' Henderson was about to say something else, but then he heard his wife, who'd finally managed to round up the kids, coming down the stairs. 'Like I say, I don't want to get anyone into trouble, but . . .' He let the sentence trail off, said his goodbyes and went back inside.

As they reached the car, Bolt looked at his watch. Twenty past eight. A thick bank of black clouds was now forming to the west, and from somewhere in the far distance there came a faint rumble of thunder.

15

We drove through a variety of back roads. I only know this because the driver kept the speed at no more than thirty and made a lot of turnings. During the whole time I remained in the same uncomfortable position, not daring to move. When I tried to speak, wanting to ask these men where they were taking me and where my wife was, I was told by the one sitting next to me to keep my mouth shut. 'We'll talk later,' came the ominous promise.

My mouth and throat felt bone dry. The only thing I'd drunk

since three o'clock that afternoon was a glass of water during the police interview. During the last five hours I'd been attacked with a knife, knocked over by a police car, accused of murder, chased by the law, and now kidnapped. It was safe to say that I'd worked up a thirst.

After about half an hour, the car slowed up and stopped. Remarkably, I wasn't actually that scared. At least these men weren't actively trying to kill me, which meant they wanted to talk. It gave me an opportunity to put my side of the case and hopefully convince them that I had nothing to do with any of this. As long as I didn't get a good look at their faces I ought to be all right. That was the theory, anyway.

The driver cut the engine, and the car was suddenly silent. I could hear the two men shuffling about, and then the blanket was pulled from my head and I was told that I could now look. As I sat back up, my eyes already accustomed to the gloom, I saw that they were both wearing black balaclavas. The one sitting next to me was still holding the gun, and it was pointing at my midriff. Outside, darkness had fallen and it had begun to rain.

They got out, and the gunman leaned back in and beckoned for me to follow. I clambered across the seats, pushing the blanket to one side, and stepped out into the open air. The rain felt refreshing on my face. We were in a small, walled parking area with room for about three cars at the back of a dirt-stained and windowless two-storey industrial building. A single flight of metal steps led up to a battered steel door that was the only sign of an entrance. There was a faint smell of old fried food coming from somewhere, and I noticed a line of overflowing dustbins against the wall.

The driver started up the steps and the gunman prodded me with the barrel, indicating that I should follow. I didn't argue.

The driver used a key to open the door and went inside, switching the lights on. Sandwiched between the two men, I was led down a narrow corridor. The smell of fried food was stronger here, and a black binliner, packed high with empty food containers and paper, was propped up outside a door on the right. A second door on the right had a gents toilet sign on it and several holes gouged out near the bottom where it looked like someone had tried to kick it in. There was no noise coming from anywhere, and apart from the smell, the place had a deserted, stale feel to it.

We stopped at a door at the end of the corridor and the driver searched for the right key. I finally risked speaking as he placed it in the lock. 'I don't know anything,' I said. 'I have no idea why people are chasing me, I promise you.'

The driver opened the door, and a breath of warm, fetid air belched out. He then turned round and, in one rapid movement that was almost a blur, grabbed my shirt at the shoulder with one hand and punched me twice in the face with the other, two savage little jabs that felt more painful than anything I'd suffered that day, mainly because they were so unexpected. I lurched, and my legs wobbled precariously, but he steadied me with a firm hand and kept me upright before swinging me round and flinging me bodily into the airless darkness of the room.

I landed hard on one shoulder blade and rolled several times along the cool concrete floor until I came to a halt, facing the ceiling. The striplights above me came on and I saw I was in a large, windowless room about twenty feet square with old floor-to-ceiling storage shelves stretching round the walls. Most of the shelves were empty but one contained a cluster of five-litre tubs of vegetable oil and a couple of sacks of rice. One of the sacks had split and spilled much of its load on the filth-stained floor.

They came into the room, the driver with a purposeful gait,

the gunman following more slowly behind. As I tried to get to my feet, the driver kicked me in the face, knocking me onto my back. I felt blood pour out of my nose and my vision turned fuzzy for a couple of seconds. But I didn't hang about, immediately rolling myself up into a protective ball as he kicked me again, his shoe striking my forearms as he tried to get me in the face again. The worrying thing was that the beating was being carried out in complete silence, with neither man feeling the need to speak. They were softening me up, breaking down my resistance, and I knew there was no point begging for mercy. I pulled my body into an even tighter ball, eyes clenched shut, as the kicks kept coming.

Then, without warning, I was hauled to my feet and dragged across the room. In front of me was a sturdy wooden chair that had been bolted to the floor. It had a high, straight back and there were looping iron shackles attached to the arms and legs. I started struggling, but a leaden punch to the kidneys, delivered with a studied ease that was almost nonchalant, took the fight completely out of me, and I was unable to resist as the driver forced me into the chair and slammed my head back against the wood, gripping my face painfully in his gloved hand. Without speaking, he used the other hand to secure my wrists with the manacles. I heard them click as they locked.

The driver released his grip, took a step back and backhanded me across the face, catching me perfectly on the fresh stitches, and reopening the wound. Drops of blood splattered onto the floor.

'Where the fuck is it?' he demanded.

'Where's what?' I gasped.

'Don't fucking play the innocent. You know what I'm talking about.'

'I don't. Honestly. I have no idea what the hell it is you want to know.'

He turned to the gunman who was standing a few feet back, watching events impassively. 'Blow his fucking kneecap off,' he said, and moved out of the way.

The gunman strode forward, bringing the gun up from his side and pointing it at my kneecap. I wriggled wildly in the seat, utterly helpless, the fear coursing through me in hot, crippling waves. The gun's barrel got closer and closer until it was only a foot away. I could hear the gunman's breathing. His eyes were grey and blank. There was no sympathy in them at all. I turned my head away so I no longer had to look into them.

'Last chance to tell us where it is,' said the driver. 'Otherwise my friend here pulls the trigger.'

'He's right, I will,' said the gunman calmly, 'and I won't lose a second's sleep over it either. You know that, don't you?'

'Please. You're making a mistake.'

'I'm going to count to five,' said the driver. 'One. Two.'

What do you say in that sort of situation? Men are threatening to maim you for life. They will probably kill you after that, and dump your body. You will never see your wife and children again. You are thirsty, you are hungry. You are in pain, and most of all you are confused. Because these men want you to tell them the whereabouts of something, and you have absolutely no idea what it could possibly be.

'Three. Four.'

I twisted, wriggled, fought against the shackles, craned my neck as far away from the gun as I possibly could, teeth clenched ready for the impact of the bullet that was going to bring hideous pain and a limp for the rest of my days, if indeed I had any days left.

102

'Five.'

'No, please!' I screamed, my words echoing around the empty room. 'Don't fucking do it!'

'Are you going to talk?' asked the driver evenly.

I turned in his direction imploringly, feeling the blood running down my face. When I spoke, the words came out in a series of pants. 'If you just tell me what it is you think I know the whereabouts of, then I can help you. I'm sure.'

The driver shook his head. 'You're fucking us about.' Then to the gunman: 'Do it.'

The gunman's finger tensed on the trigger and this time I met his eye. I was shaking my head, silently begging him. He stared back. Was there doubt there? Did I see a flicker of doubt?

A mobile rang. The tune was different to the phone I'd heard earlier at the university. The one that belonged to the knifeman. This one played 'Suspicious Minds' by Elvis Presley. It seemed very apt.

The driver reached into the pocket of his black bomber jacket and answered it, at the same time indicating for the gunman to hold his fire. He turned away with the mobile clutched to his ear. Although I couldn't hear what he was saying, his tone was respectful, and it was obvious that whoever was on the other end of the line was his superior.

The gunman took a couple of steps back and lowered the weapon to his side, looking away from my gaze. I could hear my heart thumping in my chest. My thirst was horrendous, so desperate it made it difficult to speak. It's hard to explain, but somehow it was even stronger than the fear. I would have given anything – anything – for a glass of water at that moment.

The driver came off the phone and replaced it in his pocket.

'That was Lench,' he told his colleague, and there was something close to nervous awe in his voice when he mentioned that name. 'He's five minutes away. He told us to leave this one until he gets here.'

He walked up to me, and I flinched as he brought back his hand to strike me. Then, as the hand came forward, he stopped it suddenly a few inches away, enjoying my reaction, and patted me lightly on the cheek, bringing his face so close that I could smell his sour, hot breath. He smiled, and I could see that his teeth were stained and uneven. 'You're going to talk now, mate. When Lench gets here you're going to talk, you're going to scream, and you're going to fucking beg like a dog. Because he can get information out of anyone. You'd rather sell your kids to paedophiles than hold out on him.'

'I can't tell you anything,' I said wearily, 'if I don't know anything.'

But even as I spoke, I knew the words made no difference. They would torture me until either they got what they wanted or there was nothing left of me to torture. And the problem was, I knew it was going to be the latter.

16

No-one knew him as anything other than Lench, a state of affairs he liked well enough. No-one knew his background either, nor did they enquire. People feared him, and he fed on that fear, enjoying the sense of power it gave him, aware that he was a natural predator in a world overcrowded with prey.

It wasn't simply his immense bulk that created that reaction, although it was a factor. At six feet four, and with a body made outsized and bulbous through the obsessive lifting of weights, he towered over most men, his rounded shoulders and huge, vein-popping arms giving him a vaguely primitive, ape-like appearance. Yet this was offset by the cruel, probing intelligence in his eyes. When he fixed a person with one of his unyielding stares, it made the recipient feel as if he was looking right into their soul, uncovering and devouring each and every secret. 'Snake's eyes' someone had called them once, when Lench was well out of earshot, and there was some truth in the description. They were very thin and very dark, and the skin of his eyelids hung down over them like cobras' hoods.

Lench licked his lips with a long fleshy tongue, the tip brushing along the bottom of his nose and leaving a cold trail of saliva. He didn't see the people in the other cars as he drove through the dark night streets towards his destination, nor those crowding the pavements. They didn't exist to him. If he looked their way, he saw only blurs through the rain, lit up by the watery glow of the street lights. Only those he hunted took any real shape, became flesh and blood. And tonight, he was hunting.

Lench had killed many times in the thirty-eight years he'd walked the earth. To him, torture and murder were little more than a pastime, a means of gaining pleasure. He knew that in this he was very different to other people, but he rarely thought about the reasons behind his strange, bleak desires, since he could see no point. He was what he was, and nothing was going to change that. Instead, he felt uniquely lucky in that he was paid for his crimes, and was therefore doing a job he loved. The main reason he was trusted by his employer – the only man in the world to whom he felt he owed a debt – was that he was reliable. He was imaginative in his methods, and more importantly, he didn't make mistakes. If someone had to die, Lench was the person the employer turned to. The necessary instructions would be given, and that would be the end of the employer's involvement. Lench would make all the arrangements and ensure that the job was carried out, either working alone or with help from his own people. Although on a personal level he always liked to prolong the suffering of his victims, since much of his enjoyment derived from watching them die, he knew that sometimes this wasn't possible. The key, he felt, to successful killing was making the most of your opportunities.

An old Ford Escort pulled out from the kerb in front of him without indicating, forcing him to brake. The deep, throbbing bass of some crappy hip-hop effort blasted out of the open windows, and he could see figures in the back, heads covered in hoodies, passing a joint between themselves. Arseholes, he thought, imagining for a moment cutting the driver's throat and hanging him up to bleed, but ultimately not worth bothering with. Lench never took pointless risks. Like many psychopaths, he was a pragmatist at heart, and having been incarcerated once in his life he had no desire to go back.

Tonight, too, there were bigger fish to fry. The employer had a serious problem, one that had to be dealt with decisively. Already things were beginning to get complicated. They'd had to kill Calley prematurely, and out in the open too, and now the new target, the man called Meron, had come dangerously close to slipping out of their grasp, something which couldn't be allowed to happen. At least not before they'd got their information.

He finished the call to Mantani, one of the two men currently guarding Meron, having told him to do no further harm to their prisoner, and clicked off the phone. Mantani was a reliable operative but, like Lench, he enjoyed inflicting pain and could sometimes get carried away. It was absolutely essential that Meron remained alive, conscious and lucid, so that if he was hiding anything it could be extracted from him. The boot of the Lexus Lench was driving contained a variety of implements designed to do just that. These included a remote-controlled electro-shock stun belt which delivered an eight-second 50,000-volt shock to the person wearing it; a stun baton which could be forcibly inserted into the anus, where a smaller shock could then be applied; a dentist's drill for use on teeth; and a set of six lethally sharp scalpels, perhaps his most favoured tools, which could be used to jab and pierce the ultra-sensitive nerves beneath the eyes and behind the ears.

Lench was an expert torturer with a great deal of practical experience. No-one had ever held out on him for longer than a matter of minutes. It was a record to be proud of. None had died on him accidentally either, although on several occasions they'd been finished off afterwards, as Meron would be tonight, when there was no further use for him.

He turned off the main road and into the street where the prisoner was being kept. He looked at his watch. It was 8.40 p.m. and raining hard. He was three minutes away. Hopefully, within the hour they'd have everything wrapped up.

17

'If you're holding out on us, I'd say so now,' the gunman told me, his tone that of a man trying to be reasonable.

My head ached, and it was an effort to speak, but for what felt like the hundredth time I told him I wasn't.

He nodded slowly. 'OK,' he said, 'I believe you.'

'If he is holding out, he'll get what's coming to him,' said the driver. 'Lench'll have him begging like a dog.' He sounded pleased at this prospect, and I wondered what the bastard had against me.

As I sat there chained to the seat, I was reminded of an old phrase my mother used to mutter whenever an event happened on the news where evil appeared to triumph over good. *There are none so unhappy as those who care nothing for their fellow man.* And there was some truth in that. You could almost feel sorry for a scumbag like him, so shallow was his life that his greatest joy appeared to come from beating up and doing his utmost to scare the shit out of someone he'd never met before. Almost, but not quite. I wanted to say something defiant that would demonstrate to him that I wasn't scared.

Unfortunately, the only problem was that I was scared. Terrified.

'Listen, Mantani, I need a word.' It was the gunman speaking.

Behind the balaclava, the driver's features contorted with an anger that never seemed to be far from the surface. 'What are you doing using my fucking name?'

'It doesn't matter. He's finished anyway. He obviously doesn't know anything, but he's seen and heard too much, so Lench isn't going to let him go.' He motioned towards the door. 'Come on, it's important.'

Mantani shook his head, muttered something, but started walking anyway. 'This better be fucking good.'

'It is,' said the gunman, reversing the gun in his hand and smashing the butt across the back of his colleague's head. The impact was loud in the silence of the room and Mantani fell unsteadily to his knees. With a fluid, dancer's grace, the gunman karate-kicked him in the kidneys. His victim yelped in pain before toppling over on his side and lying in a similar fetal position to the one I'd been in only a few minutes earlier. The gunman watched him thoughtfully for a couple of seconds, then kicked him in the back of the head with such force that his whole body was shunted across the grimy floor. Finally, Mantani stopped moving and the gunman put the pistol in the back of his jeans and bent down beside him, rifling through his pockets until he found a bunch of keys. Then he jumped back up and made his way over to me.

I tried to sit as far back in the seat as possible as he approached. This was a dangerous man. Even to someone as unused to violence as me, the speed and professionalism of the assault on his erstwhile colleague had been impressive. A man capable of that was capable of a lot of things, none of them nice.

But it soon became clear he had no interest in hurting me. At least not yet.

'Hold still, I'm going to let you go.' He found the key he was looking for and unlocked the shackle attached to my right wrist. 'We haven't got a lot of time before Lench gets here.'

'Have you got any water? Please, I need some water.'

'I'll give you some in the car. Now, stop moving.'

'Who is Lench?' I managed to ask.

'Someone you really don't want to meet,' he answered, freeing my left wrist, then concentrating on the shackles pinning my ankles to the chair. Finally, he pulled me up.

I was shaky on my feet, feeling very faint, but he didn't give me any time to get my bearings. Instead, he pushed me impatiently towards the door. 'If Lench finds us here like this, we're both dead,' he explained hastily, and I was surprised at the fearful urgency that cut through his own voice.

Mantani was moaning loudly on the floor. If I'd had more strength I would have kicked the bastard as I passed, but it was all I could do simply to keep upright and moving. And anyway, my rescuer had already done enough.

We moved fast down the corridor and out the door we'd come in, the gunman ushering me along by the arm. It was raining hard, and I licked at the drops as they landed on my face. But the metal steps were slippery, and as we made our descent I fell on my behind and went bumping down about three of them, just like Max liked to do on the stairs at home, before the gunman lifted me up by the collar and shoved me the rest of the way down.

He clicked off the alarm of the black Nissan 4×4 we'd travelled in and stopped and listened. We could both hear it. A car coming along the road in our direction – the only one on it by the sound of things. And it wasn't far away.

Lench.

'Get in, fast,' he demanded, running over to the driver's side.

I didn't need asking twice and hurried round to the front passenger door, praying he hadn't been lying about the water. As I pulled the door open and pushed a leg in, he slammed the gearbox into reverse and the car shot backwards out of the car park. I got a hand on the dashboard and pulled myself inside, shutting the door behind me just before it smacked into the boundary wall. The next second we were doing a three-point turn in the middle of the street – a long and dimly lit place of warehouses, vehicle repair shops and empty silhouetted concrete buildings which squatted malevolently behind fences topped with razor wire and KEEP OUT signs.

Fifty yards behind us, a single pair of headlights was approaching quickly. My rescuer cursed. He shoved the car into first and took off down the street in a dramatic shriek of tyres.

He took the first turning left, swinging the wheel so sharply I didn't think we'd make it. The back of the 4×4 slid on the wet tarmac and the rear wheel on the driver's side smashed against the kerb, jarring me in my seat. Immediately, he changed down into second, brought the car under control, and slammed his foot to the floor. At that moment the other vehicle loomed up behind us without warning, its headlights temporarily blinding me. Ten yards separated us.

The 4×4 shot forward, gathering speed, its engine beginning to squeal as the rev counter hit four thousand and kept on going, before easing a little as we hit third. The pursuing car came with us, accelerating even faster, the glare of its headlights subsiding as it came within inches of our rear bumper.

'He's going to ram us!' I screamed.

There was a major left-hand bend in the road ahead. Thirty

yards, twenty yards . . . The engine continued to protest in a banshee-like howl as the rev counter shot back up again, but the gunman kept his foot on the floor. If we weren't rammed, then we were going to smash straight into the concrete wall rising up like a wave in front of us. I clenched my teeth and put my head in my hands, praying that the car had airbags.

Suddenly, I was thrown forward in the seat, the belt not stopping me from striking the dashboard at chest height. The gunman had slammed his foot on the brakes and we were doing an emergency stop. The tyres shrieked as we went into a wild skid, and he was forced to turn the wheel sharp left to prevent it from developing into a complete pirouette. Just as I pushed myself back into the seat, trying to ignore the searing pain shooting through my sternum, the pursuing car smashed into our rear in a cacophony of shattering glass and twisting metal. I was thrown forward for a second time, this time headbutting the windscreen like an angry drunk. As I fell back, opening my eyes again, all I could see ahead was the concrete wall. Five yards, four, three, two . . . The 4×4 was swinging round with the momentum of the skid, and we were about to hit it side on. I tensed against the coming impact, wondering when this nightmare was going to end.

And then suddenly we'd stopped, only a foot or so away from the wall. The whole street became deathly silent. The pursuing car was also stationary ten yards away; it too had been knocked sideways. As I watched, the driver's door opened and an immense black-clad figure appeared in the gap. I couldn't see him very well in the darkness, nor did I make much effort to. I was too busy looking at the gun in his hand, which, as he stood up, was now pointing straight at me.

I opened my mouth to speak, but before I could get a word

out we'd shot forward again and were accelerating round the bend and out of range, like something out of a computer game. The driver ratcheted through the gears until he got to fourth, the speedometer rapidly passing fifty. As the road straightened, I looked round in my seat, saw that there was no-one following and was just about to sigh with relief when he did another ferocious emergency stop, took a right turning that seemed to have appeared out of nowhere, roared down to where it became a T-junction, and went right again. Still no-one was following, but he kept driving fast, and we'd got close to sixty when he finally jumped a set of red lights at another T-junction before slowing down as we joined a welcome convoy of evening traffic on a main road I vaguely recognized.

'Thanks for that, Schumacher,' I gasped. 'Now where's that fucking water?'

'There's some in the glove compartment. And aren't you going to thank me for saving your neck back there?'

I pulled out a three-quarter-full bottle of Evian and didn't speak until I'd downed the whole lot. 'Thanks,' I said eventually. It was only then that I asked him a question that was now really beginning to bother me.

'Who the hell are you?'

He turned in my direction as we slowed down for more lights, observing me coolly from behind the balaclava.

'I'm a police officer,' he answered.

18

Lench stood in the rain for several long seconds staring in the direction the 4×4 had taken, knowing that something had gone badly wrong. Finally, he lowered the gun and got back into the Lexus. When he switched on the ignition, the engine made an injured whine, and he could hear something rattling. This annoyed him. He liked the Lexus. It was a nice, smooth, comfortable ride and fitted his bulk perfectly. Now he was going to have to get it repaired. It might even be a write-off. Someone would pay dearly for this. But first he had to find out exactly what was going on and why the vehicle his men had been using had been fleeing the place where they were meant to be holding Tom Meron until he arrived.

He drove back to the warehouse, becoming progressively more annoyed. The car sounded like shit, and he couldn't get round the fact that somehow he'd fucked up.

He pulled into the parking area and stepped out of the car. Seeing that the door to the back of the building was open, he drew his gun, an easily concealable short-barrelled Heckler & Koch USP Compact loaded with powerful .45 ammunition that he used only in emergencies. His preferred weapon was a spring-loaded jet knife with a six-inch steel blade; attached to the inside of his forearm, it could be activated by a simple flick of the wrist. He'd only used it once, during a struggle with a target on a boat in the middle of the Irish Sea. They'd been trying to attach weights to their victim so he'd sink like a stone when they heaved him overboard into the black waters, but the bastard had made a last-ditch attempt at survival by grabbing Lench round the throat in a surprisingly powerful grip. The target had been a loud-mouthed environmental activist with useful legal and political connections, and the sort of good looks that attracted unwanted attention. He'd been determined to stop one of Lench's employer's companies from building a hotel and marina on virgin coastline south of Dublin, so he had to be made to disappear. He was young and fit, a semi-professional rugby player as well, but Lench had still been caught out by the ferocity of the assault from a man who must have known it was futile, given that he was one man against four and his legs were already partly bound. But perhaps, like a Hollywood hero, he wanted to make sure he took one of the baddies with him.

Either way, he was doomed to failure. As his grip tightened, cutting off breath, Lench had simply smiled at him, raised his left hand so that it was caressing the young man's ear beneath the vibrant locks of golden hair, and flicked his wrist with a sudden jolt. The blade drove through the soft flesh just behind the lobe and penetrated the brain instantaneously. The victim's eyes had snapped open in shock, his grip had loosened, and he'd slid down onto the greasy deck, his head disengaging from the blade with a strange sucking sound. It was a pity they couldn't have kept him alive for the actual ceremony of sending him helpless into the icy depths. The employer had wanted him to be given a gloating message so that he knew exactly why he was going to die, but unfortunately this was no longer possible. However, Lench was thankful that he had had such an ingenious weapon of surprise, and he'd kept it ever since, wearing it as often as was practical.

He crept up the steps and, hearing nothing, stepped inside. The door to the store room was half-open and the lights were on beyond it. He walked forward, making no attempt to disguise his footfalls. He had been trained in ambush techniques and building clearance and knew exactly what to look for. There were few places to hide in here, and he guessed that no ambush would be forthcoming.

He stopped at the door and saw through the gap one of his men lying on the floor, still clad in his balaclava. He was moving and making the odd quiet moan, and by the squat build Lench guessed it was Mantani.

For the first time in a long while he felt something akin to fear. It wasn't that emotion exactly, more a combination of disappointment and anxiety. He'd let down the only man he feared letting down.

Then the rage came. It was a cold yet intense anger, one that tightened the features of his face and made his eyes narrow, but which remained perfectly controllable. He knew how and where to channel the energy it gave him.

He kicked open the door so hard it slammed against the wall, then strode inside, eyes darting left and right to confirm his suspicion that no-one was waiting for him, and made directly for Mantani. The injured man's moans were louder now and he was attempting to sit up. Lench suspected this was entirely for his own benefit, a feeble attempt to show how badly hurt he'd been, so that he might be spared punishment. He must have known it wouldn't work, but most people will try anything when they're terrified.

Leaning down, Lench slipped a hand under Mantani's chin and wrenched him to his feet. He turned him round and held him steady at arm's length by the throat, using the arm with the jet knife attached. Behind the mask, Mantani's brown eyes were wide and fearful, as well they should have been. His boss was not a man to displease.

'What happened?' asked Lench in a curiously high-pitched voice that belied his bulk and physical strength.

'Daniels,' he gasped. 'The bastard hit me over the head with his gun when I wasn't looking . . . Left with the prisoner . . . It was just after I spoke to you. I'm sorry . . .'

If Lench had been a man who let his immediate instincts get the better of him, he would have used the jet knife on Mantani there and then. He could tell Mantani was afraid he still might. After all, he had been one of the people on the boat that day the knife had last been put to use. But Lench knew better than to act on instinct. Mantani had made a mistake, but then he had made one too. He should never have hired Daniels. The man was too intelligent to use as a hired thug and had clearly not been trustworthy. But Lench didn't have many men working for him who could be trusted to kill on his behalf. It takes a special type of person to murder another without compunction or remorse, while at the same time being capable of understanding and obeying orders. They were a rare breed, and Mantani was one of them. To get rid of him now would be counter-productive.

'You fucked up,' Lench said quietly. As he spoke, he increased the grip on his employee's windpipe until Mantani's breathing came out in thin, pained rasps.

'Please, sir . . . can't breathe . . .'

'I pay you well, Mantani. Better than an ex-con with no hope or prospects deserves. For that I expect some reliability. Tonight, you haven't given me that. Make the mistake again and I'll work on you until your eyes bleed. Do you understand?'

Mantani managed to nod, and Lench let go and allowed him to fall heavily to the floor. He lay where he'd been dropped, propped up on one arm, rubbing his throat, while Lench turned away.

'Go down to my car and wait for me inside,' he ordered. 'I have a private call to make.'

When Mantani had left the room and Lench could hear him going down the steps, he took out his mobile and made a call he wasn't looking forward to.

After ringing for close to a minute, the phone was picked up at the other end. There was the distinct buzz of chatter in the background, punctuated by loud female laughter. That would be the employer's wife. She'd clearly been drinking again. Over the top of the noise, the employer spoke four words: 'Have you found it?'

'There's been a problem.'

'Wait a minute, let me go outside.' There was a pause of perhaps thirty seconds, the sound of doors being opened and shut. Finally, the background noise faded to nothing. 'How bad's this problem?' the employer asked at last.

'Manageable. We've lost target one.' In keeping with operating procedure, Lench made no mention of names over the phone.

'And you're sure that's manageable?'

'He took one of our cars,' Lench answered, not adding that one of his own men had sprung him, 'but we can follow him.'

'How?'

'It's got a tracking device on it. If we're lucky, he'll lead us all the way to target two.'

'I don't want to rely on luck,' the employer said, and for the first time there was the hint of reproach in his voice. He almost always treated Lench with an unquestioning courtesy that bordered on affection, as if he was the son the employer had never had, and it was for this reason more than any other that Lench showed him such loyalty. It was also why the rebuke made him flinch.

'Don't worry. We'll get him. I swear it.'

'And when you do, make sure he talks. We have to conclude matters as soon as possible.'

'Oh, he'll talk all right,' said Lench, staring down at one of his immense gloved hands, imagining it breaking fingers one by one. 'First he'll scream. Then he'll talk.'

19

'By the way,' I told my rescuer as we drove down a quiet street of terraced housing with monolithic council blocks in the background, 'you've still got the balaclava on.'

'Oh yeah.' He pulled it from his head in one swift movement and chucked it down between the seats, revealing a dark-haired man of about thirty with the lean, wiry features of an athlete and the look of someone who'd been in the forces.

'So,' I said, looking at him, 'if you're a police officer, how come you were going to shoot me?'

'I wasn't. I was bluffing. There was no way I would have pulled the trigger. I'm here to protect you.' He checked the rearview mirror again, still concerned that our pursuer might be following, before making another turning.

I asked him what his name was.

'Daniels,' he answered. 'I've been working undercover for the man who was coming for you. Lench. I don't know his other name, but what I do know is he's a stone-cold killer. That's why I got you out.'

'You hit me in the gut out on that street,' I said indignantly, remembering the way he'd got me into the car in the first place.

'That's because I was undercover. I was playing a part. I'm meant to be a former armed robber who once kneecapped a fellow gang member. I can hardly go all faint when things turn nasty.'

'It hurt.'

'Sorry about that,' he said, not looking sorry at all. In fact, he appeared completely unruffled by events, as if a night out kidnapping and torturing was par for the course, which I suppose in his undercover role it was.

I was still very unsure of him. He could have been a copper, but then again he could just as easily be a crook. I'd run into enough of those today to know that there were plenty of bad guys about.

'You know, this whole thing took months to set up,' he said, staring at the road ahead, 'and now it's been blown. My bosses are not going to be pleased.' His tone suggested this was my fault.

'Forgive me if I don't sympathize,' I said. 'Six hours ago I was living a normal life. Now, for some reason I still can't fathom, people I've never met are trying to kill me, and my wife's missing.'

'Welcome to the big bad world, Mr Meron.'

'How do you know my name?'

He gave a hollow chuckle. 'You really have got a lot to catch up on.'

There was certainly plenty of truth in that statement, but I wondered if he was going to be the one to update me. He made another turning, and a patch of wasteland opened up to our left. I began to get an uneasy feeling.

'Where are we going?' I asked him.

'Well,' he said, reaching into the pocket of his leather jacket and pulling out a pack of Marlboro Lights, 'I'm figuring that you're telling the truth about not knowing anything about what it is we're after.' He put one of the cigarettes in his mouth and depressed the car lighter.

'I am telling the truth. And can I have one of those cigarettes?'

He proffered the pack and I took one and put it in my mouth. 'So, would you be so kind as to tell me what the *it* we're looking for is exactly?'

The car lighter clicked and he used it to spark up his cigarette before passing it across to me. I lit my first smoke for ten years and took a long drag. I felt light-headed, but then I felt light-headed anyway. I repeated the question.

'Well, that's the problem. I don't know what *it* is either. Neither does Mantani. We were only meant to get you over to the warehouse so that Lench could question you. I'm assuming he knows what *it* is.'

I shook my head, feeling utterly confused, and took another drag on the cigarette. It tasted strange. 'Then what the hell do we do now?'

'What we do now,' he replied evenly, 'is find your wife. Because I'm telling you now, if you don't know what or where *it* is, she does.'

20

Bolt and Mo arrived at the pub at five to nine. It was a small, old-fashioned place on the corner of one of the residential roads running off Highgate's main drag, the sort that's slowly being shut down to make way for the bigger, louder chains with their bars like aircraft hangars, which are steadily swallowing everything else up. The interior was threadbare, with a worn-out burgundy carpet peppered with cigarette burns, and walls and a ceiling that had long since been transformed from cream to a nicotine-stained pastiche of brown and yellow. The tables were arranged in a U-shape around a small central bar lined with a variety of draught beer pumps, behind which stood an ancient, stick-thin barman with a waxed moustache and skin the same colour as the walls. Even at this time on a Saturday night, it was quiet. A handful of older guys all of whom obviously knew each other sat on barstools chatting away to the barman, while perhaps a third of the tables were occupied by couples and groups of the same age.

Just around the corner, not quite out of sight, and occupying a large booth, was the woman they were here to see. She saw them and nodded a greeting, then waited while they bought their drinks: an orange juice and lemonade for Bolt, who would have preferred something else but felt that two officers on alcohol wouldn't look so good, and a Becks for Mo, who was officially off duty.

Tina Boyd was an attractive woman in her late twenties, but the events of the past few months had taken their toll. Her dark hair, fashioned into a jaunty bob in the *Police Review* photo, hung lifelessly, and the skin beneath her eyes was puffy and tired. Even her posture as she stood up to shake hands, slumped as if she'd just finished shrugging her shoulders, suggested she'd taken one hit too many recently. She was dressed demurely in a plain white blouse, navy-blue cardigan and jeans, and wore no jewellery or make-up. Her smile wasn't exactly forced, but nor, thought Bolt, was it on her face entirely of its own free will.

Bolt and Mo made their introductions and joined her at the table. Mo got out his cigarettes and, seeing the open pack on the table in front of Tina, offered her one.

When her cigarette had been lit, Bolt leaned forward in his seat and got straight down to business. 'So, what have you got for us?'

Tina picked up a half-full glass of wine and took a good-sized sip. Bolt noticed that her fingernails were chipped and bitten, revealing thin slithers of red-raw skin at the edges. He remembered how perfectly manicured they'd been in the photo on the cover of *Police Review*.

'How far have you got with your case?' she asked, just as directly. 'Does it look like suicide?'

'At the moment that's the official line but, as I said earlier, we were at the scene of a murder of someone close to him tonight, and that makes us suspicious.'

'You should be,' she said.

'Did you know our victim?' asked Mo. 'The Lord Chief Justice?'

She shook her head. 'No, I didn't, but I know something about him, something that no-one else knows.' She took a drag on her cigarette. 'Let me start from the beginning. You know about my ex-boyfriend, John Gallan?'

They both nodded, and Mo said that he was sorry about what had happened.

'Just after Christmas last year, John started acting a little strangely and it was obvious that he had something on his mind. Our relationship was getting quite serious, so I asked him about it, but he just told me there was nothing wrong. He could be close-lipped when he wanted to be, but it still worried me. We didn't tend to have secrets, or at least I thought we didn't, but as the weeks went by I began to get more and more concerned. He was still acting strangely, and I couldn't work out why this was. I'd even gone to the lengths of letting myself into his flat when he was out, and looking through his stuff.' She gave them a sheepish look. 'I'm not usually so paranoid, but to be honest, I thought he was having an affair.'

She sighed.

'Anyway, one evening towards the end of January, we were out for dinner and he got a call on his mobile in the middle of the meal. He excused himself and went outside to take it, and when he came back in he was really agitated. That was it, I'd had enough. I was sure it was a woman so I confronted him about it. I was surprised by his reaction. Very quietly, very seriously, he told me that a few weeks earlier he'd received some confidential information from an anonymous source about a criminal matter. He hadn't been able to talk about it until he got the necessary security clearance; he was in discussions with liaison officers from the highest echelons of Scotland Yard while they looked into it. It was one of the liaison officers who'd called, and the reason John was agitated was because the man on the other end of the phone had told him that as a result of their enquiries they weren't going to be pursuing the matter any further. They'd also told him not to talk about it with anyone, as by doing so he could be in breach of the Official Secrets Act. Naturally he was upset, and he apologized for not having told me anything earlier, which was typical of him. Even though I'd accused him unjustly of having an affair, he ended up being the one saying sorry.'

She took a drag on the cigarette and blew the smoke in the direction of a picture on the wall that showed a group of dogs playing pool. There was a deep sense of regret in her expression as she raked over the coals of her recent past, and Bolt felt for her. For a moment, he thought she might break down, but then her expression became neutral again. She drank some more wine before continuing.

'He didn't want to tell me about it, even then. Not because he was scared that he might get prosecuted – that sort of threat wouldn't have worried him – but because he was so bloody honest. He'd been told not to say anything, so he wasn't going to. He obviously wasn't in a good mood, but when we got back to his place we broke open a bottle of wine, and by the time we'd polished it off he was ready to talk.'

She took a last drag on the cigarette and stubbed it out in the ashtray.

'What he had to say . . . frankly, I found it difficult to believe at the time.' For the first time, she made the effort to look them both in the eye. Hers were dark and bleak, the pain they were reflecting almost tangible. 'I almost wish he'd never told me.'

There was silence at the table for a few seconds. From the bar came the sound of gravelly laughter. Although only a few yards away, it felt distant. Bolt knew instinctively that what was coming was both relevant to their inquiry, and bad. Neither he nor Mo prompted Tina. They simply waited.

'He told me that a man – someone I have a feeling he must have known, but who he never identified – had given him a dossier he'd compiled on a paedophile ring that had been active in south-east England in the late 1990s, and which involved several men who were high up in the establishment. This group of men had apparently murdered a young girl in 1998 and dumped her body in a lake in Dorset soon afterwards. People attached to them were also thought to be responsible for a number of murders in London late last year when they were trying to cover up the death of this girl, including the stabbing of my partner at the time, DCI Simon Barron.'

It was for this reason that Tina Boyd had got her nickname, the Black Widow. People around her had a habit of dying.

'You were working a case with DCI Barron at the time of his murder, though. Didn't you find out anything about this paedophile ring?' Bolt asked her.

'No. DCI Barron's death was, and is, officially unsolved, and there was never any evidence of a group of people matching this description. But the dossier John had named names, several of whom died in mysterious circumstances last year. They included your suicide victim, Tristram Parnham-Jones.'

Bolt was shocked. He looked at Mo, who was clearly feeling the same way. 'You're talking about *the* Parnham-Jones, the Lord Chief Justice?' Bolt knew she was, but felt he had to ask. It was that sort of revelation.

'Yes,' she said frostily, as if she felt her intelligence was being questioned. 'Your suicide victim. He was apparently involved in the murder of the girl in 1998.'

'Was there any hard evidence implicating Parnham-Jones?' asked Mo.

'The dossier contained the exact resting place of the young girl's body, and her identity. The name matched that of a girl who'd gone missing at about the right time, but the liaison officer told John that a search of the lake in question hadn't revealed any remains.'

Bolt leaned forward in his seat. 'So, it's possible – and believe me, I'm not saying it is – but it's possible that this dossier could have been some sort of elaborate hoax?'

'At the time I thought that was possible, of course I did. It was a pretty outlandish accusation. It was also obvious from what John told me that Scotland Yard had looked at it, and had probably even acted on parts of it, like searching the lake, but weren't going to devote any more resources to proving or disproving the contents. So I suppose they thought it was a hoax too. But John was convinced of its truth, and he was no fool, I can promise you that.'

'I know a little bit about his background,' said Bolt, 'so I'm aware that he knew what he was doing.'

She forced a smile, but her face remained as bleak as ever. 'He did.'

'Did you ever see the dossier?' asked Mo.

She shook her head. 'I asked to see it, but he didn't want me to. He said there was nothing that could be done so there was no point. I think it hurt him that Scotland Yard had decided against continuing to look into it. I think he also believed that they were covering things up because Parnham-Jones was such a high-profile figure.'

Bolt exhaled. 'He was certainly that. Did John make any further enquiries of his own, do you know?'

'I'm not sure. He certainly brooded over it, and he couldn't seem to let it go, but I don't know what else he did, or could have done, for that matter. I know one thing, though: it damaged our relationship, and we saw each other a lot less in February than we had done previously. I didn't like to think that events involving the top judge in our country could have ended up being connected to the murder of a young child, or of one of my colleagues, and I didn't want my boyfriend obsessing about it either. I'm a realist. I know my limitations. I don't like to see bad people get away with crimes they've committed. But at the same time I don't like to damn them when the evidence is flimsy. And in this case it was near enough non-existent.' She paused. 'But now, looking back on it, I should have done something.'

'But what could you have done?' asked Bolt, feeling the need to reassure her, the pain in her expression affecting him more than he would have liked.

'I don't know, but I know this: a month after he took that call in the restaurant, John was dead.'

'He committed suicide, didn't he?'

'That was the verdict, yes.'

'But you don't believe it?'

'John wasn't suicidal, Mike. He had a teenage daughter he doted on. He would never have left her behind. He had too much of a sense of responsibility for that. He wasn't the type either. And before you say that the people left behind always say that, I was a copper long enough to know the type. I would have seen the signs.'

'You said he was brooding, though,' put in Mo. 'Could it be possible that you . . .' He thought about what he was going to say

128

for a moment. Mo was always a diplomat when it mattered. 'That you saw the signs but didn't realize the seriousness of them?'

'He wasn't acting suicidal. He was acting as if he was obsessed with this particular case, and was frustrated by the fact that his hands were tied. But he would never have killed himself over it. I'm absolutely sure of that.'

She took another mouthful of wine, and Bolt noticed that her hand was shaking. A thought struck him.

'What was the actual cause of death?'

'An overdose of sleeping pills,' she answered. 'And that's another thing: he never took sleeping pills.'

Mo and Bolt exchanged glances. Tina picked up on this and immediately asked how Parnham-Jones had died.

Bolt sighed. 'Off the record, and it's very much off the record' – Tina nodded to show she understood – 'it was sleeping pills. Dilantin, to be precise.'

She took a deep breath. 'Snap.'

'You're saying John overdosed on dilantin?'

'Yes,' she said. 'That's exactly what I'm saying.'

Another thought struck Bolt. 'Did he leave a note?'

For the first time, he saw doubt cross her face.

'He did. A short two-liner.'

'Typed or handwritten?'

'Typed.'

'Signed?'

She nodded. Parnham-Jones's letter hadn't been, and Bolt felt his initial excitement fading a little.

'Was the signature a forgery?'

'No,' she said reluctantly, 'I saw it. It looked like his hand-writing. But there was something wrong with the letter. It was

129

the words. They just weren't . . .' She worked hard to come up with the right phrase. 'They just weren't him. He would never have said something like "I'm sorry but I just can't take the pain of living". And he would have written a lot more. He would have explained his actions, and he would definitely have made some reference to Rachel, his daughter, or he would have left her a note of her own.' She stopped speaking suddenly and looked at them both intensely. 'What is it?' she asked. 'Why are you looking at me like that?'

The excitement had returned and was racing through Bolt with a vengeance. 'Can you remember the exact words of the suicide note?' he asked, his tone as even as he could manage.

Tina lit another cigarette and looked down at the table, clearly trying to compose herself. 'I read it plenty of times,' she said eventually, 'so, yes, I remember the contents. As I told you, it wasn't very long. It went: "This letter is to all of those I care and have cared about. I'm sorry but I just can't take the pain of living. The world's problems can sometimes be too much to bear. Love" – and then he signed it with his formal signature, which again wasn't like him. He always signed his notes "John".'

Bolt heard Mo exhale. He exhaled himself. The wording was identical to that which Parnham-Jones had typed on the headed paper he'd left on the bedside table beside him as he died.

21

I stared intensely at Daniels, trying without any great success to fathom him out. We were stopped at traffic lights and it was raining hard.

'Why the hell should I help you find my wife?' I demanded.

'Because,' he said, turning in his seat and fixing me with a pretty intense stare of his own, 'at the moment I'm the only person who actually does believe you know nothing about what's going on. The whole world is after you. You need all the help you can get, and at the moment I'm it.'

I sighed and took a long drag on my cigarette as the lights went green and we pulled away. It was beginning to taste better than it had done at the beginning, but still not good enough to justify why I'd bothered getting through twenty-five of them a day during my formative years. Outside the window, the wet night streets of an unfamiliar stretch of London swept past us, the whole journey seeming nightmarishly surreal.

'Who is Lench?' I asked. 'And why would he think a man like me, a fucking software salesman, for Christ's sake, could possibly have something he wanted?'

'Lench is a hitman, a killer. We've got him down for about four murders and two disappearances, and that's just the stuff we're sure about. He could be involved in as many as twenty deaths.'

'Jesus. How come he hasn't been arrested?'

Daniels' lips formed into a thin smile. 'You've got a touching faith in the powers of the police, haven't you?'

'What? And you haven't? Great.' Today, it seemed, was definitely a day for bursting the bubbles of my preconceptions.

'We know all this,' he continued, ignoring my sarcasm, 'but the problem is Lench is careful. He doesn't leave loose ends, often there aren't even any corpses, and the only people he uses are those he trusts absolutely, and who are involved so much themselves that there's no way they'll ever testify against him in a court of law. In fact, even now we still don't know his true identity. So, you have to get someone in on the inside and gather the evidence against him that way.'

'You say he's a hitman. Who does he do his hits for?'

'He works for a very rich businessman who's involved in all kinds of projects, mainly legitimate these days. I can't tell you his name because he's someone you may have heard of, but he started out in cocaine and heroin smuggling, and rather than pissing up his profits against the wall like a lot of these guys do, he invested his money in property and built up a major portfolio. Then it was a matter of expanding into construction – so that he was building the properties rather than just buying them up – and other related businesses. He's been enormously successful, and one of the main reasons for that is the fact that he's kept to the same methods he used in his drug-smuggling days. Whenever he hits any opposition to his plans, he either bribes them or, if that fails, he gets Lench and his people to make the problem go away. We've been after this individual for years but he keeps so far away from the action we reckoned the only way we were going to get him was to secure the evidence needed to bring down Lench, and then use him to testify that our main target was the man pulling the strings. And now, suddenly, it's all fucked up.'

This information didn't make my situation any clearer. 'So, what were you told about me? How come I suddenly became a target?'

'I've been on the periphery of Lench's outfit for about six months now, doing fairly minor things. A few threats to debtors, or people who haven't been playing ball, but not really on the inside. There's only a handful of people – three or four – who are on the inside. Mantani's one of them, and I've been working mainly for him. Lately, they've been letting me in further – I've met Lench a couple of times, and he seems to approve of me – but I'm still considered a bit of an outsider. At least I was until this morning. Then Mantani and me get called in to see Lench and it's obvious something's up. He says we've got an emergency on, and that we're to stand by and wait by the phone for orders. On no account are either of us to be non-contactable, even to take a piss. He keeps Mantani back to tell him a few other things he doesn't want to tell me, but later on Mantani lets slip that the orders are coming from Lench's boss and that it's him who's in trouble. He needs to find something. I have no idea what it is, and neither does Mantani, but we both know that it's been hidden by someone, and that it absolutely has to be found, whatever the cost.'

'And that's what they're after me for? They think I've got it?'

'We got our orders at six o'clock. We had to track you down and get you over to a secure place where Lench could find out what you knew. So, yeah, to answer your question, Lench and his boss seem to think you've got it. I guess Mantani wanted to get the information out of you before Lench turned up. That way he'd earn himself some plaudits.'

I thought about the way Mantani had questioned me, never once identifying what it was he was looking for, and decided that Daniels' story was plausible. But this left me with a very grim conclusion. I didn't know where *it* was, but could it possibly be that Kathy did?

'Our instructions were very specific,' Daniels continued. 'You were named as the man we wanted. Tom Meron. You live at number two St Mary's Close, don't you?'

I nodded slowly. 'That's my address.' I thought about the man I'd seen inside my house and the 3.01 phone call I'd received from my old friend Jack Calley. I asked him what he knew about Jack's death.

'Nothing,' he answered, with a shrug of his shoulders. 'I've never heard of the guy.'

I sighed wearily. 'So, Lench is going to keep coming after me until he finds me?'

'You and your wife.'

'You don't think he's got her, do you?'

'I doubt it; we'd have heard. But I'm telling you this, Tom. He's looking now, so it's essential we find her.'

'Then what?'

'Then we put you under police protection.'

'The police still want to talk to me about a murder at the university this afternoon. A woman called Vanessa Blake was stabbed to death. She worked with my wife. You don't know anything about that, do you?'

'I know what I've told you. Nothing else. You had nothing to do with it, did you?'

'Of course not. I told you, I'm a fucking software salesman.'

'Then you've got nothing to worry about.'

'The police let me go, but I think they must have made a mistake, because as I left the station they chased after me. That was a few minutes before I ran into you.'

'Where's your wife, Tom?'

I felt a cold chill going up my spine. Something was wrong. 'If you weren't aware that the police had arrested me, how did you know where I was going to be this evening?'

He didn't miss a beat with his reply. 'Mantani took a call about half seven. They'd tracked you down to the police station. We were told to wait nearby. Then he got another call saying you were going to be released.'

'Oh Jesus, so they've got someone inside?'

'North London is our main target's stomping ground. His roots are here, and he's been doing business on these streets for close to twenty-five years. In that time he's built up a network of very good contacts, including elements within the police. Put bluntly, you're not safe in this part of town. We need to get you and Kathy to a secure venue, then my people can look after you properly.'

'And who exactly are your people?'

'The NCS,' he answered. 'National Crime Squad. Specifically, a specialist undercover team called the Guardians. You won't find us listed anywhere on the website. Our work's a complete secret.'

'Very James Bond. And is that meant to make me trust you? The fact that you work for a team that no-one even knows exists?'

He fixed me with the kind of leaden glare that demanded attention. 'You want me to let you go, Tom? Pull up here and say my goodbyes? Is that what you want? Fine, I'll do it, but let me reiterate, since you're obviously not a very good listener: a man like you isn't going to last five minutes against the people coming after your blood.'

As he spoke, he pulled up at the side of the road. It was still raining, if anything harder now, and we were on another residential road, this time dominated by modern low-rise blocks of flats that had all the aesthetic beauty of Lego houses and looked like they'd been constructed from the same material. The street was deserted.

'What I want,' I said firmly, 'is to have some proof that you are who you say you are.'

He surprised me then by smiling. 'I thought you might insist on that,' he said, switching off the engine and stepping out of the car. 'I'm going to be a couple of minutes,' he added, 'then I'll be back. You want to get out and run, now's your chance. The nearest tube's left at the end of the road and first right after the lights. But remember, you'll be on your own.'

He disappeared through the entrance of the nearest block, using a key to let himself in, and leaving me on my own in the darkness, listening to the rhythmic patter of the rain and knowing full well that he was right. Alone, I didn't have a chance. The people I was up against had, it seemed, killed many times before without suffering a single conviction, or even receiving the attention of the media. It was hard to believe, but then so had a lot of things been today, and that hadn't made them any less true. The people hunting me operated with impunity and had resources at their disposal that included hired killers and police insiders. As Daniels had pointed out, I was also severely short of friends, which was the main reason I made no attempt to open the car door and walk away. The other reason was that in the end I had nowhere to walk to, which was in some ways a more disconcerting feeling than the fact that I was being hunted.

It suddenly struck me that since being released from police custody close to an hour ago I'd made no attempt to call Kathy. I doubted if it would do any good, but I tried her again anyway. The call went straight to message, and I ended it with a frustrated stab of the thumb. I thought about phoning my mother-in-law and checking on the kids, but decided against it. There was no point alarming her, and I was fairly sure that they'd be safe in her care. No-one knew they were there, and it would be difficult to find them given that Irene didn't share the same last name as me.

When I looked up, I saw Daniels walking purposefully towards the car, speaking into a mobile. He was looking straight at me as he approached, something triumphant in his wiry features, and I wondered whether I was making the right decision, pinning my colours to his mast.

He got back in the car, flicked on the interior light and dangled a warrant card in front of my face. The photo was him all right, staring almost cockily into the camera, head tilted a little to one side, and the identification indeed stated that he was National Crime Squad. His forefinger covered the name underneath and I guessed this was deliberate. I didn't ask him to move it but inspected the card carefully, concluding eventually that it was either genuine or a stunningly good forgery.

'Satisfied?' he said, putting it in the inside pocket of his leather jacket and reaching over to the cigarettes.

'It looks real enough.'

'That's because it is.'

'Who were you talking to just now?'

'My boss. I was leaving him a message. Now, tell me, where do you think your wife could be?'

The moment of truth. For thirty-five years the path of my life had run comparatively smoothly before its sudden and violent derailment today. Its future direction would be dictated by what I did now.

'There's only one place where she might be,' I said, at last. 'If she knows she's in trouble, and I think she does, she'll be there.'

22

Bolt and Mo spent another twenty minutes with Tina. They didn't tell her about the identical nature of the suicide notes, though it was clear she'd guessed the significance. In fact they didn't tell her a lot, citing confidentiality reasons when she asked. Instead they listened as she went over everything she'd told them. There was nothing new. She hadn't found anything that backed up Gallan's claims when she'd gone through all his possessions.

The only thing was,' she told them, 'I couldn't find his personal laptop anywhere. I checked with Karen, his ex-wife, and Rachel, but they hadn't taken it.'

Bolt asked her if she thought it could have been stolen, and her answer was that it would have been typical of John to have stored all the information on the laptop and destroyed the hard copy, so yes, if someone had killed him, then it had definitely been stolen. 'Which means whoever did it took all the evidence away.'

But there were still problems with Tina's story. Whatever

John Gallan might have thought, it still seemed that he hadn't been in possession of any meaningful evidence against Lord Parnham-Jones, so why kill him and risk opening up a real can of worms? Unless he'd had something else, something that actually was incriminating.

'Didn't the police get interested in what John was investigating after his supposed suicide?' Bolt asked Tina.

'I was interviewed by the officers investigating his death, the local CID, and I told them everything I knew, but to be honest I think they thought I was mad, coming up with all these conspiracy theories. It was the way they looked at me. Like I really was the black widow everyone was calling me behind my back. I also tried to get hold of the people at Scotland Yard John was dealing with, but I didn't know their names and everyone I spoke to claimed ignorance. Then my calls stopped being returned. I was becoming an embarrassment.'

She lit a third cigarette, her expression betraying her sense of isolation.

'It was all a long way from the cover of the *Police Review*. Anyway, I became disillusioned with everything, and that's why I left the force. Last month, when the inquest came in as suicide, that was just the icing on the cake. They didn't even call me to give evidence. Just an open-and-shut case. A tragedy for all concerned.'

These last words were delivered in a tone of mocking sarcasm, and Bolt realized how badly beaten down Tina Boyd had been by the events that had befallen her these past few months. He felt genuinely sorry for her because he too knew what it felt like to have the world you'd built up suddenly collapse. It was like having every ounce of will and enthusiasm sucked out of you in one fell swoop. Your whole desire to live, to get up in the morning and follow your daily routine, disappeared, and you had to fight like you'd never fought before to bring things back on track, because the alternative . . . Well, the alternative didn't bear thinking about.

Mo, perhaps sensing that Bolt wanted to speak personally to Tina, excused himself to go to the toilet. When he'd gone, Bolt leaned forward.

'I appreciate you telling us what you've been through,' he said, putting his hand on hers in a more intimate gesture than he'd planned. 'I know what it's like to lose someone.'

Tina looked down at their hands, and then back at him. He suddenly felt self-conscious and a little foolish, and pulled away.

'I remember reading about what happened to you,' she said. 'You've done well to get everything back together.' She picked up her wine and drained the rest of the glass.

'I know you must be pissed off with the way the police treated you, and I can understand that.'

'It wasn't just that. It was everything. Simon Barron dying; being held hostage at gunpoint last year . . . It got to the point where it was no longer worth it.'

'What are you doing now?'

She smiled without humour. 'Not a lot. Spending what money I've got left and deciding what I want to do with the rest of my life.'

'When it all happened to me, I thought long and hard about leaving. Almost did it too. I was going to go travelling round the world, see if all those palm-fringed beaches and gorgeous sights could help me forget things, but in the end I stayed put. Because I always knew that some day I was going to have to come back, and then I'd still have to face the past all over again.' He saw Mo returning from the toilet. 'I heard you were a very good cop,

140

Tina,' he said, turning back to her. 'Whatever you may think now, the force needs people like you.'

'I think they said the same thing to Simon Barron to coax him back from retirement. It didn't do him a lot of good.'

Bolt wasn't offended by the cold directness of her words. He'd expected it. But he did genuinely believe what he was saying.

He stood up as Mo arrived back at the table, and put out a hand. 'We're going to need to make a move, Tina. Thanks for providing us with this information. I think it's going to prove very useful.'

She stood up and shook, her grip dry and firm. She was a woman who might be down, but he could see now that she was definitely not out.

'You know neither of them committed suicide, don't you?' she said.

'I believe it's very doubtful,' Bolt replied carefully.

She looked him right in the eye then, her expression surprisingly strong. 'Then find out who killed John. Please. He deserves that.'

'We'll do everything we can,' he told her, and turned away.

23

When they were outside and passing the window, they saw Tina going back to the bar to order another drink, the middle-aged men on the barstools moving slightly to let her in, giving her appraising glances through the fug of smoke that she either chose to ignore or simply didn't see. Bolt found himself wishing she'd go home and try to rethink her life without the benefit of alcohol. She didn't belong in a place like that.

'That was some pretty explosive stuff she came up with in there, boss,' said Mo as they made their way back to the car through the quiet, wet streets. 'Do you think all this is connected to that dossier?'

'I think that unless Parnham-Jones had amazing psychic powers, then he was murdered. And if he was murdered, then so was John Gallan. There's no other explanation for the fact that those suicide notes were exactly the same.'

'Well, they weren't *exactly* the same, were they? Our man never signed his.'

'It's still too much of a coincidence.'

Mo shook his head wearily. 'You can't believe that someone like the Lord Chief Justice would be involved in that sort of shit. It kind of wrecks your faith in the system.' He tried to light a cigarette but the rain was coming down too hard, and he replaced the pack in his pocket. 'And what about the lawyer, Jack Calley? Or our man, Meron? What part do they play in all this?'

'You know, Mo, I honestly have no idea,' said Bolt, hunching his shoulders against the rain. He thought of Tina and her grief. 'But one way or another, I'm going to find out.'

By now they were back at the car. They got inside quickly and, as Mo turned on the engine, Bolt switched his mobile back on, having turned it off for the meeting with Tina. He called DC Matt Turner, the member of his team who'd taken Parnham-Jones's home computer away for analysis. Turner wasn't answering so Bolt left him a message to check all the files on the

Parnham-Jones PC, see if there were any encrypted or otherwise interesting files, and to call back as soon as possible.

'Where to now, boss?'

Home seemed tempting. It would have been useful to take some time out to mull over everything that had happened today and to look for connections and further avenues of inquiry. The case was definitely one for mulling over, preferably with a cold beer and a Thai takeaway in the dry comfort of home, but he wasn't quite finished today yet.

He told Mo they had one more call to make.

24

The cottage in the New Forest was one of those purchases you make on a whim, without thinking through the consequences. I'm normally quite good with money, but like Kathy I got caught up in the dream, and it really did seem like a good idea at the time.

We'd been having dinner with a couple we knew from the estate, and there'd been a second couple there, people we hadn't previously met. Warren and Midge. Stupid names when you think about it, but nice people. After a lot of wine, and plenty of talk about that most boring and suburban of topics, work, Midge, who had copious amounts of curly auburn hair, lots of hippy-style jewellery and an unavoidably huge bust, and who didn't look at all like the City accountant she was meant to be, announced that she and Warren were buying a share in a holiday home. Not just any holiday home either, but a delightful 150-year-old crofter's cottage set in acres of protected forest that was barely a two-hour drive from London, and fewer than ten miles from the unspoiled Dorset coast. 'It's a piece of paradise,' Warren had exclaimed, as if quoting from an estate agent's blurb (which he probably was), 'a bolthole from all the hassles of the modern world. Our kids are going to love it.'

Something in Warren and Midge's enthusiasm had been infectious. At the time our own children were three and one, so foreign travel had lost a lot of its allure, and the idea of holidaying only two hours from home had a real ring of convenience. Plus, of course, we'd drunk a lot of wine. And lo and behold, they still needed another family to buy the last quarter share. Only £55,000, and this at the height of the property boom. For that, we'd get sole rights to the cottage for a quarter of the year, a week every month, and Christmas or New Year every other year. Warren even had the property details with him, and the cottage did indeed look idyllic. The plot was close to half an acre and included woodland, the nearest property over two hundred yards away. The price seemed a bargain – not that we had that kind of money. But within a month we'd got it, having released some of the equity in our own property, and had become the proud owners of 25 per cent of Sandfield Cottage, along with Warren and Midge, Warren's brother and his family, and one of Midge's fellow accountants at their City investment bank and her partner.

That was two and a half years ago, and I suppose, in hindsight, it had been a waste of money. It was nice when we got the chance to go there, but we used it far less than we'd anticipated. In the last year, I reckon we'd spent no more than a week there.

As with so many things, there never seemed to be enough time, which was probably why I hadn't thought of it before as a possible location for Kathy. But now it seemed like one, mainly because I couldn't think of anywhere else she might have fled to – on the assumption, of course, that she had fled somewhere and wasn't being held against her will. She'd always appreciated the fact that the cottage did indeed represent a retreat from the rat race, and the one time I'd suggested selling our share to raise some capital, she'd been against the idea. 'I need the solitude it offers now and again,' she'd told me, and I suspected that now, assuming she knew she was in trouble, she would need the solitude it offered more than ever. It was also our allotted weekend, making her presence there even more likely. I considered phoning her on the cottage landline, but I had a lot of questions I wanted to ask, and I was beginning to think that if I told her I was coming she might not hang around to answer them. Plus, the possibility that she was in the cottage gave me hope, and I didn't want that snuffed out.

At first as we drove, I asked Daniels a lot of questions about the undercover operation, trying to get as much information as I could about the man called Lench, but he was vague with his answers and didn't seem in the mood for talking. The traffic was light as we left London, heading from the M4 to the M25, and then south-west on the M3. Daniels drove fast, the speedometer regularly touching a hundred, even though it was wet outside and the rain continued to plunge out of the black night sky. I asked him on the M4 for another of his cigarettes and he told me to help myself. As the journey progressed I continued to help myself, and he had to stop at some services on the M3 to buy another pack, plus some water and chocolate. I offered him a couple of quid in payment, thinking that he wouldn't accept it, but he told me a fiver would be nearer the mark and took it without even a thanks, which I thought was a bit much. 'You don't get far in life unless you contribute,' he said, seeing my reaction.

Daniels, I had to admit, was a strange character. On the one hand he was calm and collected, his words, when he did speak, delivered in the slow, even manner of a man who always felt in control of a situation. He liked to let slip languid pieces of philosophy too, like the 'not getting far in life unless you contribute' bit, and I think he fancied himself as some sort of eastern mystic warrior, dispensing justice, righteous violence and snippets of useful advice. But there was also an air of stiff tension about him, as if there were secrets in his soul he was fighting a silent yet terrible battle to keep from view. When I looked at him driving, his jaw tight and his teeth clenched, his pale eyes concentrating hard on the road ahead, I could tell there was plenty going on in his mind.

I didn't trust him. He was too complicated, and in my experience, complicated people always have some sort of hidden agenda.

After we'd left the service station and were back on the road, I asked him why he'd allowed me to get beaten up by his colleague, Mantani, and why he'd carried out the charade of threatening me with the gun. 'You must have had some idea how scared you were making me,' I told him, between mouthfuls of Mars bar.

'I was thinking,' answered Daniels.

'That's nice to know,' I said. 'About anything in particular?'

'You know something, Meron, your problem is you mistake sarcasm for humour. Don't bother with it; I'm not in the mood. I didn't react instantaneously to your misfortune because I was thinking about what the hell I should do, and how I was going to do it. I'd spent six months weaving my way into this organization, and I still had nowhere near enough evidence to convict any of them of anything. I knew that if I pulled you out, six months' work would go up in smoke. But because you were in trouble, I made the move. Now, be thankful for it, all right? Because if Lench had got hold of you, you'd be in pieces by now.' He delivered this broadside without taking his eyes off the road once.

'OK, OK, I understand.'

'No,' he said, shaking his head, 'I don't think you do. I don't think you've got any idea what it's like to act a part every day of your life, knowing that if you make one mistake and the people you're working out find out who you really are, then that's it, you're dead. The problem with you civilians,' he continued, this time deigning to look at me, 'is that you live a nice easy suburban life and you don't see any of the shit that goes on out there in the big wide world day after day – the violence, the killing, the kids on crack who'll do anything for their next fix – because we protect you from all that. We do the hard work, we sweep away the problems that are right in front of your noses, if only you could be bothered to look for them, and we make sure they go under the carpet so you don't have to worry about any of them. And consequently, you end up having no fucking idea how lucky you are.'

I was surprised at how animated Daniels had suddenly become. It was like a pressure being released, and he seemed visibly to relax once he'd spoken.

'Congratulations, Meron,' he added. 'Today, you've seen that other world, and now you'll be a wiser man for it.'

I didn't say anything. He was probably right, but it wasn't a statement I saw much point in commenting on. I took a cigarette from the new pack. Ten years free of it, and I was already redeveloping my old bad habit. When all this was over – and for some reason, maybe the presence in the car of a hard bastard who wasn't actually trying to kill me, I was now more optimistic that it would be – I'd kiss Kathy, hug my kids, crack open a £10 bottle of wine and make a vow never to touch a smoke again.

In the meantime, though, I wasn't going to let a little thing like my long-term physical health worry me. I had to get through the short term first.

25

Forty minutes later, we turned off the A31 west of Southampton and drove into the New Forest national park. Sandfield Cottage was set back from the road behind a thick screen of pine trees in a quiet stretch of woodland not far from the village of Bolder-wood. It was reached via a potholed drive about thirty yards long that was almost impossible to spot unless you were looking for it. On my instruction, Daniels slowed up and made the turning, and as we approached along the drive I saw a light from the house appear through the trees.

There was someone there.

As the driveway opened out into the parking area and lawn in front of the cottage, Kathy's new Hyundai Coupé – her pride and joy – came into view, parked over near the fence that separated the front and rear of the property. It was the only car there, and I let out an audible sigh of relief.

'That your wife's car, is it?' asked Daniels, parking up behind it.

I nodded.

'Then I guess she's safe.' He turned off the engine.

I looked over to the cottage. The only light was coming from the upstairs bedroom. The downstairs area was in darkness, and the curtains were open. There was no sign that Kathy had heard us, and I experienced a small twinge of nerves.

'Can you let me go in first? I don't want to scare her.'

He nodded. 'Sure.'

I got out, fumbling in my pocket for my keys. I found the right one and hurried over to the front door, my shoes crunching on the gravel. It was still raining hard and I had no desire to be out in the open any longer than I needed to be.

As I passed the big bay window at the front, I looked directly into the sitting room. It was empty, but the cushions on the sofa were out of place and there was a coffee cup and an empty glass on the coffee table. Someone had definitely been here very recently.

At the front door, I bent down and opened the letterbox, peering inside. It was deadly silent in there, the only sound the relentless pounding of the rain. I wanted to call out, but something stopped me. Instead, I eased the key into the lock and gently turned it. There was a click, and the door opened with a soft whine. When it was part-way open, I slipped through the gap and stepped into the porch area. Pairs of hiking boots were lined up neatly on the floor to my left. Kathy's shoes weren't among them. I looked up at the coat rack but couldn't see her coat there either.

But her car was here so she would be too. Somewhere.

I went further inside, the sitting room opening up to my right. Beyond it, straight ahead, was the door that led through to the new kitchen/dining area that had been added to the back of the cottage as a single-storey extension by the previous owners. To the left of the door was the staircase that led up to the two bedrooms on the first floor. I walked slowly towards it, listening for any sound of human presence.

'Kathy?'

My whisper sounded artificially loud in the dead gloom of this old house with its low timbered ceilings and floorboards that creaked and sighed in time with the wind and my heavy footfalls.

The scream exploded to my left, a shocking, high-pitched screech, and a figure shot up from behind the staircase's solid-wood banister, one hand clutching a knife that gleamed viciously in the darkness.

As I threw up my hands in a desperate protective gesture, the figure vaulted the last two steps and leaped on me, the weight knocking me backwards into one of the chairs. My weight in turn knocked the chair out of the way and I landed hard on my back, one hand grabbing the knife wrist, the other encircling my attacker's throat. I squeezed hard, and would have squeezed a lot harder but for the fact that I realized I was staring into my wife's contorted, rage-filled face.

'Kathy, it's me! For Christ's sake, what are you doing?'

She was struggling like a fish on a hook, breathing in short, angry gasps, and slapping at me with a free hand, the knife still held in a stabbing position above my head, her grip on it so tight that her knuckles were white. And then, suddenly, her expression softened, her arm went limp and she dropped the knife, which clattered onto the pine flooring, narrowly missing my shoulder. For the first time, there was recognition in her face. I let go of her, but instead of falling into some kind of reunion hug she clambered off me and sat nearby on the floor, head in her hands. She was dressed in the same clothes she'd left the house in that morning: jeans, a suede jacket and ankle boots with jagged heels.

'Oh God,' she said at last. 'I can't take this any more.'

'It's all right,' I told her, getting up and putting a reassuring arm across her shoulders. I held her against me, adding soothingly that everything was going to be fine, and at that moment I meant it. We were reunited, we hadn't done anything wrong. We could dig ourselves out of this hole.

Out of the corner of my eye, I saw that Daniels had stepped over the threshold and was waiting awkwardly next to the coats.

Kathy took a couple of deep breaths and composed herself, looking at me with an expression I couldn't quite fathom. She was upset, but her eyes were dry, and there was a hardness in them I only ever recalled seeing when she was angry with me. Of relief, or any other similar emotion, there was no sign.

'I'm OK,' she said distantly. 'Are you?'

'I'm fine,' I lied. 'I've been trying to reach you for hours on the mobile.'

'It doesn't work down here, does it? There's no reception, and I've been here since this afternoon. Are the kids all right?'

'They're fine. They're at your mum's.'

I wondered then how much she knew. She couldn't have been aware of Jack's phone call, or his murder, but I assumed she must have known about Vanessa's death, as they'd both been at the university together today. But there were a lot of questions she needed to answer.

Before I could think where to start, she motioned towards the doorway. 'Who's your friend?'

'This is Daniels. He's been helping me. Daniels, this is my wife, Kathy.'

As Kathy nodded an acknowledgement, he walked into the room, switching on the light. The room suddenly seemed very bright as he came forward and put out a hand, which she took.

'Pleased to meet you,' he said, with a tight, humourless smile.

Which was the moment when Kathy snatched back her hand and the expression on her face changed completely. A new emotion now dominated it.

Fear.

26

It was ten past ten when Bolt and Mo pulled up at Jack Calley's house. Several police vehicles were still parked at the side of the road, and the glow of floodlights came through the trees up on the hill where the SOCO officers continued to work in the area where the body had been found. They were atrocious conditions to be operating in, but nothing could stop the hunt for forensic clues. Rather them than me, thought Bolt as he and Mo got out of the car. No-one seemed to be around, which was convenient as he didn't fancy having to explain himself to Lambden, who he knew would be pissed off, and might try to cause trouble.

They walked swiftly through the rain up to the neighbouring

house, where the older couple had been standing outside earlier. It was a bigger place than Calley's, a whitewashed two-storey building constructed in the style of a Mediterranean villa, with shutters on the windows and fingers of ivy running up towards the gently sloping roof. A covered porch, dotted with plant pots, ran the length of the ground floor, and two hanging lamps like orbs guided visitors to the front door. Bolt would have loved to live in a place like this, although he would probably have transplanted it to Italy or Greece, or somewhere where there was a better class of criminal.

They darted under the porch roof, dodging the streams of water running down onto the patio, and got their warrant cards ready as Bolt rang the doorbell. After a long pause, they heard footsteps coming from inside and then the door was slowly opened on a chain. The same man they'd seen earlier, silver-haired and in his late sixties, appeared in the gap, wearing a cautious expression that wasn't surprising given that they were both in civilian clothes.

'Can I help you?' he asked.

Bolt did the introductions and said that they were working on a case related to the murder. 'We know it's very late, and I apologize, but is it possible that we can come inside for a minute?'

The man nodded slowly. Behind him they heard his wife ask who was at the door. 'The police,' he answered, releasing the chain and stepping aside to allow them in.

They followed him through the hallway and into a large and comfortable sitting room whose walls were lined with numerous tourist-shop ornaments and other bric-a-brac. There were china plates with maps of Greek islands on them; wine bottles in baskets; paintings of Mediterranean beach scenes; even a couple of model donkeys. It should all have looked very garish, but somehow it managed to avoid it.

Their host introduced himself as Bernard Crabbe. His wife, a small, very round woman of about the same age who milled about them like an indecisive mother hen, was introduced as Debbie.

'We'd like to ask you some questions about Jack Calley,' Bolt told them both.

'Please, would you like to sit down?' asked Mr Crabbe.

'No, it's OK. We don't need to stay long. I'm sure you'd like to go to bed.'

'It's a bit difficult with all this excitement going on.'

'Jack was a very good neighbour,' added Mrs Crabbe. 'He always fed Monty and Horace, our cats, when we went away. It's such a tragedy to have his life taken away from him so young.'

Bolt and Mo made sympathetic noises.

'Did you know that Jack was Lord Chief Justice Parnham-Jones's solicitor?' asked Mrs Crabbe, sounding very excited by this fact.

'Yes, we did,' said Mo, who was gazing with interest at a lace doily with a pair of flamenco dancers in the middle that had pride of place above the television.

'We saw him come to the house,' added Mr Crabbe. 'Not that long ago either. Perhaps two or three weeks. I asked Jack about it and he told me that he did personal legal work for his lordship.'

'It's a tragedy about him too,' said Mrs Crabbe, who was still clucking about. 'I felt he was a very humane Lord Chief Justice who didn't pander to the demands of populism. It's about time someone stood up to the tabloids.'

Bolt wondered if she'd still say the same thing if she heard the allegations about him that had been made tonight.

'The main reason we're here,' he said, 'is to find out if you've ever seen this man with Jack at all.' He held out the photo of Tom and Kathy Meron.

'Let me get my glasses,' said Mrs Crabbe, looking around her with a sudden urgency. 'Have you seen my glasses, Bernard?'

Mr Crabbe said he hadn't. His own were hanging around his neck. He put them on and took the photo from Bolt, inspecting it carefully.

'Does he look at all familiar?' Bolt asked him.

'He doesn't,' answered Mr Crabbe, 'but she does. We've seen her at Jack's place several times, although we don't know who she is. I do know that the police who were speaking to us earlier want to find her, though.'

'Is it her?' demanded Mrs Crabbe, who was leaning across her husband, still without her glasses.

'Yes, it is.' Mr Crabbe tapped the image of Kathy Meron with a stubby forefinger. 'This woman was at Jack's today.'

Bolt and Mo exchanged glances, but it was Bolt who spoke. 'What time was this?'

'Well, this is why the other police were so interested. It was just before all this happened. I was out in the front garden and I saw her driving past. It was just after lunch, at about half past one this afternoon.'

So, Kathy Meron must have been one of the last people to see Jack Calley alive, Bolt thought. Which meant she might well have seen his killers.

Or, worse, been involved with them.

27

Kathy got to her feet and started to back away from Daniels. Daniels looked surprised, but made no effort to follow her.

'What's going on, Kathy?' I asked as I watched her retreat.

Her eyes darted down towards the knife, still lying on the floor where she'd dropped it, then she lunged and picked it up in one movement. She pointed the blade in Daniels' direction. Her hand was shaking slightly, but there was a grim determination in her eyes that I didn't like the look of at all.

'You were there, weren't you?' she hissed, addressing Daniels.

'Where?' he asked, bemused.

'At Jack's house. This afternoon. You were one of the men who came for him, weren't you?'

'I don't know what you're talking about.'

'Yes, you do.'

'I'm sorry, I think you're mistaking me for someone else.'

'Don't patronize me. I don't make mistakes like that.'

'What is this, Kathy? How do you know he was at Jack Calley's today?'

'You know how I know?' she said. The question was directed

at Daniels rather than me. She had the knife raised so that the blade was pointed directly at his throat. Three feet separated skin from steel. 'I didn't see you, because if I'd seen you I'd be dead now too, wouldn't I? I heard you. I heard you all, and I recognize your voice.'

A thin smile crossed her face as she spoke, but at the same time her expression hardened. In those moments, she didn't look like my wife at all. Even then, however, I still didn't quite make the connection, my excuse being the number of shocks I'd had that day.

'What were you doing at Jack's, Kathy? We haven't seen him in four years.'

'All right, all right,' said Daniels, stepping back and raising his hands in supplication. 'I think we may be starting off on the wrong foot here.' As quick as a flash, his hand went inside his leather jacket and the next second he was pointing the gun at Kathy.

'Daniels, for Christ's sake, don't shoot. She's my wife.'

He ignored me and released the safety catch. 'Right, let's start again. Put the knife down, Mrs Meron.'

Kathy made no move to obey. 'You killed Jack, you bastard. I'm going to make you pay for that.'

This was the moment when I finally realized the inevitable. Some might say a little belatedly. I might not have seen Jack for some years, but it was becoming clear that Kathy had been pursuing the friendship on behalf of both of us. I think deep down I'd known for a while she was having an affair. Her working hours had got longer, there were weekends away at conferences, there'd been changes in her behaviour. She'd started wearing perfume again, buying expensive underwear. But when the signs are there you don't want to admit it to yourself. You make excuses, rationalize things. That was why hearing the admission from her mouth now was like a hammer blow to the gut.

Jack. I felt dizzy. The fucking bastard.

'This isn't what you think, Mrs Meron. Now, please put the knife down, and let's talk.'

'What do you mean, it isn't what I'm thinking? I heard you torturing him on the bed.'

'I didn't touch him. I was there, but I promise you, I didn't touch him.'

'You lied to me,' I said.

The statement was aimed at Daniels, but it was Kathy who answered, although as she spoke, she kept her eyes firmly on him.

'I'm sorry, Tom. I didn't mean you to find out this way.'

'Why?' I asked, and this time it was to her, although there were probably plenty of answers to that question.

'I can't talk about it now.'

'Put the knife down, Mrs Meron.'

Kathy gave a barely perceptible shake of the head, her expression hardening. 'No.'

Daniels came forward fast, grabbing her wrist and twisting it violently. He smacked the gun barrel down on her exposed forearm and she let out a yelp and dropped the weapon. Shoving her backwards, he picked it up from the floor and flung it into the corner of the room, a long way from any of us. All this before I even had a chance to react.

For a second, Kathy looked like she was going to burst into tears, but she quickly controlled herself. I went over and hugged her, still feeling the pain in my stomach from the knowledge that she no longer loved me in the way I loved her. She buried her head in my chest, the warmth of her body comforting against my skin.

I glared at Daniels. 'So, you were at Jack's house?'

He nodded. 'Yeah, I was. I couldn't tell you before because you'd never have trusted me.'

I looked at the gun, which was still pointed in our direction. 'So, you're not a cop?'

'I am a cop. I didn't lie about that.'

Kathy broke away from me. 'You can't be. The police don't do that sort of thing.'

'I'm undercover,' he told her.

He briefly explained what he'd told me, and Kathy listened without interrupting. As he spoke he lowered the gun. 'We got a call this afternoon from Lench. Me and Mantani were to go with him over to a guy named Jack Calley's house, and we were to dress in suits and make sure we wore gloves. While we were driving, Lench told us that Calley had some information that we had to get from him. He wouldn't say what it was. When we arrived, Mantani asked him what we were going to do with Calley once we got the information, and Lench said we were going to kill him and make it look like suicide. Apparently, that's one of Lench's specialities.

'Anyway, Mantani and I knocked on the door while Lench waited round the corner. Because we were dressed in suits, we looked pretty normal, so I guess Calley wasn't suspicious. When he answered, Mantani gave him a shot of pepper spray and the three of us forced our way inside. We dragged Calley upstairs and tied him to the bed. He was coughing and choking and telling us that we could take whatever we wanted but to please leave him alone. He was really scared. Lench stuffed a golfball in his mouth, then sat on his legs and put a lighter to his balls.

'Then he took out the golfball and said, "Where is it? We know you've got it." Calley was screaming and saying he didn't know what the hell it was Lench was talking about, so Lench started burning him again, for longer this time. Then he asked Calley who he'd been blabbing to. He didn't say what about, but I got the feeling Calley knew what he was talking about.

'But he wasn't talking, so Lench put the golfball back in his mouth and told him he had five minutes to think things over, and then we were really going to get started on him. He went downstairs, and I went with him. We left Mantani on guard duty. When we were down in the kitchen, Lench put the kettle on and then came right up and looked me in the eye. He told me that to prove myself to him I was going to have to take the kettle up to the bedroom and pour the contents over Calley's face and body, before we even tried to get him to talk again. That way he'd know we were serious. Lench said he was going to film me on his phone doing it, so that I'd be completely implicated.

'I knew I was going to have to get the hell out of there, but before I had a chance to create a distraction I heard shouting coming from upstairs. That idiot Mantani had gone to take a piss, leaving Calley on his own, and he'd managed to get free. The next thing we know, Calley comes flying down the stairs and charges out the side door, with Mantani hot on his tail. Lench yelled at me to go and start the car so we could be ready for a quick getaway, and then he disappeared out the door after them.'

'I didn't hear him shout that,' said Kathy.

'So you *were* there?' I asked quietly, and with resignation.

She turned to me and nodded gently. She looked beautiful, her olive skin unblemished by the tears, her eyes radiating a warmth and intelligence that made her betrayal so much harder to accept. She was a good person, a fantastic mother. I couldn't understand how she could have done what she'd done.

'Look, Tom. I . . .'

Her words trailed off. I knew she felt sorry for me, but there seemed to be no regret, no desire to put things right. Her pain was for someone else.

'How long's it been going on?'

She sighed. 'We'll talk about it later, Tom, OK? For now, I want to know who this man is, because I still don't believe his story.'

'I'm telling you the truth,' said Daniels evenly. 'Lench and Mantani went after Calley. I had to go back to the car because we'd parked it away from Calley's house so it wouldn't get clocked by passers-by. They came back five minutes later and said that Calley was dead, but he'd told them that he no longer had the thing they were after. He said he'd given it to Tom Meron.'

I shook my head. 'But I haven't seen him for four years.'

Daniels shrugged. 'Well, that's what they told me. They also said that while he was trying to escape, Calley made a call to your house. While we were driving, Lench made a call of his own. He's got some excellent contacts because it only took him minutes to find out who your wife was and where you both worked. He got a car sent round to your house to make sure you were there when he turned up, then got us to drop him off. We were told to get rid of the car we'd been using, then to stay together and wait for further orders. The rest you know.'

'This is ridiculous,' I said, utterly confused. 'Jack Calley never gave me anything.'

'It's convenient you had nothing to do with Jack's actual murder, isn't it?' said Kathy to Daniels, an undercurrent of venom in her voice. 'Did you see what they did to him? I did. I went up into the woods to try to find him. They'd strung him up from a tree like some sort of dog. Nobody deserves that.'

Daniels ignored her. 'So, where were you all this time? I'm guessing you must have been in the bedroom. In one of the cupboards?'

She sighed. 'Jack and I were upstairs when you came to the door. When the doorbell went, Jack went to get it, and that's when I heard all the commotion and shouting coming from downstairs. I panicked and hid in the nearest place I could find – his clothes cupboard. I pushed myself right to the back, behind all his suits, and kept as quiet as I could. And then I heard you and your friends coming into the room, Jack being knocked about and tied to the bed, and then . . . And then I heard you torturing him.' Her voice cracked as she recounted the events. 'He was in agony. And no-one, none of you, seemed to care.'

Daniels didn't say anything, so she continued.

'When you went downstairs and the other man left the room too, I knew this was the only chance I was going to get to help Jack. I came out of the wardrobe and saw him lying there on the bed with the crotch of his jeans all blackened where he'd been burned. His face was screwed up in agony but he was still conscious. He motioned for me to get back inside the cupboard – he didn't want me to get caught, because he knew they'd kill me – but I couldn't leave him like that. Not helpless. I could hear the other man moving about in the toilet and it was obvious I only had a few seconds. I managed to free one of his hands, and he untied the other. We heard the toilet door opening, and Jack pushed me away and made a run for it. I heard the scuffle on the stairs and then him charging down them. And that was the extent of our goodbye.' I watched as Kathy took some deep breaths, then fixed Daniels with a hard stare. 'And I never heard anyone shout anything about going and starting the car.'

Daniels shrugged. 'That's the way it happened.'

She shook her head. 'You took part in his killing, I know you did.'

'Daniels rescued me earlier, Kathy,' I said. 'I think he's who he says he is: an undercover cop.'

'You weren't there, Tom. I was. He was a part of it, under-cover cop or not.'

'Jack phoned me, when they were chasing him,' I told her. 'He said he needed my help. The last words he said – and he said them to the people chasing him – were the first two lines of our address. Why?'

Daniels looked at Kathy. 'Maybe Calley gave the thing Lench was after to you but he didn't say anything under torture because he was trying to protect you.'

She shook her head. 'Jack never gave me anything.'

'Are you sure about that?'

She glared at him. 'I don't have to answer to you, whoever you are. Even if you have got a gun in your hand.' She turned in my direction. 'I think we need to call the police, Tom. Get this sorted out.'

'I'd advise you against that, Mrs Meron.' Daniels had raised the gun again, and I saw his finger tightening on the trigger.

'Vanessa's dead as well,' I told her desperately. 'She was murdered over at the university this afternoon.'

Kathy's eyes widened, and she looked genuinely shocked. 'Oh God, no.'

'Look, I've got to ask. Did you know anything about it?'

She shook her head. 'Of course not. Christ, what happened?' Her voice was high-pitched, distraught.

'The police didn't tell me, but I think she was stabbed.'

'Do you know anything about this?' she demanded, address-ing Daniels.

Now it was his turn to shake his head. 'I've no idea why she would have been targeted. Can you think of a reason?'

'No, I can't. She's a bloody university lecturer, for Christ's sake.' She wiped her hand across her face. 'Oh God, poor Vanessa.'

'There's something else you should know,' I said.

She looked at me quickly. 'What?'

'The knife used to kill her had your fingerprints on it.'

'No,' she said firmly. 'No way. There must be some mistake.'

I watched her reaction carefully. It's a very disconcerting feeling not being able to trust anything your wife says.

'And I'm still wondering why Jack phoned our house, and why he wanted me to help him,' I added.

'I don't know anything about that either.' But when she turned my way I could see doubt in her eyes. She was lying. I could tell.

Daniels obviously felt the same way. 'You know something, Mrs Meron, and it's in everyone's best interests that you tell us what it is.'

'What? To you? To someone who was involved in the killing of a man I cared about, who I've never met before in my life, and who's now pointing a gun at me? No, I'm calling the police. I'll talk to them.'

There was a phone in the far corner of the room, on a table next to one of the chairs, and Kathy now strode over to it.

'Don't do it, Mrs Meron,' snapped Daniels, the tension in his voice obvious. The gun was now pointed at Kathy's head.

I stepped in front of him. 'Come on, Daniels. For Christ's sake, don't point that thing at my wife.'

He shoved me aside with a hissed 'shut the fuck up', then addressed her again. 'There are police officers involved in this,

164

Mrs Meron. You talk to the wrong one, you could end up dead. Don't do it.'

'Or what? What'll you do? Shoot me?'

Daniels' features were taut and ragged. 'If I have to, yes.'

'I'm going to phone nine-nine-nine and get the police to come here. If you are a police officer, then you have to accept that, don't you?'

They stared at each other, Kathy's hand resting on the receiver. Her expression was one of grim determination. So was Daniels', but he looked to be under the most pressure, even though he was the one with the gun. I knew he didn't want to hurt her, but I wasn't sure that he wouldn't. His grip on the gun was firm. The barrel didn't move.

'Don't make me do this, Mrs Meron. If you tell me where it is, then we can sort all this out.'

Something struck me then. Something so obvious that I should have known about it right from the first minute I'd met him.

'You know what it is, don't you?' I said to Daniels. 'You know what Lench and his boss are looking for. And you want it for yourself.'

But his attention was focused entirely on Kathy.

My mind was racing. Should I rush him? Try to get the gun from his grasp? Did my wife deserve my help? I felt my legs shaking, the tension building. The room was thick with silence, no longer resembling the place where we'd spent so many relaxing evenings. My next thought, somewhat inappropriately, was that we were going to have sell our share in the cottage. I couldn't come here again, not after this.

'Please, Mrs Meron. Come over here, and let's talk.'

I leaped forward, grabbing Daniel's gun arm at the wrist and shoving it away from Kathy. With my free hand I tried to get a grip on his throat, but he danced backwards and out of reach, sending me tumbling into the banister. Then a hand slammed into the back of my skull, sending my head flying forwards into the wood with a painful thud, and Daniels' arm seemed to slip effortlessly out of my grip.

'Fuck you, Meron,' he hissed as I went down in a heap.

My head throbbed, but I ignored it, swinging round on my behind so that I could see what was happening. From my less than advantageous position, I saw that Daniels was staring hard at Kathy, the gun pointing once again in her direction. The receiver dangled limply from her hand, and her face was as pale, I think, as I'd ever seen it.

'What the fuck did I tell you?' shouted Daniels.

'Don't shoot, for Christ's sake,' I told him.

'There's no need,' said Kathy. 'The phone's dead.'

There was a long silence then. The sound of the rain crackling on the concrete outside the window was the only background noise.

Finally, Daniels spoke, and his words had a grim inevitability about them.

'They're here.'

28

Keeping low, Daniels moved to the switch on the wall by the porch and killed the lights. 'Everyone get down,' he whispered, creeping through the semi-darkness and squatting down below the bay window that looked out on to the front driveway. Slowly, he lifted his head and peered over the edge.

We obeyed his instructions. I crouched down behind the sofa, and Kathy slid down the wall and rested on her haunches. Our eyes met briefly in the gloom, and I could see the fear there. But there was nothing else, no regret, and she turned away quickly.

'Can you see anything out there?' I asked Daniels, my voice a loud whisper.

'Nothing yet, but they're there somewhere.'

'How did they find us?'

'Don't think about that now. What we need to focus on is how the hell we get out of here. Where does it lead to out the back?'

'The garden backs on to forest,' I said, 'but there are gorse bushes planted all round the border to keep people out. They're pretty much impenetrable.'

'So there's no back access at all?'

'You can get into the forest through the studio,' said Kathy. 'It's a separate building at the end of the garden. If you climb out of its rear window, you're directly into the woods.'

As she spoke, Daniels scanned the area outside, his head moving slowly. Suddenly it stopped. He was looking left in the direction of Kathy's car.

'Have you seen something?' she asked, a tremor in her voice.

Outside, the rain tumbled down relentlessly.

'I'm not sure,' he whispered, still watching the same spot. 'I think so.'

I needed to arm myself, to have something to hand that I could use as a last resort. There was a set of Japanese chef's knives in the kitchen – Midge's work colleague was an enthusiastic cook – and I decided that they would have to do. It was difficult to imagine actually stabbing someone with one of them. It was difficult to imagine stabbing someone full stop, but I was getting sick of being defenceless. Staying in a crouch, I retreated into the kitchen.

The knives – six in all, each sheathed to the hilt in a triangular slab of wood – were on the tiled work surface, directly next to the cooker. I reached out and slid a large kitchen knife with a wide blade eight inches long from the slab. The blade itself was thin but razor sharp. I'd chopped meat and vegetables with it in the past and could testify to its effectiveness. I imagined how easily it would go through the flesh of that sadistic bastard Mantani, and found myself enjoying the thought. I'm not a cruel man, and I genuinely believe I've got a strong sense of justice, but I also harbour vengeful thoughts to those who've wronged me, and there was no doubt that Mantani was one of that number. Him and my old friend Jack Calley, but Jack was well beyond my reach now.

I gripped the knife in my left hand and stood up, staring at my faded reflection in the kitchen window. Rivulets of rain ran down the glass, following uneven patterns. I still looked like shit, yet Kathy hadn't once asked me about my injuries. She didn't care. She obviously hadn't cared for a long time, but like the fool I was, I hadn't noticed.

The face shot up like a ghost behind the glass, its identity obscured by a black balaclava. Then a gloved hand appeared holding a long-barrelled pistol. Before I had a chance to react there was a loud explosion and a cracking sound behind me. The windowpane became a huge spider'sweb crack with a hole like an eye in the middle. The bastard was shooting at me! Fire shot out of the barrel and a second explosion filled the room. This time the whole window seemed to collapse, and razor-sharp shards of glass rained down over the floor like lethal snowdrops.

That was when I finally moved. I hit the deck fast, realizing with relief that I hadn't been hit, even though my attacker had been only feet away from me. Then I realized why. As I scrambled across the floor towards the doorway, ignoring the pain as my body slid over pieces of broken glass, I heard something being thrown into the kitchen. There was a loud whump, and the room was filled with light and heat. Craning my neck, I saw that a large portion of the cupboards and work surfaces were on fire, the flames licking angrily towards the ceiling. He didn't want me dead; he was trying to force us out into the open.

Thick, acrid smoke billowed towards me, and I used it as cover, jumping to my feet and running through the door back into the sitting room. At exactly the same moment the cottage's front window blew inwards in another lethal shower of glass. I saw that Daniels was already on his feet and well away from the flying shrapnel. He had the gun in his hand and was swinging it round in a tight arc, searching for a target. Kathy was also upright and standing rooted to the spot like a deer caught in headlights.

'They've got petrol bombs!' I yelled. 'The kitchen's on fire!'

A split second later, before either of them had had a chance to respond, the blast of a shotgun rang out and a huge hole appeared in the front door, just below the handle. Daniels dropped into a shooting crouch and fired three shots into the door, their noise reverberating around the room with a deafening intensity.

The shotgun erupted into life again, and the hole grew bigger. Pellets flew into the room too fast to see and Daniels yelped in pain, clutching an arm. He screamed at us to get upstairs, and I grabbed Kathy's arm and pulled her towards the staircase as he recovered himself and switched the gun to his other hand. I could see a tear in his jacket where he'd been hit, but he seemed to be holding up.

Suddenly the front door flew open, slamming against the shoe rack in the porch. The hearth was empty, the only view the rain pouring down out of the darkness onto the driveway. Behind us, the smoke poured into the room, black and choking. Daniels waited, gun outstretched in front of him, still keeping the crouching pose.

A hand came round the door containing a fuel-filled milk bottle with a burning rag pushed into it, and as Daniels pulled the trigger for the fourth time, the bottle skidded and bounced along the floor towards him. He leaped to his feet, fired a fifth shot wildly in the direction of the door, and charged towards the staircase.

'Get up the fucking stairs!' he roared, bumping into my back.

I pushed Kathy forward, and she scrambled up the staircase on her hands and knees, Daniels and I bringing up the rear. There was a second's pause, and as I turned my head away the fuel ignited and the petrol bomb exploded, a sheet of flame shooting across the wood floorboards and engulfing the sofa.

'Is there an upstairs window we can get out of?' yelled Daniels above the noise of the fire.

'The master bedroom,' I shouted in return, falling over in my haste to get away from the thick, cloying smoke. 'It faces on to the back garden. You can get out onto the extension from there.'

'Head for there, then.'

As we reached the top of the stairs, Kathy turned right onto the landing. The light was on up here and it felt unusually bright, causing me to squint momentarily. She ran over to the door of the master bedroom and flung it open. I was right behind her, so when she ran inside and suddenly cried out, I was there in seconds. Not that it did me any good.

In the darkness of the room, a masked man in black – possibly the same one who'd thrown in the first petrol bomb – had Kathy in a chokehold. In his free hand he held a sawn-off shotgun which was shoved roughly against her cheek. Both of them were facing me, and Kathy's expression was one of absolute terror.

As I came into the room, the gunman retreated slowly, barely visible in the gloom, still keeping a firm grip on Kathy, who was forced to retreat with him, her upper body bent back at an uncomfortable angle. Behind the two of them I could see that the bedroom window was open, and as I watched, a second man, identically dressed, appeared on the roof of the single-storey extension that stretched out from the old part of the house, just below the bedroom, and from which the gunman had obviously made his entry. This other man didn't appear to be armed, and as he negotiated a path along the roof, he slipped on the wet tiles and landed on his behind.

Daniels appeared behind me, and instinctively I moved aside. I heard him curse, and he raised his gun.

'Don't do a fucking thing, Daniels,' said the gunman, and I immediately recognized his voice. It was that bastard Mantani. 'Now, drop it or she dies.'

'Let her go, Mantani,' said Daniels calmly. But then he could afford to be calm. It wasn't his wife in this position. 'Let her go or I'll kill you. And you know I'd do it too.'

'Do as he says, Daniels, please. Don't let him hurt my wife.'

Mantani was still retreating with Kathy. He was only five feet from the window now. Behind him, the second masked man had found his feet after his initial fall and was approaching the window slowly.

'If you don't interfere, we'll let you go,' Mantani told Daniels. 'Even though I owe you for what you did to me earlier. We just want Meron and his missus. That's all.'

Daniels took a step forward, then another. Black, choking smoke was beginning to billow into the room now, and the crackle of flames downstairs was growing louder.

'Move another fucking inch and she dies.' Mantani pushed the barrel harder against Kathy's cheek, his face contorting into a snarl behind the mask. 'I'll kill her. I fucking will, you know. Another fucking step and she dies.'

Daniels took another step.

'What the fuck are you doing, Daniels?' I screamed in a voice far higher than I'd ever managed before. 'He'll kill her!'

'No, he won't. You won't, will you, Mantani? Because if you do, I'll kill you, and I can tell you don't want to die.'

I took a step forward myself, the kitchen knife still in my hand, wondering what the hell I was going to do next.

'Don't fucking risk it, Daniels. Please. She's my wife.'

'I'll fucking do her, Daniels. You know I will. She don't mean shit to me.'

Outside, the second man had reached the window. He saw Daniels' gun for the first time and immediately ducked out of sight. Mantani stopped and leaned back against the windowsill.

Kathy remained silent. Her jaw was quivering, her eyes racing round in fear. I'd never seen her scared before. Nervous, worried, but never terrified like this. I felt helpless. This bastard was going to murder my wife in front of my eyes. I was sure of it. And Daniels was pushing him into it. The smoke in the room was getting thicker, and I could hear footsteps coming up the stairs. We were trapped. My legs felt weak. I thought of my kids. I thought of the day Chloe, my first child, was born. The joy on

Kathy's face; the joy I knew was in mine. Holding her, together, after the first weigh-in. A new family. And now it was all going to end in a burning, smoke-filled cottage, with my wife's betrayal still acrid on my breath, and all for a reason I would probably never know.

'Last chance, Mantani. Put the gun down. Now.'

Daniels took another step forward. He was now only six feet away from his former colleague. His voice was even, yet it bristled with tension. Mantani leaned back, as if trying to put as much distance between him and his adversary as possible. It was a sign of weakness, but his grip on the shotgun remained firm.

'Fuck you, Daniels. Put yours down. You're fucking surrounded.'

The shot deafened me, and I jumped up in the air reflexively.

Mantani's head snapped back, striking the window, and a fine spray of blood covered the glass. The shotgun waved about wildly and then discharged into the ceiling with an even louder bang. His body went limp and he toppled to one side as Kathy pulled away from his grip and ran into Daniels' arms. The man outside the window jumped up. He had a gun in his hand, but instead of firing it, he ran away along the roof, slipped again, and disappeared from view. Daniels pushed Kathy away and fired a parting shot at him. I assume it missed because I thought I heard him ripping the drainpipe from the wall as he jumped from the roof.

'Get out of here now!' shouted Daniels, turning in my direction.

I ran towards the window, needing no second invitation. Neither did Kathy, who was already halfway through it.

'There's someone coming up the stairs,' I told Daniels as I passed him, choking on the smoke that was now filling the room.

At that moment, another black-clad figure loomed in the

doorway, a pump-action shotgun in his hands. But this man was different to the others. He was bigger. Much, much bigger, and even surrounded by the thick black smoke he oozed a dark, easy calm, oblivious to the drama going on around him and the death of one of his men. I knew instantly that this was the man they called Lench, and that if he got hold of us we truly had no chance.

Daniels knocked me to one side and pulled the trigger, grabbing Mantani's corpse. Lench returned fire once, the force of the shotgun blast blowing out yet another of the windows, then disappeared back behind the door. Daniels stumbled but hadn't been hit. He hauled up the corpse and crouched down, using it and the double bed as a shield, yelling at me again to move.

I scrambled past him and leaped bodily through the window, knife still clutched tightly, as Lench reappeared, firing. I hit the roof stomach first and began sliding down the tiles to the right in the direction of the guttering, using my free hand to gain some purchase and stop my descent. Directly below me was the kitchen, and I could feel the heat coming from the fire within it. This roof would collapse soon and whoever was on it would fall straight into the flames.

Kathy was a few feet above me, straddling the roof's ridgeline at the gable end, leaning forward and gripping the brickwork with her hands. She was looking down to the right where the second gunman was getting to his feet on the grass, the broken remains of the drainpipe beside him. Yet another man, the fourth, was coming round the same side of the house in our direction. He too had a gun. He pointed it up at us. From inside came more shots – the shotgun and Daniels' pistol.

'This way!' Kathy shouted, and before I could say anything she was sliding down the other side of the roof on her bottom. I followed her, throwing the knife down into the garden and swinging round so that I was hanging onto the guttering before making the final jump to the ground, not daring to look back. We both landed at the same time, a few feet apart. Fifteen yards away at the end of the lawn was the single-storey wooden studio that Midge liked to paint in. Through there lay safety.

'Run,' I hissed, fumbling in my pocket for my keys. I kept the ones to the cottage on my main ring, but couldn't remember if the studio key was still on there. I'd removed it months ago to get a new one cut, and wasn't sure whether I'd put it back or not. I prayed I had. With my other hand I grabbed the knife, and we ran like hell towards the studio door, knowing that our pursuers were right behind us.

In the darkness I couldn't see which key was which and I began to panic as we reached the wooden door. It was a smaller one than the others, I remembered that. Thin, with a round handle. I felt each one as fast as I could, praying that the damned thing was on there. Please let it be. Please. The shooting in the bedroom had stopped now and all I could hear was the driving rain and the roar of the fire as the cottage that was meant to be a peaceful retreat from the stresses of the modern world went up in a mass of unforgiving flames.

Kathy turned round. 'Hurry up, they're coming,' she screamed. 'They're coming.'

I felt a round handle between thumb and forefinger. It was the one. I shoved the key in the lock, trying to force it. I could hear their footfalls approaching fast. Someone shouted for us to put our hands up, the voice sounding muffled but close.

The key finally slipped into the lock. I turned it once and the door opened. I shoved Kathy inside and followed her into the darkness, not even bothering to remove it. I slammed the door shut and felt for the bolt that would lock it from the inside. The studio's interior smelled vaguely of varnish and incense sticks. I knew Midge smoked dope in here when she was working, not only because her abstract paintings were so bad they could only have been the product of a drug-addled brain, but also because I'd found roaches hidden away in corners of the room when I'd come in here in the past.

The door was hit bodily from the outside with a huge shunt that knocked the knife out of my hand. A gap six inches wide appeared and a gloved hand shot through it, grabbing hold of the door, and forcing it further open.

'Do something!' yelled Kathy, her voice shrill.

I pushed my full weight against the door, trying to narrow the gap.

'I've dropped the fucking knife!'

The light came on as she flicked the switch on the wall. I felt my feet sliding backwards on the bare floorboards and knew that in a couple of seconds they'd be in here. I saw the knife. It was a yard and a half away from my foot, well out of reach.

Kathy came forward fast, swept it up from the floor, and a second later she had grabbed the gloved hand by the wrist and sliced the blade deep into the bare flesh of the lower forearm. A line of blood appeared, and a shower of heavy droplets splattered onto the parquet flooring. The man to whom the hand belonged howled in pain and withdrew it with a curse. Kathy slammed the door shut, and I leaned over and shoved the bolt across.

A shot rang out, and the door splintered as the bullet passed through between us at head height. I felt a stinging pain in my face and turned away instinctively.

'Jesus!' cursed Kathy, dancing about on her feet.

I grabbed her by the arm and pulled her through the room. Abstract paintings lined the available wallspace, great mishmashes of shapeless colour that seemed to represent nothing at all. An easel and artist's chair were in the centre of the floor, and a half-finished effort in blue and green that looked like it had been put together by a boss-eyed chimp was mounted upon it.

A second shot rang out, the bullet passing straight through the painting before pinging off the far wall. We kept on going, silent now, until we reached the back window that opened directly out on to the forest. I got there first and pulled the handle. It was locked. The bastard thing was locked, and I knew for sure I didn't have a key for it. Behind me, no more than fifteen feet away, I could hear them kicking the door. It sounded like they were trying to knock it off its hinges, and with some success. We were trapped, and I had seconds to make a decision.

'For fuck's sake, break it!' Kathy shouted, looking around for something to use. She pulled a china pot from one of the shelves and heaved it against the glass. Nothing happened. The window was new, so it probably had toughened glass.

A third shot rang out, and I heard one of the hinges of the door go. I swung round, picked up the artist's chair and charged it into the window with all the force I could muster. The glass cracked, a thin line in the middle. I retreated and came forward again, hitting harder this time, and the crack widened. I was panting with the exertion. As I came back to do it a third time, I saw that the door was now hanging inwards on its frame, one hinge gone, the other just about to go. Both men were partly visible in the gaps, and one was poking a gun through.

Summoning everything I had, I smashed the chair into the window a third time, and this time the glass broke into two pieces and fell outwards with a clatter. A large shard was still poking upwards so I hammered it side-on with the chair and most of it flew off.

Behind us there was a crash as the door flew open completely. They were in, and in the light of the room we were sitting ducks. But this time there was no way we were stopping.

Dropping the chair, I grabbed Kathy, lifted her up (thank God she was slim) and heaved her bodily through the window before she had a chance to protest. I took three steps back and, ignoring the footfalls coming across the floor, and the strangely muffled shouts to put my hands up coming from my pursuers, ran forward and did a flying dive through the gap, experiencing a sharp, hot pain like a burn as what was left of the lower shard tore through my clothing and the skin of my stomach.

I landed hands first, beyond the panes of glass lying on the grass, and somersaulted over, my legs hitting Kathy as she got to her feet. I was up in an instant, grabbing her by the hand and running through the soaked undergrowth, the cool air filling me with an exultant relief. She stumbled; I pulled her up. We went through a bramble bush, jumped over a fallen log, kept accelerating. Knowing that we were free. That we'd beaten the bastards. We'd actually beaten them. In those moments, nothing else mattered.

Behind us, the shouts of our pursuers faded into the rain.

29

Lench jumped back onto the landing, using the bedroom door as cover, Daniels' bullet narrowly missing him. He knew that the trap he'd set had failed. Knowing that Daniels was armed, and that a full-frontal attack would cost him men, Lench had decided to send Mantani round the back of the house to climb up onto the single-storey roof and get inside that way. Then, by simultaneously firebombing both ends of the house, they would drive the three either out into the open or more likely up the stairs, where Mantani had been ordered to ambush them and despatch Daniels so that the Merons would have no choice but to surrender.

Lench had assumed that Daniels would take the lead and be the first of the three upstairs, making him a comparatively easy target, but that hadn't happened, and now Mantani was dead, and Lench himself was having to pick up the pieces. Far better, he thought as he stood outside the bedroom door, to have simply firebombed the place and waited for them to exit the building, choking and vulnerable. In the battlefields of Croatia and Bosnia all those years ago, they'd taught him always to keep plans simple. Elaboration wasted time. Human beings, particularly civilians, were essentially cowardly creatures given to panic. Surprise and overwhelming force were all that was needed to subdue them. He'd ignored that advice tonight by trying to be clever, and now it had cost him. But the situation was redeemable. If he moved fast.

He dived low into the bedroom, all the time facing the badly damaged and blood-stained bedroom window. Meron was scrambling out of one end and onto the roof while Daniels crouched a few feet away in front of the shattered middle pane. He had a gun in one hand and was using the other to pull up Mantani's balaclava-clad corpse under the arms, trying to use him as a shield.

Lench pulled the trigger while he was still in mid-air. So

did Daniels, three times, the bullets cracking like whiplashes through the room. Each man's shots missed the other. Lench landed on his side and the shotgun discharged again, this time accidentally, blasting a tight circle of penny-shaped holes in the ceiling above the bed. Dust and plaster sprinkled down. Daniels fired two more shots in return, both of which hit the lower part of the wall near Lench. Then there was silence. Neither man could see the other. Lench could hear Daniels shuffling along the line of the window, presumably making for the part that was open so he could make his own escape. He'd fired thirteen shots. The weapon was a Glock that Lench had supplied, which carried a fifteen-round magazine, with one in the breech. That left Daniels with three more bullets. Enough still to be dangerous. Lench only had two shells left himself, and he wasn't carrying spares. Another lesson from the Yugoslavian war zone he'd failed to heed: always prepare for the worst-case scenario.

But whatever faults Lench possessed, the fear of death was not one of them. In one surprisingly athletic movement for a man so large, he leaped to his feet, calculating accurately Daniels' position, and opened fire without hesitation.

Daniels stumbled backwards with the force of the shot, but he was crouched low behind Mantani and it was the dead man who took the force of the blast, his masked face disappearing in a cloud of blood and bone, much of which sprayed over the undercover cop. Daniels let go of Mantani's body and pulled the trigger of the Glock wildly, cracking off two shots, neither of which went anywhere near their target, before Lench discharged the shotgun for the last time.

The shot caught Daniels in the centre of the chest, driving him hard against the broken glass of the middle pane, the gun flying uselessly out of his hand. Mantani's ruined corpse slipped out of view and hit the floor with a dull clump. At the same time, Daniels let out a pained gasp that filled Lench with the kind of warm, easy glow that ending a life always gave him. Daniels was unsteady on his feet, stumbling badly, but Lench wanted him conscious for these last few moments so that he could hold him close as his life ebbed away. He dropped the shotgun and with an animal howl sprang across the bed.

But for a dying man, Daniels still had something left, and he moved to one side and avoided the full force of the attack. Lench managed to grab him with one arm, though, and pull him into the beginnings of a bearhug. Daniels fought back, a punch coming out of nowhere and catching Lench across the cheek.

The two men struggled as Lench manoeuvred the arm to which his jet knife was attached so that it was against Daniels' belly, close to the appendix. But as he pushed against his foe's torso, he realized that it felt solid. The bastard was wearing a bulletproof vest. No wonder he was still fighting. Lench shifted the knife so that it was wedged in underneath Daniels' armpit, but the other man suddenly bucked wildly, pushed himself away from the open window and grabbed the knife arm by the wrist, yanking it away from his body.

Lench punched him hard in the face with his free hand, twice in quick succession, and flicked the wrist of the knife arm so that the six-inch blade shot out, ripping a huge gash in Daniels' thumb and narrowly missing his neck. Dazed, Daniels stumbled backwards, still clinging to Lench's wrist. Lench knew that there was no point in continuing to toy with his victim. He had to make the kill. And quickly. Smoke was filling the room, and he could hear the sounds of shouting outside as the other two men gave chase to Meron and his wife. He needed to bring the situation under control, and now.

Daniels had also grabbed his free hand by the wrist so that Lench couldn't punch him again, so instead he shoved Daniels hard, bending him backwards over the windowsill. Using all his weight, and his advantageous position looking down on the other man, Lench tried to force the knife downwards into his throat. Daniels bent his body back through the open window in a desperate bid to avoid the blade as it inched closer and closer. His face was bloodied where he'd been hit, and his eyes were wide with nervous tension. The arm holding the knife away from him was the one that had been hit by shotgun pellets, and it was shaking wildly. Any moment now it was going to give, and then death would be inevitable. The tip of the blade was just three inches away from Daniels' Adam's apple, and Lench smiled down at him.

'Time to die, my friend,' he whispered gently. 'Time to spill some blood.' His voice was thick with gloating.

Then, suddenly, he gasped in shock as Daniels drove a knee up into his groin. Lench felt his whole body go slack, and before he could right himself Daniels had slammed his knife arm against the window frame, risen up from his supine position and headbutted him on his upturned chin. Lench lost his footing and Daniels shoved him away, managing to put a couple of feet of space between them, then turned and slid out of the window onto the single-storey roof. Lench grabbed wildly for one of his legs, ignoring the pain in his groin, but Daniels kicked the hand away and began crawling along the ridgeline, making for the edge.

Thin lines of smoke seeped through the gaps in the roof's tiles, and Lench realized that it was going to collapse at any moment. But he couldn't let his quarry get away. Clambering up onto the window ledge, he leaped through the air, landing on Daniels' back, knees first. There was a loud crack beneath them as the badly weakened roof buckled under the strain, but Lench ignored it and pulled Daniels' head back by the hair, the knife raised ready to slash his throat. Something else cracked.

But Daniels was a formidable opponent who didn't seem to know when he was beaten, and he shifted violently onto his side, bucking like a donkey and knocking Lench off balance. The two men rolled down to the guttering, and suddenly they were falling through the air.

They landed hard, Daniels on top. Lench exhaled violently, winded by the fall, but still had the presence of mind to lash out with the knife, the blade narrowly missing his opponent's cheek. But Daniels was already struggling free, and he ducked away from the second slash of the knife and jumped unsteadily to his feet.

He started running towards the bushes, but then abruptly changed direction as two of Lench's men emerged from the timber-framed summerhouse ahead of him, and instead made for the wooden fence that separated the back garden from the driveway. He jumped up, grabbed the top with both hands, and used his arms to lift himself up and over.

Lench watched him negotiate the fence, realizing not only that it was possible the Merons were escaping, but so was this bastard, Daniels. A man who was his own responsibility. This couldn't be. Failure was not possible. Not tonight.

One of the two men coming out of the summerhouse made a gesture at Lench to let him know that their quarry had escaped. Lench cursed, slid the blade of his knife back into the handle, then ran over and grabbed the pistol of the nearest man.

'Where the hell have they gone?' he demanded.

'Into the woods,' answered the one whose pistol he'd taken,

managing to keep his voice free of nerves. He was afraid of Lench, as all who knew him were, but was also aware that he needed both of them right now, so he wouldn't do anything rash. 'There's no way we're going to get them out there. They've got fifty yards on us, probably more.'

Lench told them to wait where they were, then ran over and vaulted onto the fence. He sat astride it and spotted Daniels through the rain running unsteadily across the driveway, ten yards short of the 4×4, the keys to it in his hand. He took aim carefully, squinting as he sighted his eye down the barrel. The distance was fifteen yards. Handguns are notoriously inaccurate over distance, but Lench was an excellent shot. He'd learned to shoot pistols in Croatia in 1991, and had practised regularly ever since, often travelling to a shooting range in Normandy where he made use of his wide collection of licensed firearms. The Glock 17 he was holding now was one of them, brought back into the UK illegally amid a shipment of computer chips some months earlier. He picked out the back of Daniels' head and held the position. His quarry seemed unaware that he was being targeted. Lench's arm was perfectly steady. The distance between Daniels and the Lexus decreased to eight yards, then seven. Lench pulled the trigger. A second later, Daniels pitched forward and fell flat on his face on the gravel, arms spreadeagled.

Lench allowed himself a small triumphant smile. Another to add to the list of his kills. He remembered all his victims individually, could bring up a picture in his mind of every one of them, as well as the circumstances of how they'd died. Sometimes, when it was possible, he took a trophy. He still kept a lock of thick, raven-black hair spun through a small gold wedding band in a drawer beside his bed, a constant reminder of his single most enjoyable encounter to date – a stunningly attractive, newly-wed Muslim girl of barely eighteen with the bluest eyes he'd ever seen. He'd invaded her home in a village near the Bosnian border town of Banic in the winter of 1992, and had snuffed out her existence in a bloody bout of sexual ecstasy that had probably lasted only a couple of hours but which had felt like a whole joyous lifetime.

Daniels didn't move. He was dead, of that there was little doubt. Now he could do no further damage. But the problem was, the people who could do real damage – Tom and Kathy Meron – had somehow got away again.

Lench looked up towards the leaden sky. It was as if he was sniffing the wet night air. In the distance he could hear the sound of sirens, and he knew they were coming here. The house was now completely ablaze, flames licking the brickwork, their heat spreading in thick, comforting waves. The fire, coupled with the gunshots, would have been more than enough to attract the attention of anyone living within a half-mile radius.

He slid down the fence and jogged over to the other two men. The Merons, he knew, were lost to them for the moment.

It was time to up the ante. It was time to call Dorriel Graham.

30

Mike Bolt had a theory about detective work, and it was this: the detective could never explain everything. He might have a good overall idea about a criminal's motivations, but rarely, if ever,

did he have the full picture. It was the same with the circumstances of a crime. Sometimes things happened that defied logic.
Like a woman in a university library murdered with a knife that
held the prints of a work colleague who several hours earlier had
been ten miles away at the home of a man who was murdered in
entirely different circumstances, almost certainly by different
people, in a case that may or may not have been connected. The
way forward in something like this was not to rack your brains
trying to come up with theories, but to get hold of live witnesses
who could fill in the gaps for you. And this meant finding the
Merons.

They stopped at the HQ and picked up Bolt's car, saying their
goodbyes at just before eleven o'clock.

'I'm sorry I messed up your night,' Bolt told Mo as he got out
of the car.

Mo smiled. 'You didn't. It's everyone else. If they weren't
dying in mysterious circumstances and leaving behind secret
pasts, I'd be tucked up at home with a beer in front of *Match of
the Day*.'

'Well, go home now, get some rest. I'll call you in the morning.'

'Sure. Are you going to put out a bulletin on the Merons?'

'I'll put a call in on the way home.'

Bolt shut the car door and watched as Mo drove away. The
rain had stopped, and the clouds were breaking up in the
orange-tinted night sky. He was exhausted. This was a case like
no other he'd investigated, with wildly disparate pieces appearing
all the time, and events moving at breakneck speed. Bolt was
more used to cases lasting months, involving a long, patient
build-up of evidence against elusive and very careful targets, not
a sudden and explosive series of crimes that might be linked to
individuals right at the very heart of the establishment, and

where suspects and victims alike appeared, on the face of it, to be ordinary, hard-working people.

Bolt wondered if the key to this set of events was the man whose apparent suicide they were currently investigating. One thing was certain: if Parnham-Jones had indeed been part of a ruthless paedophile gang there would be some record of his hobby somewhere. Most likely on his computer.

As he walked over to the Ford Orion he was driving these days and opened the door, he put in another call to Matt Turner. For the second time, it went straight to message. Once again he left a voicemail asking him to call back, whatever time it was.

He flicked off the phone and started the car. His stomach growled but he no longer felt hungry. He'd gone beyond that stage. Now he just felt empty. Empty and tired.

He put the car in gear and pulled away.

31

The forest ran uninterrupted for more than a mile behind our cottage before giving way to agricultural land. We ran through the rain and undergrowth for what seemed like hours, battered, exhausted and shocked by the events of this bloody day, ignoring the tight coils of brambles that ripped at our clothes and exposed skin, knowing that in order to survive we had to keep going. Because for the first time in our lives, there were people out there who wanted to kill us.

Finally we reached the edge of the forest and sank to our knees in the darkness, just inside the treeline. Beyond it was a quiet country road, little more than a track, and then a huge wheat field that ran in a dip along a quarter-mile stretch to where the trees started again. We'd walked here a few times before with the kids in happier times, and I knew that there were storage sheds hidden away from the road on the other side of the field. The sound of our heavy breathing seemed to fill the air along with the constant pattering of the rain and the faint noise of sirens somewhere in the distance behind us.

After a few seconds, Kathy stood up and looked my way. Her expression looked worryingly like pity. 'Oh Christ, Tom, I'm sorry I got you involved in all this.' She was fitter than me so I was still on my knees, panting. I didn't say anything, but I guess my own expression must have said it all. 'I didn't know they'd be after Jack,' she continued. 'I was just there because, you know . . .' She let the words trail off.

I pictured her and Jack on his big double bed – I knew it would be big – him on top. Fucking her. My wife. Our love life had become sporadic of late. In fact, it had been sporadic for a long time now. This was why. The betrayal felt like a physical weight bearing down on me.

'How long's it been going on?' I asked, still on my knees. It felt like an apt position to be in, fitting my humiliation perfectly.

'A while,' she answered. 'Almost two years.'

It came as a bit of a shock when she said this – and yes, even now I was still capable of receiving one. Of course I'd had my suspicions, but two whole years? This made it even worse.

The rain dripped down my forehead and onto my face, and I wiped it angrily away.

'With my best friend,' I said.

'I didn't plan it like that. It just happened.'

'How?'

'I met him at O'Neills in Harrow. I was out with people from work.'

'Classy.'

'Don't start getting like that, Tom. This is one time when we really don't need your sarcastic humour. And you're not exactly holier than thou, are you?'

She had me there. Five years ago, I had a brief affair with a girl at work. Her name was Bev, and she was seven years younger than me. It had started almost by accident, after a few drinks too many at one of those pointless team-building weekends that companies like you to go on these days, where you learn skills such as orienteering and rock climbing that you know you're never going to use again. A few fumbles after work in the office and a night away in a hotel room in Brighton had followed, but I don't think either of us was ever that interested, and I was finding the guilt hard to handle, so when she finished it – somewhat undiplomatically, citing boredom as the main reason, and adding nothing about wanting to remain friends – I was actually quite relieved. At least, that is, until it became clear that someone – God knows who, I'd never found that out – had told Kathy what had been happening. We'd split over it for a couple of weeks, but she'd finally managed to forgive me, although thinking back now, I wonder if it may have been the catalyst for everything else. Either way, I was never going to get away from it entirely.

'OK, OK,' I said, 'point taken. So, did you start a relationship with him straight away?'

She gave me a look that cut me dead, her dark eyes full of

contempt. 'Is your opinion of me really that low? Of course I didn't. We had a chat for a little while, he bought me a drink, then we said our goodbyes, and I didn't see him again for a long time after that. Months, probably. But then we ran into each other in the street one Saturday when I was without the kids, and we went for a coffee. We got on well, and arranged to go out to lunch a couple of weeks down the line. We went out a couple of times like that.'

'Behind my back.'

'That's right, Tom. Behind your back. We weren't getting on well at the time. We haven't been getting on well for a long time now. Or hadn't you realized that?'

I didn't say anything. I suppose things hadn't been as good between us as they had been before the children were born, but I'd assumed that was natural. Part and parcel of the whole kids thing. I guess I'd been wrong. It looked like I'd been wrong about a lot of things. Delusional, even.

'Jack made me feel good, Tom. That's all I can say. We had a platonic relationship for a long time, but eventually it turned into something else.'

Typical Jack Calley. He'd always been persistent. That was why he'd been so successful. Not just in romance, but in everything in his life. I could just imagine what he'd been thinking as he pursued my wife. Easy does it. Be patient and she'll relent. They always do. Pay her compliments. Tell her how pretty she is. How taken for granted she is in her marriage. He'd bedded dozens of girls that way down the years. I'd even admired him for it, once upon a time. Now I knew he was simply being a selfish bastard. It was sad to only find this out now, after he was dead. It would have been nice to have had the opportunity to tell him what an arsehole he was. I couldn't believe the extent of his betrayal. Choosing Kathy over me and sacrificing a lifelong friendship as if it was nothing.

'I'm sorry,' she said, 'I really am.' And she was, I could tell.

I sighed. 'Were you ever going to tell me?'

'We talked about it, but there never seemed to be the right time. And I didn't want to do anything that would affect the kids. It was just . . . I don't know . . . a separate relationship to the one I had with you and the family. It existed in parallel.'

'It existed for a long time.'

'Yes,' she said, 'it did.'

At that moment we heard the sound of a car coming down the road, its tyres hissing in the wet. It was coming slowly, the headlamps lighting up the trees. Instinctively, we both crouched down and stayed absolutely still as it came past. I didn't get a good look at it – there was a thick holly bush in the way – nor did I want to try too hard, in case I got spotted by whoever was inside. They might have been perfectly innocent, but I'd had enough scrapes today to know that it was better to be safe than sorry.

'What do we do now?' Kathy whispered, standing back up as its lights faded into the distance.

'We need to get out of this rain. Then we need to call the police. You've got a lot of explaining to do.' I stood up as well and pulled out my phone, but there was still no reception. 'Something else, too.'

'What?'

'They found a pair of my gloves at the scene of Vanessa's murder. They had bloodstains on them. I think someone's trying to set me up.'

She looked shocked. 'Do you have any idea how they got there?'

'None at all. Luckily, the police don't know they're mine, but there's probably tests they can do to find out, and I really don't want to end up spending the next twenty years of my life in prison for something I didn't do.' I paused. 'So, you know, if—'

'I didn't have anything to do with Vanessa's murder, Tom. I promise you that. And I don't know how the hell my fingerprints got on the knife either. You trust me, don't you?' She sounded like she needed that trust.

'Why did Jack phone me, Kathy? When they were after him? And how much do you really know about all this?' I'd raised my voice and was aware that we were sailing very close to an argument, which, under the circumstances, really would have been foolish.

'I had nothing to do with any of it,' she said firmly, 'and I don't want the police to frame me with Vanessa's murder either.'

'We're both going to have to talk to them eventually. And, to be honest, who else is going to protect us?' Calming down, I walked over and put an arm around her shoulders, burying my face in the crook of her neck. It was wet and I couldn't pick up her usual fragrant smell. I kissed her gently. 'It's going to be all right, don't worry,' I said, somewhat optimistically. 'Now, let's get out of this rain. Then we can decide what to do.'

We fought our way through the bushes at the edge of the treeline, crossed the road and climbed over the fence into the wheat field. It had been ploughed recently and was muddy underfoot, slowing our progress. I could see the two large wooden storage sheds in the distance. A tractor was parked on a concrete forecourt in front of the first, but there was no sign of activity. As we ran across the field, I turned and looked back. In the distance, beyond the pine trees, the sky glowed and flickered at the spot where they'd set the cottage ablaze. I thought of

Warren and Midge, and wondered what their faces would look like when they found out what had happened. I'd gone off them since we'd bought that quarter share, because I felt they'd taken us and our money for granted, but I still felt bad for them. They loved that place.

I was panting again by the time we got to the first storage shed. I ran across to the huge double doors and was pleased to find they weren't locked. With a heave, I pulled one of the doors open, and the two of us stepped inside out of the rain. The place smelled of dry hay and motor oil, but felt hugely inviting after the other places I'd been in tonight. I found a light switch on the wall and flicked it on. The room was cavernous, with huge empty shelving units on either side going up to the roof and a space on the ground easily wide enough for driving a tractor in and out. A solitary Land Rover was parked opposite us in front of the far wall, and I walked towards it with Kathy following, pulling off my wet coat at the same time.

I looked at my phone again. There was still no reception. It pissed me off. This area must have been about the last in the country where it was impossible to get a mobile phone signal. On those few weekends when we'd actually made it down here to stay, this had seemed something of a boon. We'd never given out the number of the cottage so it was impossible for either of our employers to reach us, which meant we could take time out and relax. Now, trapped in the middle of nowhere with hostile forces searching for us, it was proving to be a real problem.

It was too much to expect that the Land Rover would have the keys in it, but at least the door was open, and there was a thick sweater draped over the front passenger seat. I climbed inside and offered the sweater to Kathy. She peeled off her suede jacket and blouse, both of which were soaked through, and took it with a whispered 'thanks'.

'Can you get a reception on your phone?' I asked her.

She shook her head, and undid her bra to reveal pert breasts with cherry-red nipples. She had a slim, toned body with skin like pale gold, and I gazed at it for a moment, full of regret, before she pulled the sweater down over her upper body and clambered in the other side.

'God, I'm tired,' she said, closing her eyes.

'We can't really stay here,' I told her, but it was clear she wasn't moving anywhere.

'I need to think,' she added, her voice heavy with weariness.

I needed to think too, but I didn't want to, because there were holes in Kathy's story and I knew there were things she wasn't telling me. I found a tartan dog blanket in the back of the car and silently thanked the owner for his level of preparedness. By the time I'd removed my clothes and settled back in my seat with the blanket covering me up to my chin, Kathy had fallen asleep and was breathing softly through her mouth. I moved closer to her and tried to cuddle up, but evidently she wasn't completely gone because she moved away.

A few moments later I heard her weeping, and my heart sank. My marriage was over, and for the last however many years my wife, the woman I genuinely loved, had been living a complete lie.

The question was, would I ever know the extent of that lie?

Part Two

SUNDAY

32

Sinking his shapeless, slug-like bulk into the specially reinforced chair in front of his state-of-the-art computer system, twenty-nine-year-old computer hacker Dorriel Graham began the hunt through cyberspace that would find the information his client was looking for. His client was Lench, but neither man knew the other's real identity, nor had they ever met. Graham was simply a mobile telephone number that could be called at any time, while Lench was Lima 2, a customer who used his services periodically, and who could be trusted to pay for them.

The virtual world of the Internet was Graham's life. He was a techno-mercenary, his speciality being the ability to use his hacking skills to track down anyone. The average UK citizen over the age of eighteen has his or her personal details held on scores, sometimes hundreds, of electronic databases. Even those who never take part in telephone questionnaires, who actively avoid giving out information to anyone, and who try to register as little as possible in their own name, leave their virtual foot-prints everywhere. If you use a credit card or debit card, there'll be a record held in someone's database of where and when it was used, and what you bought. If you use your mobile phone and the person looking for you has the number, there will be a record. Only the most serious and organized criminals, who know all the tricks, pay with cash for everything and have literally nothing registered in their own name, represent a more taxing proposition. But even they can be traced. It's just a matter of using their family and friends who aren't as careful.

The point is, you can find anyone if you know where to look, and Dorriel Graham always knew where to look. Tonight he'd been given two names, Thomas and Katherine Meron. He'd been told to find out where their close relatives lived, starting with the nearest first. It was, Lima 2 had added, a rush job; he'd been given a time limit of two hours. Usually, he would have told the client to forget it – after all, there was plenty of demand for his services, and he didn't have to put himself out unless he wanted to – but he'd been promised a hugely inflated fee of three grand for this work, and he knew Lima 2 would pay it.

Taking a huge bite of the kingsize Snickers bar he was holding in his left hand, Dorriel started with Thomas Meron. A quick Google search revealed that he worked for Ezyrite Software Services based in Harrow, and had been there for eight years. The next step was to break into Ezyrite's employee database. Dorriel assumed that, being an IT company, this would be a harder proposition than might otherwise have been the case, but his assumption was wrong. Their main firewall was full of holes and it took only eleven minutes before Meron's details were up on his screen. These gave Dorriel the names of Meron's parents and younger brother. He then perfectly legally accessed the electoral roll and discovered that the parents now lived in Sidmouth, Devon, while his brother resided in east Kent.

Katherine Meron turned out to be a tougher proposition. He

located her place of work quickly enough, but the university employee database proved surprisingly hard to crack, and it took him twenty-seven minutes before he finally got inside. She had one older sister who didn't turn up on the electoral roll or in a Google search, and Dorriel was forced to use more basic tactics by accessing Friends Reunited. Like millions of other people wanting to catch up with old friends from school, she used the site and had helpfully posted the information that she now lived in Sydney, Australia, with a wonderful husband, John, and 'her babies', two Dalmatian dogs called Harry and Spike.

With that, Dorriel had found out everything he needed, and it was only an hour and twenty-two minutes after receiving his instructions from Lima 2 that he called him back with the information requested. Not once did he consider what the information could be used for. Dorriel was not a people person and, frankly, he didn't care. It was one of the reasons he was considered so reliable.

'Have you got what I need?' asked the voice at the other end.

'Yes,' said Dorriel, shifting his bulk in the chair while logging on to a favoured porn site. 'I've been through all the relatives, and the nearest one is Katherine Meron's mother, Irene Tyler. Do you have a pen? I'll give you the address.'

33

DI Mike Bolt lived in the heart of London. Nestled in the quiet area of streets that sprouted from either side of the Clerkenwell Road between the points where the West End finished and the financial district of the City of London began, Clerkenwell was about as central as a man could get. At one time it had been home to the printing and brewing industries, but in recent years it had undergone a prolonged period of gentrification as the fashionable young rich moved in, creating residential lofts and apartments among the old warehouse buildings.

Home for Bolt was an attractive studio apartment on the third floor of a converted warehouse near the jewellery district of Hatton Garden, not far from Farringdon station. He'd lived there for a little under two years, and rented it from a Ukrainian businessman called Ivan Stanevic. It was a stunning place, done out to the highest specifications. Long and spacious, with polished wood floors and an open-plan mezzanine containing the bedroom. The windows that ran its entire length faced east on to the bright lights of London, the towers of the Barbican reaching up like stubby fingers from behind the buildings opposite. Stanevic, a property developer, could have got £500 a week for the place easily, probably more, but instead he charged £150 a month. The reason: Bolt had once done him a big favour. An extremely big favour.

Two and a half years earlier, not long after Bolt had been seconded to the NCS, Stanevic's twelve-year-old daughter had been snatched from the street outside her Chelsea school by business rivals, who'd then threatened to strangle her unless her father signed over the deeds to his share in a hotel complex in the south of France. After the intervention of his wife, Stanevic reluctantly brought in the police, and the case had been handed to an NCS team led by Bolt.

A meeting was set up between Stanevic and the kidnappers at a café in Tottenham, during which the deeds were duly signed over. Unfortunately, just to make sure that nothing got in the way of their plans, the kidnappers decided to take Stanevic prisoner too, while the transaction was being processed, so that they could then sell their new share of the business on to another party. But the meeting was being monitored by Bolt and his team. Rather than intervene, he'd ordered that they allow Stanevic to be taken and follow the kidnappers at a safe distance to find out where they went.

It was the most difficult piece of surveillance Bolt had ever overseen. The targets had been trained in anti-surveillance techniques, and during the forty-five-minute journey through the centre of the city they'd double-backed, performed illegal U-turns, had at times hit speeds of seventy miles per hour down Islington backstreets (a near physical impossibility, and something Bolt had never seen since), and had even gone the wrong way up a one-way street. All to make sure they avoided being followed. They were almost successful too, but somehow, using a combination of CCTV cameras and a lot of shouting down various different phones, Bolt kept them covered all the way to their destination – a basement flat in Fulham.

Bolt scrambled all available officers to the flat, and at the same time called up SO19 specialist firearms units to assist in any possible rescue.

It was his call. Should he adopt a wait-and-see approach, or should he go in hard, assuming that the girl was in the flat as well? He was well aware that the kidnappers could kill the girl and her father even as he waited. The Russian mafia were ruthless operators.

In the end, Bolt decided on a third way. He got British Telecom to supply him with the number of the flat's landline, and, with the firearms team in place, he phoned the kidnappers from his control room at Scotland Yard, assuming that curiosity would lead to one of them picking up. He guessed right. The kidnappers' leader did the honours, and in a marked departure from the rulebook Bolt told him that he was never going to get the deeds to the hotel, he was never going to sell them on, he was never going to escape from the situation he'd put himself in, because no-one in Britain ever negotiated with kidnappers, and if he killed either of his prisoners he'd never see the outside of a prison again. However, if he released them both unharmed, there was a possibility that a judge would treat the case leniently. He said all this before the man on the other end had a chance to reply, and it was a massive gamble because the girl might already have been dead: having alerted the kidnappers to the fact that the police had them in their sights, they might have decided they had nothing to lose by going for a shoot-out. Bolt wouldn't have called himself a gambler by nature, but he was decisive, and not afraid to take responsibility for his actions.

And, on that particular occasion, it worked. The kidnappers were badly spooked, and after further telephone negotiations, during which Bolt repeated the fact that they were surrounded and didn't have a leg to stand on, they surrendered, releasing both prisoners unharmed.

Stanevic had never forgotten what Bolt had done, and credited him with saving both his and his daughter's life. They'd remained in occasional contact after that, and when Stanevic heard that Bolt was looking for a place to live, he'd offered to help out by letting him stay in one of his properties rent-free for as long as he liked. Bolt should have said no since it was against all the rules, and was a sackable offence if anyone ever found out. But at the time, pissed off with life, not too bothered with what the rulebook said and, most importantly, flat broke, he'd accepted, although with one proviso: he wanted to pay something at least. Stanevic didn't want to accept a penny, but Bolt didn't want to feel like he was in hock to anyone, and they'd finally agreed on the £150 figure, with Bolt moving in soon afterwards.

It had just turned midnight when, having trudged up the stairs to the third floor with a bag full of Thai food, he finally closed the front door of his apartment behind him. Coming back to the dark emptiness of his home occasionally gave him a deflated feeling, particularly after he'd had a busy day, and tonight was one of those nights. As he turned on the hall light, he thought of Tina Boyd, of the loneliness he'd seen in her dark eyes, and wondered if the same emotion had been reflected in his.

He put the bag on one of the metallic kitchen tops and cracked open a Stella from the fridge, taking a much-needed gulp straight from the can. He moved into the middle of the room, away from the kitchen area, and stood in the semi-darkness, looking through the window at the orange glow of the city at night, savouring the faint sounds of people and traffic from the street below as they rose up to drive away his gloom. Bolt had lived in London for almost twenty years, and he still felt a frisson of excitement whenever he stood here, knowing that he was in the centre of one of the oldest, most vibrant cities in the world. Plenty of people criticized London, and he'd be the first to admit that there were things wrong with it – the horrendous crime rate, for one – but he still couldn't imagine living anywhere else. It gave him a sense of security and belonging that he couldn't quite explain, but which, to him, were as tangible and obvious as the wooden floor he was standing on. The city was his crutch.

He was used to being on his own now. Although it had been thrust upon him suddenly and in a way that no-one would ask for, he found that it quite suited him. He didn't have to justify his comings and goings, could cook what he wanted when he wanted, and could make as much noise as he liked. The location, with so much on his doorstep, also assuaged the worst of the loneliness and melancholy that afflicted him whenever he thought too much about that night three years ago. And for the moment, at least, he had no desire to change his situation.

Or so he liked to convince himself.

He was just serving up the food – sea bass in tamarind sauce with coconut fried rice – and taking another long pull on the can of Stella when his mobile rang.

It was Turner. He told Bolt he'd been out to the cinema and had only got back a little while earlier. He'd been to see the new Tom Cruise movie. 'It was bloody terrible as well. And the girl I took said she was really tired and wanted to go home straight afterwards. I think the film put her off relationships for life.'

Bolt leaned back against the kitchen top and drank again from the can. 'Ah, my friend, there's no justice in this world.'

'Too right, and life's too short to waste evenings like that. I ought to sue.'

'Who? The girl or the film company?'

'Both.'

Bolt laughed. He liked Turner. The guy was an acquired taste, there was no doubting that, and clearly his date tonight hadn't acquired it. Prematurely balding, with a long, hangdog face, he rarely bothered with a smile, preferring to rely on a bone-dry, cynical wit that was always delivered in the same deadpan manner. Why he'd chosen to be a copper was anyone's guess. He certainly didn't attempt to connect with the general public, who he viewed with a general disdain bordering on dislike. But he was bright, could pick up bullshit a mile off, and was an expert with computers. Plus, he was dedicated enough to phone his boss back after midnight on a weekend.

'You obviously got my message, then. Have you had a chance to look at Parnham-Jones's laptop yet?'

'There wasn't one.'

'Do we know whether or not he used a laptop?'

'Not at the moment, no. I just assumed he didn't. We can easily find out, one way or another.'

'I'll call his cleaner tomorrow.'

'There was a PC, though. I had a quick look at it this afternoon, but when I got your message tonight I had a much closer inspection.'

'Anything on it of interest?'

'Yes,' Turner said after a pause. 'There is.'

Bolt tensed. 'Go on.'

'There's an email. It was saved in a folder in his personal filing cabinet, the only thing in there. What caught my attention was that it was password-protected. I broke through the security easy enough – it wasn't designed to deter anyone who knew what they were doing – and I've just finished reading it now. It's a blackmail note.'

'Have you got it in front of you? I'd like to hear what it says.'

'It's short and to the point. "Dear Lord Chief Justice. We know everything. All the details. 1998. The girl. Her father's dead too, isn't he? Hanged himself in jail. If you want to avoid spending the rest of your days rotting behind bars as well then we will need to make some arrangements. Otherwise we're going public. You will be hearing from us soon."' Turner paused again, but Bolt didn't say anything. 'And that's it,' he added. 'I've no idea what he's meant to have done. There's no other mention of anything untoward anywhere else on the PC that I can find, and no other emails from the blackmailer.'

'Have you checked Parnham-Jones's Internet history?'

'I've had a cursory look. He doesn't seem to surf the net too much, and none of the sites are out of the ordinary. Amazon, the BBC, stuff like that. And he likes to read articles about himself. Were you expecting to find something else, then?'

'No,' Bolt lied. 'Just checking.' He was still thinking about the absence of a laptop. Could Parnham-Jones have had one which he used for his more nefarious pursuits? Perhaps one that had been stolen by his murderer, as appeared to be the case with John Gallan?

'I've just forwarded the mail to you,' Turner told him.

'No idea who it's from, I suppose?'

'The address is a hotmail account. It's already been closed down, and if the blackmailer knows what he's doing he'll have sent it from an Internet café, which means it's going to be very difficult to track down.'

'But you can tell when it was sent, can't you?'

'Yes, it's dated the eleventh of May. Ten days ago.'

Recent, then, and almost certainly connected to Parnham-Jones's death.

'I suppose this puts a different slant on things, doesn't it?' said Turner rhetorically.

'It certainly does.'

'No idea what that bit about the dead girl and her father is all about?'

'Not yet,' answered Bolt, lying for a second time. He asked Turner to continue his search of the PC's hard drive to see if there was anything on there that could be connected to the ransom note, thanked him and hung up.

He looked down at his food with only vague interest. It smelled good, but he was too busy thinking about this latest information. He was convinced now that the Lord Chief Justice had been murdered. He was also nearly certain that John Gallan had been murdered by the same person or persons several months earlier. The connections between the two were too great for it to be otherwise. Gallan's murder had surely been carried out to put an end to his investigation into the allegations of paedophilia and murder that had been levelled against Parnham-Jones, but this begged the question why Parnham-Jones had also been murdered. It could have been to silence him and therefore prevent his potentially explosive secrets being made public. In which case the killer was likely to be one of his fellow paedophiles, or possibly even someone from within the establishment trying to snuff out a potential government-toppling scandal.

But this theory begged another question. The person with the most obvious motive for killing Parnham-Jones (i.e. to hush up the scandal) would not have been blackmailing him. Quite the reverse. He would have been going out of his way not to panic him into foolish action.

So who the hell had sent the email?

34

It was just after 3 a.m. and the street was silent.

A black cat crept out of the bushes near Irene Tyler's front door, took one disdainful look at the masked man in black who'd loomed up in the darkness, and scuttled across his path before disappearing. Lench couldn't remember whether such a thing was a sign of good or bad luck, nor did he care. He wasn't superstitious, and always marvelled at the rank naivety of those who were. Individuals made their own destiny by their actions alone. Luck was random. There was no afterlife, no spiritual world. If there had been, Lench would have been haunted by the ghosts of each and every one of the forty-three people he'd murdered in his lifetime, and yet he slept soundly each night and felt at home in the darkness.

He removed the skeleton keys from his pocket and started on the five-bar lock on the front door. It took just under a minute to undo. Then it was the turn of the Yale lock, which took a matter of seconds. Slowly, he pushed the door open. It was on a chain. He slid the bolt cutters from his pocket and cut it in the middle. Irene Tyler was obviously more security-conscious than most, but it made no difference. Any house could be broken into if the intruder knew what he or she was doing, and Lench had had plenty of lessons. He'd seen that the property had a burglar alarm as he approached it, so now he pocketed the bolt cutters and took out a laser pen. These days, a lot of homeowners turned on their burglar alarms at night, activating the ground-floor sensors only, and given the fact that she'd double-locked the door and put the chain across he had to assume that Irene Tyler had probably done the same. Inching his way through the door and into the hallway, Lench spotted the flashing motion detector on the wall to his right. After a couple of seconds' careful manoeuvring, the laser pen's beam found the centre of the detector's red light, effectively blinding it.

Shutting the front door with his foot, Lench kept the beam in exactly the same position and moved sideways across the floor, one easy step at a time, until he reached the bottom of the staircase. He mounted the first three steps until the angle of the laser became too narrow to keep still, but he knew that by this time he was safe. He switched it off, replaced the pen in his pocket and carried on climbing.

He found Irene Tyler's room on his first try. It was spacious and warm, and he could see her in the eerie blue-white light of the streetlamp outside. She was lying on her left side, tucked up beneath the covers of her double bed, her long silver hair loose, snoring lightly. He shut the door behind him and crept wraith-like over to the bed, his heavy boots making barely a sound. He could smell her vaguely perfumed scent. She was perhaps sixty-five, her skin lined and sagging a little at the jaw, but she was not unpleasant to look at.

He leaned down until he was only inches from her face, so close now that he could suck in her deep, slumbering breaths. His eel-like tongue slipped out from his mouth, its tip creeping along the line of her aquiline nose, almost, but not quite, touching it. He so desperately wanted to lick her, to taste the warmth of her skin, as he'd done sometimes with his female victims back in the anarchy of Bosnia, an intimate gesture that he believed drew him closer to them, and thereby increased his power when he finally snuffed out their lives.

But he had to be careful tonight, knowing that he couldn't afford to leave any trace of DNA. Instead, he pushed back her silver hair and touched a gloved finger to her fleshy earlobe. Irene flinched but didn't wake up, so he rammed the finger into her ear and that did the trick. Her eyes shot open and she tried to sit up but he shoved her back down and put a hand over her mouth. With the other hand he produced a long stiletto knife which he gently ran across her throat.

'Is the burglar alarm on?' he hissed. 'Nod your head for yes, shake it for no.'

She made some muffled noises and nodded her head.

'When I remove my hand, you're going to give me the code. If you delay or give me the wrong one, I'm going to cut one of your eyes out.'

He spoke calmly, almost with reassurance, in a slightly high-pitched Home Counties accent which utterly belied his huge, looming bulk and somehow made the words he spoke even more terrifying. The knife slid across the skin until the tip was pressed against the loose fold of skin just beneath her right eye. There was no doubt whatever that his threat was serious, and she nodded again, this time to show she understood. Lench's hand slipped away from her face, although the knife remained where it was, causing her to squint.

'Five-two-eight-one.'

'Good.' He took the knife away. 'Turn over.'

'Take what you want, but please don't hurt the children.'

So they were here. That was useful. 'I'm not interested in them,' he lied, keen to secure her co-operation. 'Now, do what I say.'

She rolled over onto her front and he produced two pairs of plastic restraints, one of which he used to bind her wrists, the other her ankles. She didn't resist, but repeated that he could take anything he wanted as long as he didn't hurt her grand-children. 'Open your mouth wide,' he told her, and when she did so he slipped in a golfball, which he secured in place with a piece of masking tape.

When he was satisfied that she was helpless, he left the room and went back down the stairs. He allowed the motion detector to pick up his movement this time, and the alarm went off in the house. He made his way over to the keypad and fed in the numbers, automatically turning it off.

Now he was ready to move. Pulling a mobile from his pocket, Lench made a quick call. 'Bring the van round the front in one minute and keep the engine running,' he told the person at the other end, before starting up the stairs again. The people he was using tonight were reliable, and proven killers, but he also knew they had grave doubts about involving children. Lench con-sidered this a weakness. In his world, there was no such thing as a boundary that could not be crossed. It was one of the lessons he'd learned during his four years in the killing fields of the former Yugoslavia, fighting for whichever side paid him the most money. Everyone, young and old, was potential prey. All just bags of blood. But not everyone understood that, and in order to stave off any potential mutiny from his men he'd had to double their money for the night's work.

The boy and girl were fast asleep in a bunk bed in the back bedroom, which had been decorated with Disney characters on the walls and was full of toys and fluffy animals. It was obvious, even to someone like Lench, that Irene Tyler doted on them. He crept through the gloom and lifted the boy from the top bunk. He stirred but didn't wake, and Lench carried him silently through the house. He could hear Irene Tyler writhing around on her bed through the door, but knew she was in no position to do anything.

As he approached the front door, he heard the Bedford van pull up outside. He pushed open Irene Tyler's front door with his foot and hurried down the path, the child asleep in his arms. There were two men in the van, and the passenger got out and opened the double doors. He was no longer wearing a balaclava but had a baseball cap pulled down low over his forehead to avoid detection. In the back of the van were two bare mattresses. Lench placed the boy on one, then headed back inside, checking for lights in any of the neighbouring houses. There were none.

The girl turned over and fidgeted in her sleep as Lench approached the bottom bunk. It looked like she might wake up. If he had to, he would tape her mouth shut and fit her with one of the restraints, but he wanted to avoid this since it might create a problem with his accomplices. But she remained asleep as he lifted her up and took her down with him.

'I don't like this,' hissed the man in the baseball cap as he closed the double doors of the van, the children safely inside.

'They'll be fine,' Lench told him, 'but don't fuck up. You've got one hell of a lot to lose.' Lench had things on both men that would put them in prison for life, and they knew it.

The man in the cap grunted something and climbed back in the van. A second later it pulled away, accelerating slowly down the street and out of sight. The houses were all still dark. No twitching curtains could be seen. Lench slipped out of the light of the streetlamp, then walked slowly back to the house, experiencing a familiar frisson of excitement like soft, cold fingers dancing upon his groin.

He didn't have to kill Irene Tyler. After all, she hadn't seen his face and would be able to describe nothing about him with the possible exception of his voice, which would be of no great use. He could simply have left her there, trussed up like a pig, unable to raise the alarm.

But that would have been a terrible waste. His opportunities to indulge were so rare these days. And, as his commander had told him years earlier in a burnt-out Muslim village in western Bosnia while casually surveying a pile of corpses, the last stiffening remains of a family of ten:

'The dead can't point the finger.'

35

I slept a grey, dreamless sleep. I vaguely remember half-waking up at some point with a sore shoulder, but not really paying much attention to it or my many troubles. I was too tired for that, and I'd slipped under again within moments.

When I woke up properly, it was my face that was sore where it had been cut with the filleting knife in the university library the day before. The knife that held my wife's fingerprints. Kathy was curled up in the passenger seat with her head propped against the window. She'd taken most of the blanket – a habit of hers throughout our years of marriage – and even looked quite comfortable. I wondered whether or not it was the sleep of the innocent.

I yawned, feeling cold and a little sick, and looked at my watch. It was twenty to seven. Outside, it was light. I was thirsty, and hungry too. I'd hardly eaten a thing since yesterday lunchtime, a period which felt like a whole lifetime ago. Before I'd gone to sleep the previous night, I'd taken off my shirt and jeans and put them in the back of the Land Rover to dry out, but when I put them back on now they were still wet and clammy.

I opened the door and stepped out onto the stone floor of the barn, stretching my legs. Why didn't Kathy want to go to the police? That thought worried me more than any other. Was she really involved in Vanessa's murder? I couldn't see how she could have been, but I still kept coming back to the big, immovable question: what the hell were her prints doing on the knife? It was a question the police would be asking and one she didn't seem to want to answer. But we were both going to have to face the music at some point, and it might as well be now. I was going to turn myself in, even if Kathy was against the idea. That way at least I could get some protection, both for myself and the kids.

The kids. In all the drama of the previous day, they'd slipped my mind. Now I realized I missed them. It was time to end all this.

The passenger door opened and Kathy stepped out of the Land Rover, looking bleary-eyed. 'Morning,' she said, taking slow, faltering steps in my direction.

'Hi.'

'Look—'

'We need to go to the police,' I said.

She seemed to think about this for a moment.

'I'm going to go, even if you're not.'

She nodded slowly. 'I'll come with you.'

Even after everything she'd been through, and a night of crap sleep in a car, she still looked good, and I felt an aching for her that made my throat go dry. I think if I'd been capable of it I would have cried, but for some reason domestic woes have never been able to bring tears to my eyes. I rarely cry, and when I do it's usually about something I can do nothing about, like my grandma's death fifteen years ago, or a bad result in a hugely important football match, and it only happens when I've had too much to drink, which I guess says something about me. As we stood there facing each other, I wondered at which point in our marriage it had all gone wrong. When she'd ceased to see me as her lover. If I was honest, it was probably a long time before she'd met Jack Calley.

'How are we going to get to the police station?' she asked.

'Have you still got the keys to your Hyundai?'

'They're in my coat. Are you saying we should sneak back to the house and drive it away? The police'll be there, won't they? There were a lot of gunshots last night, not to mention the fire.'

'Well, if they are, that'll solve our problem, won't it?'

She nodded, but didn't look entirely convinced.

It took us fifteen minutes to retrace our steps back to what was left of the cottage and when we saw it we were both shocked. The whole top floor was gone. All that remained were four exterior walls, now uneven and charcoal-stained, barely a few feet high in places. Smoke still rose in thin plumes from the gutted interior. Yellow police crime-scene tape surrounded the whole thing.

We moved through the undergrowth until we were level with the front of the property. A police car was parked in the front drive, but it was unoccupied, and whoever had turned up in it was nowhere to be seen. Kathy's Hyundai Coupé was also still there, the maroon paintwork grimy and dull from the smoke but otherwise looking largely undamaged.

'Give me the keys,' I said, putting out a hand.

'No way,' she snapped. 'I'm driving. Come on, let's go.'

Before I could protest, she took off across the driveway, running in her typically gangly fashion, her heels crunching on the gravel. I had no choice but to run after her. When I caught up I was surprised to see that she had a grin on her face.

There was a shout to our left and a uniformed copper appeared from round the side of what was left of the cottage, about ten yards away. He was about two stone overweight with a round, pink face and didn't give you much faith in the future of crimefighting in the south of England. It looked like we'd just disturbed him taking a leak.

Kathy had the keys in her hand, and she flicked off the central locking and ran round to the driver's-side door.

'Oy, stop right there!' the copper called out as he lumbered towards us.

I stopped, but Kathy didn't. She jumped in the car and switched on the engine.

'Kathy, for Christ's sake, what are you doing? He's the police.'

'All right, sir, stay there,' panted the copper as he ran up towards Kathy's door.

The Hyundai slammed into reverse and roared backwards up the driveway in a shower of loose chippings, the copper following in its wake.

I made a snap decision. Whatever was happening, I still didn't know the half of it, but I had a strong feeling Kathy did, and unless I went with her it was possible, even likely, that I wasn't going to find out the truth. So I ran after the car.

Spotting that I wasn't hanging around either, the copper turned in my direction and spread out his arms like a basketball player defending the basket. He made, I have to say, a pretty ludicrous sight, and I had to resist the urge to laugh. Instead, I sidestepped him easily, and though he got a hand on my jacket I brushed it off and kept running, breaking into the kind of sprint that, with the exception of the previous night outside the police station, I hadn't managed since my school days.

Kathy kept reversing up the drive, at the same time motioning for me to keep coming, and after another ten yards she slowed down and flung open the passenger door. I could hear the copper behind me but I knew I was outpacing him. The Hyundai slowed to walking pace and, as I grabbed the open door and scrambled inside, Kathy suddenly accelerated again, reversing out onto the road in a screech of tyres. The last I saw of the copper, he was standing uselessly in the middle of the drive, frantically talking into his radio. Then Kathy shoved the gearstick into first and with a maniacal laugh took off up the empty road.

You know the feeling you get sometimes when you wake up in the darkness of an early morning, and in those first few moments you're not quite sure if you're still in a dream or not? I had that feeling now. My wife, thirty-five-year-old college lecturer and mother of two, was behaving like some sort of lunatic. I could offer no explanation, other than, like her, I had to be going mad.

'What the hell is going on, Kathy? We're meant to be handing ourselves in, not doing some sort of fucking Thelma and Louise.'

She grinned at me. 'Don't you like taking a bit of a risk now and then, Tom? You don't, do you? You were never much of a risk taker.'

'I don't go running away from the police, no. Not when we need to speak to them. You might have forgotten, but your work colleague and your lover are dead.'

The smile left her face in an instant, but the expression it left behind was hard and determined, and totally unlike the Kathy I knew. Or didn't, as the case might be. 'When we give ourselves up to the police, I want to do it on my terms,' she said. 'I want to walk into a police station in front of plenty of witnesses so nothing can happen to me. I'm not just walking up to the first overweight plod I see. Do you understand?'

'No,' I said, 'I don't think I do.'

Before either of us could say anything else, my phone rang. Ten seconds later, so did Kathy's. We were obviously hitting a reception area. I pulled mine out, flicked it open, and saw that I had a message from my voicemail service, as well as a video message. The sender had withheld his number. A prompt on the screen asked me if I wanted to play it. I wondered if it was some sort of spam thing. There was only one way to find out.

I pressed play.

A second later my two young children appeared on the screen, their expressions confused and scared. Chloe looked like she'd been crying. They were in a room I didn't recognize, sitting on a double bed. The wall behind it was painted orange, and there were no pictures or ornaments visible. The video concentrated on the children for about five seconds. During that time they remained still and said nothing. Then the camera moved left and a man dressed from head to foot in black, the now standard balaclava hiding his identity, stood against one of the other blank orange walls. It could have been one of the men from last night; it was difficult to tell. It didn't matter either. The message was clear: my children were now in the hands of some very ruthless people.

The video ended, and I felt my whole body sag. A black mix of gloom, helplessness and terror filled my insides, its weight crushing me from the inside out. Not my kids. Please, anything else, but not my kids. Not the most precious, innocent people in my life. For a parent there is no worse feeling than knowing your child is in grave danger and being unable to do anything about it. Your utter impotence tears you apart. All your resistance evaporates. You are a pliant, begging wreck, which I guess is exactly what they must have been banking on.

Beside me, Kathy pulled up to the side of the road, and I heard her groan as she looked at the video on her own phone. I couldn't even turn my head in her direction. All my energy seemed to have gone, and this time I really did weep. I prayed too. Prayed that they wouldn't be hurt, offered a God in whom until this moment I hadn't believed in for close to thirty years anything he wanted if he'd just let them go. I would go to church, give all my money to charity, work with the poor in Africa . . . anything. But don't hurt them.

'Oh God,' I heard Kathy say. 'Oh God. Not my babies.'

I wiped my eyes and tried to calm myself down. So far, Max and Chloe were unharmed. We had to make sure the people holding them got what they wanted, and this time there could be no bullshit. I assumed they'd left some sort of message to go with the video, so I dialled 121, and sure enough a man's voice I didn't recognize came on the line. 'You know what we have,' he said in the tone of someone describing the stock in his shop. His voice was perfectly ordinary, if a little high-pitched. 'Call this number now if you're interested in having them back whole.' He reeled out a mobile number, and hung up. As I hunted in the glove compartment for a pen and paper, the time of the message was given as 5.53 a.m. – a little over an hour ago. I found a pen but no paper, so when I listened to the message again I wrote down the number on the back of the Hyundai's logbook.

'They want us to phone them,' I told Kathy, staring out of the windscreen into the empty tree-lined road ahead.

'You do it,' she said, weeping quietly.

'Whatever they want. Whatever you know, give it to them. OK?' I still didn't look at her as I spoke.

'Sure.'

'Don't sure me. Yes. I want you to say yes.'

'Yes, yes, yes. Just phone them . . . please.'

I wanted to tell her that this was her fault, but I didn't. I took a deep breath and dialled the number. It rang five times before it was picked up.

'I'm glad you called,' said the man on the other end, the same one who'd left the message on the voicemail. 'We need to get this matter concluded as soon as possible.'

'Are our kids OK?'

'They're fine.' His voice sounded confident, but it was impossible to know whether to believe him or not. 'Now, tell me. Where are you?'

'About a mile from the cottage, the one near Bolderwood. In a car.'

'Whose car?'

'My wife's. We went back there to get it.'

'And you weren't seen?'

'I don't think so, no.'

'Good. I have a set of instructions for you. If you follow them to the letter, your children will be released safe and well. As soon as this phone call ends, you are to delete the video message that was sent to you and switch off your mobile phone immediately. Your wife is to do exactly the same with hers. Then you are to throw them away, somewhere where they're not likely to be found. And don't try any tricks, like keeping the phone with you and switched on. The same person who gave us the identity and address of your mother-in-law will be calling the numbers periodically over the next hour. He has access to technology that will tell him whether or not your phone is transmitting a signal. If he finds that you have disobeyed my instructions, one of your children will lose an ear. You'll be able to choose which one.'

'Don't harm Max and Chloe, please,' I said, using their names in a desperate effort to personalize them in their captor's eyes, even though I was sure it would do no good. 'No-one is going to mess you about this time, I promise. Whatever you want from us, you'll have.' Out of the corner of my eye I saw Kathy nodding in numb agreement, tears streaming down her face.

'Nothing will happen to them if you do what I say. Have you got a pen and paper?'

'Hold on.' With my free hand I picked up the pen and the Hyundai logbook again. My hands were shaking but my voice remained artificially calm as I told him I was ready.

'Listen carefully. Once you've got rid of the phones, you're to drive up the M3 to Basingstoke, then take the A33 towards

Reading. Go through Reading and take the road to Henley-on-Thames. At Henley take the road to Marlow. Three miles along that road there's a left turning to a village called Hambleden. Have you got all that?'

I was writing furiously. 'Yes. Yes, I have.'

'Park in the village square. There's a phone box there. In just over an hour, at eight fifteen, it will ring. I'd advise you to hurry, because if it's not picked up by you I will have to make sure that one of your children pays the price for your delay.'

'We'll be there, OK? Please, don't do anything to them. We'll be there.'

'You'll then receive further instructions,' he continued, completely ignoring my pleas. 'At this time on a Sunday morning you should have no trouble making it by eight fifteen, and if everything goes to plan you'll be reunited with your children before midday. But remember this, and remember it well: deviate even slightly from what you've been told, get caught by the police before you arrive here, or try to enlist the help of anyone, and your children will die alone and screaming.'

The words were like punches, each one sapping my strength and driving me further and further into a darkness from which I could see no escape. 'I understand,' I said, my words little more than a croak.

'Is my mum all right?' asked Kathy, her words seeming to come from some distance away. 'Ask him if my mum's all right.'

'Don't even bother asking that question,' said the man on the end of the phone, who'd obviously heard her.

I knew then that Irene was dead, but didn't really take it in. There was too much else to think about at that moment.

'Get rid of the phones and get to Hambleden now. I'm looking forward to seeing you again.' With that, he rang off.

Kathy grabbed me by the arm, bringing her face close to mine. I'd never seen such pain in her dark eyes, a pain I was sure was right there in mine too.

'What did he say?' she demanded.

'The kids are fine. I don't know about your mum.'

'Oh God. They've killed her, haven't they? Haven't they?'

'I don't know. Now, give me your phone. He wants us to turn them off and throw them away so that the police can't use them to follow us. Then we've got to drive up to a place called Hambleden, near Henley.'

Kathy pulled the phone from her pocket and handed it over. 'They're going to kill us, you know. When we arrive. They'll never let us go, not after this.'

'We're out of choices, Kathy,' I said, meeting her gaze. 'They've got us over a barrel this time.'

I got out of the car and walked into the trees at the side of the road. I switched off my phone and threw it into a fern bush. Then I switched off hers. But I didn't throw it away, because I knew Kathy was right. When we turned up to wherever it was our tormentor – and I could only guess it was the man Daniels called Lench – wanted us, and he'd got the information he wanted, we'd be surplus to requirements, loose ends to be dealt with. But it wasn't that which bothered me; it was the fact that they might also get rid of Max and Chloe. Our whole family wiped out, like we'd never existed. I didn't know who could help, but I did know without a doubt that if I threw away Kathy's phone, that would be the end of our last lifeline.

I placed it in my pocket and headed back to the car.

'Head for the motorway,' I told her, and without another word she pulled away, driving north.

It had just turned ten past seven.

36

Bolt was woken up by the shrill blasts of his mobile as it vibrated away like an enthusiastic sex toy on his bedside table. After a long yawn, he reached over and picked it up. He still hadn't even opened his eyes when he heard the angry tones of a voice he didn't immediately recognize.

'I think you owe me a very fucking big apology, DI Bolt. What is it with you? Do you think because we're based in the suburbs we're so utterly incapable that we're not worth bothering with? That you can run roughshod over our investigation and not bother to keep us informed of what you're finding out?'

Bolt inched open an eye, saw that, according to the alarm clock, it was 7.17 a.m. and realized that he was talking to the man in charge of investigating Jack Calley's murder.

'Ah, DCI Lambden. You're up early, sir.'

'Don't piss me about, Bolt. I've just been talking to Calley's neighbour, Bernard Crabbe. He tells me you and your colleague came to see him last night, with a photograph of Tom and Kathy Meron.'

Bolt sat up in the bed, fully awake now. 'How did you know about them?'

'Not through you, that's for sure. I suspect we found out the same way you did. We checked Mr Calley's phone records and saw that his last call was made to the Meron address. Bet you didn't think we could manage that, did you?'

'Listen, I'm not trying to hide anything—'

'We also found out that Mrs Meron appears to be wanted in connection with the murder yesterday of a Vanessa Blake,' continued Lambden, still sounding extremely irate. 'So, we're not as pig-ignorant as you might think.'

Bolt rubbed his eyes. 'I never said you were.'

'Actions speak a lot louder than words.'

'If you give me a second, I'll tell you everything I know.'

'Good. Fire away.'

'First of all, I'm sorry. Everything was moving so fast yesterday, I got ahead of myself. I was going to call and update you this morning.'

'OK, apology accepted,' he said, without missing a beat. 'Now, what can you tell me that'll make my job of finding whoever strung up Calley easier?'

Bolt knew he was going to have to give Lambden something decent if he was to get him to remain onside. So, as he got out of bed and walked into the bathroom, he told him that Parnham-Jones's suicide was looking like murder, and that at the time of his death he was being blackmailed. He didn't mention the child abuse allegations since there was still absolutely nothing tangible to back them up. 'I don't know what connection the Parnham-Jones death has with Jack Calley or the Merons, but the timing's extremely coincidental,' he concluded.

'Someone's looking for the Merons,' said Lambden. 'I found

out this morning that a cottage they part-owned in the New Forest got burned down last night, and there were reports of gunfire coming from the area. The local police have got SOCO teams going over there this morning to sift through what's left of the wreckage and see if there are any bodies in there.'

'If they're dead, we're in trouble. I can't think of anyone else who's in a position to explain why Jack Calley and Vanessa Blake were murdered. Have you put out traces on their mobiles?'

'That's another of the reasons I was calling you,' said the DCI. 'You know how hard it is to get authorization for a trace. We need one on Kathy Meron's phone, and you, being NCS, have got a better chance of getting it than me. If you can do something on that score, it'd be a big help.'

Bolt poured himself a glass of water. 'Leave it with me. I'll keep you posted of how I get on this time as well, OK?'

'Thanks.'

'No hard feelings, eh?'

'None at all.' It sounded as though Lambden meant it as well, which made Bolt feel a little guilty. Perhaps he'd judged him too harshly yesterday. Lambden gave him Kathy Meron's mobile number and hung up.

If either Tom or Kathy had their mobile phones with them, and they were switched on, it would be possible for the network provider to pinpoint their exact location simply by tracking the phones' signals – something that Jean Riley could probably sort out in no time, with her contacts. But in the UK Police Service there are always hurdles to jump, and Bolt would have to go right up the chain of command to the head of the NCS, Detective Chief Superintendent Steve Evans, in order to gain approval for such a course of action. He called Evans now.

The DCS was a renowned early riser, a habit he'd picked up in his previous life in the military, and he answered on the second ring, as if he'd been waiting for exactly this call. Bolt was swift and to the point. He wanted a trace on both the Merons' mobile phones, and explained his reasons.

Evans listened patiently, and when Bolt had finished the DCS was also swift and to the point. 'I'm going to give you verbal authorization for a trace on Kathy Meron's phone, not Tom's,' he said. 'There's not enough probable cause on him.'

Bolt didn't argue. There was no point. Evans was sticking his neck out as it was. He thanked his boss for his help.

'Keep me informed of your progress,' Evans told him, 'and we'll sort out all the paperwork later.'

Next, Bolt called Jean Riley, waking her up. She sounded awful, hardly able to string a sentence together. 'It's twenty past seven, guv. What are you doing? I've only been in bed three hours.' At twenty-four, Jean Riley was something of a party animal who liked to let her hair down when she wasn't working. She was the complete opposite of Matt Turner, which was probably the reason they got on so well.

'Emergency, Jean,' Bolt said unsympathetically, filling her in on what he needed and ignoring her hangover-induced groans and occasional bouts of rasping coughs.

'Blimey, this case is taking on a life of its own, isn't it?' she said, waking up at last. 'Any ideas what the hell's going on?'

'Plenty, but whether they're the right ones is anyone's guess. Call me back as soon as you've got a trace on Kathy Meron's phone.'

Then, having flung on a dressing gown and made some strong coffee, he called Mo and updated him on the new developments, from the blackmail email Turner had discovered on Parnham-Jones's PC to the burning down of the holiday cottage in the New Forest. It was breakfast time in the Khan household, and he could hear the sound of Mo's kids charging about and Saira trying, with only limited success, to keep order. The raucous noise made a stark contrast to the silence in Bolt's kitchen.

'So someone else knew about P-J's little sideline?'

'It looks that way. Turner's trying to track down the source of the email and he'll be getting back to me later. The reason I called was just to keep you in the loop. I don't need you to do anything today. Spend some time with the family.'

'Thanks for that,' said Mo, and told him to hang on a moment. Bolt heard a door shutting and the background noise fading out. 'Listen, boss,' Mo whispered, 'I don't want to miss out on anything, not on a case this big. If you need me, let me know, all right? We're just planning a quiet morning here, so you won't be disturbing anything.'

'No problem. If anything serious comes up, I'll be on the phone. But you go and enjoy yourself, OK?'

'Do you think the Merons are dead?' he asked.

'They could be,' Bolt admitted, 'because whatever they know is obviously worth killing them for. And if they are dead, their secret's going to die with them, and I've got a horrible feeling that'll put us straight back to where we started.'

They fell silent for a moment.

'Anyway,' said Mo eventually, 'you know where I am.'

37

'I think you owe me an explanation,' I said at last when we were on the M27, heading east towards Southampton and the M3. In the twenty minutes up until that point we'd driven entirely in brooding, fearful silence.

Kathy sighed, shifting uncomfortably in her seat, avoiding my gaze. I had a feeling she'd avoid my gaze now for the rest of her life – however long that was going to be.

'When I was at Jack's yesterday, he gave me a key. It's for a safety deposit box in King's Cross.'

'What's in it?'

'He didn't tell me. He said that if anything happened to him I was to go down there, take out the contents, and make them public. He said he couldn't do it himself because it would be unethical.'

'Since when did he ever worry about being unethical? It's unethical to sleep with your friend's wife. That didn't seem to bother him.'

'I'm telling you what he said, all right?'

'This is what they're after, isn't it? Whatever's in that box?'

'I don't know. I suppose so.'

'And you never asked him what was in it?'

'I did, but he just said it was something that belonged to a client. And before you ask, I don't know who the client was.'

I shook my head in disbelief. 'And you took it? The key? Why did you have to get involved? What the hell did any of it have to do with you?'

'Listen, Tom, I know I made a mistake, OK?'

'Is that what you call all this? A fucking mistake? It's a little bit more than that, love. At least three people I can think of are dead, and now some sadistic bastard's got our kids. All because you had to have an affair with that cheating, lying bastard.'

'I know, Tom, I fucking know. You don't have to keep reminding me.'

I took a deep breath, willing myself to calm down. 'And you really have no idea what's in that deposit box?'

Kathy seemed to calm down as well, and when she replied her voice was softer. 'I don't, and I've got no desire to find out either. Whatever it is, they're welcome to it.'

'Why didn't you say something earlier, then?'

'When did I get the chance? After Jack got killed, I didn't know what to do. I panicked and just drove down to the cottage. I was trying to work out what to do. Then when you came down with that man who claimed to be a policeman—'

'Daniels.' In all the excitement, I'd forgotten about him. He'd saved our lives the previous night, and I wondered if he too had made it out.

'Yes, him. When I recognized his voice from Jack's place, it threw me completely. I was sure he was after whatever was in the box, and I thought that once he found out about it, and we were no longer any use to him, he'd get rid of us.'

It sounded like a plausible story, though God alone knew what the box contained. Something explosive, I had no doubt about that. But why had Jack given the key to Kathy? His excuse about ethics was just that, an excuse. He'd given it to her for a reason, and again I felt sure she wasn't telling me the whole truth.

I asked her once again how her prints got on the filleting knife.

She said she honestly didn't know. 'You do believe I didn't have anything to do with Vanessa's death, don't you?' she said. 'Because the man who killed her attacked you. But you still don't believe me?'

'I don't know what to believe any more,' I answered, and it was true. I didn't.

Once again we fell into a tense silence as both our minds focused on the most important thing: the welfare of our kids.

38

Bolt drank two coffees, ate the leftovers of his Thai takeaway and a banana, showered, and was in the process of getting dressed when his mobile rang again.

'Bad news and good news.' It was Jean Riley, and she was sounding a lot more sprightly than earlier.

'Give me the bad.'

'They can't get a trace on Kathy Meron's number. It's switched off.'

'And the good?'

'It's unlikely they're dead. Or at least Tom Meron isn't. I managed to get a check done on his records and a call was made from his mobile at 7.08 this morning, lasting ninety-eight seconds. The location was just outside Bolderwood in the New Forest. The number being called was a pay-as-you-go mobile, not registered to any individual.'

Bolt looked at his watch. 8.05. Less than an hour ago. 'Can you get a trace on that one?'

'You'll need to speak to the big boss to get that.'

Bolt knew it was doubtful that DCS Evans would approve a trace on a number called from Tom Meron's mobile when he wouldn't approve a trace on Meron's own phone. And if the number belonged to the people who were after the Merons, it was likely that it would already be switched off. But the fact that a call had been made at least gave him room for some optimism.

'Do me a favour, Jean.'

'Another one?'

'The last, I promise. You've got to make sure that you know the minute Kathy Meron's phone emits a signal, and tell me straight away. And if you can do some begging and pleading, and see if you can get your contact to let you know if Tom's gets switched on, even better.'

'That's two favours.'

'Well, they're the last two. I know it's not strictly above board, but see what you can do. I'll stand you drinks all night the next time we all go out.'

'You know,' she said, 'I'd settle for knowing exactly what it is the Merons have got to do with the Lord Chief Justice's suicide.'

Wouldn't we all, thought Bolt as he hung up.

39

The village of Hambleden, perched at the edge of the Chilterns, is quintessentially English and has been used as a backdrop for numerous films and TV programmes. I know this because I've seen some of them. It's got a small, attractive square with a fourteenth-century church, a village shop, a family butcher's and a pub on the corner called the Stag and Huntsman. The houses are quaint, old and very attractive. A couple of them even have thatched roofs.

It was 8.13 when Kathy pulled up at the side of the road, directly outside the phone box. I got out of the car without looking at her, and stepped inside. The interior of the phone box smelled a little stale, but was remarkably free of the usual stench of urine you get in the ones in London. Perhaps they preferred using toilets out here.

I stood there, cold and still, watching the second hand ticking on my watch. It made it to the top and kept going. 8.14. One more minute. Thank Christ Kathy had driven like a maniac. But I couldn't help thinking that it might be too late. My children, my precious children, might already be dead. A five-year old and a four-year old – everything to me, yet just an inconvenience and a bargaining tool to the men who'd taken them. And put in this position all because of the treachery first of my former friend, then of my wife. I didn't care what was in that fucking safety deposit box at King's Cross station. It meant nothing to me. All I wanted was to get back to where things were before, when my marriage was good and the world was fine, and my children were laughing and happy. But as the second hand ticked relentlessly on, passing the six, I knew that whatever happened the past was gone for ever. And that the future for all of us might well be very short and very dark.

The phone rang, shrill and loud, startling me. I stole a glance at Kathy. She was staring through the windscreen, her features rigid and haunted, having aged ten years in the past hour. I picked up. My throat felt dry, and when I spoke my voice was a croak.

'Tom Meron.'

'You've made good time,' said the man I'd spoken to earlier. 'I trust you've followed your instructions.'

'Yes, I have.'

'You switched off the phones and got rid of them?'

'I did. I'm not going to do anything that risks my children's lives.'

'Very wise. I have further instructions for you. You are to walk north through the village square in the direction of the Stag and Huntsman pub. It will be on your right as you pass it. Continue on the road as it goes up the hill, and you'll be met by someone on the way. That person will have his identity concealed, and you will go with him. If there's anyone tracking you, we'll know about it, and one of your children will be sacrificed as forfeit.'

I shivered visibly, knowing that he meant what he said, and feeling physically sick with fear. 'We're not going to try anything, I promise.' But I was already speaking into a dead phone.

I stepped out of the phone box and motioned for Kathy to park up properly. She found a spot next to the wall that lined the village's graveyard, and got out. Her movements were unsteady as if she might collapse at any time, and her face was ashen, but I had no sympathy. She'd got us into this.

'This way,' I told her, pointing up the hill past the pub and the family butcher's. 'We've got to hurry.'

She fell into step beside me and we strode up the road in silence. A white-haired man in his seventies appeared in the front door of one of the cottages. He was dressed in a tweed jacket and tie, and he smiled and gave us a small wave. Instinctively, I waved back and managed a weak smile in return, feeling hugely jealous of anyone who had anything to smile about on this particular day.

The road became steeper and was lined with overhanging trees as we passed the pub, and soon the terraced cottages gave way to a wooded hill of oaks and beeches, with just an occasional house appearing through the greenery on either side. The only sounds were the squawks of pheasants and the faint but ever-present roar of planes passing above the ceiling of unbroken white cloud above us. Then, suddenly, from the garden of one of the houses, came the laughing shouts of young children. I felt my insides constrict so tightly it was difficult to breathe. My legs felt weak, but I forced myself to keep walking, wanting to get as far away as possible from the sound and what it reminded me of. Kathy kept pace, her features contorted into a frozen expression of deep animal pain. I knew that this was tearing her apart as much as it was me.

As we walked, and the road got so steep that it began to resemble a climb, I slipped a hand into the pocket of my still damp jacket and felt Kathy's phone. The woods around us were silent now, the houses gone, the road gradually becoming little more than a potholed track. I looked around, trying to spot anyone monitoring our progress, but if anyone was there, they were well hidden. Kathy's mobile was a fliptop like mine, so I flicked it open inside the pocket and, finding what I hoped was the on switch, pressed my thumb on it until it made a tiny muffled bleep.

We reached the brow of the hill, maybe four minutes after leaving the car, and the road flattened out ahead of us. There were still trees on either side but they were more spaced out now, making concealment that much more difficult. Beyond them, fields were visible as well as several farm buildings. I could still see no-one.

I felt with my finger for the number two button on the phone. Kathy had never been good at remembering numbers and her code to unlock the SIM card was a simple 2222. Four pushes on that button and the phone would start broadcasting a signal. I'd read somewhere that this was enough for a phone company to track its location, often down to within a few feet. I was taking a terrible risk, and a voice in my head told me that by switching the phone on I was sentencing my children to death. Deeper down, instinct told me that unless I made some effort at providing a clue to our whereabouts, then we – the whole family – were finished. But if I was searched, and they found the phone, then there really would be no way out. I needed to ditch it somewhere, but it was going to have to be somewhere close to our destination. The problem was that with every step I took, the prospect of my discovery became that much more real.

Even now someone could be watching me through binoculars, following my every move.

I pressed the numbers and flicked the phone shut, clutching it in my palm. Then I slipped my hand from my pocket and, as I drew level with a thick puddle of mud formed in a divot at the side of the track, let it slip from my grasp. At the same time I moved closer to Kathy, putting an arm on her shoulder, and said, louder than was necessary, that everything was going to be OK. 'Of course it's not going to fucking be OK,' she answered, without bothering to turn in my direction. But at least she didn't hear the phone hit the ground.

I immediately regretted my action, but it was too late to worry about that now. The die had been cast. You make split-second decisions, and sometimes they can have life-changing results; the point is, you still have to make them. I kept walking, not breaking my stride, not giving anyone watching even the slightest hint that I might be up to something. I said nothing further to Kathy and she said nothing to me.

The woods ended and became fields, the track continuing to run through them in a straight line before disappearing as the land dipped downwards. A house stood alone, just back from the track, about a hundred yards' distant.

'OK, stop where you are,' said an unfamiliar voice a few feet to my right.

I did as I was told and saw a thin man in a Homer Simpson face mask appear from behind a thick holly bush that partly obscured a timber-clad, single-storey building a few yards behind him. The man held a pistol with a long, cigar-shaped silencer that dwarfed his skinny, hairless wrist. He was dressed in jeans and a black, pulled-up hoodie with the word SURF written on the chest in jaunty script. I couldn't see his face, but I could tell he was young – probably early twenties. There was something in his overall demeanour – a little gawky and skittish – that suggested he wasn't a hundred per cent confident in what he was doing.

He waved us over with the gun, and when we reached him he pushed us behind the bush so that we were out of sight of the road.

'Empty your pockets,' he demanded, waving the gun around as he spoke.

We did so. There wasn't much. I had a pen, some loose change, and my credit card wallet. Kathy didn't have anything. She tended to keep her personal belongings in a handbag, which I guess had been left at the cottage and had subsequently been turned into charcoal.

'Chuck it all on the floor.'

I let the stuff drop from my hands and lifted my arms away from my sides as he patted me down in an amateur fashion, before turning his attention to Kathy. She glared at him, and pushed her legs tightly together as he subjected her to a slightly more detailed search.

When he'd finished, he told me to pick my stuff back up. 'All right, get inside,' he said, pushing first Kathy and then me in the direction of the single-storey building. He made a point of pressing the gun hard into my back, and I assumed he was enjoying his little bit of power. It depressed me that the world seemed so full of individuals who gained enjoyment and satisfaction from inflicting pain.

The building was obviously a fairly recent and expensive barn conversion which made it look similar to a high-spec log cabin. The front windows were large and double-glazed but the curtains were drawn, making it impossible to tell who was inside.

We followed a cobbled path down to the front door, and when we were two steps away it opened with a flourish. The huge balaclava-clad man who'd come into our cottage's master bedroom the previous night holding a pump-action shotgun loomed over us, this time unarmed. The man Daniels had called Lench. He was still dressed in the same black clothes, flecked now with pale mud, and his immense bearing and long, ape-like arms, bulging with muscles like cannonballs, gave him the appearance of an executioner from a medieval history book. Behind the mask, he radiated a cold confidence that had the entirely natural effect of making other men feel weaker. I'd met the occasional man like him in the business world, although never one his size. They were invariably highly successful, and, just as invariably, psychopaths.

'Come inside,' he said in an ordinary, slightly feminine voice that did nothing to detract from the air of menace that surrounded him.

I was first in, and he pointed me in the direction of a large and very modern kitchen, all done out in pine, with an oak dining table in the middle that seated eight. There were pots and pans lining the walls, all in order of size and make, and everything was spotlessly clean and tidy. I went over to the far window and looked out across the field. Kathy followed me over, while Lench took a seat at the head of the table facing us. The younger man who'd searched us stood near the door, the gun held by his side, the Homer Simpson mask giving us a dozy smile.

'You know what I want,' said Lench, without preamble. 'And one of you knows where it is. Our mutual friend, Jack, said that it was you, Tom, but I have a feeling he might have been protecting someone.'

He smiled behind the balaclava and looked at Kathy. She held his gaze, the fear that had been so prominent on her face earlier now giving way to a quiet rage that sat behind her eyes. Her body was tense, and I thought for a moment that she might do something stupid, like charge him. But she stayed where she was and remained silent.

'I've been thinking about it ever since yesterday afternoon. When Jack knew we were about to kill him, he tried to think of a way to protect the woman he was fucking, so he told us that it was her husband who had what we were looking for. That's how you came to be involved in everything, Tom. All very unfortunate, really.' He leaned forward in the seat, resting his elbows on the table, and regarded us both in turn. 'And now the moment of truth. Does a child die, or do you tell me where it is?'

I looked at Kathy, but she continued to stare at Lench.

'You murdered Vanessa, didn't you?' she said.

'Are you talking about the woman at the university? That was a case of mistaken identity, I'm afraid, and it wasn't me. One of my colleagues was dealing with that. He ran into her while looking for you. It didn't take us long to find out who you are and where you worked. But I'm not interested in discussing this. You know what I want. Now, are you going to tell me where it is?'

Hatred flared in Kathy's face, and once again I got the feeling she might try to do something stupid. I moved in closer and put a hand on her shoulder.

'Remember, Mrs Meron, your children are depending on you.'

She glared at him defiantly for several seconds before finally reaching down and pulling up the leg of her jeans a couple of inches. She unzipped one of her ankle boots and pulled a small gold-coloured key from inside her sock. She put it down on the table and slid it across in Lench's direction. 'Jack gave me this yesterday, before you killed him. It opens a safety deposit box at King's Cross station. I don't know what it is you want, but I'm guessing it's there.'

'Number three-two-eight,' said Lench quietly as he examined the key. He reached into the pocket of his jacket and pulled out a mobile. As we watched he called a number. When the person at the other end picked up, he reeled out a set of instructions, keeping his voice low and turning away so we couldn't hear what he was saying. A few seconds later, he replaced the phone in his pocket. 'Our man will be at that deposit box in about forty minutes. As soon as he's verified the contents we'll let you and your children go. But if you haven't been entirely honest with us, on every matter' – he seemed to look right through me as he said this – 'then you all die.'

I thought of the phone sitting in the mud fifty yards away, and wondered whether it would save or condemn us.

40

Twenty minutes after Jean Riley had called Mike Bolt, she phoned him again. By this time he was pacing up and down in the sitting area in front of his kitchen, half-watching Sky News, desperate to be doing something. The reporters were dissecting the previous day's big football match. As was often the case, England had lost to supposedly weaker opposition, the final score being 2–0. Bolt had missed the last goal – a goalmouth scramble after a terrible keeping error – which Sky helpfully showed for him. Schoolboy defending, said the reporter, using a well-worn phrase that Bolt had to admit was an apt description.

So far, there'd been no mention of the Jack Calley murder, or that of Kathy Meron's colleague at the university. Clearly no-one in the media had made the connection yet between Jack and Lord Parnham-Jones, and as for the other killing, a mundane stabbing all too common in London, it would be lucky to make the local news.

Bolt picked up the mobile on the first ring.

'They've got a signal on Kathy Meron's phone,' Jean told him. 'A place called Hambleden, seven or eight miles off the M40 in Buckinghamshire.'

'I know it.' Bolt had been there once before with his ex-wife on one of the occasional day trips they used to make to places outside the city. He remembered it as a very pretty village with good walks in the surrounding countryside. 'How close can you pinpoint it?'

'We've got it down to the top of Ranger's Hill, which runs up from the north end of the village. You'll need to look at a map to get an exact spot. Are you going to drive over there?'

There was, of course, no way Bolt could have said no. 'Yeah, I think I'm going to take a look. I'll let the big boss know where I'm going, and if I get a location on Kathy Meron, I'll call for back-up. Keep me posted of any changes.'

He knew that there was no point trying to get additional resources to help him, not with knowing only the location of Kathy Meron's mobile. He also didn't want to flood the area with local police, just in case the couple were in danger and their safety was compromised.

When he'd hung up, he called DCS Evans, but his line was

busy so he left a detailed message before ringing Keith Lambden to let him know about this new development.

'She drives a maroon Hyundai Coupé apparently,' Lambden told him. 'A witness called the incident room an hour ago to say she'd seen it parked behind some trees about twenty yards down from Calley's house, and only just visible from the road. This was at about half past one yesterday.'

'So, just after the neighbours saw her drive past? That's strange. The neighbours, the Crabbes, said they'd seen the woman they identified from the photograph as Kathy Meron with Jack Calley several times before, so I'd assumed they were having an affair.'

'I think it's a fair assumption to make.'

'But if that was the case, why didn't she park on his driveway? There's room for at least three cars on it, and Calley's only got one. Why park your car twenty yards away, and out of sight?'

'Maybe someone else was there.'

'Or maybe,' Bolt said, 'she didn't want to be seen.'

41

The wait seemed interminable, the minutes dragging by in slow motion. Kathy and I avoided looking at each other. For the most part we stood where we were, utterly helpless, but occasionally one of us would pace round our end of the table a little, or sit down in one of the chairs, always avoiding Lench's mocking gaze.

Lench himself never spoke. He sat where he was, hardly moving. Waiting with the confident patience of a cat stalking prey. There was no point begging him for mercy. Both of us, I think, knew that. Here was a man utterly at ease with his cruelty. We were nothing to him, not even cardboard cut-outs. Neither were our children. He would kill every one of us without a second's thought. We weren't even worth speaking to, except to provide him with the information he was after. I doubt if there were many people with as cold a heart as his walking this world, and I cursed my bad luck that our paths had crossed.

After a while he left the room, his chair scraping loudly on the tiled floor, and only the gunman in the Homer Simpson mask remained. He was silent too.

I went over to the window and looked out again. The view was green and pretty. Normally, I'd have appreciated it. Today, I wished I was looking at something ugly, something more in tune with my feelings. A scrapyard or a slag heap. A landfill site. I wondered if anyone was responding to my SOS, moving in on us right now. 'Get real,' I told myself. 'No-one's coming. You're on your own. You've always been on your own.'

I looked at my watch yet again. Ten past nine. The forty minutes were up. The person Lench had sent would be at King's Cross by now, and the moment of truth with us soon. Which probably meant death. Yet it wasn't that that occupied my thoughts. Because something was bugging me. Something Kathy had said that didn't ring true. I played back my conversation with her in the car earlier. She'd admitted to me that Jack had given her the key to the deposit box, and that it contained something important belonging to one of his clients. She'd told Lench this too, and where the box could be found.

No, it was something else . . .

I looked down at her. She was sitting with her head slightly bowed, eyes downcast. Both her hands were flat on the table, palms down. One thumb moved left and right in a steady windscreen-wiper-like movement, the only visible sign of the tension I knew was coursing through her. She wasn't a fidgeter like me; she tended to simmer silently and without moving. It had always been an aspect of her character that unnerved me.

Her fingerprints had been on the knife that killed Vanessa. But she wasn't the killer. I'd seen the killer, and Lench had not denied that one of his people had done it. Therefore it wasn't Kathy. But her prints were on the knife.

Then it hit me. Last night she hadn't asked me about the injuries I'd received from the filleting knife or how I'd sustained them. Daniels hadn't said anything about them either. So she couldn't have known that I'd been attacked by Vanessa's killer. Yet when we were speaking this morning she mentioned the attack, had even talked about my attacker being a 'he'.

How the hell had she known?

I racked my brains to think of when I could have let slip something, but there'd been very little time for me to have done so, and I was almost certain I hadn't. Which meant only one thing.

She'd been at the library yesterday afternoon.

42

From Clerkenwell, Bolt drove up to Angel Gate and turned left onto the Pentonville Road, heading west. The Pentonville Road became the Euston Road, then the Marylebone Road, and finally the A40. Usually this route was heavily congested, but before nine on a Sunday morning it was quiet, and Bolt was on the M40 within twenty minutes.

Fifteen minutes later, having driven consistently at speeds over a hundred miles per hour, he came off at junction 5, High Wycombe, and took the A404 to Marlow. The phone didn't ring during the entire journey, which he found vaguely reassuring. It meant there were no new developments. Either Jean had gone back to bed or Kathy Meron's mobile was still on and not moving from its current location.

He continued to drive fast, breaking the speed limit, and it was ten past nine, just about forty minutes after he'd set off, when he finally turned onto the country road that ran for a little over a mile down to Hambleden village.

It had been the summer before her death that he and Mikaela had driven down here for the day. The weather had been mild and sunny, and there'd been a cricket match in progress on the green at the edge of the village. They'd eaten at the pub, sitting outside in the beer garden, basking in the sunshine and feeling at peace with the world. It had been such a contrast to the noise and fury of the big city that for a moment he'd dreamed about living out here, away from it all. Mikaela had obviously been thinking the same thing. 'If we ever have kids, this is where I'd like them to grow up,' she'd said, sipping from her wine and looking out across the rolling green fields, her long blonde hair almost white in the glare of the sun. 'We could have a bit of land and keep chickens.'

He'd known for months by then that she'd wanted kids. It had come up more and more in their conversations. Personally he'd been far less sure. He loved her, there was never any doubt about that, but children . . . They were a huge tie, and with the job he did, he just hadn't been sure he, or they, were ready for it. 'Let's leave it a while. Give it a year or two. There's no hurry,' he'd said, delaying things, knowing all the time that one day he was going to have to choose between starting a family and losing her.

He drove over the old stone bridge that led into the village square and almost immediately spotted the maroon Hyundai. He made a note of the plate. It was Kathy Meron's car. He carried on driving, up past the family butcher's and the pub on the right-hand side, to the point where the road began to climb as it left the village. He could see from the map on the car's satellite navigation system that this was the beginning of Ranger's Hill, but instead of driving up it, he turned right into the village car park, where a loose group of middle-aged ramblers in shorts and hiking boots stood next to their cars, chatting loudly among themselves. Bolt decided to make the rest of the journey on foot. His approach would be less conspicuous that way.

He stepped out of the car, put his mobile on to vibrate, and started walking, wondering what it was he was going to find.

43

I could hear my heart beating loudly in my chest, a rapid rat-tat rat-tat that would have had any self-respecting doctor writing out a prescription for beta blockers. Each minute now was a lifetime. A lifetime filled with fear, confusion and betrayal. My children were in terrible danger. My wife had been living a lie that seemed to grow larger and blacker with each new layer of treachery I uncovered. How could I not have seen it? Kathy was – or rather, she had been – a good person. A loving mother, a friend to the people she met, someone everyone seemed to like. More than they ever did me. But underneath it all, something had been terribly wrong. She had been at the library yesterday, I was convinced of that now. Her prints were on the filleting knife, and it would explain the presence of my gloves. Once again, I looked over at her, but she didn't seem to notice my gaze and continued to stare at her hands.

I looked at my watch. 9.20. It would all be over very soon, one way or another. If they let my kids go, then that would be enough for me. I know it sounds a weird thing to say, but at that moment in time it would almost have been a relief to have the gun put against my head and the whole thing ended. Before I found out any more grim facts about the way my life had been knocked totally and utterly off course. As long as I knew that my kids were OK.

The door opened and Lench came back into the room. It was difficult to read his expression behind the mask, but something told me he was not pleased about something. He stopped on the other side of the table and looked across at Kathy.

'You told me you never knew what was inside the deposit box,' he said darkly.

'That's because I don't,' she answered, looking up. Her tone was one of righteous indignation.

It didn't work. 'Our man's recovered the contents of the box,' Lench said, making no effort to hide his irritation. 'It's what we were after, but we think there may be more. And we think you know where they might be.'

'I don't know what you're talking about.'

'I think you're lying to me, Mrs Meron.' There was something chilling in his voice. An undercurrent of excitement, as if he was pleased with her defiance because it gave him an excuse to hurt her. He moved slowly around the table in her direction.

She seemed to sense this, and when she spoke again, her defiance was faltering. 'I'm not lying, I promise you. I was just looking after the key for Jack Calley.'

'Listen, Kathy, if you're hiding anything, just tell him, please.' I suddenly felt hugely protective towards her, though God knows why. Not after everything that had happened.

Lench stopped several feet from her. 'I want to know if there are any copies.'

'Copies of what? I don't know what you're talking about, I promise.'

'Tell him, for God's sake. He'll get it out of you one way or another.' I put an arm on her shoulder, gripping her tightly. 'Please.'

Lench turned my way, then looked back over his shoulder at Homer Simpson. 'Take him outside,' he said, motioning dismissively towards me.

Homer Simpson moved away from his position against the wall and walked over to me. I looked imploringly at Kathy, but once again she didn't meet my gaze. Homer grabbed me roughly by the arm and pushed the silencer against my back, pulling me in the direction of the door.

'Kathy, for Christ's sake, he's got our children! Just tell him what he wants he know. What the fuck is wrong with you?'

Something was burning deep inside me. Rage. Rage aimed at Lench, Kathy, the man in the crappy Homer Simpson mask pushing me around. The whole fucking world. As Homer pulled me again, I shoved him away, ignoring the fact that he had a gun in my back.

'Don't try anything, Meron,' snapped Lench. 'Like you say, we've got your little brats, and we'll cut them to pieces if we have to.' Then to Homer: 'Get him out of here. If he fucks you about, kill him. We don't need him any more, so if he wants to commit suicide, that's up to him.'

The rage continued to simmer, and as Homer half-led, half-hauled me out of the room I aimed one more comment at Lench. 'If anything happens to my kids, they'll hunt you down to the ends of the earth. You know that, don't you? They don't like child killers in this country.'

But Lench simply turned his back on me as if I no longer mattered and reached towards Kathy with an immense gloved hand. Her dark eyes flashed with fear.

The kitchen door was opened and I was pushed out into the hallway. 'You want to be associated with child killers, do you?' I said over my shoulder at Homer as he manhandled me into a sitting room which, like the kitchen, had windows facing out over both sides of the property. Like the kitchen, too, it was immaculately neat and tidy, with expensive leather furniture and a plasma TV on the wall, but utterly devoid of character.

'I couldn't give a fuck,' Homer answered casually, kicking the door shut behind him, and I could tell immediately that he genuinely didn't. My kids were nothing to him. Nor was my pain, or Kathy's.

It was obvious I'd always viewed the world and its people in too much of an optimistic light. I had always believed that people were, by and large, good at heart. But it was becoming clearer to me by the second that there were evil bastards out there who were devoid of any positive attributes at all, who lived by no rules and cared nothing for their fellow human beings. And this ignorant piece of dirt was one of them.

The rage exploded within me then and my actions became utterly instinctive, no longer the slaves to conscious thought and the attendant fear that always comes with thinking. As Homer pushed me towards a low-slung black leather sofa that would have probably cost me a month's wages, I swung round without warning, knocked his gun to one side with a contemptuous slap and, before he had a chance to react, smashed my forehead into the bridge of his nose. There was a crack as it broke. It sounded like a gunshot when you were as close as I was to it, and blood squirted out of his nostrils. He stumbled backwards like a drunk, eyes wide and unfocused, and banged his head against the skirting. But he still had hold of the gun, so I grabbed his wrist and yanked it upwards so that the silencer faced the ceiling, then ripped the mask from his face and butted him again, three times in rapid succession, every blow landing in roughly the spot where I'd done the initial damage. His head was already back against the skirting so he was unable to move, and thus took the full force of my attack. At the same time I punched him in the gut, then the balls. He groaned and his wrist went limp, giving me the chance to yank the gun from his grip by the silencer. I pointed the gun back in his direction, viewing the unmasked features for the first time. His face was pallid and pockmarked, belonging to an unattractive and now only semi-conscious young man in his early twenties. It was stained and splattered with blood, and I kicked it hard as his body slipped down the wall to the thickly carpeted floor, cracking another bone.

The whole attack had been carried out in near silence, but I wondered whether I'd been quiet enough. We were only a matter of a few yards and a couple of walls from where Lench had my wife.

I looked down at the gun in my hand. It shook just a little. I looked down at Homer Simpson. He was out for the count. I asked myself a simple question: what the hell do I do now?

And then I heard a shot ring out, the sound of glass smashing, and suddenly the question was answered for me.

44

When Bolt reached the top of the hill at the point where it flattened out, he stopped and listened but could hear nothing other than the natural sounds of the woods: leaves rustling, the singing of birds, the odd squawk of a pheasant. He knew he was in the right place. This was the top of Ranger's Hill and Kathy Meron's phone would be round here somewhere. There was, however, no sign of Kathy herself. Through the treeline he could see the outline of buildings thirty yards or so away, and he made his way towards them, moving away from the road and quietly from tree to tree in his approach.

When he reached the edge of the trees, he found himself faced with a freshly mowed back garden belonging to a Norwegian-style wooden lodge. There didn't seem to be anyone about. Nor were there any other buildings visible. Bolt looked at his watch. 9.20. The phone was still emitting a signal from somewhere very close to here. It didn't necessarily mean that Kathy was also here. The phone might have been abandoned, but even so, he felt it must have been abandoned for a reason. To leave some sort of clue. Which meant he needed to check the house out.

Coming out of the trees and keeping low, he crept slowly towards the nearest window, using a pampas bush and then a loveseat as cover. He knew he was going to look like a right idiot if he was spotted by the owner sneaking through his back garden, but the worry lasted as long as it took to cover four of the five yards to the window. When there was only that one yard remaining, Bolt froze. He could see a man dressed in a black balaclava standing inside. The man had a gun in his hand and it was obvious he was talking to someone out of sight. The gun arm was straight, the barrel pointed at a slightly downwards angle, the man's demeanour perfectly calm.

Bolt felt a rush of elation. His hunch had been right. He was already crouching back down again and reaching into his pocket for his mobile to summon help, when in one of those perverse twists of fate the man for some reason looked his way. Their eyes met, and even from behind the double-glazed glass of the windowpane Bolt recognized instantly that they belonged to a killer. Knowing that he was hopelessly exposed, he dived to one side as a shot rang out and glass cracked. The bullet whistled past his head and disappeared off into the trees. Bolt's flight mechanism kicked in and he rolled over in the grass, jumped to his feet and ran for the safety of the trees. A second shot rang out, and this time it passed so close to his shoulder that he felt its draught. He jumped to one side and smashed bodily into the loveseat, careering over the top of it and landing on his belly half a yard from where the treeline began.

He waited an interminably long second for a third shot to ring out, but when it did it was muffled and seemed to be fired from inside the house. He scrabbled round onto his back, flicked open the mobile and dialled 999.

45

Occasionally in life you're faced with choices you know you should never have to make, and this was one of them. If I charged into the kitchen, gun in hand, I risked dying. I also risked putting Kathy's life in further danger. If I was successful and killed Lench, I risked sentencing my children to death. If I stayed where I was, I risked all three. It was, of course, no choice. All these thoughts shot across my mind and were computed in the space of a second, and, before they'd had too much of a chance to slow me down, I ran out of the lounge, across the hallway and straight through the kitchen door, not knowing what the hell it was I was going to see in there.

I yelled out some incoherent battle cry as I charged inside, waving the gun wildly, just as a second shot rang out. I saw immediately that Lench had his back to me and was firing out of the window. Kathy, meanwhile, was still in her seat but leaning away from him, her face a frozen mask of fear and confusion. As she saw me with the gun in my hand, she screamed, 'Don't do it! We need him!'

I hesitated, not knowing what to do, and as I stood there,

Lench swung round with surprising speed, one hand lashing out like a tentacle to grab Kathy by the shoulder. He pulled her towards him in a grip that looked unbreakable, and arced the gun round in my direction.

The world became slow motion for me as I watched the barrel line up against my chest. My whole body felt weak and exhausted, a stark and terrible contrast to Lench's casual, cat-like grace. If I fired, my children might die; so might my wife. If I didn't, I knew I certainly would. I don't know if it was reflexive or not – I like to think that it was – but I pulled the trigger anyway. Three times, one after the other, aiming above Kathy at Lench's head and shoulders, surprised at how mild the kick on the gun was. The bullets made an aggressive hiss, like air escaping from a balloon, as they flew out of the gun, while the whole room seemed to reverberate with Lench's third shot.

Somehow, incredibly, it had been me who'd fired first, and by some wondrous quirk of fate at least one of my rounds had found its target. Lench swivelled on his feet, his boots squeaking on the tiled floor, and seemed to lose his footing, while his own bullet went wide, shattering one of the plates on the wall. He let go of Kathy, who was still screaming, then she ducked as I fired a fourth shot, which struck the window and immediately made a spider's-web crack. Lench slipped over and landed on his side, still pointing the gun in my direction, and I was forced to dive into the kitchen units as he fired again.

We were operating on instinct now. I had no idea how many bullets were still in my gun but I knew that in an enclosed space like this I had to keep shooting. I didn't think about the fact that I was killing a fellow human being. I'd gone way beyond that now, and anyway, I didn't want to kill him. I just wanted to make him helpless so that he'd have no option but to tell me where my children were.

From my position on the floor I could see him under the kitchen table rolling onto his back to face me, the gun flashing silver in his gloved hand. I didn't have time to look for Kathy. I vaguely remember seeing something moving very slowly along the floor out of the corner of my eye, then I took as good an aim as I could and fired.

I hit him in the sole of his boot, making a penny-shaped hole that immediately started smoking. He shrieked out in pain, and pulled the trigger himself. There was a deafening explosion just above my head and the sound of wood splintering. My ears were ringing and I scrunched myself into a ball, trying to make myself as small a target as possible, at the same time unloading two more shots. But he was already moving, rolling away once again, then jumping unsteadily to his feet and hobbling towards the door. I fired at his legs, my bullets striking kitchen cupboards, the washing-machine window, the fridge door. Everything but him. Then, as he came round the edge of the table, we were suddenly only six feet apart. He leaned round to fire, his gun hand still remarkably steady, the barrel pointing directly into my eye, and in that moment I knew I was finished. For the first time in the last few minutes, I felt abject fear.

Kathy screamed, her sound not as high-pitched as the noise Lench had made when I'd put a hole in his shoe, and I swung my own weapon round, taking aim with a terrified desperation.

'Armed police! Drop your weapons!'

The shout came from somewhere outside the kitchen door, and Lench hesitated for a split second, his head inclining slightly in the direction of the shout. Because of this, his shot missed me, and he lost his balance, falling to one knee. I lost my nerve then, the realization that I, a lowly software salesman, was involved in a gunfight with a man far stronger and ruthless than me suddenly proving too much. I scrambled under the table in Kathy's direction, knocking the heavy wooden chairs out of the way, waiting for the inevitable agony when Lench's next bullet caught me between the shoulderblades.

'Come out with your hands up now! You are surrounded!'

The bullet never came. I grabbed hold of Kathy and pulled her under me in a protective gesture, holding her in a desperate, exhausted embrace.

And then the kitchen window exploded.

46

As soon as he heard the shout 'Armed police!', Lench experienced a flash of panic for the first time in years. Even the sudden burst of resistance from Tom Meron which had left him in the embarrassed position of being wounded for the first time in his life had only temporarily fazed him. The injuries – a flesh wound in his knife arm, and the bullet in the foot – could be treated and would heal. He'd always known that Meron, although a spirited fighter, was an amateur with a shot that was lucky rather than proficient, and so the final outcome of their shootout had never been in doubt. Lench would have finished him, then killed the wife. She'd already told him what he needed to know, so his use for both of them had run out. The wife had known that as soon as she gave out her final piece of information she'd be dead, which was why she'd held back. Lench admired her for that. She had guts. But it made no difference. The plan had been to kill them, then kill Grellier, the man in the Homer Simpson mask he'd brought with him today, hoping that he would then be saddled with the blame for the Merons' deaths. Grellier was new to the organization, a petty criminal with no ambition but the right kind of evil streak, and was therefore considered totally expendable. Unfortunately, this morning he'd proved exactly why he was totally expendable, allowing himself to be over-powered and disarmed by a frightened office worker.

But everything had still been under control until the moment Lench heard the shouts of the police. His one great fear, that of incarceration without limit, rose up and stared him right in the face. He'd planned for this day, knowing that it was inevitable, so he immediately reverted to the set of procedures he'd drilled into himself for just this kind of eventuality. First, he let the gun clatter to the floor. It was no use to him now. Then he unclipped the wristband to which the jet knife was attached and let this too fall to the floor. It was cleaned and sterilized regularly, the last time only hours ago, so would no longer contain traces of the blood or body matter of any of his victims, thus making it useless to the police. The gloves went next. They would carry traces of gunshot residue, but he would deny they were his. Now he no longer carried any incriminating evidence. It was his word against the Merons. They had nothing on him. And within hours, his employer's team of lawyers would be arriving at the police station to demand to know on what charges he was being held, and to badger the arresting officers into releasing him.

But as Lench got to his feet, wincing with pain, he realized that there were still problems. Grellier was probably still alive and might talk. The phone on which he'd received Tom Meron's call was still in the house. The balance of probability was still against him. It was potentially enough for charges. Even if his employer's people could reach the jury, as they'd done before, it might not be enough. Better to leave the evidence here and attempt to escape. That way he would have done all he could.

'Come out with your hands up now! You are surrounded!'

He staggered towards the window, grabbing a chair as he went and sending it smashing into the window at the rear of the kitchen with such force it went straight through. Which was the moment when Lench realized that the police almost certainly didn't have the back of the house covered – either that or they weren't armed – because no-one had reacted to the chair's exit. Without looking back, he hoisted himself onto the worktop, looked out into the empty garden, then went head-first through the hole he'd made.

Getting up again immediately, he half-hopped, half-ran, towards the field beyond. No-one tried to stop him. No further shouts of 'armed police' came from either his left or right. He kept going, ignoring the pain.

He sensed freedom.

47

The moment Bolt heard the sound of further gunshots coming from inside, he got to his feet and ran round the side of the house, the phone to his ear. As the operator came on he gave his name and rank and told him hurriedly that he needed armed police and an ambulance to a house at the top of Ranger's Hill in Hambleden. 'I don't have the address but I can confirm shots have been fired and it's a possible kidnap situation. Repeat: shots have been fired. You need to get ARVs here fast.' He put the phone back in his pocket, not wanting to stay on the line and have to concentrate on two things at once. Unarmed and alone, he was undoubtedly risking his life, but he also felt that he had to do something. There were almost certainly people dying in there.

He reached the front door. It was shut. Pulling open the letterbox, he decided bluffing was his only chance. In such situations you rarely have time to think things through. If you did, you'd never go up without a gun against half the villains the job threw up.

Another loud shot came from inside, mixed in with quieter ones that Bolt knew were being muffled by a silencer. He could hear the pings the bullets made as they struck wood and metal. 'Armed police! Drop your weapons!' He shouted the words with as much authority as he could muster, and hoped for the best.

The gunfire stopped. Straight away. Bolt waited for two seconds, just to make sure that they weren't suddenly going to change their minds and aim their guns at him, then looked left and right. No-one was sneaking up on him. 'Come out with your hands up now!' he called out. 'You are surrounded!' He didn't know what on earth he was going to do when they did actually come out with their hands up. He didn't even know who the villains were. But of one thing he was sure: if he sounded confident enough and they did indeed step outside with their hands pointing skyward and their guns nowhere to be seen, he could probably handle them until the cavalry got here.

He moved away from the door, ready to give the first man out a helpful slap if he saw the extent of Bolt's lack of resources and proved troublesome, but a second later he heard the sound of a window being smashed. After a further, longer pause, a male voice called out to say that he was unarmed and that the man they wanted was getting away. It might have been a trick, but the voice sounded genuine, so Bolt opened the door and ran inside, turning in the direction from where the shots had been coming.

There were two bodies lying on the kitchen floor, partly obscured by the kitchen table, arms entwined in a position that looked both unnatural and uncomfortable. They were staring up at him, and though their faces were grimy and drawn, like startled scarecrows, he recognized them immediately as Tom and Kathy Meron. They appeared unhurt, and there was a pistol – a Browning or similar – with a four-inch silencer attached, lying a few feet from Tom Meron's hand. On the floor in front of Bolt was a silver Walther PPK that was still producing a thin line of smoke, and next to it a pair of discarded gloves and a knife.

'He's getting away,' yelled Meron, extricating himself from his wife's embrace, his eyes wide and desperate. 'He's got our kids. You've got to do something.'

Bolt looked at the window from where the man in the balaclava had fired at him only a minute or two earlier. There was a huge hole in it, easily enough for a man to get through. He ran over and saw his attacker limping towards the end of the garden where a waist-high fence led to a fallow field and woodland beyond. He was obviously hurt but moving fast, and with reinforcements still realistically at least five, more likely ten, minutes away, there was every chance that he would indeed get away.

'Where are the rest of you?' demanded Tom Meron, coming up beside Bolt and following his gaze out of the window.

'It was a bluff,' Bolt told him. 'I'm on my own.'

'You've got to stop him!' shouted Kathy Meron, getting to her feet. 'If he escapes, our children die. That's how he got us here.'

'I'm going after the bastard,' said Meron, and he turned away.

Bolt pulled him back. 'Stay here, I'll go,' he said. 'I'll be able to stop him.'

He hurriedly pulled on a pair of scene-of-crime gloves and grabbed hold of the Walther and the Browning, pushing them both into the pockets of his suede jacket, not wanting them to stay in the hands of the Merons in case they did something stupid. Then he ran out of the front door, round the back of the house, and started after the man in black.

By now, Bolt's target was negotiating the fence and was trying to drag his bad leg over it. He was having some difficulty. Twenty-five yards separated them. Bolt had given up smoking five years earlier, visited the gym two, sometimes three, times a week, and at school had been a champion sprinter. He knew he was going to catch his quarry, but behind him he could hear the sound of footfalls and heavy breathing. Tom Meron was coming. Maybe Kathy too. If he wasn't careful, they could fuck this arrest up royally.

The man in black got his leg up and eased himself down the other side of the fence before stumbling away. He had seen his pursuer but was still trying to get away, even though he must have known he didn't have a chance.

Bolt accelerated, reached the fence, took it in an athletic one-handed bound that impressed even him, and charged down his target, now only feet away. The target was a big man. So was

Bolt, but this guy had a couple of stone on him, and most of it looked to be muscle. The man in black started to turn, but his bad leg went from under him and he fell onto his good knee. Bolt had spent more than ten years in the Flying Squad chasing down armed robbers and was well used to dramatic and violent arrests, so he kept coming, jumping up and using his momentum to kick the man full in his balaclava-clad face. He shot over backwards and Bolt rolled him over, drove a knee into his kidneys and twisted a muscular arm up behind his back, encountering little resistance.

He leaned forward so his mouth was next to the target's ear. 'You're nicked, son,' he hissed.

'Sure,' came the reply. The word was delivered with deliberate casualness, even though it was obvious the man was in pain. 'No problem.'

'I'm arresting you on suspicion of attempted murder and kidnap,' he continued, reeling out the standard police caution.

Bolt then heard Tom Meron coming over the fence and running up to them. 'Keep back!' he shouted at him. A few yards further on he could see Kathy approaching too, her progress slower. She looked like she might collapse with exhaustion at any minute.

Meron ignored him. 'Where are my kids?' he screamed, kneeling down beside the man in black's head and trying to wrestle off his balaclava. 'Where are my fucking kids? Tell me or I'll kill you!'

'Please get him off me,' said the other man calmly.

'Leave him, Mr Meron. Let me handle this.'

Their faces were only inches apart and Bolt could see the anguish carved deep into Meron's every pore. He seemed to radiate pure animal fear, like electricity. Even his hair was standing upright. Bolt knew that he was beyond reasoning, and who could blame him?

'His name's Lench and he's got my kids. We've got to find them. Please!' As he spoke, Meron finally tore free the balaclava and scratched ferociously at the other man's face. 'Tell me where my fucking kids are! Tell me!'

Lench tried to pull free but was unable to. For a moment, Bolt made no effort to stop Meron as he gouged chunks out of the pale, pockmarked face beneath him.

'I don't know what the hell he's talking about,' said Lench, trying to look at Bolt.

His eyes were dead onyx, utterly emotionless. Bolt had seen similar before, in various cells and interview rooms. Killer's eyes.

'He's assaulting me while I'm in your custody. Stop him or I'll be on to the IPCC.'

Bolt was in no mood to help this arrogant bastard, who clearly knew the law and its limitations inside out, but as Kathy Meron arrived and aimed a kick into Lench's ribs, shrieking that she'd kill him unless he talked, he knew things were getting out of hand.

He made a decision.

'Tom, get Kathy away now,' he ordered. Their eyes met and a message passed between them. The message said that, one way or another, Bolt would get them the information they needed so badly. 'Back to the house. Right away.'

'I don't know anything about their kids,' said Lench.

'Help me, please,' pleaded Tom Meron.

Bolt nodded, and watched as Meron got to his feet and threw his arms around Kathy before she could land another kick. 'What the hell are you doing?' she called out as he dragged

265

her away. 'He's the only one who knows! We can't let him go!' Meron whispered something in her ear, and her resistance seemed to disappear. Bolt watched as they climbed over the fence together.

Bolt's mobile rang. He let it go to message. He couldn't hear any sirens yet. Only three or so minutes had passed since he'd made that initial call but the cavalry would be here soon. Especially as he was no longer answering his mobile phone.

'Tell me where the kids are, Lench,' he said evenly, using both hands to push the other man's arm high up his back.

Lench grunted in pain, and tried without success to resist. 'This is a case of mistaken identity,' he repeated. 'I don't know what they're talking about. Now, let me go. You're assaulting a prisoner.'

'If anything happens to them, you'll never see the outside of a prison again. Do you understand that? Every day for the rest of your life you'll be looking at the world through a set of bars, knowing that the view is never going to change.' Bolt continued to apply the pressure on the arm, positioning it at an ever more precarious angle. Much more force and it would break.

'I'm definitely going to have you for assault now,' hissed Lench, through gritted teeth. 'My lawyers are fucking Rott-weilers. They'll have your arse in a sling for this. You know you've got nothing on me.'

In the distance, Bolt heard the first sounds of sirens across the valley. They'd be here soon. Two or three minutes at most.

'Where are the kids?' he asked once again. 'Tell me or I'll bust it.'

'Bust it and you can kiss goodbye to your pension. You'll never be able to explain away a broken arm.' Even though he was in obvious pain, Lench somehow managed a small laugh. He knew damn well that Bolt's threat was impotent, and that every second he didn't talk brought him closer to his lawyers.

The DI had met plenty of men like him before. Hardened career criminals. Men with a degree of intelligence and street cunning who knew the weaknesses of the system back to front. Who knew that the greatest mistake they could make was to admit to anything. Who knew that even the best evidence could be torn apart in court by clever, well-educated defence barristers. Who knew that plenty of trials collapsed on legal technicalities because judges, in their wigs and gowns, followed the law to the letter, even if it clashed with common sense. Who knew that juries could be bribed and intimidated if the person doing the bribing and intimidating was determined enough. Who knew, ultimately, that the law was weighted in their favour. What, then, was the point in admitting to anything?

Bolt released the pressure and stood up. Lench rolled over so that he was facing the man arresting him. His face was small and round, the features cruel and unhealthy. His pale, dead-looking skin was lined and cratered with acne scars and stretched tight over uneven and prominent cheekbones that served to obscure the cold, slit-thin eyes. As they faced each other, and Lench rubbed his arm, his bloodless lips spread in a knowing sneer.

'You'll pay for doing that,' he said, more confident now. 'Maybe when all this is over, I'll come and do something to your kids.'

'I haven't got any.'

'Pity. One day, eh?' Lench sat up, still rubbing his arm, and looked down at his injured foot. 'Get me an ambulance. I need this foot looked at.'

Bolt had learned to be patient in the face of the abuse of those he'd nicked. Every copper had to be. To react, especially in an age when there were cameras everywhere, was potentially disastrous. Most of the time the abuse was just bluster, and he was able to brush it off, knowing that the guy was likely to be going down; but with this man, Lench, it was different. The bastard knew the odds were stacked in his favour. He also knew that any mention of the kids and their whereabouts would incriminate him hugely. Bolt thought about what might happen to the Meron children. The people who held them were ruthless. It would probably be easier to get rid of the children rather than let them go. Murder them and make their bodies disappear.

Bolt thought of Mikaela, pictured her as she was. Wondered what she'd advise him to do.

'One of these sirens better be an ambulance. This foot needs looking at.'

Bolt turned around. He could no longer see Kathy and Tom Meron. He guessed that they were back at the house, waiting for him to get the information out of Lench, trusting that he could deliver. The emergency services sounded like they were coming into the village now. Time was running out.

His mobile started ringing again.

The kids could die. They might already be dead. Or they might already have been released. He just didn't know, and the man in front of him, sitting there with the cocky look on his face, was the only one with the information.

Bolt pulled the pistol with the silencer out of his pocket, and released the safety. He pointed it at Lench's lower abdomen.

A flicker of doubt crossed Lench's face but disappeared so fast it could almost have been something Bolt imagined.

'Tell me the location of the kids now or I put a bullet in you.'

Bolt's arm was steady and his face impassive, but inside he was a maelstrom of conflicting emotions and desires, knowing that what he was about to do would put his whole career and even his freedom at risk. He was threatening to shoot a prisoner. He'd never done anything remotely like this before. He'd killed a man once during his Flying Squad days, but that had been an ambush and his victim had been armed, resisting arrest, and pointing a sawn-off Remington automatic at Bolt's head. In other words, what he'd done was justified. But this . . . this was different. But still he kept his arm steady.

Lench sighed in the manner of a primary school teacher showing exasperation at a particularly irritating pupil. 'So now I've got you on threats to kill as well as assault. You're in a lot of trouble.'

Bolt pulled the trigger and shot him in the gut. Lench's upper body was knocked backwards by the momentum of the bullet but he remained upright. He gasped frantically and his eyes flew wide open, then he clutched at the wound, trying to do something to ease the pain. Finally, he rolled over onto his side, moaning loudly.

Bolt leaned down and grabbed him by the scruff of the neck, pulling him round so they were facing each other. 'Tell me where they are or the next shot's into your bollocks.'

'Fuck you,' Lench spat, blood dribbling out of the corner of his mouth.

Bolt shoved the silencer against his crotch. 'Last chance not to talk like a two-year-old girl for the rest of your life.' He pushed down on the gun. 'I'm already fucked. Nothing's going to stop me fucking you too.'

Their eyes met. It was easy to tell that Bolt wasn't lying.

'Twenty-four Limestone Street in Hendon. The ground-floor flat. That's where they are.' More blood leaked out of Lench's mouth, running down his chin. He started coughing, and said something about an ambulance, but Bolt couldn't make it out amid the choking sounds.

Bolt stood back up. The emergency services were coming up the hill now, only a matter of yards away. As many as four different sirens shrieking. Enough to have the ramblers dispersing for miles.

'Armed police!' he shouted without warning. 'Drop your weapon, now! Now!'

Lench rolled over so he was lying on his back, staring up at Bolt, his expression suddenly calm. He knew what was happening. That this was the end of the road. If anything, it was a relief.

'Armed police!' Bolt screamed again, and shot Lench in his left eye. Blood sprayed the grass behind his head, and he went into convulsions.

At the same time, the DI threw the Walther PPK on the ground next to the dying man's uninjured arm and reached into his pocket for his mobile. He speed-dialled Mo Khan's number, willing his partner to pick up the phone.

He did, after three rings. Once again the noise of kids filled the background.

'Hello, boss, any news?'

Bolt spoke rapidly. 'Call nine-nine-nine anonymously and tell the police that you've just seen two young children being manhandled into a flat at twenty-four Limestone Street in Hendon, and you're absolutely sure that they're being held against their will. Have you got that?'

'No problem. Do you want me to go over there?'

'Yes, go and check the place out, but don't get involved unless there's no choice.' He could hear cars pulling into the driveway at the front of the house now. 'And one other thing: we never had this conversation. Understand?'

'Sure, boss, whatever you say.' He hung up without another word.

Bolt exhaled loudly. Mo would do what he'd been requested to do, he was sure of that. But their relationship had, in those few moments, changed for ever.

He put the mobile back in his pocket and turned away, feeling unsteady on his feet. He couldn't believe what he'd just done. It made him want to throw up, but he held himself together, knowing that only by keeping his wits about him was he going to get out of this situation in one piece.

He clambered over the fence and began to walk slowly up the garden towards the two black-clad armed police officers moving carefully towards him, rifles outstretched.

48

I was at the front of the house, holding Kathy tightly, telling her that the plainclothes cop who'd rescued us would find out where Chloe and Max were being held while praying I was right, when two police cars pulled into the driveway, sirens blaring, followed by an ambulance. All three vehicles screeched to a halt and three guys with rifles who looked like something out of *Robocop* jumped out of the first.

'We've had an emergency call,' shouted one of them, a bullet-headed guy in his thirties. 'Can you please put your hands on your heads and step apart.'

'It's not us,' shouted Kathy in return, her face dirty and tear-stained. 'They're at the bottom of the garden.'

'Please do as we say, madam,' demanded the cop, remaining about twenty feet away. Although his weapon wasn't trained on us, it wasn't exactly pointed away either. Behind him two more officers, unarmed this time, stepped out of the other car. The ambulance crew remained in their vehicle. More sirens blared in the near distance.

We followed their instructions and kept our hands firmly on our heads. It struck me that this was the fourth time in less than twenty-four hours that someone had pulled a firearm on me.

'Now, can both of you get down on your knees, please?'

Kathy cursed audibly. She'd always had a rebellious attitude to the police, her being a college lecturer and all. But these guys didn't look like they were in the mood to be argued with, and I was long past arguing anyway. I went down to my knees, and a second later she followed.

'Is anyone hurt?' asked the cop.

'We're OK,' I answered, 'but the detective who rescued us ran round the back after the man holding us.'

'He's got our kids,' added Kathy. 'The man who was holding us has got our kids. Please make sure you don't kill him.'

'Is he armed?'

'Yes,' we both said. 'And there's another man in the cottage as well,' I added, 'but he's unarmed. And hurt.'

'Has he been shot?'

'No.'

'We had reports of a gun battle. Who else was involved?'

I briefly told him what had happened, and he gave me a puzzled look, as if he couldn't imagine a man like me with a gun. I could see his point.

'OK, we're going to secure the area,' he told us. He then spoke hurriedly to his two armed colleagues, who disappeared round the back of the house.

Meanwhile a police Range Rover had pulled up on the side of the road outside and disgorged a further three armed officers. They came onto the drive and, after speaking to the bullet-headed cop, two of them peeled off and came over to me. I was told to get to my feet again and was quickly and silently frisked for weapons. 'He's clear,' called out one of the officers, and I was told I could go, although quite where I wasn't sure.

I walked forward and waited while an unarmed female officer who'd appeared out of nowhere quickly frisked Kathy. She gave her the all-clear and the two of us were led over to the ambulance, where the two-man crew asked if we were all right.

'We just want our kids,' I said, looking back over my shoulder.

'I'm sure they'll be fine,' said the older of the two.

'How the hell do you know?' demanded Kathy.

His colleague, a stocky guy in his twenties with a South African accent, told her that the police were doing all they could. His voice was soft and soothing, and as he spoke he sat Kathy down on the driver's doorstep and crouched down to check her out. I hoped he was right. When the detective who rescued us had told me to get Kathy back to the house, there'd been something in his lean, scarred features and sky-blue eyes I don't think I've seen too many times before. It was moral strength. This guy had signalled to me that he could handle things. That he would somehow make the cold-hearted thug talk. I'd known better than to doubt him.

But had he succeeded?

The older ambulanceman had an arm on my shoulder and was

273

offering me a bottle of water. I took it with a nod of thanks and drank deeply, still looking back towards the house.

And then the detective came round the corner, several inches taller than the two armed officers flanking him. One of them was holding the pistol with the silencer in one hand. The detective's eyes met mine and he looked grim-faced.

'Did he tell you where my kids are?' I asked, breaking free from the ambulanceman.

The armed cop who wasn't holding the pistol put out an arm to move me aside, but I brushed it away and stopped in front of him.

The detective stopped too. We were only three feet apart.

'He was armed. I had no choice but to shoot him.'

'Is he dead?' I asked incredulously.

He nodded. 'I think so. I'm sorry.'

I charged forward before either of the two cops could stop me, grabbing the detective by the collar and shoving my face towards his. 'Bastard!' I shouted, but I made sure my ear was by his mouth so he could speak.

He said three words that filled me with elation: 'I've sorted it.' Then something that sounded like 'I've got a guy going over there.'

I was pulled off him and shoved away violently by one of the armed cops. Kathy came running up to me.

'What's happened? What the hell happened?'

I yanked her as far away from any witnesses as possible. 'Act upset,' I hissed at her, and she seemed to understand. 'He says it's sorted, that Lench told him where the kids are. He's got someone going over there.' I pulled her close and whispered that Lench was dead.

'Good,' she said, and then, with an acting skill that I have to say surprised me, she fell to her knees, crying.

Seconds later, the South African ambulanceman was down comforting her and he and the woman police officer who'd searched her a couple of minutes earlier helped her to her feet.

I turned away and saw our detective being put into one of the police cars and the pistol with the silencer being bagged by an officious-looking man in a raincoat who'd also appeared from nowhere. The bottle of water was still in my hand and I took another long drink, hoping he'd be all right.

But had I been a betting man I wouldn't have put money on it.

49

Mo Khan pulled into Limestone Road just before ten, a little over twenty-five minutes after Bolt had called him. It was a quiet residential road of post-war semi-detached housing that had probably seen better days, and straight away he saw a small cluster of police cars and ambulances double-parked on the right-hand side about halfway up. They were blocking the road and it was obvious there was no way past, but Mo drove up anyway.

A young uniformed officer broke off from a small knot of police gathered round the back of one of the ambulances and walked into the middle of the road, holding up his hand. His expression was irritated. Mo came to a halt a few feet in front of him and let down his window. The officer came up to the driver's side and Mo gave him a disarming smile.

'Excuse me, officer, I live down here. Is there a problem?'

The officer lost his irritated look. It was, thought Mo, always amazing what politeness could do to win people over.

'I'm sorry, sir, there's no access. We've got an operation ongoing.'

Mo feigned surprise. 'Nothing serious, I hope? This has always been a quiet street, and I've got kids. I wouldn't like to think there's anything going on that could affect them.'

'It's nothing for you to worry about, sir. I can promise you that.'

'It's not drugs, is it? Tell me it's not drugs.'

The officer leaned down closer and gave him a conspiratorial look. One man to another. 'To be honest, it looks like a home-alone case. A couple of children were left in the house down there. Young ones.'

'God, how awful,' said Mo. 'Who the hell would do something like that?'

'Well, we got an anonymous call from someone who said he saw them being dragged into the house. That's why we've turned up in force.'

'They're OK, though, are they? The kids?'

'They're fine. A bit upset, as you'd expect, but no physical injuries. They're in the back of the ambulance at the moment, but there was no-one in the house with them. I think it must have been a concerned neighbour who called, and he said that it was a kidnap just to make sure we turned up.' He shrugged his shoulders to signify that this explanation would satisfy him.

'As long as they're all right, that's the main thing,' said Mo. 'Thanks for letting me know.'

He said his goodbyes and reversed up the road. He'd done

what his boss had asked him to do, but he now wondered what on earth had happened to lead the DI to the two kidnapped children. He guessed that they were the Merons' kids, but the way this investigation had twisted and turned he wouldn't have been surprised if they'd turned out to be Lord Chief Justice Parnham-Jones's illegitimate children from an affair with the Prime Minister's wife.

Mo had known Mike Bolt for over two years. He trusted him completely and had always been loyal to him. Even so, he was worried. The boss had insisted he make the call to the police anonymously, rather than go through the established channels. There would only have been one reason for this: Bolt didn't want anyone to know that it was he who'd got this information. Which meant that he had to have got it illegally.

Mo wasn't naive enough to think that corners never got cut in the pursuit of results. They did. He'd cut them himself on occasion. So had the boss, who because of his background in the Flying Squad had come up against some pretty vicious villains. But something in his tone of voice when he'd called Mo, the quiet desperation underlying the curtly delivered orders, made him feel that this time it was different. That this time the corners had been cut drastically. He'd reserve judgement until he found out more, but he didn't like the feeling he was getting.

As he drove, he called the boss's mobile on hands-free for an update on the situation, but it was switched off. He didn't leave a message.

Someone had once said to him that a man's first loyalty was to his family, his second to his friends. The authorities, the state, the law, all of these came a long way down the list. But this wasn't what concerned Mo Khan. Mike Bolt was his friend, but if he had to lie to protect him and by doing so perjure himself, would he not be risking his career, and therefore the wellbeing of his family?

It was a choice he hoped he didn't have to make.

50

The next hour passed in a blur. Kathy and I were both given a cursory examination at the scene by a white-haired doctor who kept muttering to himself. He pronounced us both fit and well, which suggested a lack of observational skills on his part, before disappearing round the back of the house to take a look at Lench.

Kathy was then arrested by the officious-looking detective in the raincoat on suspicion of the murder of Vanessa Blake. She tried to protest, but did so without looking at me, and she didn't resist as she was led away. She was driven off in a marked police Escort with me following in a separate car. I was informed that we were both being taken for separate questioning at Reading police station. Officers from Reading CID wanted to interview me about what had happened at the house; Southampton CID were also interested in having a chat about events at our cottage the previous night. Apparently, the body of a man had been pulled from the wreckage and they wanted, quite reasonably I suppose, to find out how he'd got there. I asked about Daniels but neither of the officers driving me knew anything about that. I assumed that meant he'd escaped. I hoped so. There'd definitely been something not quite right about him, but he'd saved my life at least once, possibly twice, and you've got to give a person credit for that.

Five minutes from the station, as I sat in the back of the car, still trying to come to terms with the fact that I'd beaten a hardened criminal senseless and traded gunfire with a proven killer, the police radio crackled into life, the voice on the other end asking the driver if I was in the car. The driver said I was, and the voice then informed us that Max and Chloe had been found safe and well at an address in Hendon and had been taken to the Royal Free Hospital as a precautionary measure. As soon as I heard that, I'm not ashamed to admit that I cried for the second time that day, so huge was my relief.

'It's OK,' said the officer in the front passenger seat, putting a hand on my shoulder. 'Let it all out.'

So I did.

51

At the station, I was given a cup of strong black coffee and told that the body of Irene Tyler, my formidable mother-in-law, had been discovered in the bedroom of the house where Kathy had grown up. We'd never got on, as I've already said, but the news still hit me hard. Harder, I think, than I would have expected. It was one more tragedy in a twenty-four hours that had been full of them. They wouldn't tell me how she'd died, just that they were treating it as suspicious.

After I'd finished the coffee I was taken to one of the interview rooms, where a male and a female detective wanted to hear everything that had happened to me since my release from custody the previous evening. They said that as soon as I'd finished I'd be taken back to London and reunited with my children. 'What about my wife?' I asked, but they wouldn't answer that one, so I let it go, and just told them the whole story. Occasionally they stopped me to request certain details or to get clarification of one of my points, but for the most part they just let me talk, expressing no obvious scepticism at my version of events, even when I told them how I'd shot at Lench in self-defence, wounding him in the foot. I thought they'd ask me more about the detective and how he'd come to kill Lench, but they skirted around that particular topic, so I volunteered the information that the detective had chased him and that Lench had been armed, adding that neither Kathy nor I had seen what happened after that. I hoped that this way I was helping him.

As for Kathy's role in the whole thing, I told the truth, mainly because I didn't see any alternative. I said she'd been having an affair with Jack Calley and that he had given her the key to a safety deposit box which apparently contained something from one of his clients. Other people had clearly been very interested in getting hold of it, and had tortured then murdered Jack in an effort to find the box's location. They'd then come after Kathy and me, and had finally caught us.

'And you have no idea what the safety deposit box contained?' asked the female detective, a DI in her forties with a severe haircut that didn't match her personality.

'It's something you can make copies of,' I said, remembering Lench's earlier interrogation of Kathy.

'And do you think your wife knows?' pressed the female detective.

'No,' I answered, but in reality I wasn't so sure.

'What about the client? Have you any idea who he, or she, might be?'

I shook my head. 'The only names I was given were Daniels, the undercover cop; Mantani, who was one of the people who kidnapped me; and Lench. He was the one who got killed this morning.'

'How do you know he was killed?' asked the male detective, a much younger guy with a very high hairline and the air of someone who felt sure he was going places a lot more important than a provincial copshop. He reminded me a little of my boss, Wesley 'Call me Wes' O'Shea. A smug, self-righteous go-getter who, if he'd been in the military, would undoubtedly have been shot by his own men.

'The detective who rescued us told me at the scene.'

The two of them turned to each other, then back to me. I looked at my watch. It was ten past eleven. I'd been in this room for three quarters of an hour and I was suddenly exhausted.

'I've told you everything I know,' I said wearily. 'I just want to see my kids.'

The female detective nodded. 'OK. Interview suspended at 11.11 a.m.'

'By the way,' I said, 'before you turn the tape off I just want to say that my wife did not have anything to do with Vanessa Blake's death. The man who attacked me in the library, and who was armed with the murder weapon, killed her.'

'We'll let the investigating officers on the case know your

comments,' she told me sympathetically. 'Thanks very much for your co-operation.'

I nodded and shook her outstretched hand. The male detective didn't bother putting out his. It was clear he didn't believe everything I'd told him. Well, fuck you, laughing boy, believe what you want. When you'd been through what I'd been through in the past day, it took more than some fast-track graduate with a sharp suit and a cocky attitude to scare you.

When I was outside in the main reception area, I sat down on one of a row of empty seats to wait for the lift back to town the female detective had promised me. The place was quiet, courtesy, I suppose, of it being a Sunday morning – not a peak time for criminal activity. No-one was being booked in and there was only the odd hooded delinquent hanging around, waiting to be seen by his bail officer. I remembered that I'd started smoking again, and experienced an unwelcome urge for a cigarette, although even if I'd had any it wouldn't have made any difference. This part of the station was non-smoking, which seemed a little unfair to me. The least you could offer a person you were incarcerating, potentially for some time, was a smoke to ease them through the situation.

'Mr Meron, how are you doing?' said a voice nearby, interrupting my thoughts.

I looked up to see DCI Rory Caplin, one of the two men who'd interviewed me about Vanessa Blake's murder, seventeen hours and a lifetime ago. His red-grey hair was looking even more dishevelled than usual and he was dressed casually in jeans and a black leather jacket that was too short to be fashionable.

'I'm here to give you a lift over to the hospital to see your kids,' he said with the kind of sympathetic smile I'd been getting from people all morning. On him, though, it could just about pass for genuine.

I yawned. 'I'm surprised they're using a man of your seniority for that.'

'My colleagues are interviewing your wife, and doing a fine job of it. I've got to get back to the station, and it's on the way.' He had his keys in his hand. 'Come on. I've got a lot on today.'

'Have you found the guy who attacked me in the library yet?' I asked as we walked out together through the main doors.

'Not yet, no. We haven't had any witness sightings of him either, and we've already taken a number of statements.' He made little attempt to hide the scepticism in his voice.

'I'm not making it up, Mr Caplin. I was attacked by a man who was holding the murder weapon. The filleting knife you showed me yesterday in the interview.'

'The one with your wife's prints on it. Yes, I know. But the answer remains that we haven't found him yet.'

We walked towards Caplin's car. It was a green-gold Toyota saloon with plenty of mud stains up the sides. He unlocked it, and we both got inside. It smelled of air freshener and smoke.

'Have you found any other clues that might lead you to the killer?' I asked.

'Yes, we have,' he said, starting the engine and pulling away.

There was a silence.

'Care to elaborate?' I said eventually.

'Vanessa Blake was having an affair. We discovered correspondence at her house that suggested very strongly that she and her married lover were going to be moving in together in the very near future.'

'And have you questioned him yet?' I asked as we pulled out onto the road.

'We're questioning her now,' he answered, and this time the expression on his face really did convey genuine sympathy. 'I hate to have to say this, Mr Meron, but the lover in question was your wife.'

52

Mike Bolt had interviewed dozens, scores, hundreds of criminals down the years and he knew every interrogation technique backwards. Just like, he suspected, the man he'd killed an hour earlier. The secret was to believe the story you were telling. And if you go over it in your head enough, you will do, even if it's a lie. And what Bolt was saying was definitely a lie.

When they brought him to Reading police station for questioning – he wasn't actually arrested, but realistically he'd had little choice in the matter – his interrogators, men from Reading CID, had questioned him repeatedly about his version of events, trying to sound like they were his friends, but also trying, like any good coppers, to find holes in his story. But he'd stuck to it like glue. The man he'd shot – armed, and dressed in a balaclava – had jumped through the kitchen window and fled through the garden of the property and into the field beyond. Knowing that the suspect had a gun and was prepared to use it, he, Bolt, had picked up the Browning with the silencer that Tom Meron had allegedly fired in an exchange of shots with the suspect, and given chase. Because the suspect was already wounded, his progress was slow and Bolt had quickly got to within a few yards of him. At this point they were in the field and he had already shouted to him twice to drop his weapon. The suspect had then swung round, gun in hand, looking as if he was going to shoot. Bolt, still moving, had fired off a round that had caught him in the belly. However, the suspect was still upright and pointing his own weapon in Bolt's direction, so he'd come to a halt, taken aim and fired again, this time hitting him in the head. The suspect had fallen and, hearing the arrival of police reinforcements, Bolt had walked briskly back in the direction of the house to call for first aid.

It was a plausible enough sequence of events, and with Bolt making no mistakes in his recounting of it, the interrogating officers had no grounds for further action. It was an extremely unorthodox situation however, and no-one in the British police service likes those. He was informed that the matter had been referred automatically to the IPCC, the Independent Police Complaints Authority, and that he would have to make himself available to them whenever they wished to speak with him. He told them that he understood all that, and was advised to remain in the interview room because his boss from the NCS, DCS Steve Evans, had just arrived at the station and would shortly be on his way over to speak to him. He took the cup of coffee on offer, his third, and waited.

He didn't feel bad lying, but he did feel depressed that he'd been put in a position where he'd had to kill a man, essentially in cold blood. He felt a sense of shock at what he'd done because ending someone's life, however much they might deserve it, is always a terrible act that hits any man with a conscience very hard. You have destroyed someone, taken away every dream, emotion and memory that person ever had. It was an awe-inspiring thought, and for Bolt perhaps even more so, as it went against all his training as an enforcer of the law. But it had been done, and he hoped that as a result two innocent lives had been saved.

They hadn't told him whether or not the Merons' children had been freed safely, and he hadn't asked, because in his version of events he hadn't spoken to the gunman, but his gut feeling was that they were OK. No criminal wants to murder two young children unless he absolutely has to. The fall-out is simply too great. But Bolt hadn't wanted to take the risk. He told himself once again that he'd done the right thing. He kept repeating it. Staring at the coffee and repeating it over and over in his mind. You did the right thing. He deserved it. You did the right thing.

There was a knock on the door and DCS Evans came into the room. He was a short, compact man in his late forties with a well-groomed military-style moustache. Even today, on his day off, he was sporting a neatly pressed suit, shirt and tie. If either his first or last names had begun with a D he would forever have been lumped with the prefix 'dapper', but Dapper Steve didn't have much of a ring to it, so he remained plain old DCS Evans. Bolt had met him on several occasions and was confident that, unlike a lot of the senior figures in the police service, he had the best interests of his men at heart, and was prepared to stand up for them. Which, under the circumstances, was no bad thing.

Bolt stood up as he entered and they shook hands. The DCS's grip was only one rung down from painful, his palm dry.

'Hello, Mike,' he said, looking Bolt squarely in the eye. 'Bearing up?'

'Just about. It's not a lot of fun being on the wrong end of the questions for once.'

Evans moved past him and took a seat at the other end of the table. Bolt took a sip from his coffee. It was tepid and weak, but he took another sip anyway.

'It's always a tough call having to make the decision to pull the trigger,' said the DCS. 'Very few of us ever get put in that position. Even fewer get put in it twice.'

Bolt didn't say anything. There wasn't a lot he felt he could say. He knew that as a young man Evans had served in the Falklands, and was a veteran of the battle of Goose Green, where he'd undoubtedly had to make the decision to pull the trigger, so at least he wasn't spouting the usual 'I feel your pain' bullshit you got from some of the Brass.

'Because this is the second fatal shooting incident in your career,' Evans continued, 'and because you were using an un-authorized weapon when you opened fire, there's going to be even closer scrutiny of your actions than would otherwise be the case. The PCC are going to be going over your story again and again. You've got to be prepared for that.'

'I'm prepared, sir,' said Bolt. 'I didn't do anything wrong.'

'I'm not saying you did, Mike. In fact, I'm sure you didn't. You've had an unblemished career spanning seventeen years, and you're a hugely valuable member of our team. But not everyone thinks like we do, and at the moment, given the circumstances, I've got no choice but to suspend you from duty on full pay.'

Bolt shook his head angrily. 'Don't do this to me, sir. You know how long the investigation'll take. Those bastards don't do anything quickly. I could be off duty for months. Years even.'

'Once the air's cleared, we'll petition to put you back on the job, but we've got to be seen to be acting decisively.'

'The guy was armed. He was pointing a gun at me. What the hell was I meant to do? Stand there and let him use me for target practice, so that everyone could turn round afterwards and say what a hero I was for acting with such restraint? He can be proud of himself except, oh shit, he's dead.'

'Listen,' said Evans, sitting forward and raising his voice, 'my sympathies are with you, Mike. They are. I've got no doubt the bastard deserved it. There you are, I've said it. But that's my personal opinion, not official policy, and my job, unfortunate though it may be, is to follow official policy. I'm sorry, but that's the way it is.' He sat back again and sighed. 'I'll do everything I can to get the suspension lifted over the next few weeks, so bear with me, OK? In the meantime, have a rest, and make sure you have a federation representative present whenever you talk to the PCC. Co-operate, but don't make it easy for them.'

Bolt was surprised by his words. Not because the DCS's opinions were particularly controversial, but because he was prepared to speak his mind, and you didn't get that very often from senior officers. Most of them believed one thing and spouted another. He was also relieved that Evans was coming out so obviously on his side.

'OK,' he said, 'I'll have a rest, but I don't want to be resting for too long. We've got a lot of work to do.'

Evans nodded. 'One other thing I think you ought to know,' he said. 'Because of the tangled nature of this case, the NCS are taking overall control of it. We're now in charge of the investigations into the murders of Jack Calley and Vanessa Blake, and all the other investigations linked to it, including the suicide of the Lord Chief Justice.'

'And I'm not going to be a part of it?'

'As soon as I get you back from suspension, you'll be involved.'

'I know as much as anyone, probably more than anyone, about what's been going on. You need me.'

'I know that, but there's nothing I can do about it. I've explained the situation.'

Bolt knew there was no point arguing. 'If that's how you want it,' he said, picking up the coffee.

Evans's mobile rang. 'Excuse me,' he said, looking vaguely embarrassed.

He was on the phone for maybe a minute, no more. During that time his expression became progressively more concerned, and the lines on his face deepened. 'Are you sure?' he asked once. Then he sighed, cursed, and ended the call.

'What's happening?' asked Bolt, intrigued.

Evans got to his feet. He looked worried and just a little unsure of himself.

'We've got a situation,' he said. 'A potentially serious one.'

53

DCI Rory Caplin's revelation about Kathy, the latest in a long line, was the final straw for me. What next? I thought. The news that she'd been bankrolling al-Qaeda for the past ten years? That she was hiding Nazi war criminals? For one of the few times in my life I was shocked into absolute silence.

'I'm sorry,' declared Caplin as we drove through Reading's deserted town centre in the direction of the M4. 'I suppose you would have found out sooner or later, but it might have been easier once you'd recovered from everything else.'

I stared out of the passenger window as we passed the drab, redbrick Huntley and Palmers biscuit building. The sight of it seemed to suit my mood.

'You said you discovered correspondence at Vanessa Blake's house.'

'That's right.'

'What kind of correspondence?'

'Among other things a joint mortgage application in both their names, which they'd both signed. We checked the signatures. They were genuine. There were other bits and pieces as well. Photographs of them together. One or two of them, er . . .' He cleared his throat for maximum effect. 'Intimate.'

'All right, all right, I get the picture.'

But I didn't. I didn't get the picture at all. I thought that Kathy had been in love with Jack Calley. That's what she'd admitted to me the previous night. Their relationship had been so intimate that he'd entrusted her with that fateful key. She'd even wept over his passing. But had she? Maybe she'd been weeping not for Jack but for Vanessa. Maybe she hadn't even been seeing Jack. The only confirmation I had that she had been was what she'd told me, but it could just as easily have been a lie. In the end, it was impossible to know what to believe.

All I knew for certain was that I needed to see my kids, kiss them both, and then go to sleep for twelve hours. And maybe, just maybe, I'd feel a lot better about everything when I woke up.

An unwelcome image of Kathy and Vanessa in bed together crossed my mind, slowed down and stayed where it was. Vanessa had never been my cup of tea. Knowing that she couldn't stand me and wouldn't touch a man if her life depended on it had seen to that; but in fairness she wasn't unattractive, and unwelcome or not, for a few moments I couldn't get the sight of the two of them naked out of my mind.

Shaking my head at the baseness of my instincts, I turned to Caplin. I wondered if he and his colleagues had had a laugh about my wife's extra-curricular activities. I suspected that they had, and felt vaguely embarrassed that I was going to be stuck in the car with him all the way back to London.

'Have you got a cigarette?' I asked.

'I didn't think you smoked,' he answered, reaching into the waist pocket of his leather jacket and pulling out a crumpled pack of Rothmans and a lighter. He pushed them in my direction, asking me to light one for both of us.

I did, and handed his back to him. He put it to his mouth and took a long, tight drag that seemed to hollow his cheeks. At the same time, his jacket sleeve rode up, revealing a thick white bandage, yellowing in places and still flecked with vivid droplets of blood, wound around his wrist.

That bandage hadn't been there yesterday afternoon in the interrogation room.

Caplin moved the cigarette away from his lips. He winced slightly as if he'd been stung, then, as casually as possible, rested his hand on his thigh. The sleeve rode back down. I stared at it for several seconds before looking away. My chest felt tight as the adrenalin began to kick in.

We came to a set of red lights. There were two cars queueing in front of us. Caplin dragged again on the cigarette and put his hand on the wheel. The sleeve rode up for a second time.

The bandage had darkened on one edge.

Drip.

A perfectly rounded droplet of blood fell down from it and landed on his jeans. He looked down at it. So did I. Then we both looked up and our eyes met. And I knew without a doubt that he'd been the man Kathy had cut with the kitchen knife at the holiday cottage last night.

And that was the moment the whole thing came together. Suddenly I knew who'd killed Vanessa Blake, who'd attacked me in the library, and very possibly who'd been involved in the kidnapping of my children.

But it was too late, because the fact that he also knew that I knew all this was now written all over his face.

Drip. A second drop of blood fell onto his jeans. Once again we both watched its descent through the stale, smoky air of the Toyota. Ahead of us, the lights turned green and the first car pulled away.

I went for the door. Fast, the cigarette falling from my hand. But not fast enough. He clicked on the central locking and I found myself pulling uselessly at the handle. The car in front of us moved forward. I turned back towards him and saw that he'd shoved the cigarette into his mouth and was going for something in his inside pocket. I'd been through enough to know what it was going to be. I'd also been through enough to know that I had to react. So, as he pulled the pistol free, I punched him in the side of the face with one hand and grabbed his injured wrist – the one holding the gun – with the other, squeezing with as much force as I could muster.

He let out a squawk of pain and the gun went off with a deafening blast, putting a hole in the middle of the windscreen. He reached round with his other arm to land a punch on me but I didn't give him a chance, hitting him again with an upper-cut, this time in the jaw. His head was knocked to one side, and he cursed loudly. I punched him a third time, pressing my advantage, feeling a terrible elation, wanting to knock the living shit out of the bastard who'd sat interrogating me less than twenty-four hours ago, even playing the role of good cop, while all the time knowing that I was completely innocent. I imagined him taking my kids from Irene's house, and that really got me. I grabbed at his hair and gave it a vicious tug, then tried to slam his head into the window, but this time I over-reached myself, and I wasn't prepared for the way he lurched forward in the seat and drove his gun arm round in a sudden movement that caught me off guard.

The gun went off again, and this time I felt the rush of air as the bullet tore past my face, breaking the window behind me. The noise was deafening, the smell of cordite intense. My cheek stung where it had been burned by gunpowder residue. I was thrown off balance. This time Caplin punched me and the blow sent my head flying back into the broken passenger window. Instinctively I relaxed my grip on his gun arm and he jerked his hand away, freeing it.

The driver in the car behind us, clearly a brave man, tooted his horn, leaning on it for a good five seconds. At the same time I blinked against the pain of the blow and saw that Caplin's gun was now pointed at my midriff. Strangely, I didn't feel any fear, just a sense of resigned weariness. I no longer had any energy left to fight. If it was time to die, then so be it.

'You fucking idiot,' he said contemptuously. 'You never know when to stop, do you?'

'Were you lying about Kathy?' I asked. 'Her affair?'

The guy behind us, who was either very shortsighted or suicidal, blasted away on the horn again.

Caplin looked at me as though I was mad to ask this question at such a fateful point in my life. 'No,' he answered. 'I wasn't.' Then he did a strange thing. He apologized. 'I never wanted to get your kids involved. You've got to know that. I don't hurt kids.'

I wasn't sure what to say. Instead, I looked at the gun, which was still pointed at my midriff. In the end I settled for a heartfelt plea: 'Don't shoot me.'

'I'm not going to,' he said. Almost to himself, he added, 'Christ, why the fuck did I offer you a lift?'

Then, turning the gun round, he put it in his mouth and pulled the trigger.

54

'So, where am I taking you to?' he asked.

I had to think about it for a moment. 'Home,' I said, but I wasn't really sure that it was any more. I asked him if he knew how to get there.

Bolt nodded, and opened the driver's-side door. 'I was there last night.'

'Is the place OK? Someone, one of Lench's people, broke in yesterday afternoon. I saw him inside.'

'It's secure,' he answered, getting in. 'They've had a police guard on it.'

I got in the other side and he switched on the engine. The clock on the dashboard said 14.35. As I fastened my seatbelt, Bolt drove out of the car park and through Hambleden village. There were more people around than earlier – talking in small groups, some on doorsteps – and two uniformed police officers were speaking to someone outside the pub. There'd been a lot of drama here this morning. You don't expect a gun battle in a picturesque village, but then things seemed to be changing a lot these days.

I asked if he minded if I smoked. I'd been given a pack of Benson and Hedges earlier by a sympathetic detective when I'd been taken back to the station after the incident with Caplin, and I now found that I was desperate to have another. A bad sign.

Bolt gave me a mildly disapproving sideways look, and sighed. 'I guess after all you've been through it'd be a little bit cruel not to let you. Can you open the window, though?'

I did as he asked and lit up, taking a long draw. It tasted good, but I noticed that my hands were still shaking a little. It had been a long twenty-four hours. They'd released Kathy on unconditional bail, and without charge, an hour earlier and she'd driven her car back to London to get the children, telling me that I could come back to the house later. She'd looked pale and drawn, the shock of the deaths of her mother and two lovers carved deep into her face, but remained remarkably lucid and calm. She hadn't explained herself, just given me a small nod to acknowledge my hurt before turning away with her solicitor in tow.

I'd had to stay behind to answer questions relating to the death of DCI Caplin, and had given a lengthy statement. There was a sense of shock among the officers questioning me that one of their own could have been involved in the bloody events that had started a day earlier. This shock had become pronounced when I'd suggested that I thought Caplin's colleague, DC Ben Sullivan, might also be involved. It struck me in the midst of my confrontation with the DCI that Sullivan matched the height and build of the man who'd attacked me in the library, and who'd appeared at the holiday cottage the previous night with Lench, Mantani and Caplin. I didn't know whether anyone had been sent to interview or arrest him, so I asked Bolt.

'I wouldn't know,' he told me. 'I've been suspended.'

'I'm sorry about that,' I said, and I genuinely was. I owed Bolt a huge favour, and in the end, suspended or not, he was the only man I actually trusted to drive me back to London on the second attempt. The Reading police hadn't been too happy about this, but I'd insisted, and they'd given us both a lift back to his car in Hambleden.

I took another draw on the cigarette. I felt like talking. 'You know, I don't know what the hell I'm going to do now that me and Kathy are in the situation we're in.'

'Do you think it's redeemable?' he asked. 'You and her?'

'I don't think so. Not after all this. I don't think I even know her any more.' I sighed, trying to articulate my current emotions. 'It's a strange feeling, you know. Empty. Like my life – everything I knew, everything I loved, everything – it's like it's all just ended.'

'It's a shock, Tom. But you'll get over it.'

'Easy for you to say, Mr Bolt.'

'You're not my prisoner. You can call me Mike.'

'Well, Mike, put bluntly, I'm fucked, and I don't think anyone knows exactly how that feels. Even you.'

Bolt didn't say anything for a few moments as he pulled out onto the main road, heading north towards High Wycombe and the M40. The road was busier, filling up with Sunday drivers enjoying the greenery of this pleasant pocket of England now that the sun had managed to break through the worst of the clouds.

When the detective next spoke, his words were thoughtful and tinged with a melancholy I wouldn't have associated with a man like him. 'The thing about life is that it can run in a smooth line for years on end, so smooth sometimes that you take the whole thing for granted. Tragedies happen in far-off places, involving people you don't know. Then, bang, out of the blue you hit a bend in the road and suddenly your whole life's been turned on its head. That's what's happened to you, and three years ago that's exactly what happened to me. So, yeah, take my word for it, Tom. I know what you're going through.'

We slipped into an uneasy silence. Eventually, my interest pricked, I asked him what had happened to him.

'My wife was killed in a car crash,' he answered, without looking at me.

'I'm sorry. I didn't know.'

'The reason I'm telling you this is that life does come back to you. It takes time, it's a hard, lonely road, but eventually you learn to get back some normality.'

'I'm sorry,' I said again.

'So am I. I was driving.'

I was shocked. 'Jesus, that must have been hard.'

'It was. Even now, three years on, I have no recollection of the crash itself, or what led up to it. We'd been for dinner at a friend's place. I remember arriving there, and I remember the first half an hour or so of the evening, but then the whole thing's a blank until I woke up in hospital twelve hours later. I had severe abdominal injuries and internal bleeding, but my wife was worse, a lot worse. Her parents agreed to turn off her life support system three days later. I was too ill to make the decision. I was too ill even to leave my bed and see her. We'd been married four years and she was two months pregnant.'

'Christ, Mike, I don't know what to say.'

He sighed, and I saw his expression harden. 'You've been through one hell of a lot in the past day. More than most people will ever go through in their lives. You're lucky to be alive. So was I. When they pulled me from the wreckage of my car, it was touch and go. I didn't think I was so lucky at the time, though. As soon as I heard what had happened to Mikaela, I wished I was dead. No question. The six weeks I spent in that hospital, lying there helpless while my injuries slowly healed, were the worst of my life. The next six months, sat at home on sick leave with all the reminders of our time together, weren't much better either. But eventually I got back to work, I moved house . . . I moved on, I suppose. I still think about Mikaela every day. I still wonder what would have happened if we'd stayed in that night, how life would have turned out. Family, children, a house in the suburbs. But I try not to dwell on it. Life goes on. You've got no choice but to get on with it.'

'Is that how you got those scars? In the car accident?'

He nodded, touching a finger to the S-shaped pink slash that ran above his jawline. 'A constant reminder,' he said. 'In case I ever get too complacent.'

I took a last drag on my cigarette and chucked it out of the open window. 'I think I'm going to change jobs,' I announced. 'I hate being a fucking software sales manager.'

I thought of Wesley's oily smile and horseshit motivational speeches, and remembered that today I'd shot a man, and that somehow this meant that Wesley could never intimidate me again. I imagined standing up during the next weekly sales meeting and, instead of going through a list of frankly imaginary current business prospects in the hope that they'd be enough to appease him, simply announcing that I had none whatsoever, and what's more I was quite happy with this state of affairs, before sitting back down with a big grin on my face. I could imagine the look of shock on his face as he realized that his supreme authority as Vice-President Sales of Ezyrite Software Services was being challenged, and that when it came down to it he wasn't as charismatic, popular and invincible as he'd always thought.

'Do you enjoy being a copper?' I asked Bolt.

He appeared to think about this for a few moments. 'I do when I get a result, because then you can see that you're making some sort of difference. But I don't like it when I can't get a complete line on what's going on. When there are loose ends that need tying up. Like this case. Why don't you fill me in on what you know?'

'But if you're suspended, surely it won't make any difference. I've already said everything I know in the interview.'

'Humour me,' he said. 'We've got a forty-five-minute drive ahead of us.'

I was reluctant to go through the story again. I didn't much like being reminded of all the details. But Bolt struck me as the sort of man who didn't very easily take no for an answer, and who would probably take my reluctance as a sign of guilt. So I went through everything in chronological order, with him regularly interrupting with perceptive questions.

When I'd finished he asked me why I thought Jack Calley had called me even though we hadn't spoken in four years, particularly as he was having an affair with my wife.

'He said he wanted me to help him.'

'What possible help could you provide? I don't mean that in a derogatory way, but I don't see how you, a man ten miles away from where he was being chased, could assist him in any way. If I was him, I would have dialled nine-nine-nine.'

I shrugged. 'So would I, but who knows what goes on in the mind of someone in that situation?'

'Well, you must know,' he said. 'You've been in that position several times over the past twenty-four hours and you've told me that when you were being interrogated and threatened with torture, if you'd known what the hell your interrogators wanted you'd have told them everything straight away. But it sounds like Jack didn't.'

'He got freed by Kathy. Then he made a break for it.'

'But he was tortured prior to that, and then, what did you say was the last thing you heard him say on the other end of the phone? Your address, wasn't it? He gave them your address.'

I nodded slowly. 'That's right.'

'Why? If what you say is true—'

'It is true.'

'If Calley had handed the key these men were looking for to your wife, why not just tell them that your wife was in the house with him? Why give them your address?'

I'd been thinking about this for a while today. 'My guess is he was trying to protect her. Throwing them off her scent by sending them to our house. Perhaps he thought that if he could let me know what was going on, that they were after Kathy, I could get her away from there.'

'Perhaps,' he mused, although something in his tone suggested he wasn't entirely convinced.

I played Jack's final phone call over in my mind, and wondered whether he'd been trying to warn me when he'd shouted out my address to his pursuers. To let me know they were coming so I could get out. The last act of a man who'd once been my best friend. I liked to think so, but, as with everything else, I couldn't be sure.

300

I decided it was time to ask Bolt a question since he clearly had doubts about the reasons behind the call. 'You're the detective,' I said. 'What do you think?'

'I think,' he answered, looking at me out of the corner of his eye, 'that your wife's hiding something.'

I gave a humourless laugh. 'I think she's been hiding a lot of things.'

55

Bolt cooked himself pasta sauce that evening – a slow dish of tomatoes, Spanish ham from the local deli, fresh garlic and spring onions, chilli and parmesan. He served it on a bed of penne with a glass of dry Aussie Chardonnay on the side. He tried to forget that he'd killed a man that morning. It wasn't easy, but at least the food tasted good and the wine went down well. He wondered what he was going to do now that he was suspended. He'd missed his Dorset fishing trip; a few days' salmon fishing in the west of Ireland to make up for it sounded an attractive proposition. He knew he needed the break, and thanks to his single status and the ultra-cheap rent on his apartment he wasn't short of cash. He would have to make himself available to the PCC, but that didn't mean that he had to sit on his arse at home waiting for them to call. The speed they usually worked, it would probably be August by the time they turned up with their reams of questions and stern, officious stares. He might as well do something productive in the mean-time.

But, as he'd said to Tom Meron, he didn't like loose ends, and elements of this case still bugged him. It also bugged him that he was no longer privy to the information being garnered by the various investigation teams. He was out in the cold. It made trying to find the solution to what had happened – what the safety deposit box actually contained, who the hell wanted its contents so badly, and why – near enough impossible.

He finished the Chardonnay, and his thoughts turned to Mikaela. He was surprised he'd told Meron as much as he had. It wasn't like him to talk about what had happened that night. He'd always preferred to take the exact opposite of the route the bereavement counsellors recommended, and brood alone. But he'd felt sorry for Meron, sitting in the passenger seat, his face hollow with the shock of the seismic changes in his life, and the loss that was a part of it. He hadn't told him everything, though. There were secrets he kept that no-one would ever know. That he hadn't wanted the child Mikaela was carrying, had still felt he wasn't ready; how unsupportive he'd been as a husband in those final weeks, even though he'd agreed to go through with starting a family; how at the time he was in the habit of drinking at, or occasionally above, the drink-drive limit when he was out for the evening; and how he still wasn't sure whether or not he'd had alcohol on that fateful night. How the couple whose house they'd been at – Mikaela's friends Chris and Sharon – had avoided him ever since the accident, and how he was never sure whether or not they blamed him for what had happened. He never told anybody about these things, or about the occasional crippling attacks of guilt he experienced when he went over them in his mind. Nor would he ever do so.

He felt an attack coming now, a leaden cloak of melancholy that left unchecked would drag him down into a slow depression. In an effort to stave it off, he walked over to the window and looked down at the bright lights of the street below. It was quieter than usual, being a Sunday evening, but people still wandered up and down. A bus snaked past and stopped outside the Feathers, the pub he drank in sometimes. Two young couples disembarked, their laughter drifting up towards him, and walked to the Thai place, thirty yards further down the road. One of the girls leaned into her boyfriend and whispered something in his ear. They kissed, and Bolt looked away, feeling like an interloper.

He refilled his glass and took a long sip, wondering whether it might be worth popping down to the Feathers for a couple of pints. He knew the landlord pretty well and he was usually good for a chat when the bar was quiet. He could do with the company and it would help to take his mind off things.

His mobile rang. He went over to the table in the lounge area and picked it up.

It was Mo. 'Hello, boss, everything OK?' His voice seemed flatter than usual, the tone cautious.

'Mo, how's it going?'

'I'm OK. I've been busy. What about you? I heard about the shooting this morning.'

'He had a gun,' Bolt said, maybe a little too quickly. 'I gave him a chance to surrender.'

'DCS Evans says he's hoping you'll be back on duty soon.'

'Him and me both. I'm not the kind of person who likes sitting around twiddling his thumbs. You made the call to the police then, about the kids?'

'Just like you said.'

Bolt knew his friend wanted to ask him how he'd come by the information he'd called in, so he told him. 'The guy I shot told me where the kids were. I shot him once in the belly when he aimed his gun at me, and when he went down I asked him where they were being held. He told me, but then he went for the gun again. That's when I shot him a second time.'

'Why didn't you make the call yourself? And why did you want it done anonymously?'

'I didn't have time to make it myself, and I didn't want people asking me how I got the information. You're not meant to interrogate a wounded man.'

There was a painful silence down the other end of the phone. Bolt could tell Mo was having difficulty believing him. Finally, he said: 'The man you killed: fingerprint records confirm that his name was David Harrison. He was an ex-soldier who got involved in the Yugoslav conflict, and who was meant to have been killed in Bosnia more than ten years ago, but obviously wasn't. He had an old record for sexual assault, and was named as a war crimes suspect by the UN in 1995. Apparently, he'd been involved in several massacres of civilians. Meron said that he was referred to by the men working for him as Lench, but we can't find any record of anyone using that name or alias.'

'Do we know who he was working for?'

'From what we're hearing, his boss was a London-based businessman called Paul Wise.'

'I've heard the name, but I don't know where from.'

'Probably from the *Sunday Times* Rich List. He's a seriously wealthy guy, with some very aggressive ways of doing business. Also, the body of another man was found in the burnt-out wreckage of the house, and he's been ID'd through his DNA as a Peter Mantani, an ex-con with a whole raft of convictions for violence. Mantani's name appears on the payroll of a company linked indirectly to Paul Wise. It's not a lot to go on, and it wouldn't do a scrap of good in court, but it's something.'

It made sense to Bolt. The reason Lench had been so confident when he'd thought he was going to be arrested was because the person he worked for had a lot of power. Bolt now remembered reading an article on Wise in one of the Sunday papers several years earlier. It had detailed his steady rise to becoming one of the UK's top self-made businessmen. The reporter doing the story had dropped the odd vague hint that there was a dark side to Wise's wealth, but Bolt had thought little of it. There's no shortage of people out there whose money comes from nefarious business dealings.

'Meron said something about being rescued by an undercover guy from the NCS with the codename Daniels,' Bolt said. 'The last he saw of Daniels was at their place in the New Forest. He was taking on Lench and his cohorts. Do we know anything about that?'

'There's been no undercover NCS operation against Paul Wise,' said Mo. 'Whoever Daniels was, he definitely wasn't NCS.'

'Strange.'

'Also, you ought to know that Kathy Meron gave a full and detailed statement.'

Bolt felt an icy chill go up his spine. What did that mean exactly? 'Are you able to tell me the details?'

'She confirmed that the man you shot had kidnapped their two children and was armed and threatening to kill both of them, as well as her and her husband, unless she revealed the whereabouts of a key to a safety deposit box.' Bolt resisted sighing with relief. So, Kathy hadn't put him in the shit either.

'She also told us that the deposit box contained a tape and a laptop, both of which belonged to Calley.'

'Really? So she did know what was in it?'

'That's right, but she kept quiet because if the people after her thought either she or her husband knew anything, she knew they'd kill them.'

Bolt was intrigued. 'So, are you going to tell me? What was on the laptop and tape that was so important?'

'According to Kathy, the tape contained a partial confession from Tristram Parnham-Jones about his involvement in a child abuse ring. The same one Gallan had been investigating. It also named names, the majority of whom are dead, but including one man who isn't.'

'And what's his name?'

'Paul Wise.'

'Jesus, so he's one of them as well. No wonder he wanted to get his hands on that tape.'

'That's what it looks like,' answered Mo. 'But Kathy's admitted she's never actually heard the tape. She just knew about what it contained because Calley had told her. Apparently, all the details of the allegations were held on the laptop. They'd been compiled by Calley over a period of some months.'

'But Calley was Parnham-Jones's solicitor. What was he doing putting together a case against his biggest client?'

Mo sighed. 'It seems that Jack Calley was one of that rare breed: a lawyer with a conscience. When John Gallan first went to his superiors in January, they did start a formal investigation into Parnham-Jones, and obviously the Lord Chief Justice involved his solicitor. Although the investigation was dropped a few weeks later due to lack of evidence, Kathy Meron says that Calley became convinced of his client's guilt and that the fact that he was helping to keep a dangerous paedophile out of jail worried him immensely. He even resorted to taping several of his private meetings with Parnham-Jones, and in one of them the Lord Chief Justice actually let slip comments that confirmed his role in some of the alleged crimes. Because of client confidentiality, the information Calley had couldn't be used in an open court, but he was so concerned he told Kathy, who was having an affair with him at the time. She thought he should air the allegations somehow, but in the end he decided against it, and a few weeks later the affair fizzled out.

'It was about this time that Kathy started another affair, this time with her work colleague Vanessa Blake. And it was now that things started to go wrong. Kathy told Vanessa what she'd heard about Parnham-Jones, and Vanessa, who was something of a political activist, was very keen that this information got out into the public domain. Apparently, she told a reporter she knew about the existence of this confessional tape, and although she didn't name names herself, the reporter started digging around for details. Kathy says she stopped Vanessa from going any further but she thinks that word got out about the tape, and that possibly several of the people involved came to hear of its existence, including Wise.'

'Do you think Wise had anything to do with Parnham-Jones's death?' Bolt asked him.

'It looks likely, doesn't it? It's safe to assume that Wise's people got rid of John Gallan, so maybe they decided it was too much of a risk keeping the Lord Chief Justice alive. What we do know is that Jack Calley phoned Kathy on hearing of Parnham-Jones's death. This was yesterday morning. She said he was sounding very worried. He was sure that it wasn't suicide, but murder, and he was worried that, as the owner of the tape, he might be a target. He was also concerned that Kathy might be too. She said she thought he was being overly paranoid, but she did agree with him that it was now a good time to make the contents of the tape and the allegations public. But, as Parnham-Jones's lawyer, Jack obviously couldn't do that. He wanted Kathy to do it. He'd placed the tape and laptop in a deposit box and he asked her to come over to his house so he could give her the key, telling her not to park outside. That was apparently how paranoid he was, but it was this paranoia that saved her life. While she was there collecting the key, this guy Lench and his friends turned up. Kathy hid, but as we know, they got Calley up in the woods, and it seems that he gave them Tom's name, as well as the Merons' address, before he died.'

'I still don't know why he gave them Tom's name. The poor bastard had nothing to do with any of this.'

Mo thought about that for a moment before replying. 'Maybe Calley felt that if he was going to survive, he had to give them something. He didn't want to name Kathy but he'd have been under so much pressure he wouldn't have been able to think of anyone else fast enough, so maybe he just let slip Tom's name. Now that he's dead, I suppose we'll never know for sure.'

'What about Vanessa Blake? Did Wise's men find out about her as well?'

'Kathy says Lench told her that Vanessa's murder was a case of mistaken identity. It looks like the killer turned up at the university looking for her and stumbled on Vanessa instead. Apparently, the filleting knife she was killed with was actually Vanessa's own. Like Calley, she was also very paranoid after Parnham-Jones's death, especially as she was the source of the leak, so she'd taken to carrying the knife around with her as protection. That's why Kathy's prints were on it. She'd used it for cooking in Vanessa's kitchen during their time together.'

Now it was Bolt's turn to sigh. 'All those dead people. Someone's going to have to pay for it. Has Wise been brought in for questioning yet?'

'On what grounds? There's no sign of the tape or the laptop anywhere. The deposit box has been checked and it's empty.'

'Fuck. So, he gets off?'

'There's no evidence against him. Just some bits and pieces of hearsay. Not enough to do anything with.'

Bolt fell silent. He believed Kathy Meron's story. It made sense. Not that it made any difference to him. He was still suspended. He wondered whether the man he'd killed – David Harrison, Lench, or whatever his name was – could have provided any of the answers that would have built up a case against Wise. It was doubtful. He didn't seem like a man who would have crumbled under interrogation and tried to save his own skin. And anyway, there was no point thinking about it now. He was dead. It was irrelevant.

'Can I ask you a question, boss?'

Bolt knew what it was going to be. 'Sure, go ahead.'

'There was no other way, was there?'

'What do you mean?'

'You had to shoot him, right? This man Lench. He would have killed you otherwise. That's how it happened, isn't it?'

Bolt knew how hard it was for his friend to ask this. They trusted each other. But what had happened this morning had changed things.

'I wouldn't ask, you know, but . . .' He paused. 'I feel I've got to know.'

'There was no other way, Mo. I promise you.' The lie came

309

easier than Bolt had expected. 'He went for the gun, and I pulled the trigger. I guess he didn't want to go to prison.'

He heard Mo sigh with relief down the other end of the phone.

'I didn't doubt you, boss, but the circumstances were . . .' He searched for the right words. 'They were strange, weren't they? And it's all a bit of a shock.'

'This whole weekend's been a bit of a shock. Get back to your family, Mo. Take it easy.'

'And you, boss.'

'Don't worry about me, I'll be OK.'

And he would be too, he knew that. He, Mike Bolt, was a survivor. He'd fought back from the brink before, from the physical and mental wreckage of the car crash that had killed his wife, and had emerged stronger. But the parameters that guided his life had changed again. He'd killed a man in cold blood – justifiably, to his own mind, but justification didn't alter the trajectory of a bullet. His victim was still dead. And he'd still been unarmed. Like most people's, Bolt's hands had never been entirely clean. Until now, however, they'd not been too dirty either. It would take some getting used to.

He put the phone down on the coffee table, picked up the wine and switched on the TV. He'd done enough thinking for one day.

56

Being reunited with Max and Chloe was, without doubt, one of the best moments of my life. As soon as I came in the door, they ran, laughing, into my arms, and the three of us held each other in an unbreakable clutch. For a while, nothing else mattered. The bloody events of the past twenty-four hours faded away; my broken, battered marriage suddenly didn't matter. I was home.

When Chloe finally pulled away from the embrace, she gently touched the bandage on my face and asked me how I'd hurt myself. I told her I'd fallen over and scraped my face on a nail.

'Ah,' she said, 'poor Daddy,' and kissed me gently on the cheek. 'Do you know what happened to us?' she asked, wide-eyed.

'No,' I answered, feigning ignorance. 'What happened to you?'

'A man in black came and kidnapped us from Grandma's,' she explained, excitedly.

I flinched. I knew they hadn't been told about their grandma yet. I was hoping not to have to do it now. 'Yes, I heard all about it.'

'I cried. But only a little.'

'I didn't cry,' piped up Max. 'I told him off.'

'Well, you don't have to worry now,' I said. 'The naughty man's in prison.' But, as I said the words, I wondered if all four men at the cottage last night were now accounted for. Lench, Mantani and Caplin certainly. I still wondered if the fourth was DC Sullivan and, if so, what had happened to him.

But, for the moment, it was time to forget all that.

It was the opinion of the child psychologist at the hospital that Max and Chloe had been only very mildly traumatized by the ordeal they'd undergone, their age, the fact that they'd been together, and the relative shortness of their incarceration preventing the effects from being much worse. And certainly, as we played together back at the house that afternoon and they charged, shrieking, around the garden with me giving chase, they seemed just the same as they'd ever been. We'd been told to let them talk about it, but neither of them seemed that interested in doing so, so I didn't mention anything, preferring – hoping, I suppose – that we could consign it to history.

Kathy held back from the games, and I could see that she was finding it hard not to crack. Three people very close to her had been murdered in obscenely rapid succession. All she had left was her family, although I had to wonder if this still included me.

After we'd put the two of them to bed, and I'd read them stories, I came back downstairs and joined Kathy in the kitchen. She'd opened a bottle of red wine and I saw that she'd poured a glass for me. Her eyes were dry, but the strain in them was obvious. I couldn't help thinking how beautiful she looked, even after all this.

'I think I owe you the truth,' she said, handing me the wine.

I took a big gulp, figuring that I deserved it. 'Tell me when you're ready,' I said, looking at her over the top of the glass, trying to work out whether our relationship was retrievable. The expression in the smooth, olive contours of her face didn't tell me one way or another.

'I'm ready now. Are you hungry?'

I shook my head. 'I ought to be, but my appetite seems to have gone absent without leave.'

'I'm the same. All I feel is empty. Come on.'

She took my hand, her touch giving me a small crackle of excitement, and led me through to the lounge. We sat next to each other and, with her hand still in mine, she told me everything. How she'd been unhappy in the marriage for a long time, and had started affairs first with Jack, then with Vanessa. How, during her relationship with Jack, she'd found out about the allegations against one of his major clients, the Lord Chief Justice, Tristram Parnham-Jones no less (I'd never liked the look of that guy), and the existence of his taped confession; and how, finally, we'd all become targets as Lench, Mantani and whoever they were working for raced to find the tape before it could be made public.

'I'm so sorry for involving you in all this,' she said when she'd finished recounting the story.

'In the car this morning, Caplin told me that the police found a joint mortgage application in your name and Vanessa's during the search of her house.' I couldn't bring myself to mention what he'd described as the 'intimate' photos.

Kathy let slip a small, melancholic smile. 'No, it wasn't a mortgage application. It was a mortgage enquiry.' I couldn't quite see the difference, but she explained it for me. 'Vanessa was pushing to make the relationship more serious, move it to a higher level. I was infatuated with her, but I think she might actually have been in love with me, and, being single, she had a lot less to lose.'

I began to experience some less than charitable thoughts about Vanessa, but remembered that she was dead, so had ended up with a pretty raw deal herself.

'I knew I should have been trying to calm things down,' continued Kathy, 'but with everything else going on it was difficult, so I went along with things.' She looked at me, her doe eyes suddenly very doe indeed. 'I really wish you hadn't had to find out about her, Tom. I tried to keep our affair a secret right up to the very end, especially after you'd found out about Jack.' She gave my hand a squeeze. It felt good. Maybe I'm a bit naive where women are concerned, but at that moment I really thought there might still be something there.

When Kathy finished speaking, I shook my head with what can only be described as weary sorrow. It was Jack I was thinking about now. Jack, my old friend. Jack the traitor.

'Did he ever say anything about me?' I asked.

'He said that sometimes he felt guilty about what he was doing.'

Somehow I doubted that. There was no room for guilt in someone like Jack Calley. He followed his instincts in everything he did, often without any real thought for the consequences for himself or those around him. Jack's instincts told him he was all-powerful. That was why he could ride the near vertical slope at Sketty's Gorge. It was why when the two of us were nine years old and three older kids had accosted us in the local park and demanded that we give them our money, Jack had charged them, fists flailing, rather than pay up. And so many times, his instincts had been right too. The three kids had given us a bit of a beating (Jack especially, since he'd offered the most resistance), but they hadn't got our money.

Yet, when he'd needed it the most, his luck had finally run out. I thought back to that day in the park. How we'd returned home bruised and battered, arms round each other's shoulders, united and triumphant, with me thinking how glad I was that he was my friend. Even now, after everything he'd done to me, I couldn't help but mourn his passing just a little. Underneath it all, he'd been a good man. When he could have kept his mouth shut about the terrible crimes his biggest client had committed and carried on taking his money, he'd done the right thing, and the right thing had cost him his life. And in a way this made his betrayal even harder to take. The fact that, in my case, he'd allowed his honour to slip, as if I wasn't an important enough person to justify it. That was what hurt the most.

'Have I really been that hard to live with these past few years?' I asked.

She sighed and flicked a lock of dark hair out of her eyes. 'It's not just been you. It's been both of us. We've grown apart. We don't talk, and when we do, it's usually shouting.'

I hadn't remembered it being as bad as this, although I think my ignorance owed more to a desire not to confront the truth of the situation rather than a better reading of it. We had had some pretty big fights of late.

'I suppose,' she continued, 'it was inevitable that something would happen, but I never intended it to be as bad as this. I can't tell you how sorry I am, Tom. If I could turn back the clock, I would.'

'Is there any way we can get back to how we were?'

The $64,000 question. Suddenly, nothing else mattered. More than anything, I wanted to go back in time to the point when we still loved each other. I needed her. I needed my whole family. Without them, I was nothing.

'I don't know,' she answered, which wasn't quite what I was hoping for.

'Well, I want to try,' I said, leaning forward like a kid on a first date. I went for the full-on lips kiss, and saw with a heavy heart that she was inclining her head slightly and I was being presented with the old platonic cheek.

As I gave it a peck and she squeezed my hand once again, the phone rang a few feet away. It was the first time I'd heard it ring since Jack's fateful call the previous afternoon. That call seemed like a lifetime ago now. Slowly, I got to my feet, feeling inexplicably nervous. I knew it was all over, but if nothing else, my experience had taught me that life is never predictable. It can throw up plenty of surprises, many of them extremely un-welcome.

'Hello?' I could hear the nerves in my voice.

'Tom, how are you?' came a loud, confident voice with artificial American inflections that made it sound like the person it belonged to was stuck somewhere out in the mid-Atlantic. Wesley O'Shea had always wanted to be American, and it was a source, I suspect, of everlasting shame to him that his place of birth was actually Leamington Spa. 'Are you OK, bro? I've just heard all about what's happened to you. The cops just called me, and frankly I'm speechless.' Wesley then showed me exactly how speechless by launching into a long series of questions about my ordeal, and when my answers were deemed too brief and evasive, he responded by telling me about a supposedly similar incident that had happened to a cousin of his in New Jersey back in the early 1990s.

'Wesley, thanks a million for your call,' I said, interrupting him as he got to the bit where the SWAT teams were just about to go in, 'but I'm extremely tired, as you can imagine. Do you mind if we talk about this later?' I turned to Kathy and made the universal jerk-off gesture, and she smiled.

'Sure, Tom. I understand. Listen, take the day off tomorrow. Maybe even Tuesday as well. Ezyrite Software wants you back on the job fit and well.'

'That's very kind of you, Wesley.'

'Please, Tom, we're friends. Call me Wes.'

'Well, that's very kind of you, Wes. I appreciate it.'

'Er, also, Tom . . .' His voice suddenly sounded uncharacter-istically shaky.

'Yes, Wes?'

'Er, is it true what I'm hearing? That, you know, you actually shot someone?'

'Twice,' I said, and hung up.

When I put the phone down, I looked at Kathy, knew that one way or another we'd make it, and for the first time in as long as I can remember, actually laughed out loud.

57

When DC Ben Sullivan got out of the car, he looked nervously both ways down the deserted night street before running up the steps that led to safety. He opened the front door to the flats and stepped inside, waiting for the click of the automatic lock as the door shut behind him. He was in trouble, big trouble. He was sure that after Caplin's death they would be looking for him; they might also have him down as Vanessa Blake's killer. He knew the evidence against him was flimsy, but he wanted some time to think before he answered any of their questions, and that meant getting out of the country for a while.

A part of him knew this was a foolish move, an obvious declaration of guilt, but he wasn't in the right frame of mind for an interrogation. Yesterday afternoon he had killed for the very first time, stabbing to death a woman for money. They'd promised him £20,000 in cash for the job, and he'd received ten grand already. It was a lot of money. But there was no way he was going to be getting the other ten, because Vanessa Blake, his actual victim, was the wrong person. He'd been sent to the university to intercept a woman he'd never met before called Kathy Meron, having been told that she was possibly in possession of a key to a safety deposit box. If she was there, he was to get the key off her, get the box's location, and then kill her; if she didn't have it, he was to find out who did, then despatch her. He was told that he'd be supplied with a pair of her husband's gloves which had been taken from the family home, and which could then be used to frame him.

But everything had gone wrong when he'd been disturbed by Vanessa Blake and, in the ensuing struggle, had killed her with her own kitchen knife.

And now the guilt was kicking in. He wished he'd never got involved. He blamed his former colleague and mentor, Rory Caplin, for tempting him with talk of earning large amounts of money on the side, and he also blamed his girlfriend, Janet, for her expensive tastes. If she hadn't wanted all those clothes and furniture and exotic foreign holidays, he would have been able to get by. In fact, Ben Sullivan blamed everyone other than himself. It was a long-standing trait of his that did little to endear him to people.

He flicked on the hall light and walked down the corridor past the staircase to the door to Flat One, Janet's pad. They didn't live together – Sullivan preferred his independence – but he paid the rent on the place, and had done ever since she'd lost her job in the hotel months earlier. Stupid cow, he thought irritably. How the hell do you lose a job as a receptionist in a hotel? It was hardly a challenging role. All you had to do was answer the fucking phone. And this place wasn't cheap either. Seven fifty a month, even though it was only one bedroom, and in one of the cheaper areas of Hendon. The cost of living in London was extortionate. No wonder he'd had to do other, more lucrative, work.

Janet was out tonight, meeting friends in the West End, a situation that suited him fine. The ten grand was in a holdall in the top of her bedroom wardrobe, underneath a pile of blankets, along with a further four thousand in cash he'd made for other tasks he'd performed on behalf of his unofficial employers. More than enough to get him out of the country and somewhere warm, where he could plan his next move. She'd be getting a shock, though, when rent day came round. From now on, he wasn't paying it. Fuck her. Let her get off her arse and find another job giving out room keys. Consider this goodbye, love, he thought.

But as soon as he'd shut the door to Flat One and flicked on the lights, he knew something was badly wrong. The living-room carpet had been covered by a thick sheet of black tarpaulin that crinkled underfoot. More tarpaulin had been taped to the back of the door and the adjacent wall. It even covered the sofa in the middle of the room. A man was standing behind the sofa, facing him. As their eyes met, the man let slip a thin, humourless smile and raised a gun with silencer attached, pointing it at Sullivan. Eight feet separated the end of the barrel from its target.

'You,' said Sullivan, recognizing his killer straight away, even though his hair was now a different colour and he'd taken to wearing thick-rimmed glasses.

'It's always me,' said the killer, and shot Sullivan once in the leg, just above the kneecap, the bullet making barely a sound.

Sullivan fell backwards against the door, grabbing at his injured leg as it went from under him. He ended up in a sitting position, his teeth clenched against the pain.

'You've got something I want,' said the killer calmly. 'Two things, actually. A tape and a laptop. Where are they?'

'I don't know what you're talking about,' hissed Sullivan.

'Yes, you do.' The killer shot him in the other leg, and Sullivan gasped painfully.

'They're in my car. I was going to bring them back.'

'Sure you were,' said the killer, and pulled the trigger for a third time, sending a bullet into Sullivan's forehead. The dead police officer slumped forward with his head bowed, the blood splash from the bullet's exit wound caught by the tarpaulin on the door.

The man Tom Meron had known only as Daniels unscrewed the silencer and placed it and the gun in the pocket of his jacket. He knew the value of the tape and laptop that Sullivan had liberated from the deposit box at King's Cross station, and knew too that they implicated his employer, multi-millionaire businessman Paul Wise. It was why from the start he'd wanted them for himself. It was why he'd risked his life to get hold of them. Because he knew they represented the biggest potential pay day of his career.

Things had very nearly gone disastrously wrong at the Merons' cottage, when they'd been ambushed by Lench and his men, and he had to admit that Lench had proved a worthy and resilient foe who'd almost hit him with the shot he'd fired in the cottage driveway. But now he, Mantani and the rest of the employer's people were dead, and Paul Wise no longer had any protection.

Which made him rich pickings.

When Daniels had finished wrapping Sullivan's corpse in the tarpaulin, he tied it up at both ends and with some effort carried it out to Sullivan's own car, depositing it in the boot. He had a contact in Essex who disposed of bodies with no questions asked, and who would also get rid of the car. Daniels had called ahead and told him to expect a delivery.

The laptop and tape were under the front passenger seat. He started the engine and placed the tape in the car's player. Five minutes later, and two miles away, he was convinced he had all he needed. He parked up at the side of the road and dialled a number on his mobile.

If Paul Wise thought his problems were over, he was in for a major shock.

They were just beginning.

Epilogue
THREE WEEKS LATER

Bolt had done a lot of thinking since his suspension. It was difficult to avoid it when you had so much time on your hands. You get the full understanding of what it's like to be lonely when you're at home all day, and most evenings too. He'd made it across to Cork for some fishing, which had taken his mind off things a little, and he'd spent more time in the Feathers than he was used to, putting on close to half a stone in the meantime, even though he'd doubled his visits to the gym. And all the time he'd been thinking. Thinking about the man he'd killed, thinking about the case he'd been involved in, thinking about the individual alleged to be behind it all: Paul Wise. The man who'd got away.

More details had emerged about Wise's operations over the past three weeks. There had actually been an NCS investigation into his business dealings some months earlier which had inexplicably been wound up, even though Mo had said that he was suspected of involvement in as many as five murders – and this before the events of three weeks ago – as well as extortion, fraud, even non-payment of tax. It was amazing that someone so crooked could not only rise so high within the establishment, but also remain there unmolested. Not quite a pillar of the community, but not far off it either. But then, Wise had some powerful friends, people who did him some big favours. Bolt wondered how many more there were like Parnham-Jones, people right at the top of the pile who shared his perverted tastes. It was a thought that pissed him off, because he suspected there were a few.

There was something personal about all this too. It was Paul Wise who'd given Bolt sleepless nights by putting him in a position where he'd had to shoot dead an unarmed man, and where he'd had to break the very law he'd spent so much of his adult life upholding. He wanted to make the bastard pay for that. But it looked like he was going to have to wait. Wise was clever, and he kept his hands scrupulously clean. What evidence there was against him was still so patchy as to be unusable. For the moment, at least, he was safe, although, as Mo had said, now that he was suspected of a whole new raft of killings it meant that the investigation into his affairs was going to be reopened, and with significantly more resources. One day, like most criminals, he would pay a price for his crimes. It was just that it might not be any time soon.

Three weeks into his suspension, on a warm summer's afternoon in June, Bolt walked into a café on Camden High Street. The interior was quiet, and once again she had arrived before him, and was sitting at a corner table at the back. Bolt gave her a nod, ordered a regular filter coffee from a young eastern European girl behind the counter, and made his way over.

'You're looking well,' he said as they shook hands.

And she was too. Her skin was tanned and healthy-looking, her black hair a little longer and a lot more lustrous, and the eye shadow she was wearing seemed to accentuate the brightness in her eyes. She was dressed in a white lace top with short sleeves that showed off the tan, a simple silver chain with one of the smaller Tiffany hearts around her neck.

'Thanks,' said Tina Boyd, and sat back down. 'You're not looking so bad yourself.'

'So, where have you been?'

'Holiday. Two weeks in Mexico. I felt like I needed the break.'

'I think you did. It seems to have done you a lot of good.'

'I heard what happened to you. I'm sorry.'

'The suspension is a formality. I've done my interviews with the PCC, and it doesn't look like they've found anything untoward, so I'm starting back on the job next week.'

'Same rank?'

'Exact same rank.'

She smiled. 'Good. The Brass spend too much time hanging good officers out to dry. It's a wonder they've got any left.'

'You thought any more about coming back?'

She considered that one for a moment. 'Part of me has. But I'm still not sure.' There was a pause. 'So tell me,' she said, changing the subject, 'Parnham-Jones. Was it suicide or was it murder? I've fallen behind on everything.'

'No-one knows for sure,' answered Bolt truthfully as the coffee arrived.

He then told her what he knew of the story, but didn't mention Paul Wise by name. As he spoke, she listened raptly, occasionally shaking her head at some of the grimmer details.

'So John was right. There was a paedophile ring involving Parnham-Jones and others.'

'It certainly looks that way.'

327

'And one of them's still out there evading justice. And you know who he is.'

Bolt nodded. 'We've got a suspect who could have been behind John's murder,' he said carefully, 'but we've got no proof.'

'And you also think he had Parnham-Jones killed. Is that right?'

Once again, Bolt nodded. 'I think the Lord Chief Justice was the weak link. He had to go. Let's assume he had been involved in the murder of that child years before. He thought he'd got away with it, then a few months ago it becomes clear that the secret's out, and that there's a detective sniffing around, asking questions. He calls on one of his associates, someone who was also involved in the murder – let's call him Mr W – and asks him to sort it out. A few weeks later, the detective ends up dead. Now the judge can breathe a sigh of relief, but not for long. Because word gets out that there's a tape recording of him confessing to the crime, or at least to being involved with child abuse, and then, to top it all, he gets an anonymous email from someone telling him they know the details of his crime. We found it on his desktop PC. So, more sleepless nights. My guess is he was beginning to panic as his murky past finally caught up with him, and his associate finally decided that it was simply too dangerous to keep him alive. They use the same people who killed John, and rather than vary their modus operandi, the perpetrators stick with a formula that's worked before and kill Parnham-Jones in exactly the same way, trying to make it look like suicide.'

'And someone's got away with it,' said Tina, taking a pack of Silk Cut from her pocket. 'Your Mr W.'

'The people who actually carried out John's murder are

almost certainly dead. As for Mr W himself, his card's marked. He won't get away with it for ever.'

'Well,' she said, lighting a cigarette, 'our Lord Chief Justice certainly deserved what he got, the bastard. He ruined a lot of lives, but at least John can rest in peace now.'

Bolt nodded. He agreed with her. 'There's only one mystery left,' he said, taking another sip from the coffee.

'What's that?' she asked.

'Who sent the email to Parnham-Jones a week or so before he died? The one saying they had all the details on his crimes?'

They looked at each other for a long moment. Tina held his gaze, giving nothing away, the expression behind her eyes impossible to read. Then she let slip a small smile that managed to be both confident and vulnerable at the same time.

'You know I sent it, don't you?'

'I've thought about it a lot,' Bolt said, giving her a small smile of his own to show that he understood what she'd been through and why she'd done it, 'and I couldn't work out who else it could have been.'

She sighed and dragged on the cigarette. 'The problem was, I thought he'd got away with everything. And I suppose at the time, he had. I just wanted to make him suffer some of what I was suffering. I only ever sent him that one mail, and I realized afterwards how stupid I'd been, and what a risk I was taking. Is it likely to be traced back to me?'

'Where did you send it from?'

'An internet café from a hotmail account I'd set up.'

'I talked to the guy who was looking into it a couple of days ago,' said Bolt, recalling a conversation he'd had with Matt Turner, 'and he hadn't turned up anything. So I think it's very unlikely.'

'Good. Not that I regret sending it. He deserved it. I just wish I'd thought of something more effective.'

'You didn't have to in the end, did you?'

'I suppose not.' She stubbed out the cigarette in the ashtray and eyed him carefully. 'This'll be our secret, though, yes?'

'Scout's honour.' Bolt made the sign. 'But that's not the only reason I came here.'

She looked wary. 'So, what else is there? Anything I should be worried about?'

'Maybe,' he said, but once again he was smiling. 'I've come to offer you a job.'

'You're joking, aren't you? I'm not even on the force any more.'

'No, I'm not joking. I'm very short on numbers for my team, and I know that you'd be welcomed back at any time. Your record's excellent, and you're the sort of person I need. A fighter.'

'You're serious, aren't you?'

'Absolutely.'

She brushed a hand through her hair. 'It's an interesting offer. But aren't the NCS going to be disbanded next year?'

'That's next year. Come on, you know you belong with us.'

'I'll give it some thought, OK? But I don't want to make an on-the-spot decision. You understand that, don't you?'

'Sure,' he said, feeling vaguely disappointed.

The reason he wanted her on the team wasn't just because she was a good copper. When he'd first met her three weeks ago, she'd seemed vulnerable and in need of comfort. He'd responded to her pain, perhaps seeing something of himself in her. But he realized afterwards that he was also attracted to her. Seeing her now, tanned and pretty, only accentuated those feelings.

He stood up, trying to brush off the disappointment, although with only limited success. 'You've got my number, haven't you? Let me know when you can.'

She nodded. 'I appreciate the offer. I'll tell you by the end of the week.'

They shook hands and said their goodbyes. Bolt left a couple of pound coins on the table for his coffee and walked out into the street. The sky was a faded blue, and the sun shone amid the long, crooked fingers of cloud.

The disappointment faded. It was time to move on.

Author's Note

Some astute readers will notice that I've taken a few liberties with the village of Hambleden in order to further the plot. For instance, there's no phone box in the village square anymore, and no such place as Rangers Hill. However, the pub's real enough, and it serves good beer, too.